Centerville Library
Washington-Centerville Public
Centerville, Ohio

DISCARD

W9-BMI-605

image comics presents

ROBERT KIRKMAN
CREATOR, WRITER

CHARLIE ADLARD
PENCILER, INKER

CLIFF RATHBURN
GRAY TONES

RUS WOOTON
LETTERER

CHARLIE ADLARD
&
CLIFF RATHBURN
COVER

IMAGE COMICS, INC.

® **Robert Kirkman** - chief operating officer
Erik Larsen - chief financial officer
Todd McFarlane - president
Marc Silvestri - chief executive officer
Jim Valentino - vice-president

ericstephenson - publisher
Joe Keatinge - pr & marketing coordinator
Branwyn Bigglestone - accounts manager
Sarah deLaine - administrative assistant
Tyler Shainline - traffic manager
Allen Hui - production manager
Drew Gill - production artist
Jonathan Chan - production artist
Monica Howard - production artist
www.imagecomics.com

THE WALKING DEAD, VOL. 10: WHAT WE BECOME. First Printing. Published by Image Comics, Inc. Office of publication: 2134 Allston Way, 2nd Floor, Berkeley, California 94704. Copyright © 2009 Robert Kirkman. All rights reserved. Originally published in single magazine format as THE WALKING DEAD #55-60. THE WALKING DEAD™ (including all prominent characters featured in this issue), its logo and all character likenesses are trademarks of Robert Kirkman, unless otherwise noted. Image Comics® and its logos are registered trademarks and copyrights of Image Comics, Inc. All rights reserved. No part of this publication may be reproduced or transmitted, in any form or by any means (except for short excerpts for review purposes) without the express written permission of Image Comics, Inc. All names, characters, events and locales in this publication are entirely fictional. Any resemblance to actual persons (living and/or dead), events or places, without satiric intent, is coincidental.

PRINTED IN CHINA

ISBN: 978-1-60706-075-8

International Rights Representative: Christine Jensen (christine@gfloystudio.com)

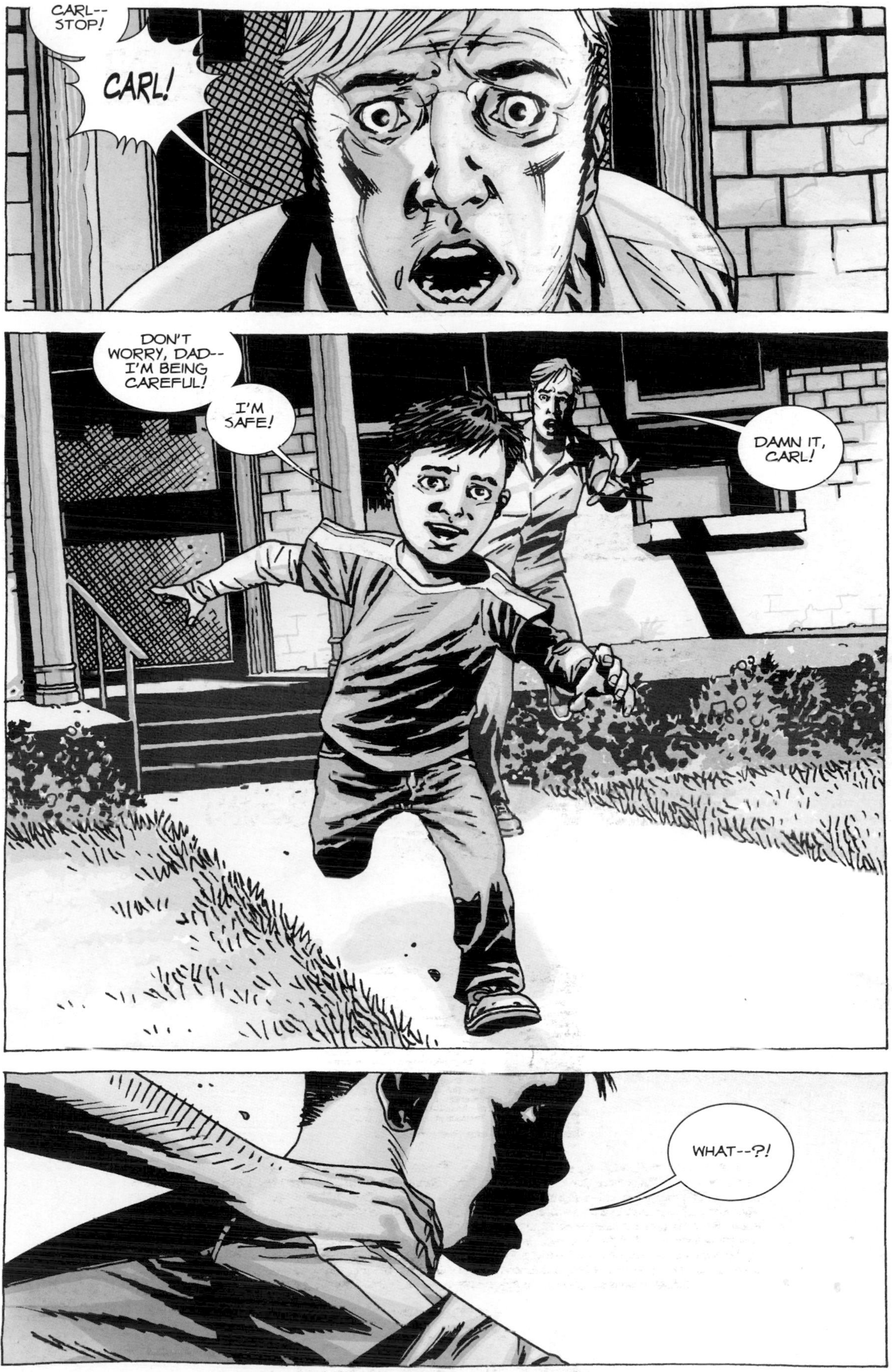
CARL--
STOP!
CARL!
DON'T WORRY, DAD-- I'M BEING CAREFUL!
I'M SAFE!
DAMN IT, CARL!
WHAT--?!

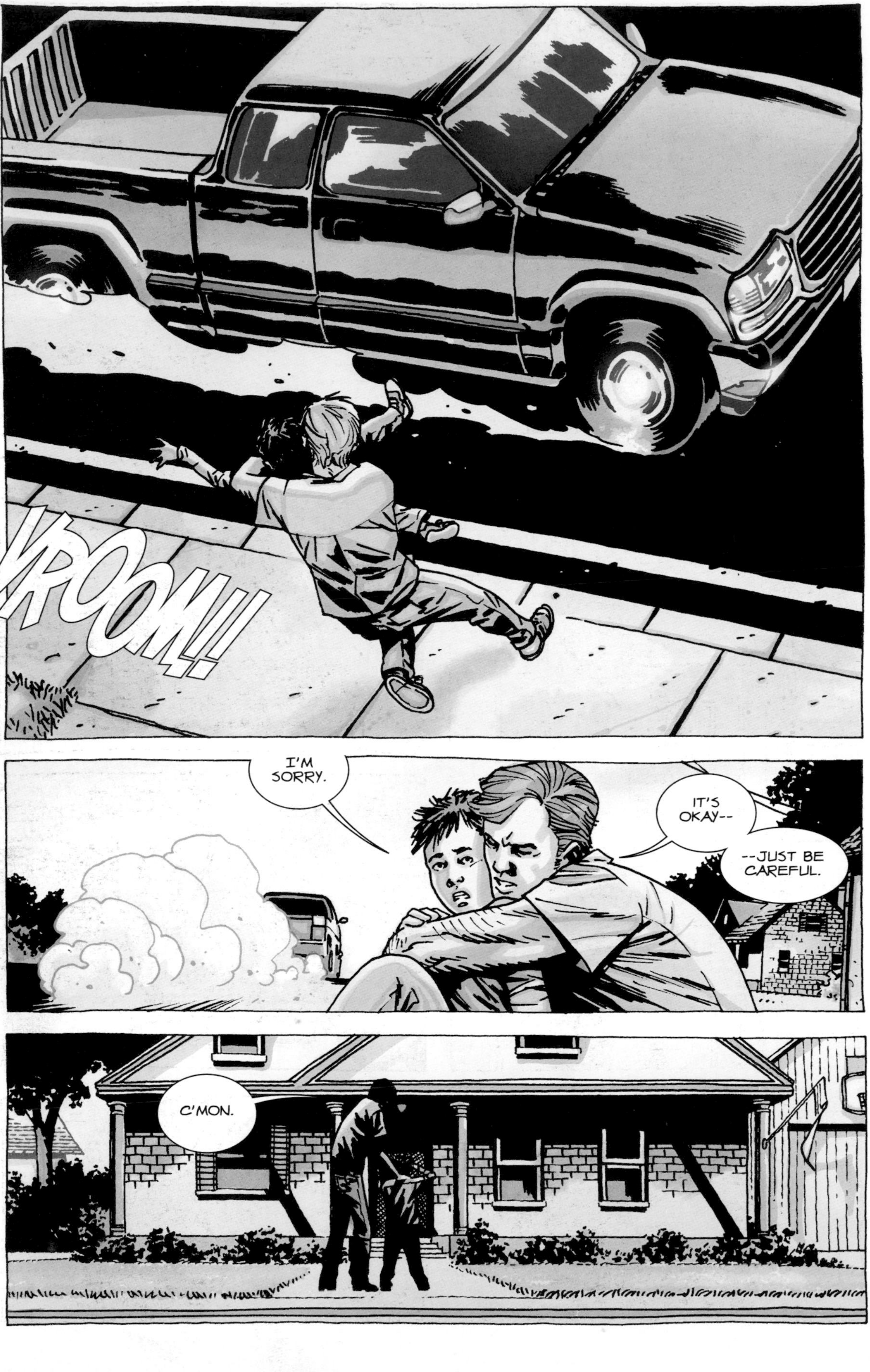
VROOM!!
I'M SORRY.
IT'S OKAY--
--JUST BE CAREFUL.
C'MON.

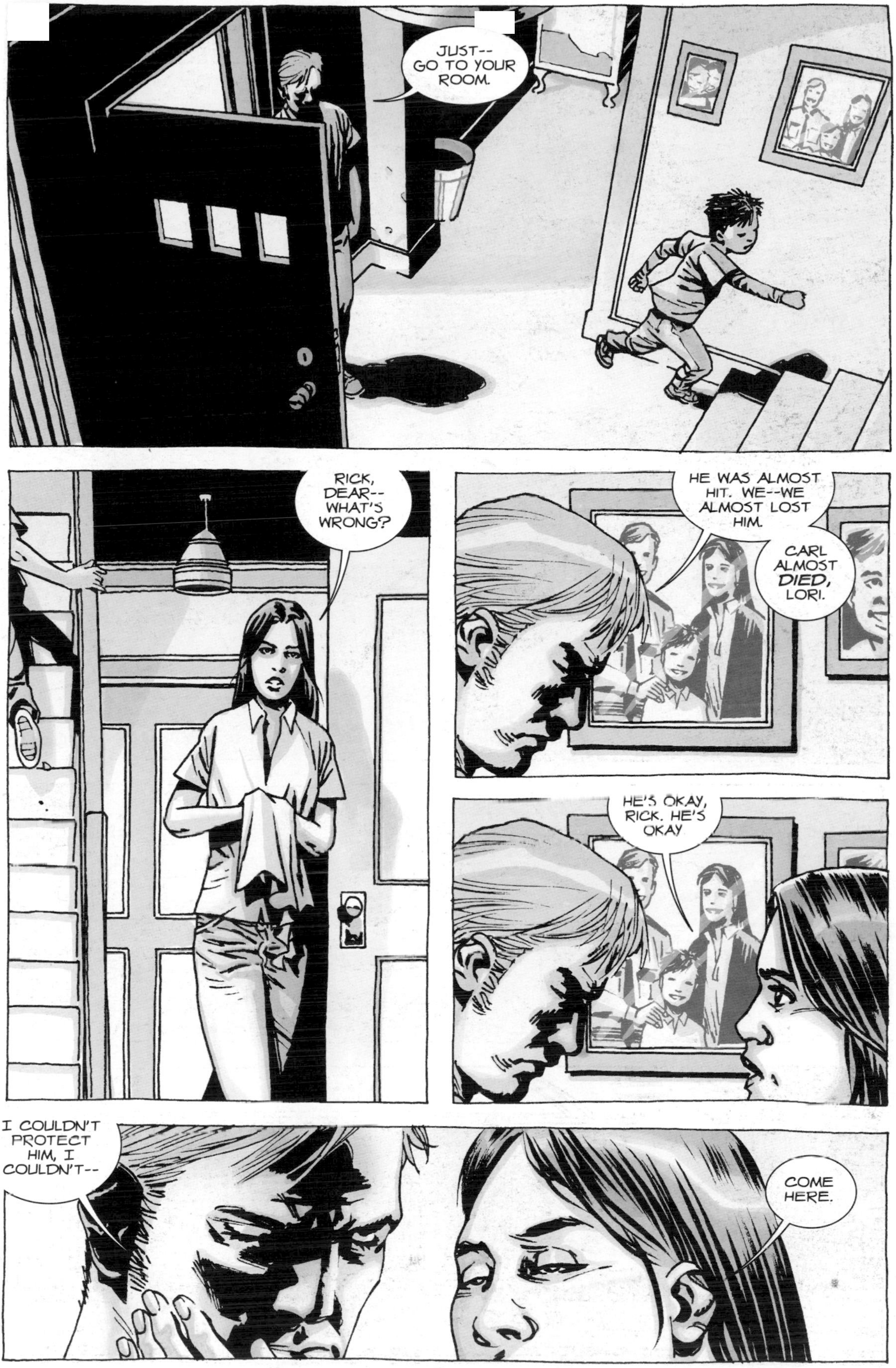
JUST--
GO TO YOUR ROOM.
RICK, DEAR-- WHAT'S WRONG?
HE WAS ALMOST HIT. WE--WE ALMOST LOST HIM.
CARL ALMOST DIED, LORI.
HE'S OKAY, RICK. HE'S OKAY.
I COULDN'T PROTECT HIM, I COULDN'T--
COME HERE.

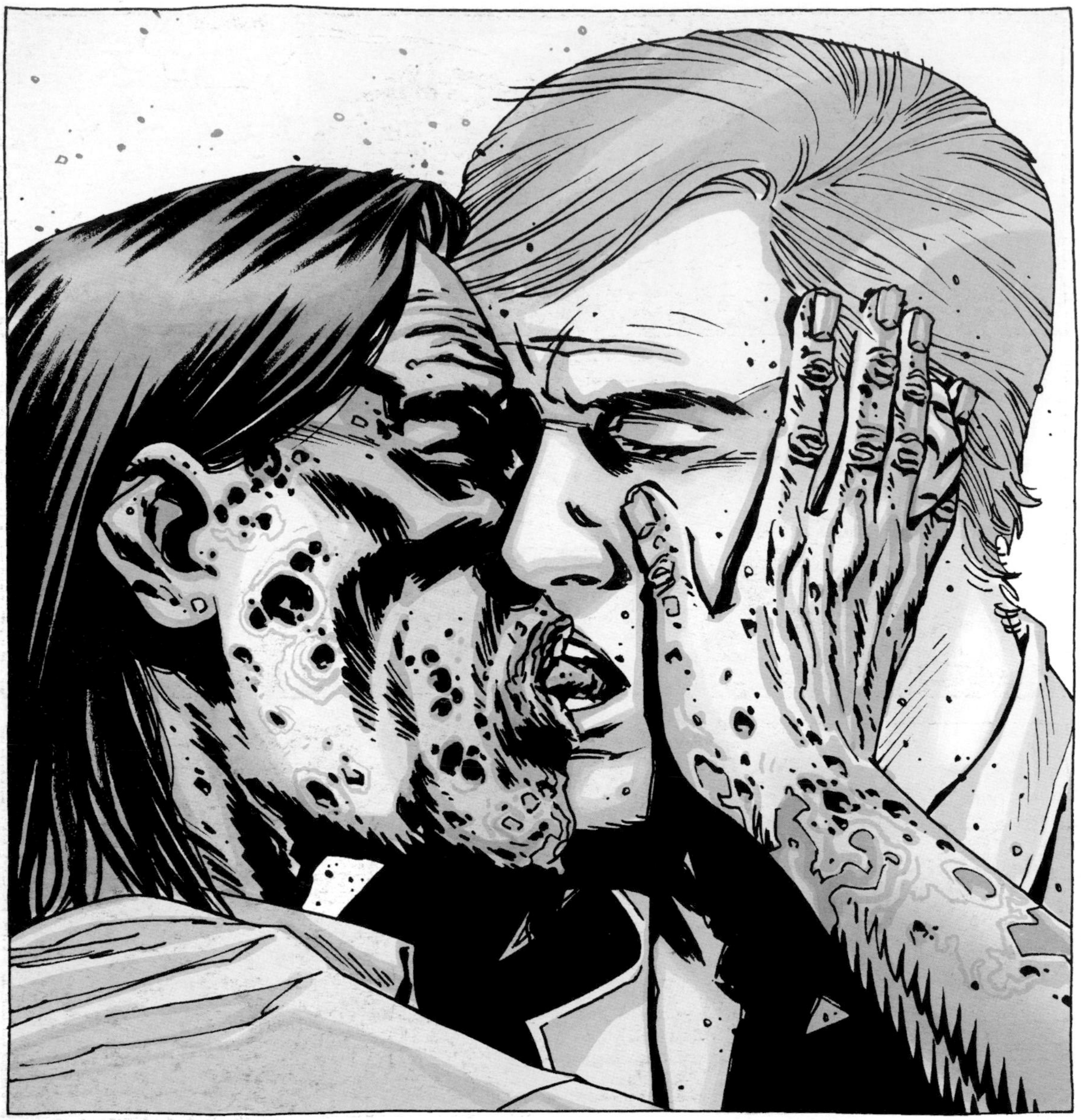

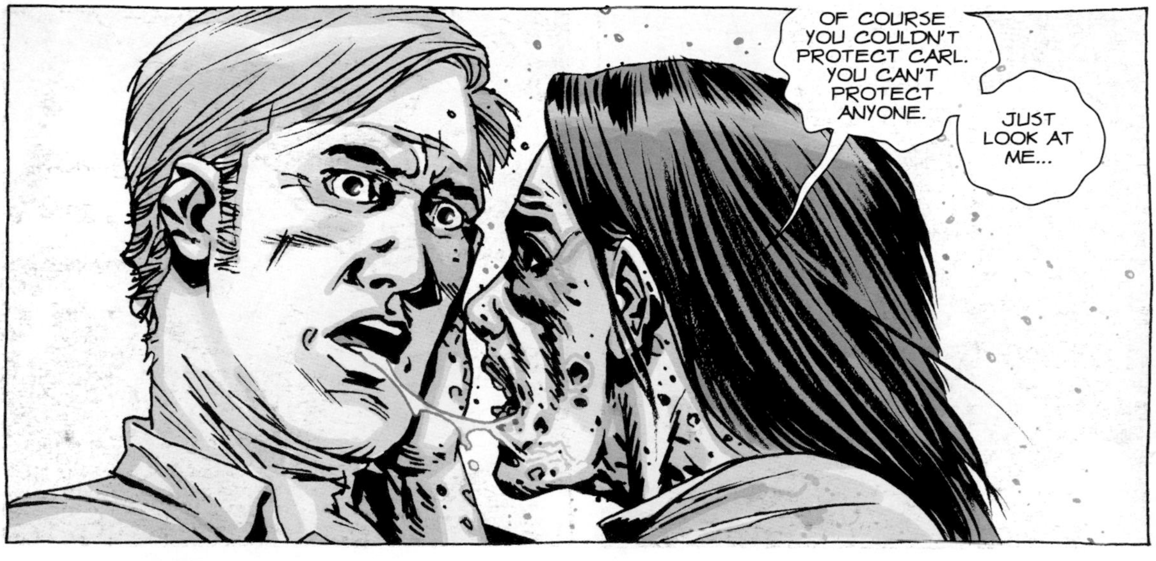
OF COURSE YOU COULDN'T PROTECT CARL. YOU CAN'T PROTECT ANYONE.
JUST LOOK AT ME...

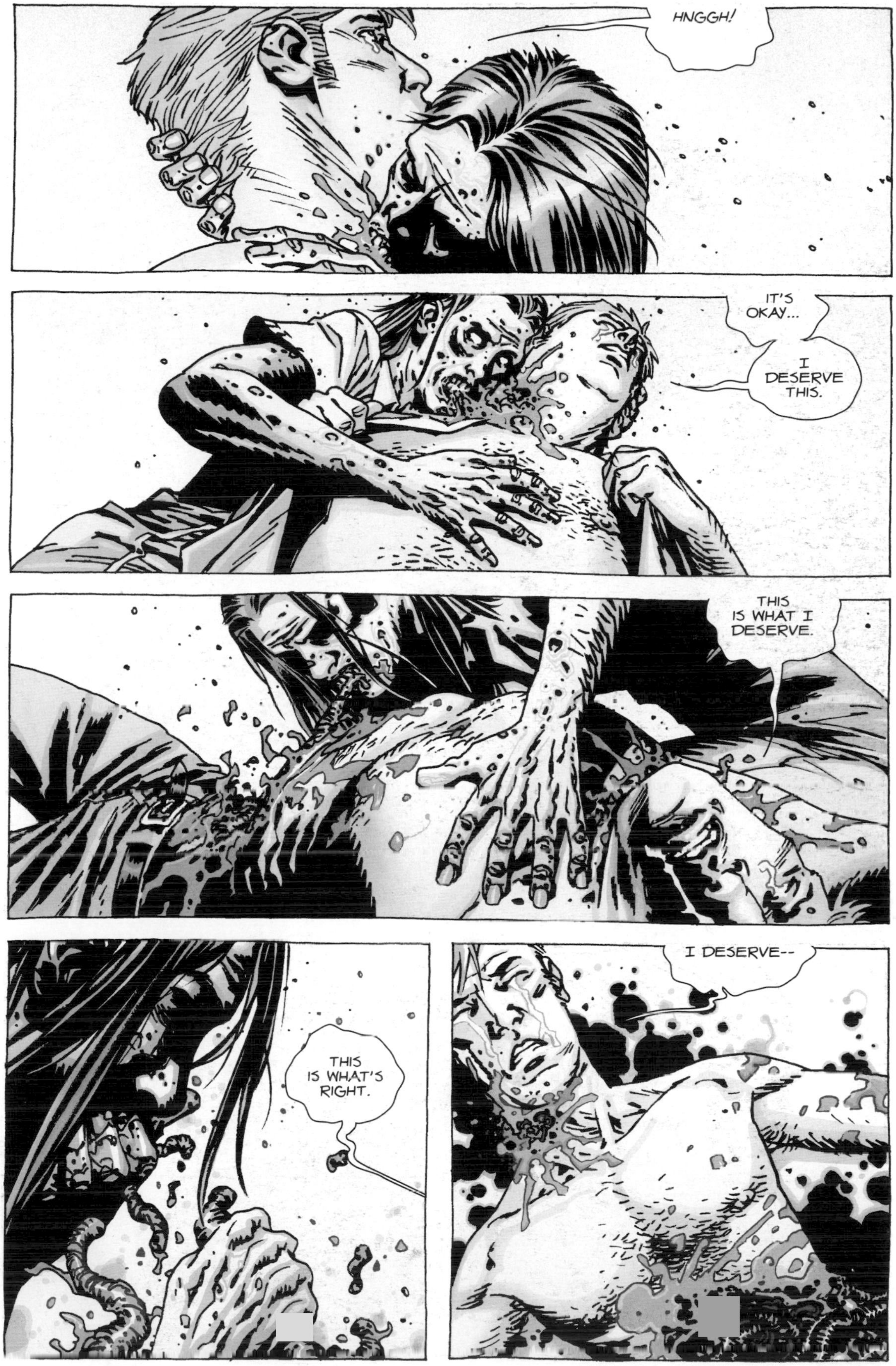
HNGGH!
IT'S OKAY...
I DESERVE THIS.
THIS IS WHAT I DESERVE.
THIS IS WHAT'S RIGHT.
I DESERVE--

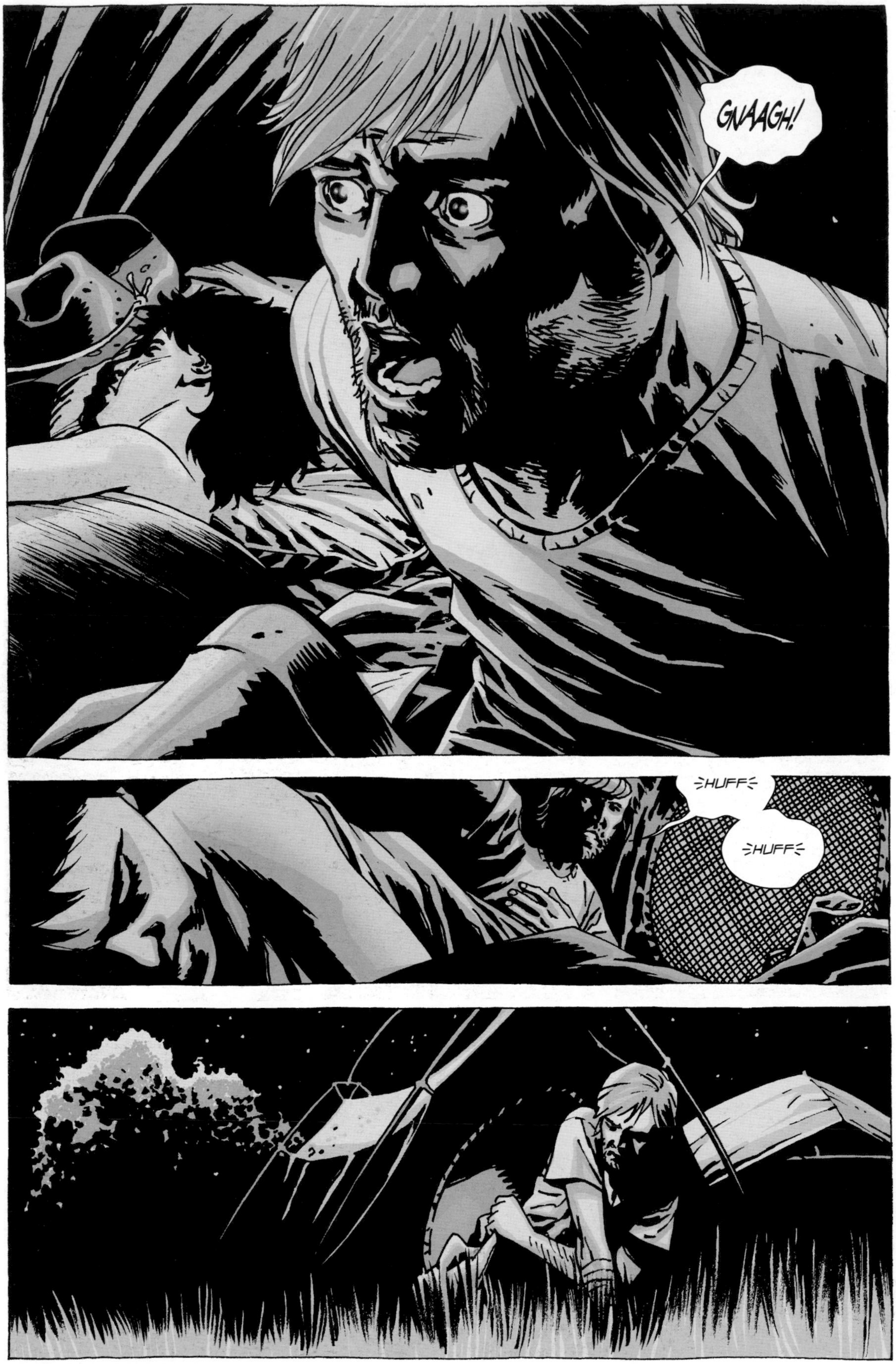
GNAAGH!
HUFF
HUFF

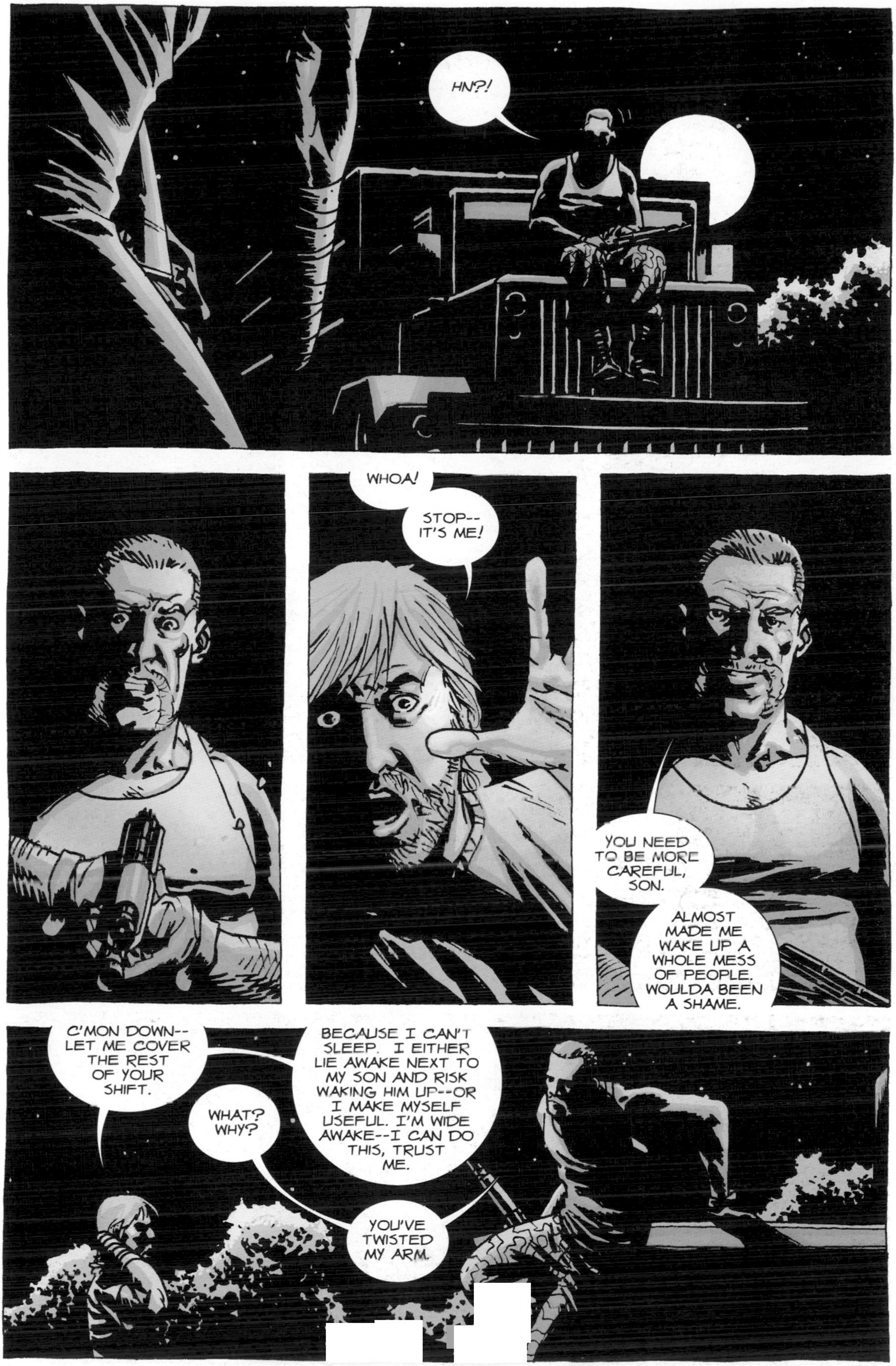
HN?!
WHOA!
STOP-- IT'S ME!
YOU NEED TO BE MORE CAREFUL, SON.
ALMOST MADE ME WAKE UP A WHOLE MESS OF PEOPLE. WOULDA BEEN A SHAME.
C'MON DOWN-- LET ME COVER THE REST OF YOUR SHIFT.
WHAT? WHY?
BECAUSE I CAN'T SLEEP. I EITHER LIE AWAKE NEXT TO MY SON AND RISK WAKING HIM UP--OR I MAKE MYSELF USEFUL. I'M WIDE AWAKE--I CAN DO THIS, TRUST ME.
YOU'VE TWISTED MY ARM.

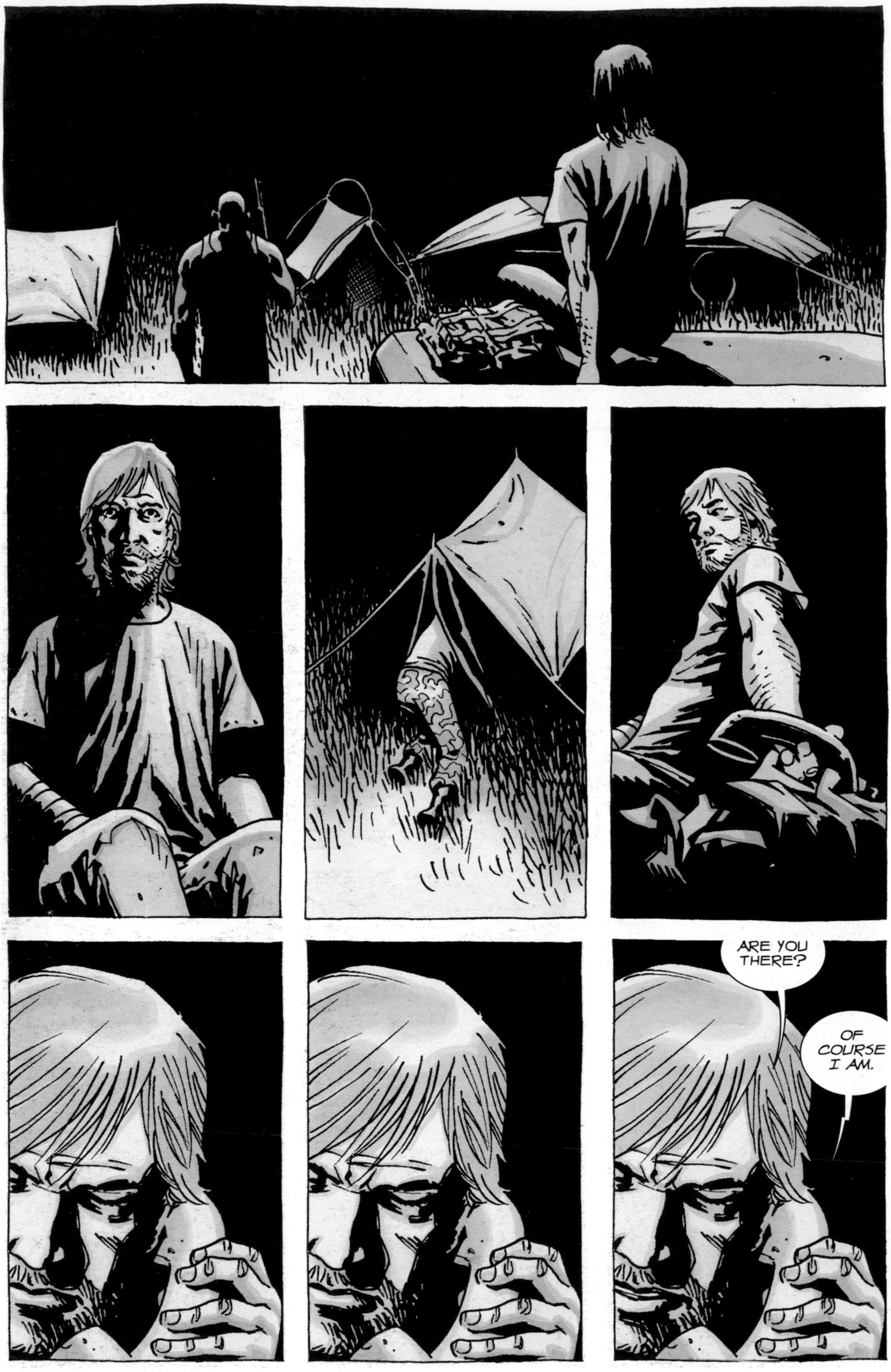
ARE YOU THERE?
OF COURSE I AM.

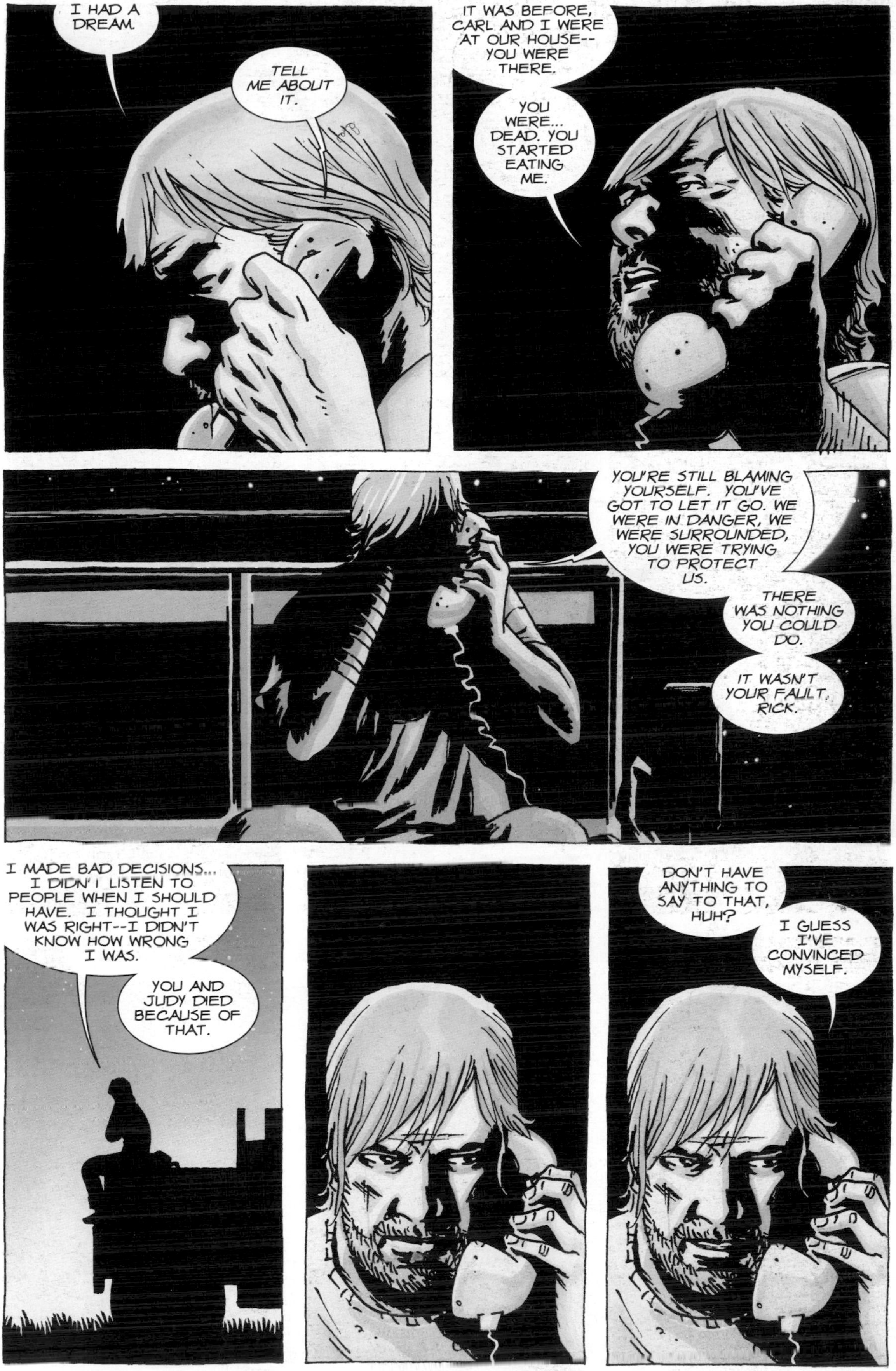

I HAD A DREAM.
TELL ME ABOUT IT.
IT WAS BEFORE, CARL AND I WERE AT OUR HOUSE-- YOU WERE THERE.
YOU WERE... DEAD. YOU STARTED EATING ME.
YOU'RE STILL BLAMING YOURSELF. YOU'VE GOT TO LET IT GO. WE WERE IN DANGER, WE WERE SURROUNDED, YOU WERE TRYING TO PROTECT US.
THERE WAS NOTHING YOU COULD DO.
IT WASN'T YOUR FAULT, RICK.
I MADE BAD DECISIONS... I DIDN'T LISTEN TO PEOPLE WHEN I SHOULD HAVE. I THOUGHT I WAS RIGHT--I DIDN'T KNOW HOW WRONG I WAS.
YOU AND JUDY DIED BECAUSE OF THAT.
DON'T HAVE ANYTHING TO SAY TO THAT, HUH?
I GUESS I'VE CONVINCED MYSELF.

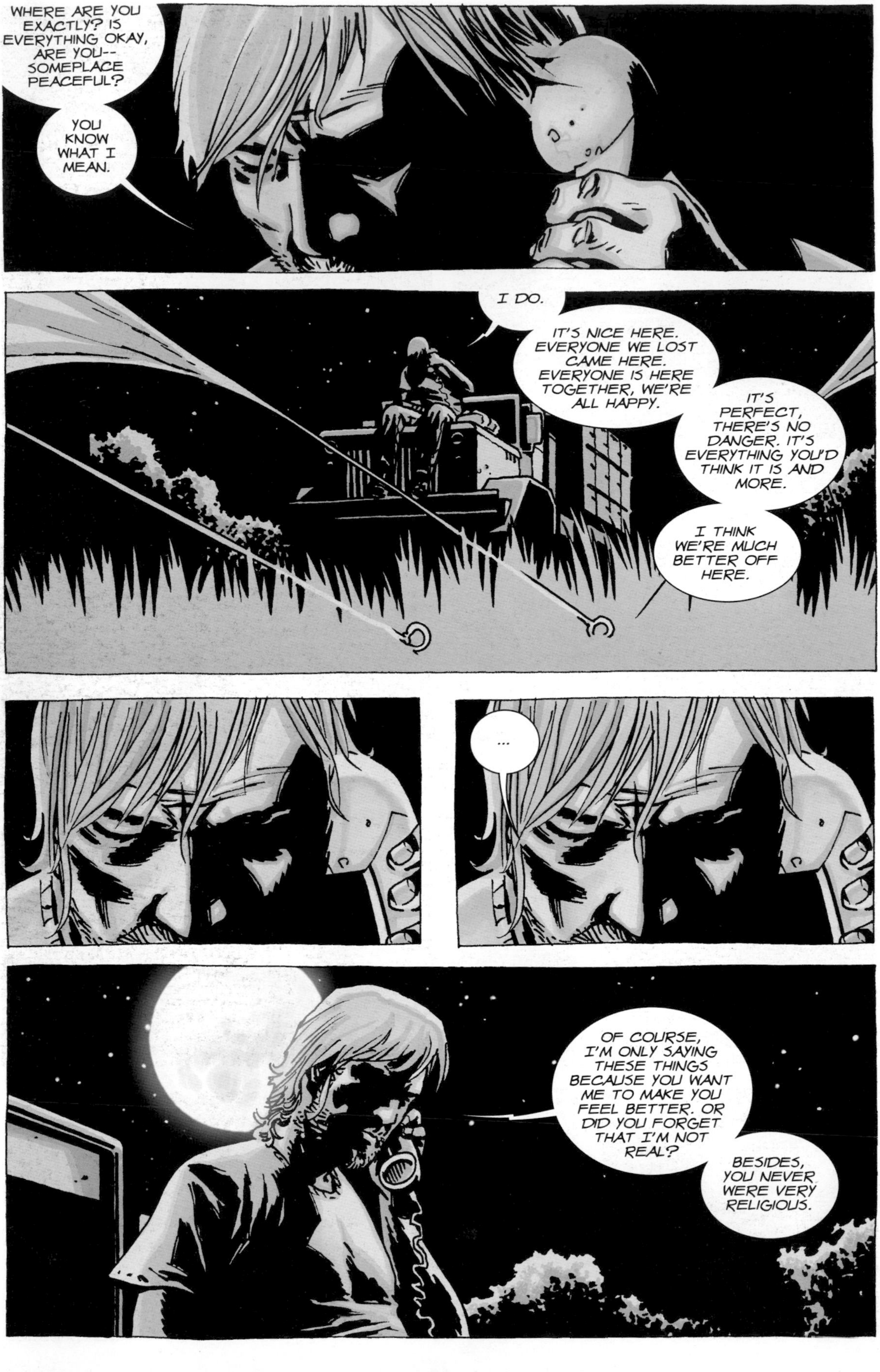
WHERE ARE YOU EXACTLY? IS EVERYTHING OKAY, ARE YOU-- SOMEPLACE PEACEFUL?
YOU KNOW WHAT I MEAN.
I DO.
IT'S NICE HERE. EVERYONE WE LOST CAME HERE. EVERYONE IS HERE TOGETHER, WE'RE ALL HAPPY.
IT'S PERFECT, THERE'S NO DANGER. IT'S EVERYTHING YOU'D THINK IT IS AND MORE.
I THINK WE'RE MUCH BETTER OFF HERE.
...
OF COURSE, I'M ONLY SAYING THESE THINGS BECAUSE YOU WANT ME TO MAKE YOU FEEL BETTER. OR DID YOU FORGET THAT I'M NOT REAL?
BESIDES, YOU NEVER WERE VERY RELIGIOUS.

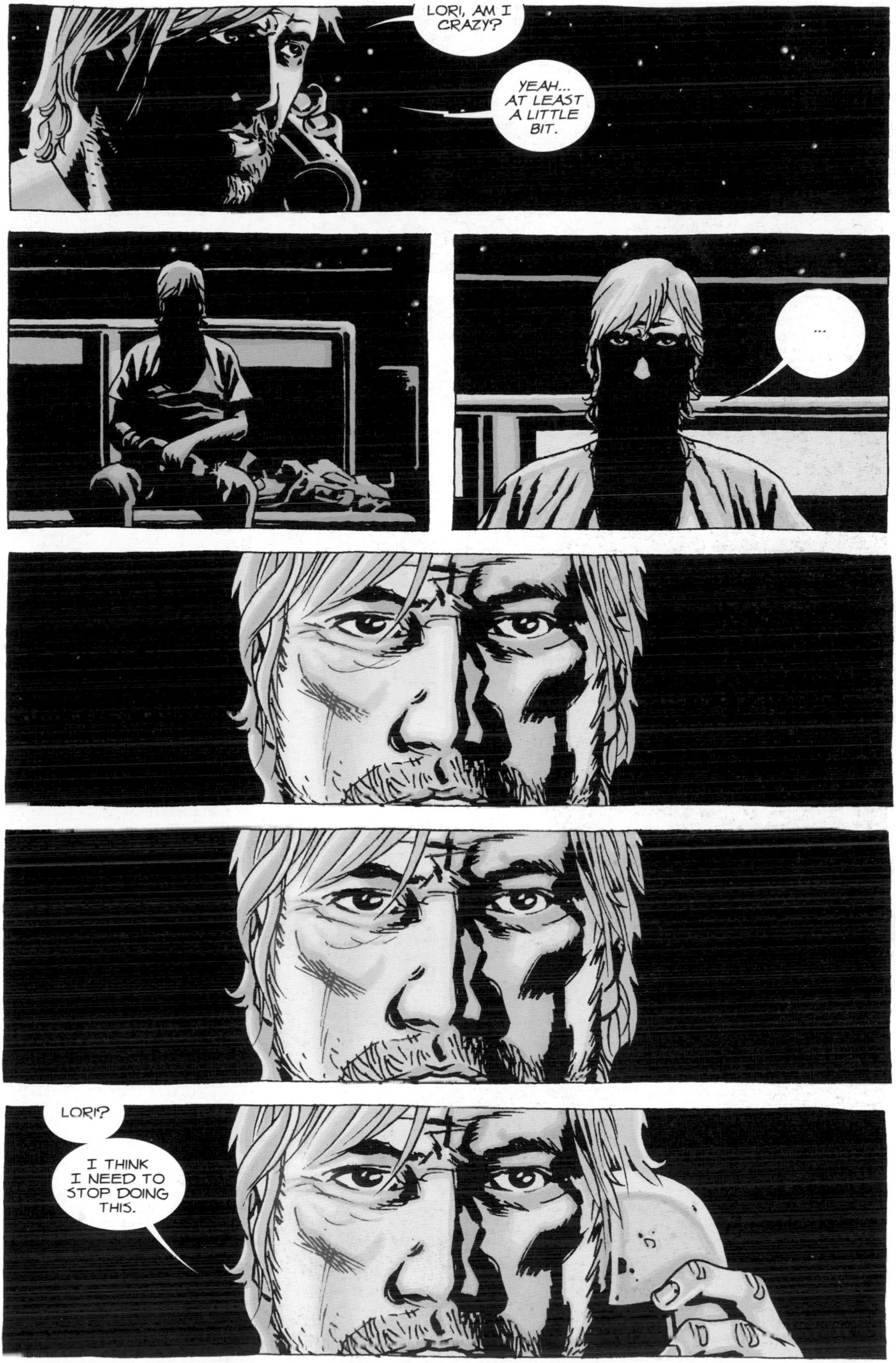
LORI, AM I CRAZY?
YEAH... AT LEAST A LITTLE BIT.
...
LORI?
I THINK I NEED TO STOP DOING THIS.

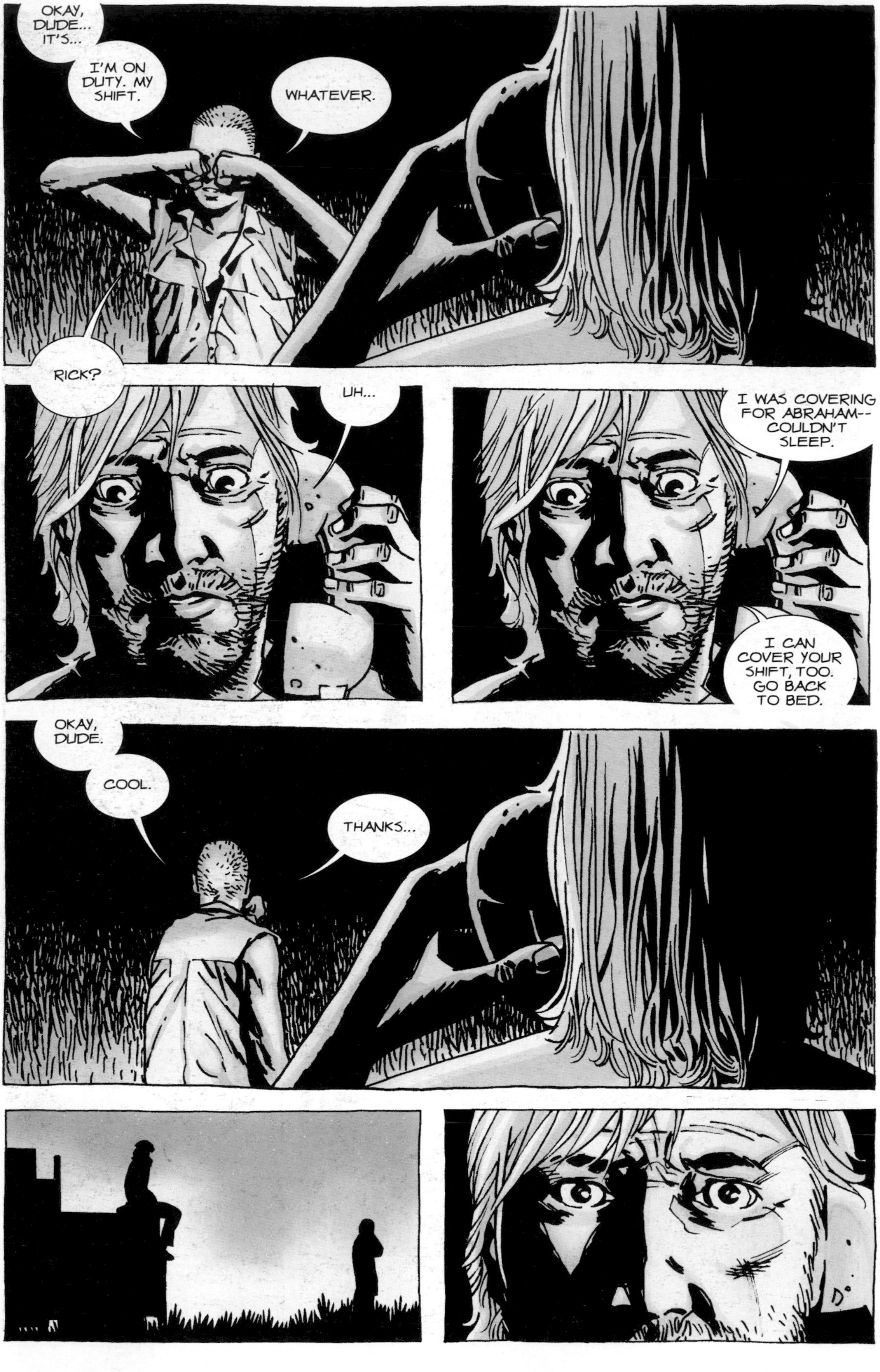
OKAY, DUDE... IT'S...
I'M ON DUTY. MY SHIFT.
WHATEVER.
RICK?
UH...
I WAS COVERING FOR ABRAHAM-- COULDN'T SLEEP.
I CAN COVER YOUR SHIFT, TOO. GO BACK TO BED.
OKAY, DUDE.
COOL.
THANKS...

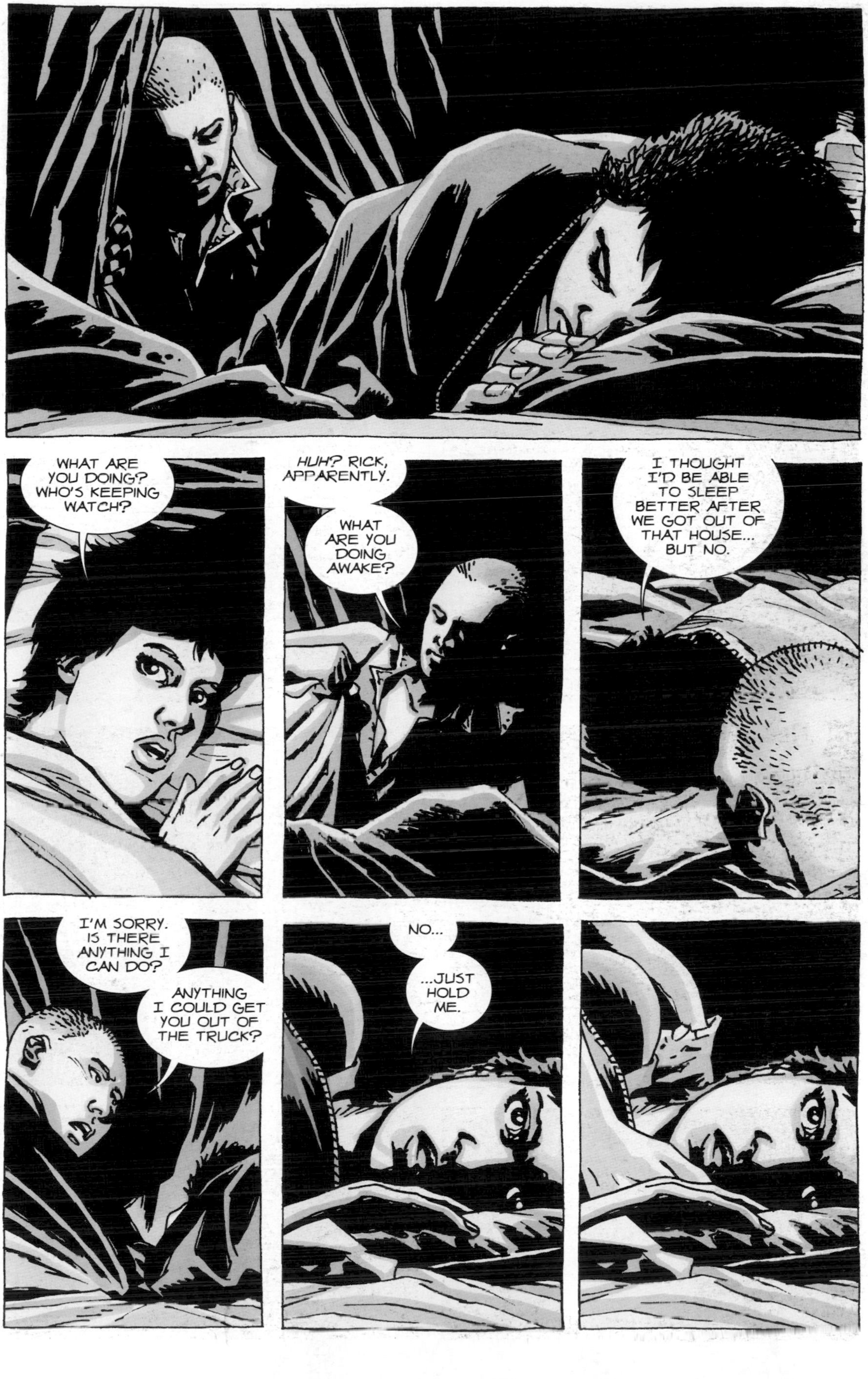
WHAT ARE YOU DOING? WHO'S KEEPING WATCH?
HUH? RICK, APPARENTLY.
WHAT ARE YOU DOING AWAKE?
I THOUGHT I'D BE ABLE TO SLEEP BETTER AFTER WE GOT OUT OF THAT HOUSE... BUT NO.
I'M SORRY. IS THERE ANYTHING I CAN DO?
ANYTHING I COULD GET YOU OUT OF THE TRUCK?
NO...
...JUST HOLD ME.

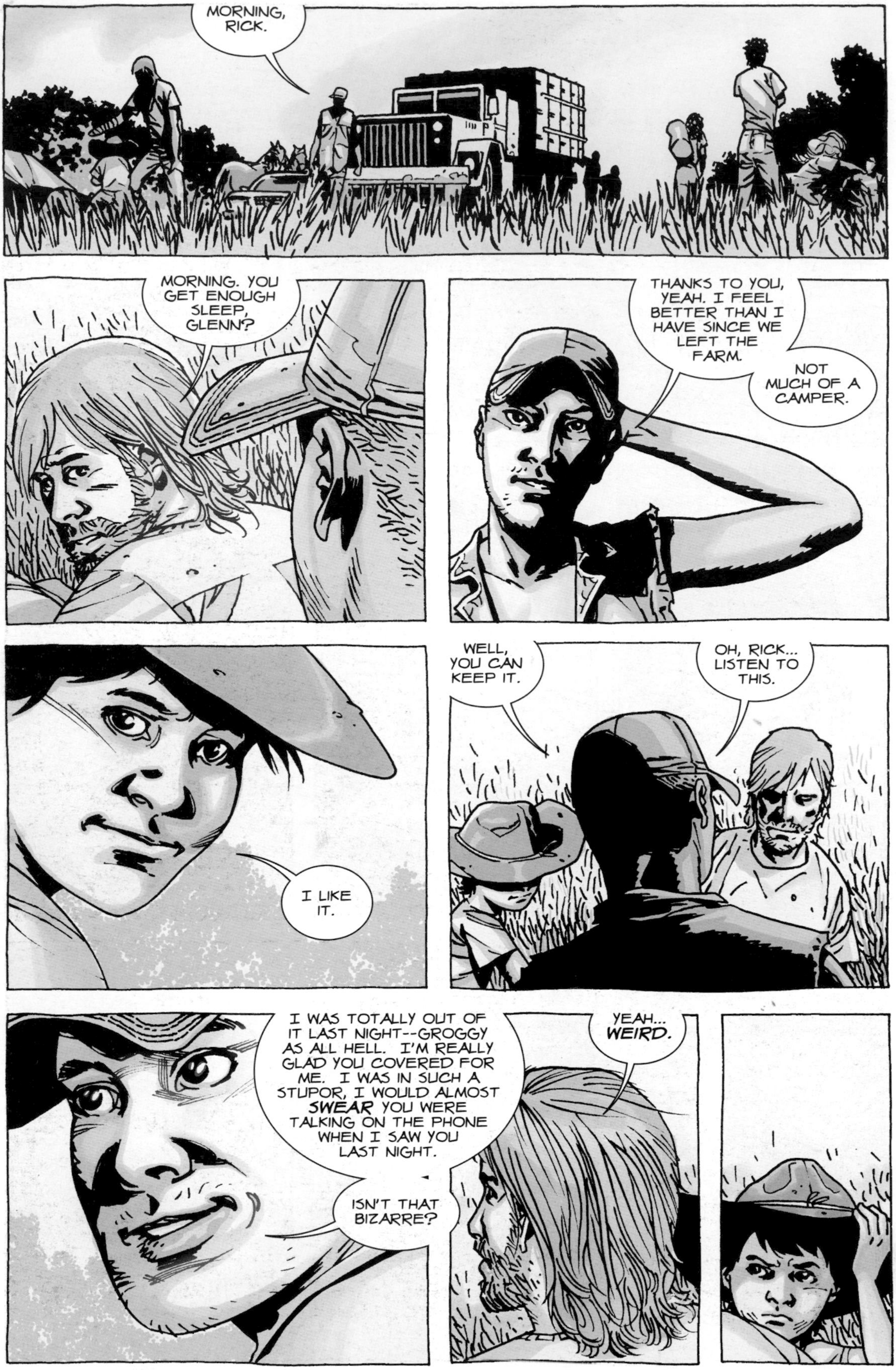
MORNING, RICK.
MORNING. YOU GET ENOUGH SLEEP, GLENN?
THANKS TO YOU, YEAH. I FEEL BETTER THAN I HAVE SINCE WE LEFT THE FARM.
NOT MUCH OF A CAMPER.
I LIKE IT.
WELL, YOU CAN KEEP IT.
OH, RICK... LISTEN TO THIS.
I WAS TOTALLY OUT OF IT LAST NIGHT--GROGGY AS ALL HELL. I'M REALLY GLAD YOU COVERED FOR ME. I WAS IN SUCH A STUPOR, I WOULD ALMOST SWEAR YOU WERE TALKING ON THE PHONE WHEN I SAW YOU LAST NIGHT.
ISN'T THAT BIZARRE?
YEAH... WEIRD.

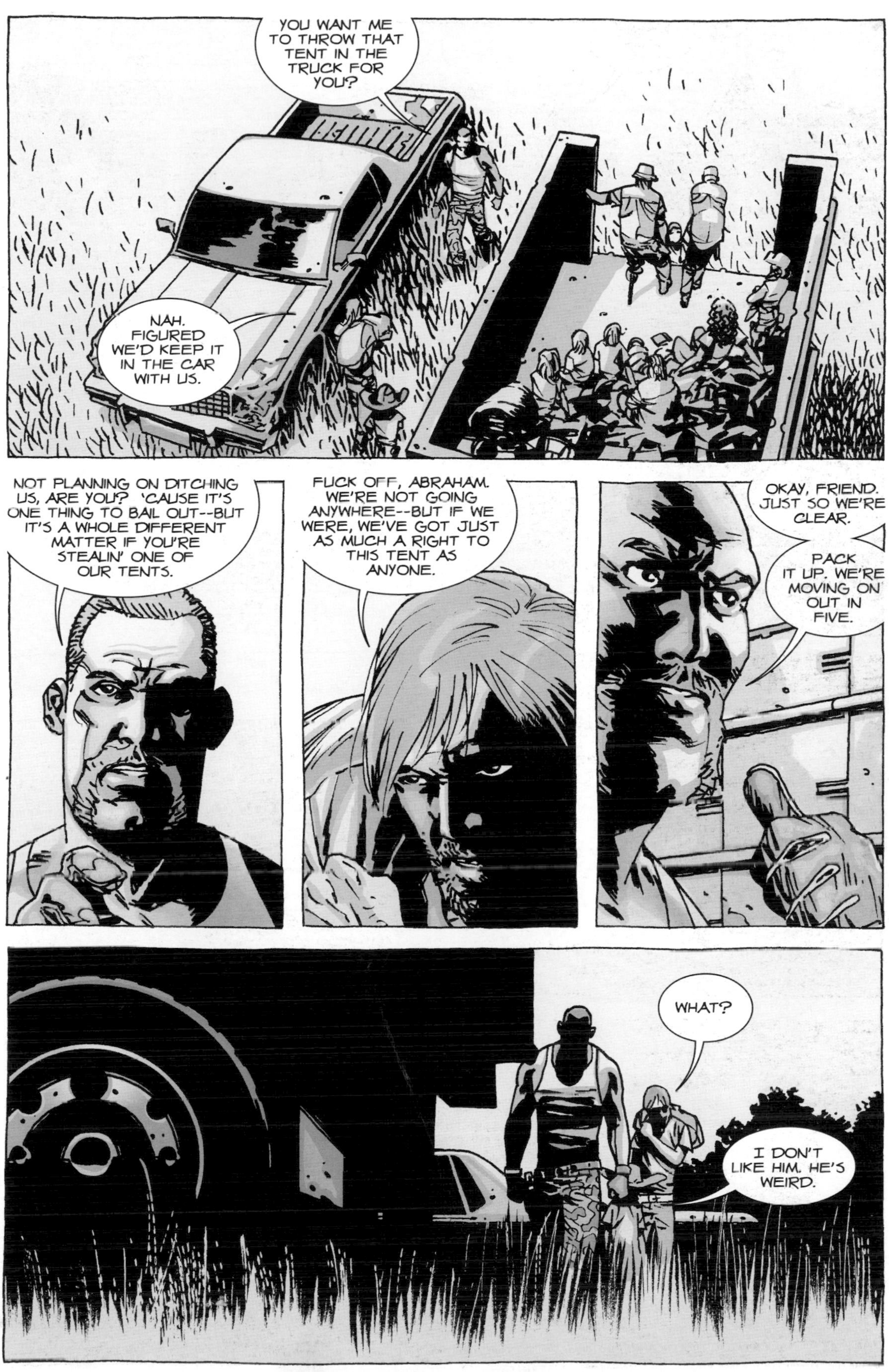
YOU WANT ME TO THROW THAT TENT IN THE TRUCK FOR YOU?
NAH. FIGURED WE'D KEEP IT IN THE CAR WITH US.
NOT PLANNING ON DITCHING US, ARE YOU? 'CAUSE IT'S ONE THING TO BAIL OUT--BUT IT'S A WHOLE DIFFERENT MATTER IF YOU'RE STEALIN' ONE OF OUR TENTS.
FUCK OFF, ABRAHAM. WE'RE NOT GOING ANYWHERE--BUT IF WE WERE, WE'VE GOT JUST AS MUCH A RIGHT TO THIS TENT AS ANYONE.
OKAY, FRIEND. JUST SO WE'RE CLEAR.
PACK IT UP. WE'RE MOVING ON OUT IN FIVE.
WHAT?
I DON'T LIKE HIM. HE'S WEIRD.

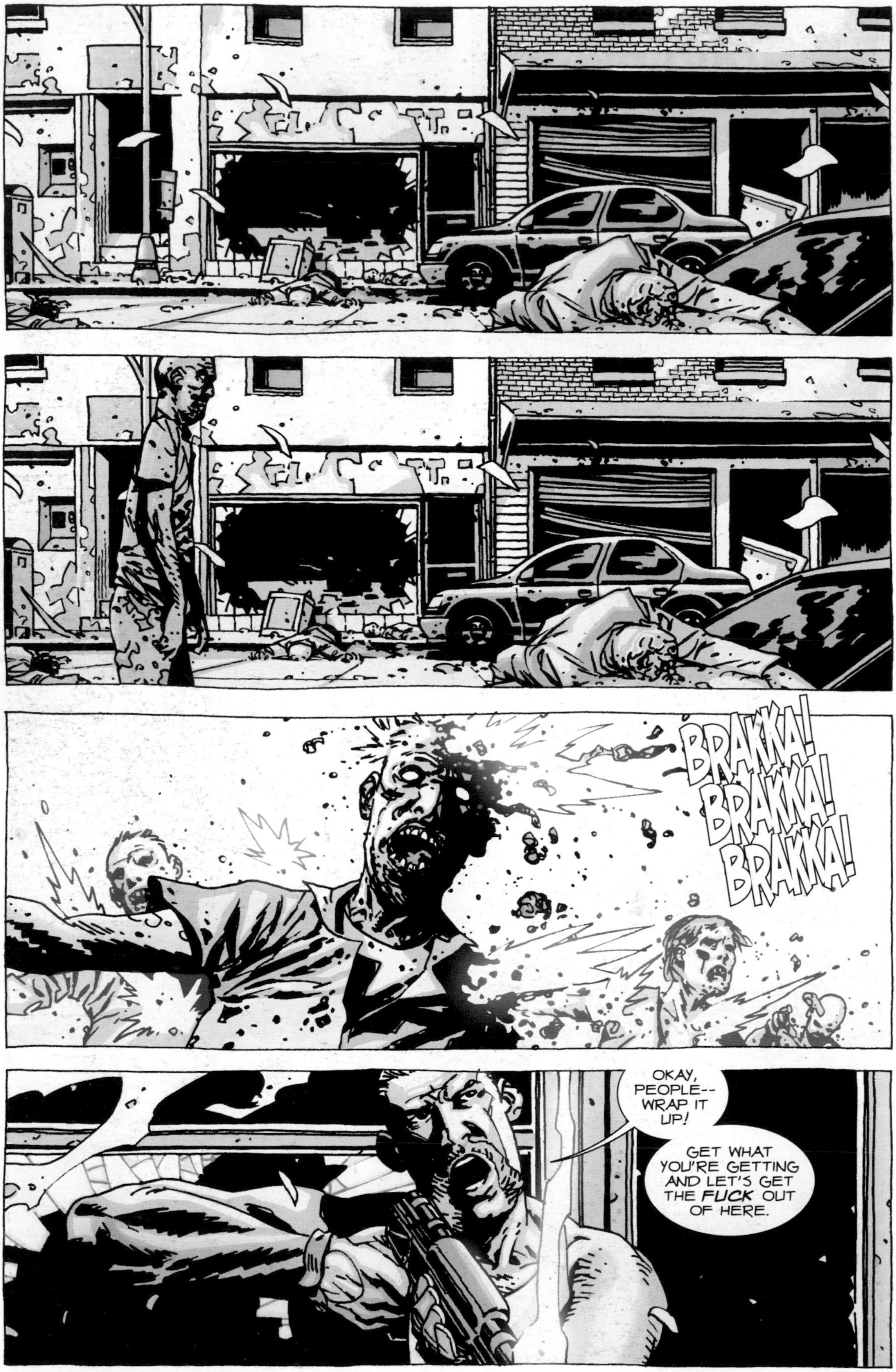
BRAKKA! BRAKKA! BRAKKA!
OKAY, PEOPLE-- WRAP IT UP!
GET WHAT YOU'RE GETTING AND LET'S GET THE *FUCK* OUT OF HERE.

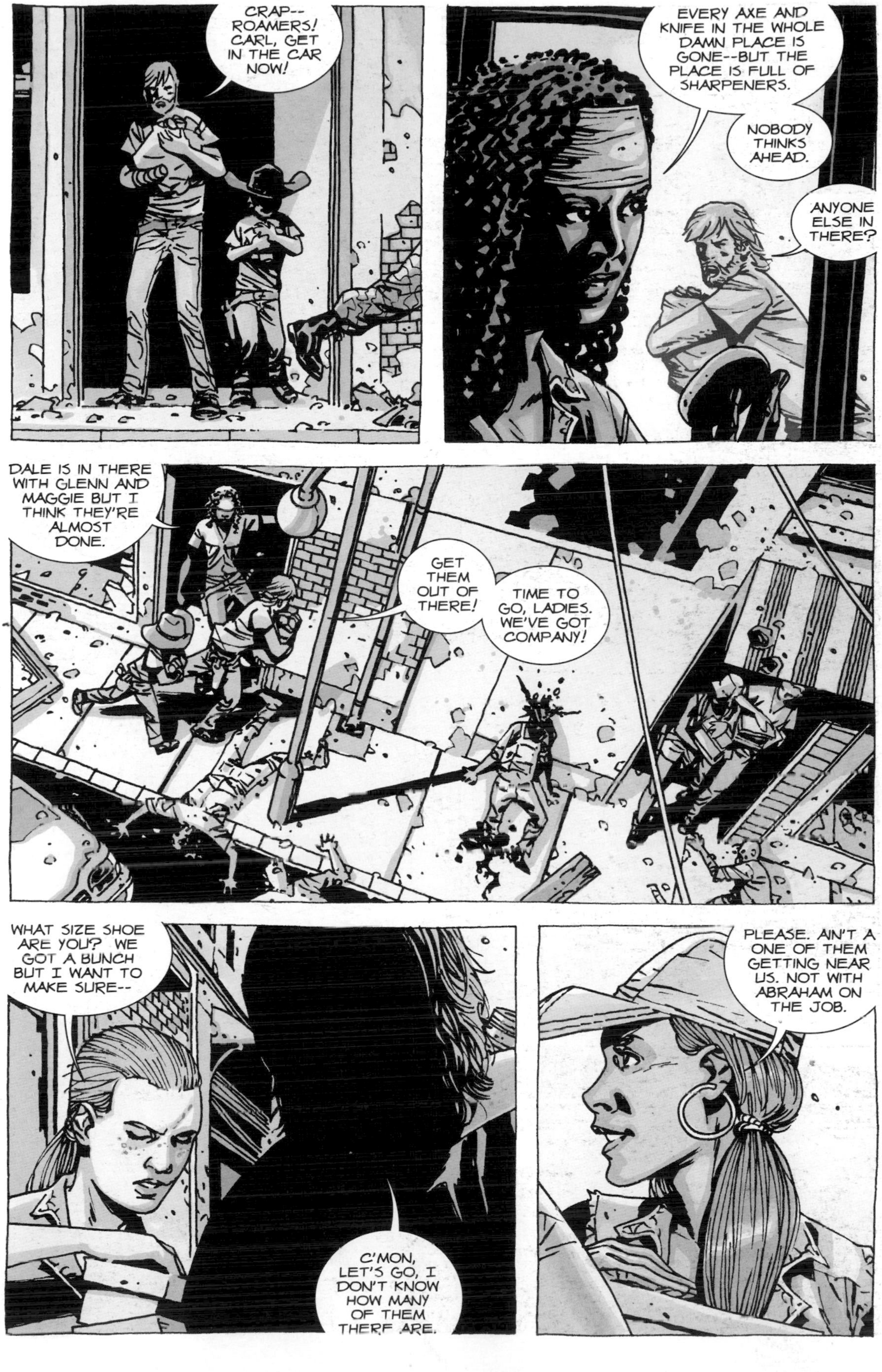
CRAP-- ROAMERS! CARL, GET IN THE CAR NOW!
EVERY AXE AND KNIFE IN THE WHOLE DAMN PLACE IS GONE--BUT THE PLACE IS FULL OF SHARPENERS.
NOBODY THINKS AHEAD.
ANYONE ELSE IN THERE?
DALE IS IN THERE WITH GLENN AND MAGGIE BUT I THINK THEY'RE ALMOST DONE.
GET THEM OUT OF THERE!
TIME TO GO, LADIES. WE'VE GOT COMPANY!
WHAT SIZE SHOE ARE YOU? WE GOT A BUNCH BUT I WANT TO MAKE SURE--
C'MON, LET'S GO, I DON'T KNOW HOW MANY OF THEM THERE ARE.
PLEASE. AIN'T A ONE OF THEM GETTING NEAR US. NOT WITH ABRAHAM ON THE JOB.

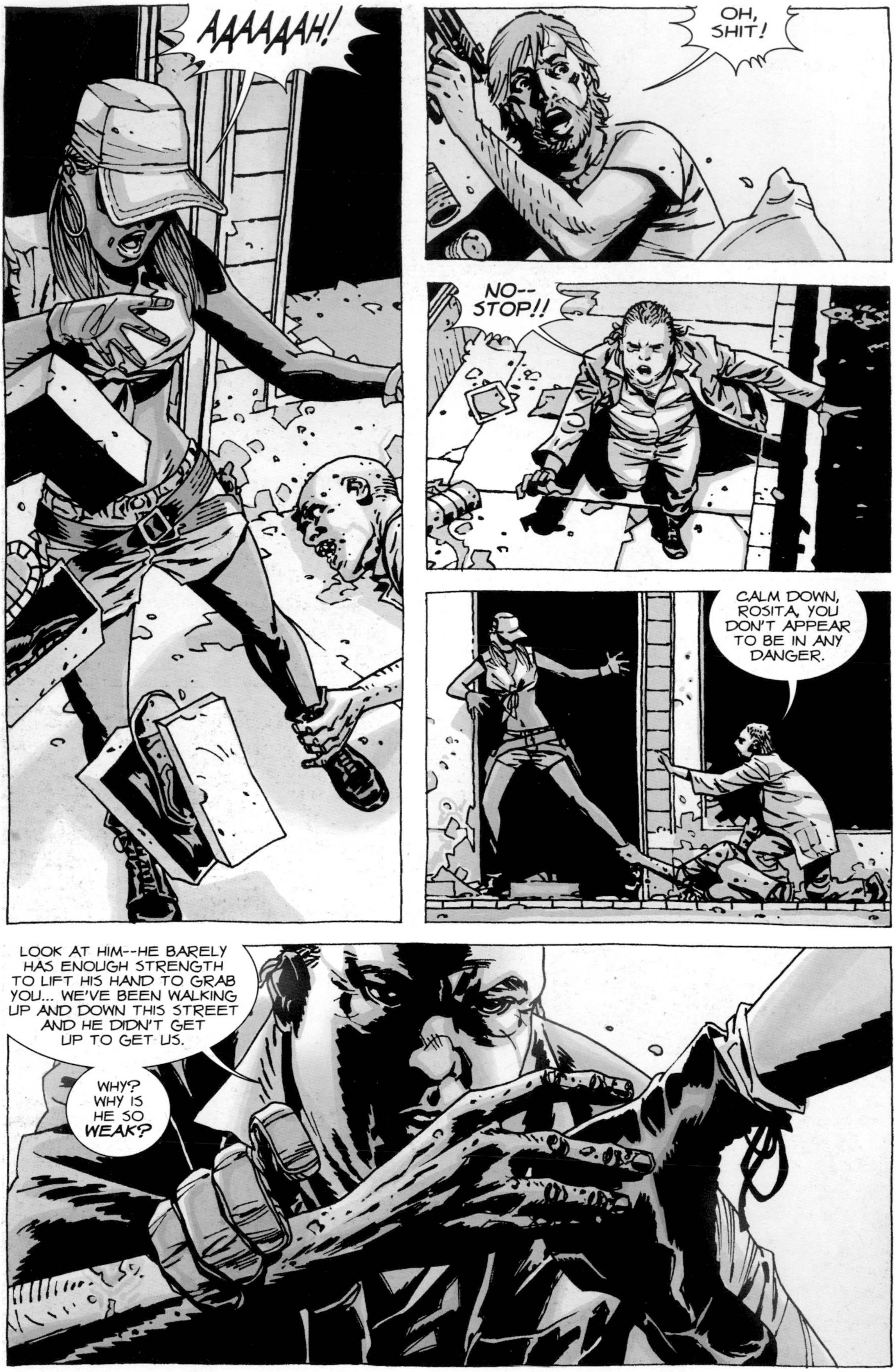
AAAAAAH!
OH, SHIT!
NO-- STOP!!
CALM DOWN, ROSITA, YOU DON'T APPEAR TO BE IN ANY DANGER.
LOOK AT HIM--HE BARELY HAS ENOUGH STRENGTH TO LIFT HIS HAND TO GRAB YOU... WE'VE BEEN WALKING UP AND DOWN THIS STREET AND HE DIDN'T GET UP TO GET US.
WHY? WHY IS HE SO WEAK?

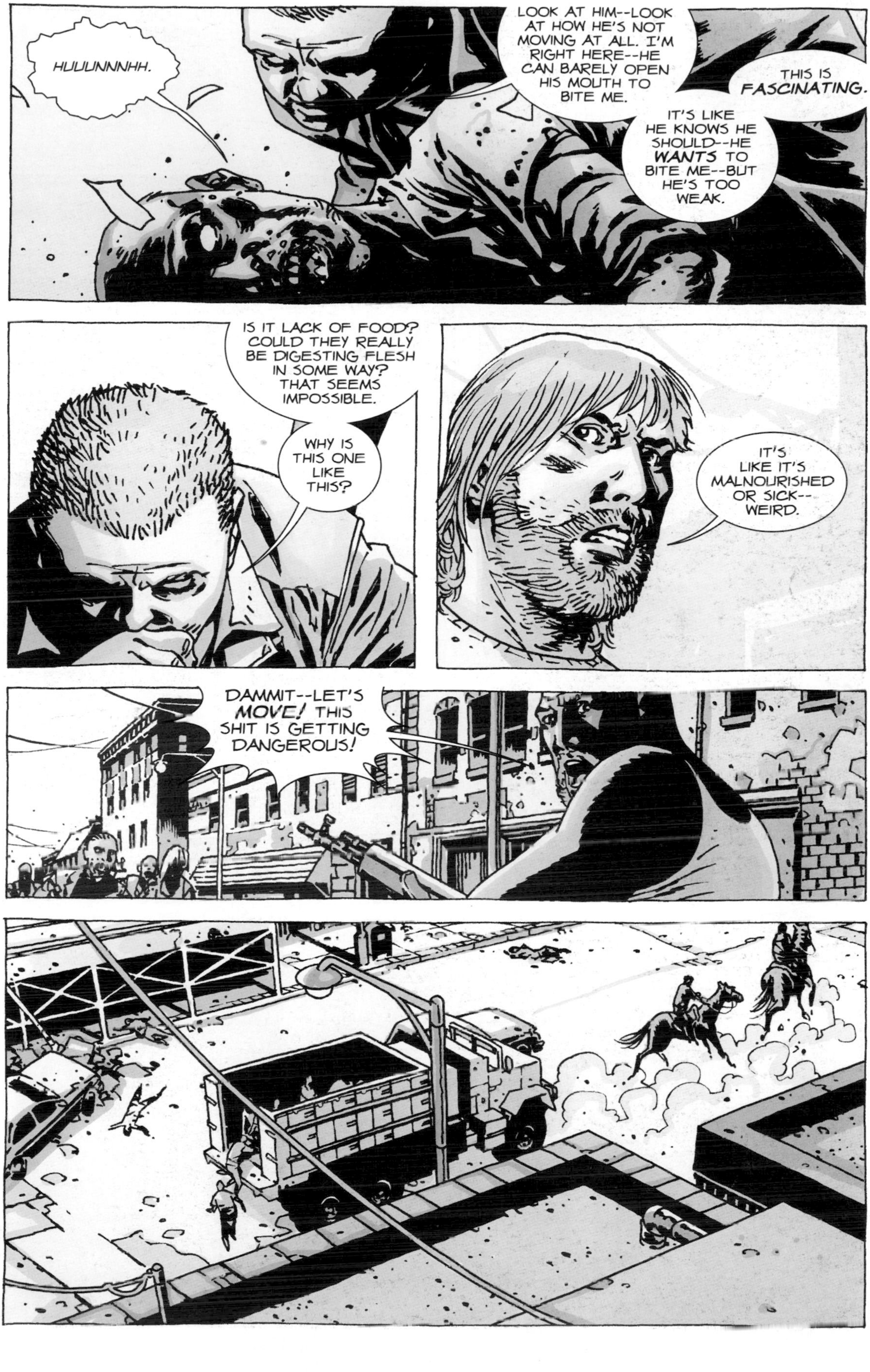
HUUUNNNHH.
LOOK AT HIM--LOOK AT HOW HE'S NOT MOVING AT ALL. I'M RIGHT HERE--HE CAN BARELY OPEN HIS MOUTH TO BITE ME.
THIS IS FASCINATING.
IT'S LIKE HE KNOWS HE SHOULD--HE WANTS TO BITE ME--BUT HE'S TOO WEAK.
IS IT LACK OF FOOD? COULD THEY REALLY BE DIGESTING FLESH IN SOME WAY? THAT SEEMS IMPOSSIBLE.
WHY IS THIS ONE LIKE THIS?
IT'S LIKE IT'S MALNOURISHED OR SICK--WEIRD.
DAMMIT--LET'S MOVE! THIS SHIT IS GETTING DANGEROUS!

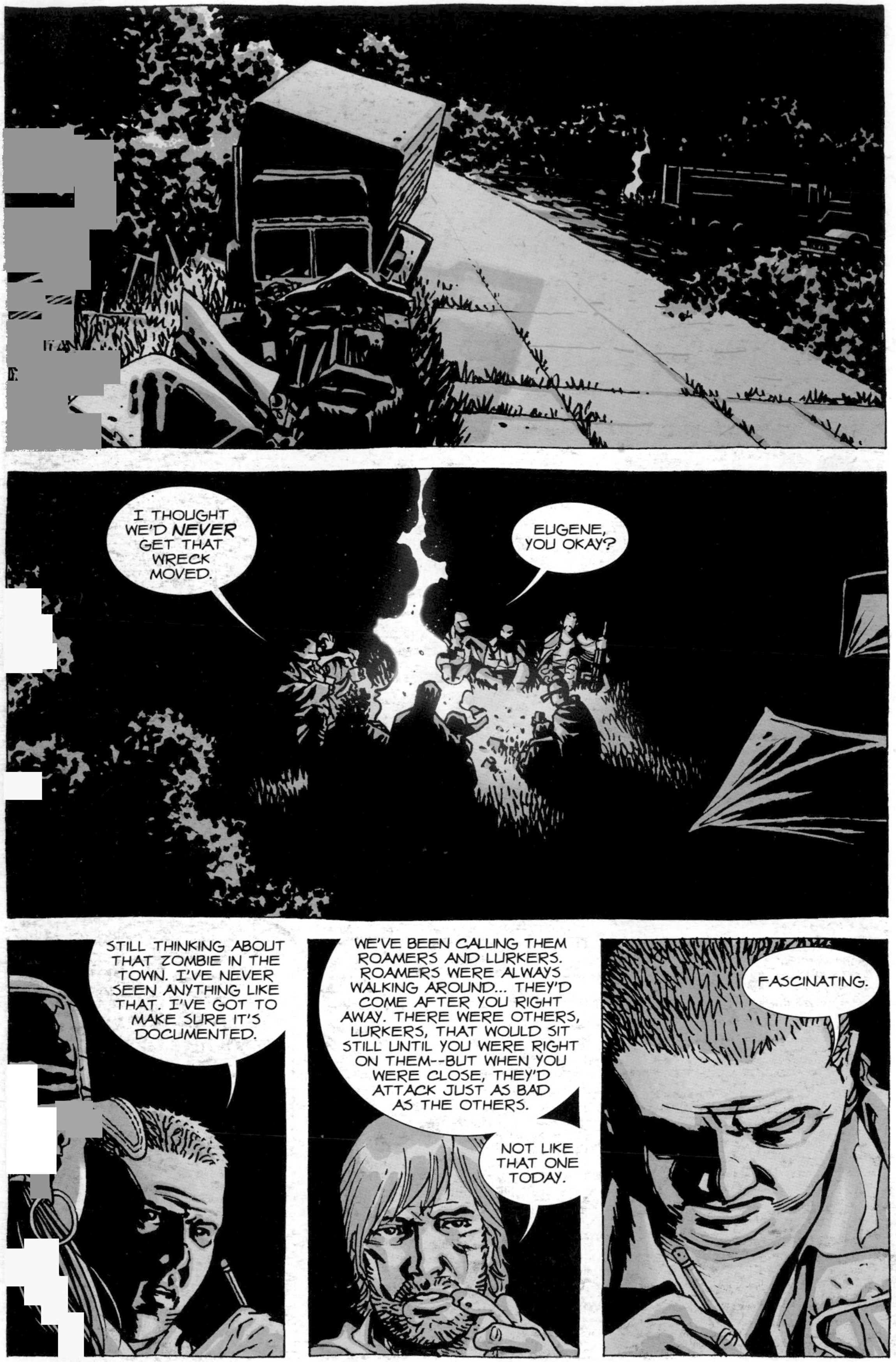
I THOUGHT WE'D **NEVER** GET THAT WRECK MOVED.
EUGENE, YOU OKAY?
STILL THINKING ABOUT THAT ZOMBIE IN THE TOWN. I'VE NEVER SEEN ANYTHING LIKE THAT. I'VE GOT TO MAKE SURE IT'S DOCUMENTED.
WE'VE BEEN CALLING THEM ROAMERS AND LURKERS. ROAMERS WERE ALWAYS WALKING AROUND... THEY'D COME AFTER YOU RIGHT AWAY. THERE WERE OTHERS, LURKERS, THAT WOULD SIT STILL UNTIL YOU WERE RIGHT ON THEM--BUT WHEN YOU WERE CLOSE, THEY'D ATTACK JUST AS BAD AS THE OTHERS.
NOT LIKE THAT ONE TODAY.
FASCINATING.

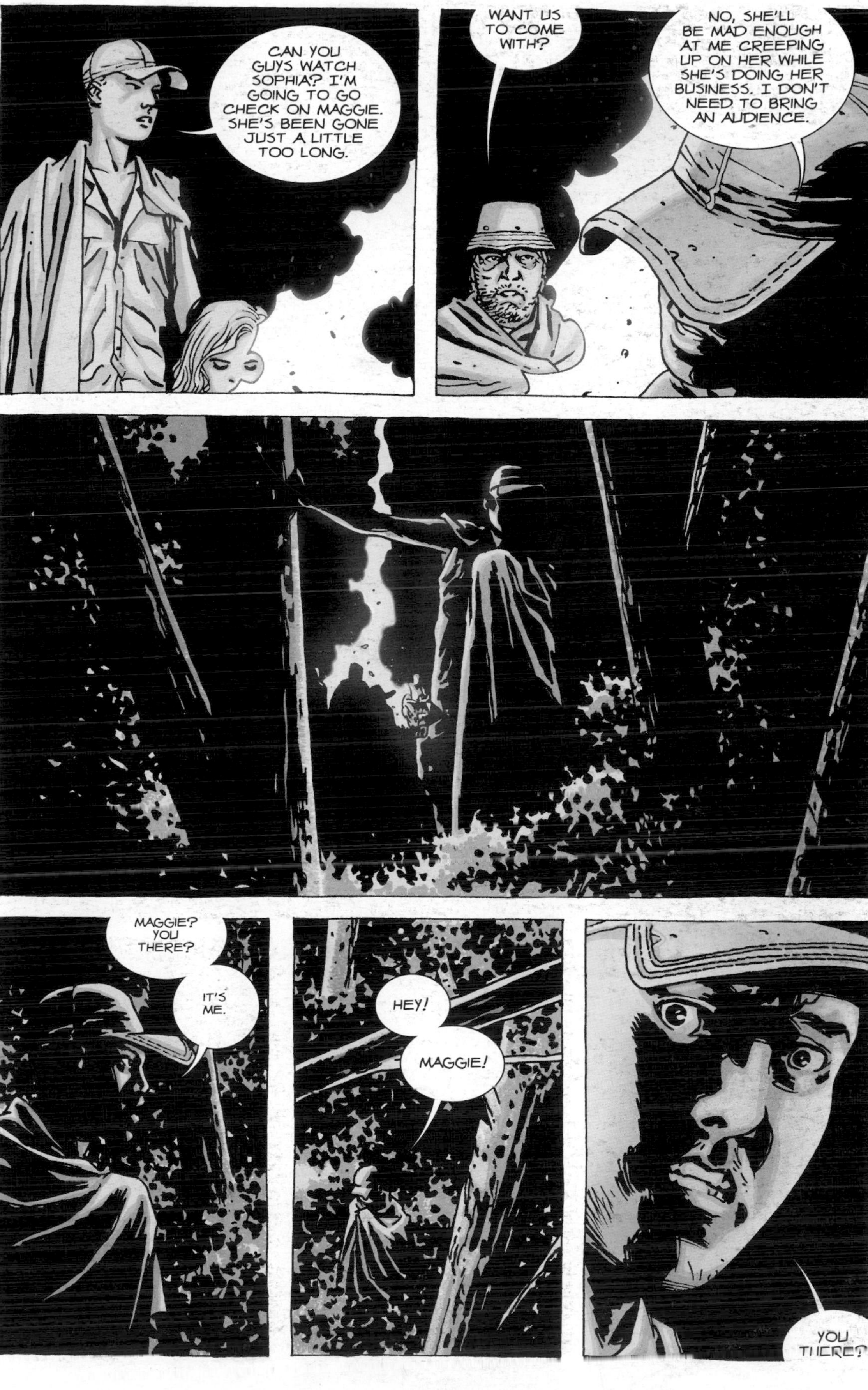
CAN YOU GUYS WATCH SOPHIA? I'M GOING TO GO CHECK ON MAGGIE. SHE'S BEEN GONE JUST A LITTLE TOO LONG.
WANT US TO COME WITH?
NO, SHE'LL BE MAD ENOUGH AT ME CREEPING UP ON HER WHILE SHE'S DOING HER BUSINESS. I DON'T NEED TO BRING AN AUDIENCE.
MAGGIE? YOU THERE?
IT'S ME.
HEY!
MAGGIE!
YOU THERE?

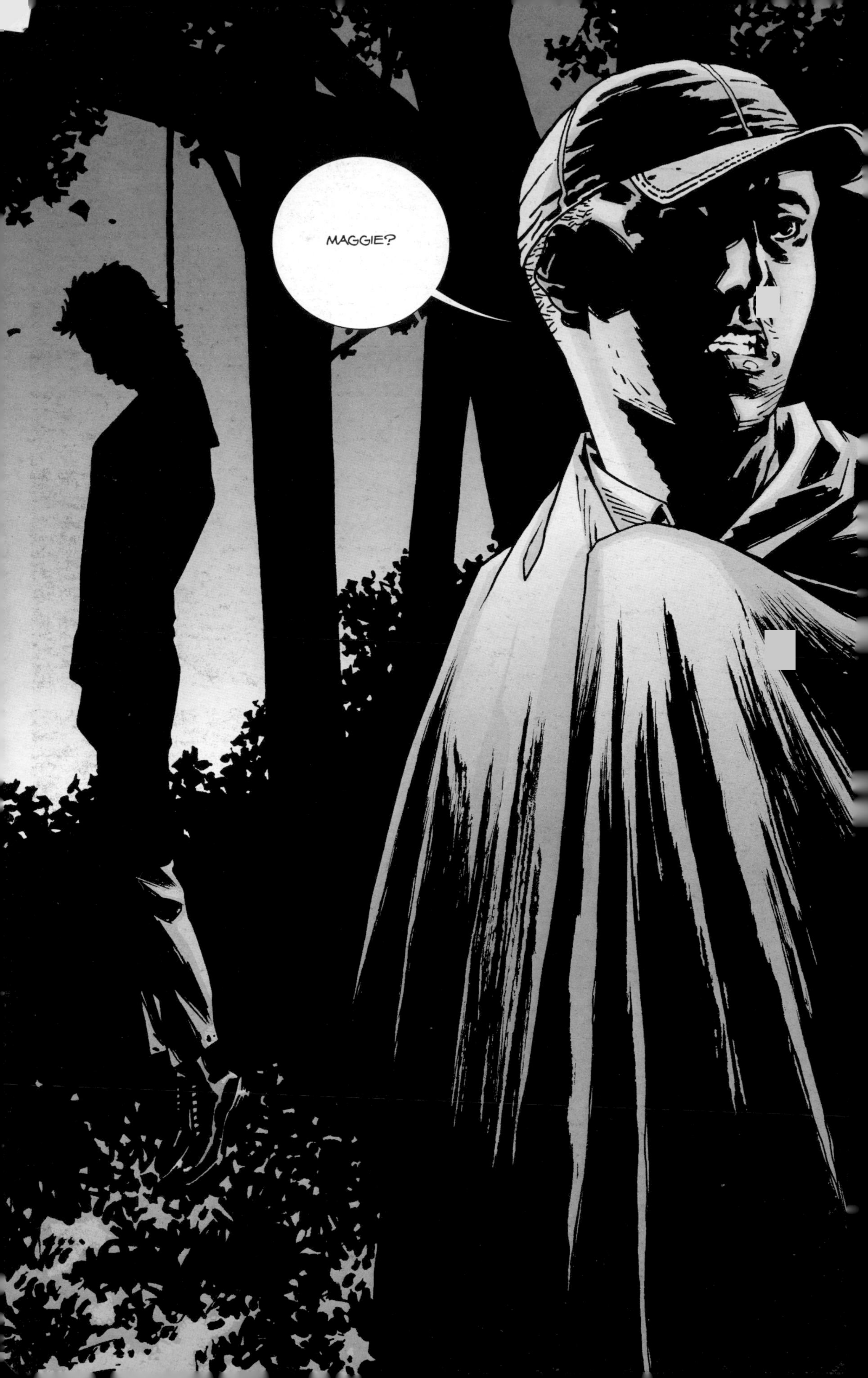
MAGGIE?

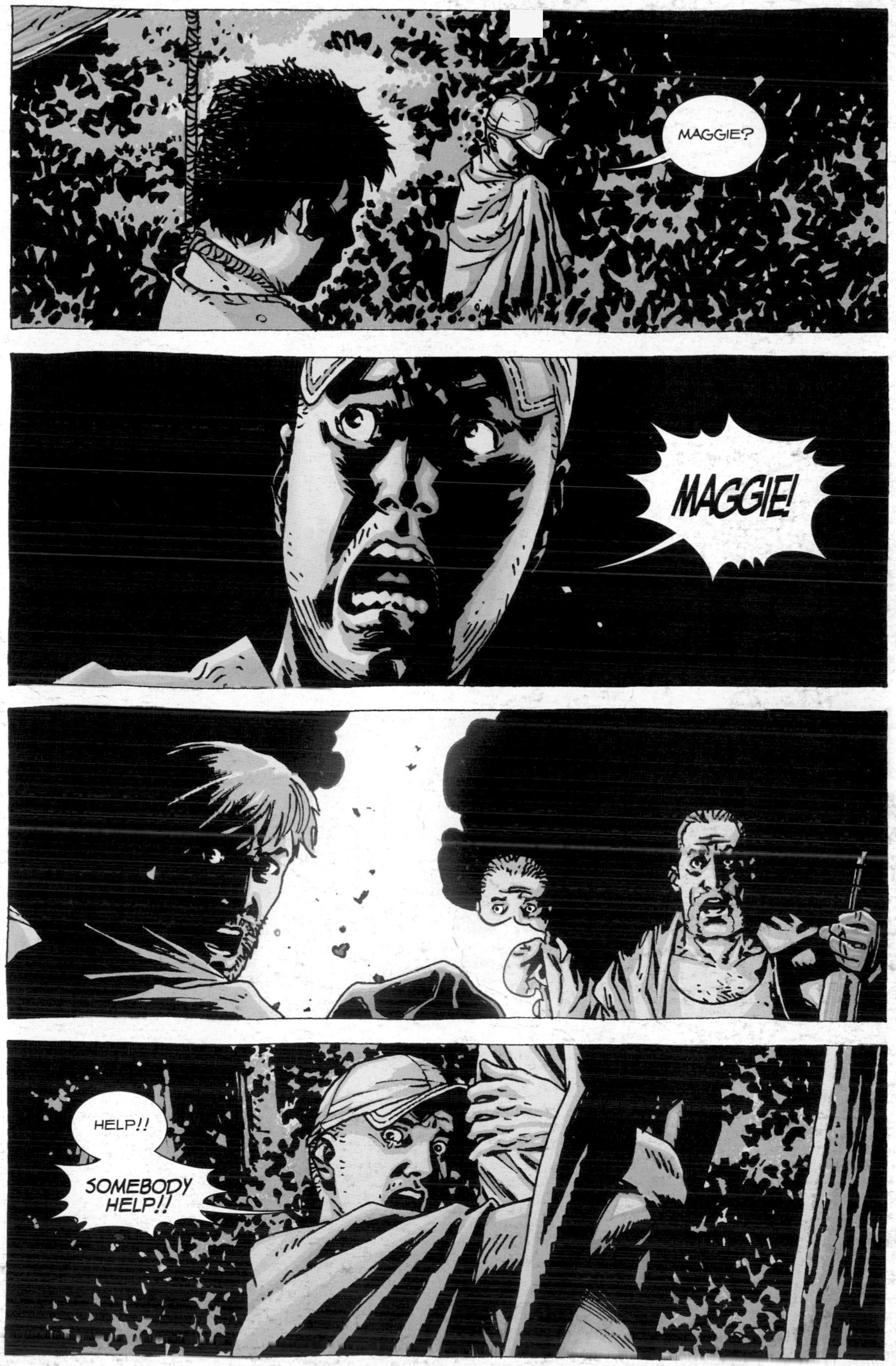
MAGGIE?
MAGGIE!
HELP!!
SOMEBODY HELP!!

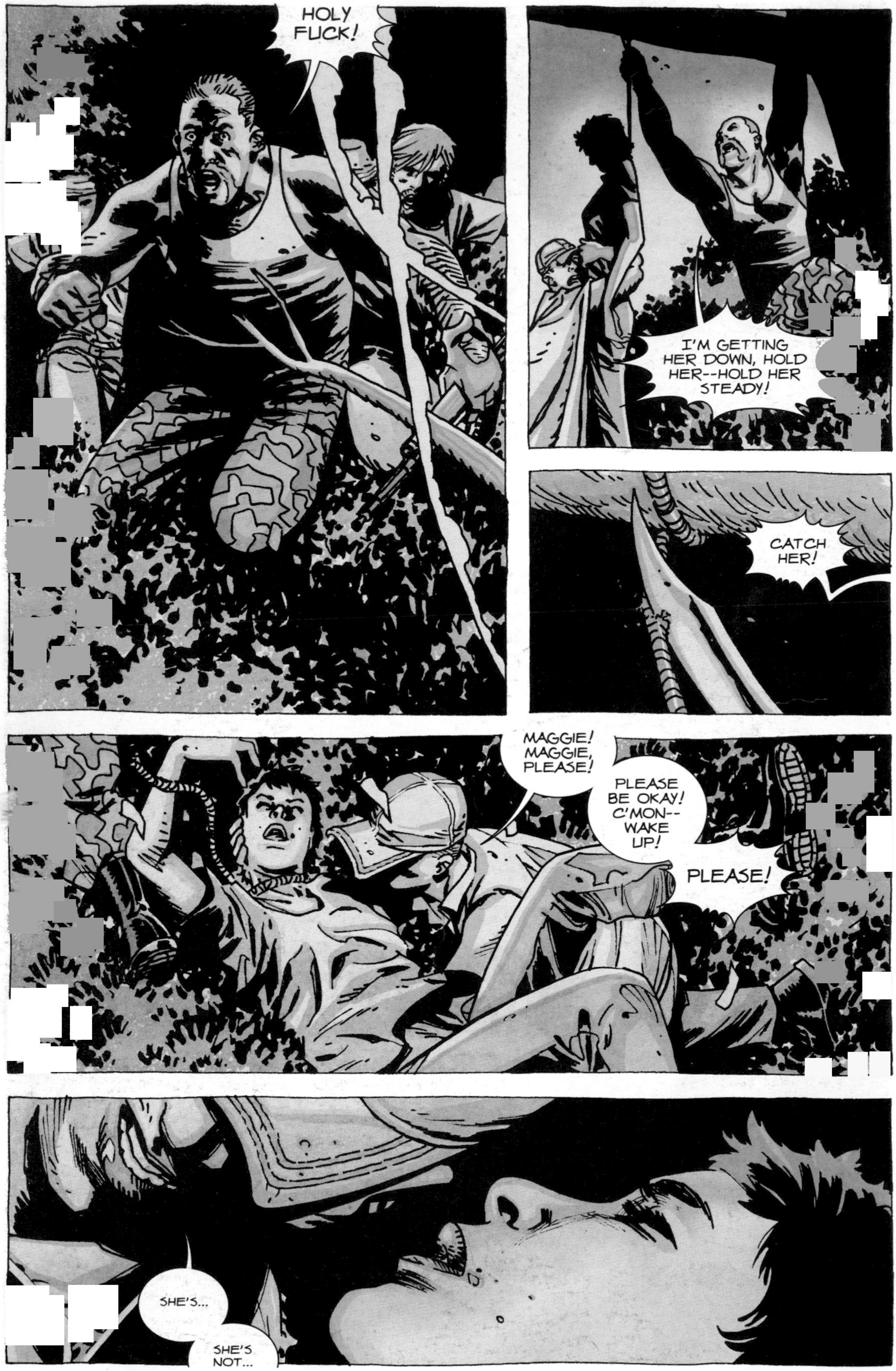
HOLY FUCK!
I'M GETTING HER DOWN, HOLD HER--HOLD HER STEADY!
CATCH HER!
MAGGIE! MAGGIE, PLEASE!
PLEASE BE OKAY! C'MON-- WAKE UP!
PLEASE!
SHE'S...
SHE'S NOT...

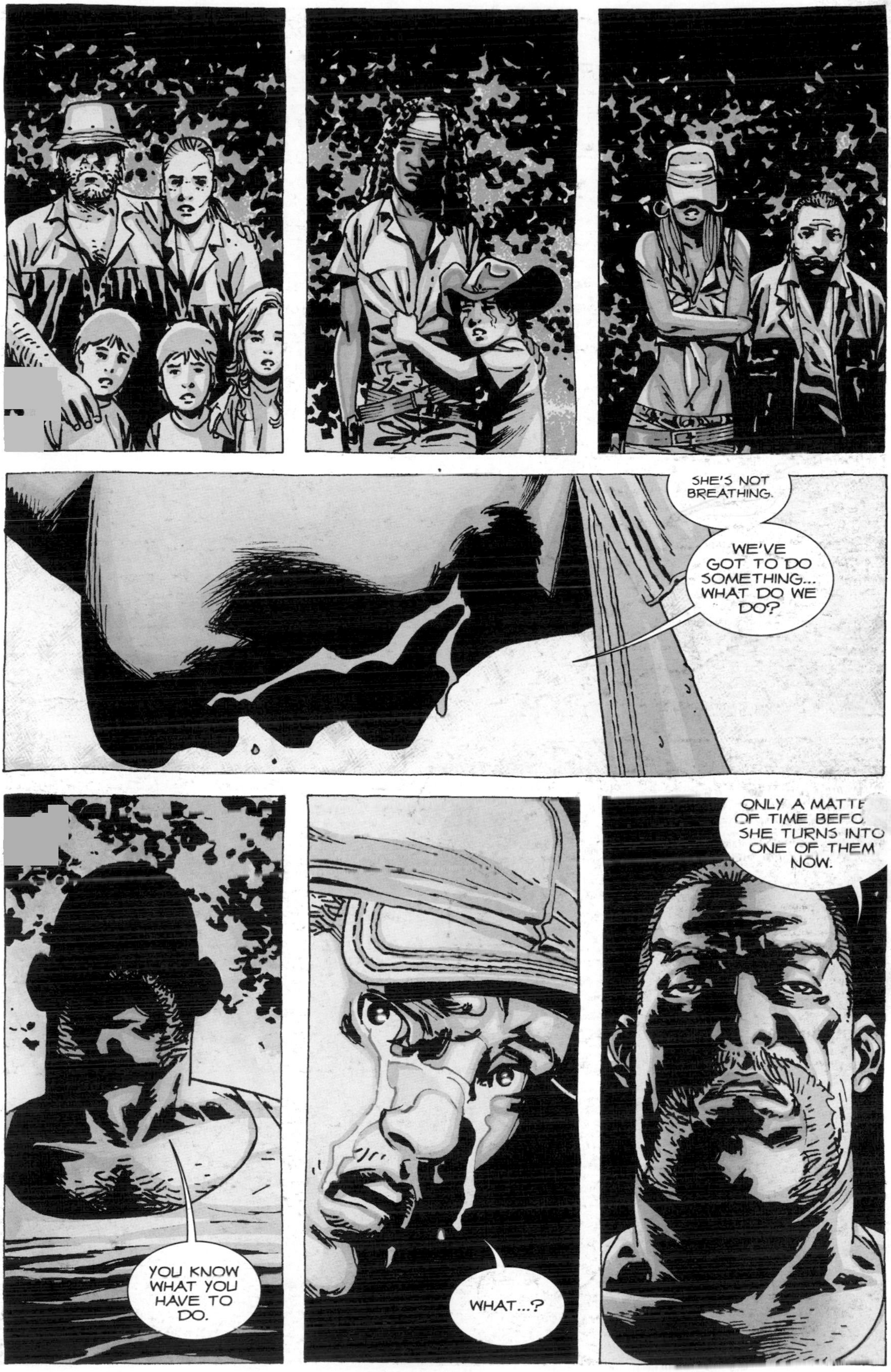
SHE'S NOT BREATHING.
WE'VE GOT TO DO SOMETHING... WHAT DO WE DO?
YOU KNOW WHAT YOU HAVE TO DO.
WHAT...?
ONLY A MATTE OF TIME BEFO SHE TURNS INTO ONE OF THEM NOW.

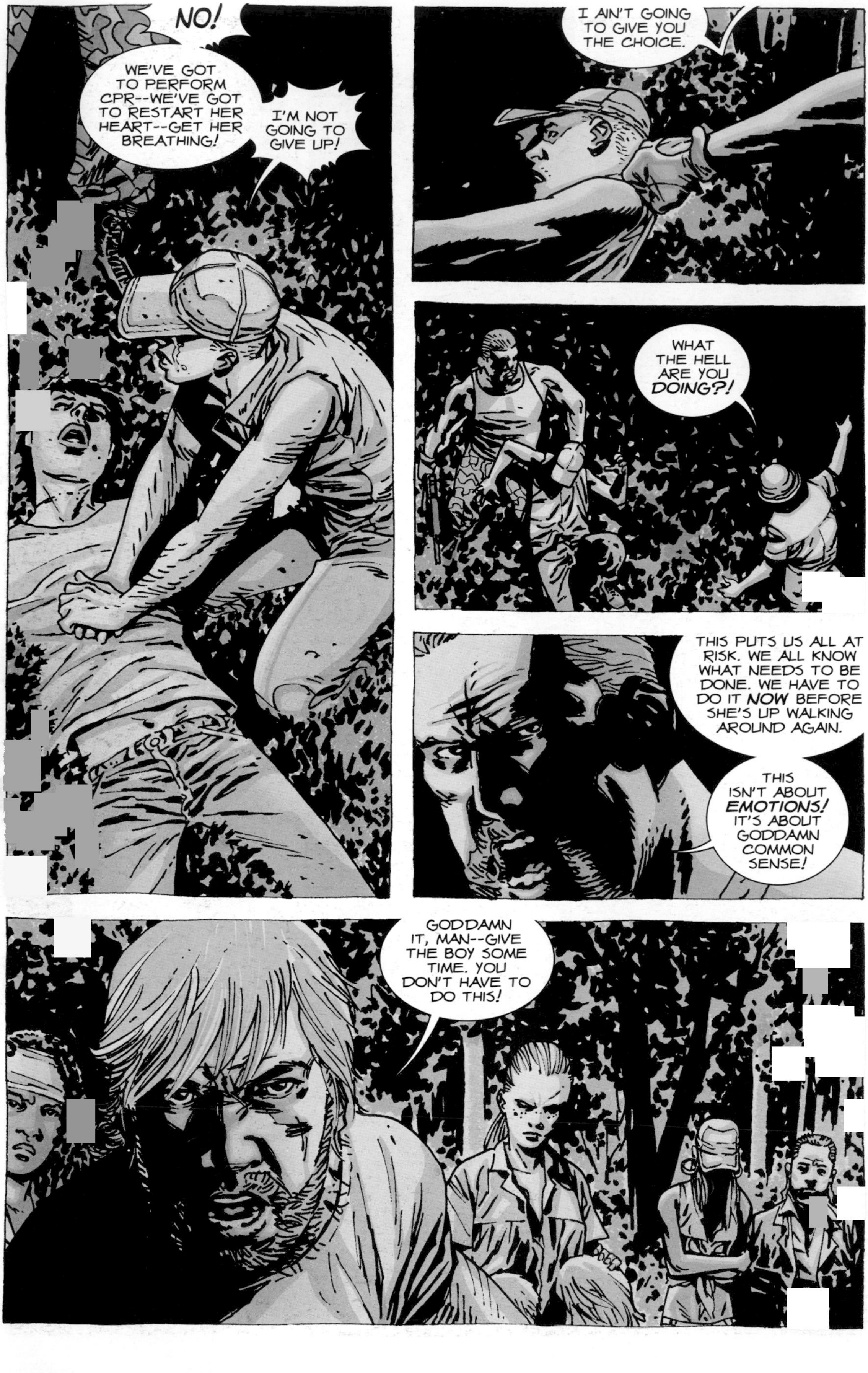
NO!
WE'VE GOT TO PERFORM CPR--WE'VE GOT TO RESTART HER HEART--GET HER BREATHING!
I'M NOT GOING TO GIVE UP!
I AIN'T GOING TO GIVE YOU THE CHOICE.
WHAT THE HELL ARE YOU DOING?!
THIS PUTS US ALL AT RISK. WE ALL KNOW WHAT NEEDS TO BE DONE. WE HAVE TO DO IT NOW BEFORE SHE'S UP WALKING AROUND AGAIN.
THIS ISN'T ABOUT EMOTIONS! IT'S ABOUT GODDAMN COMMON SENSE!
GODDAMN IT, MAN--GIVE THE BOY SOME TIME. YOU DON'T HAVE TO DO THIS!

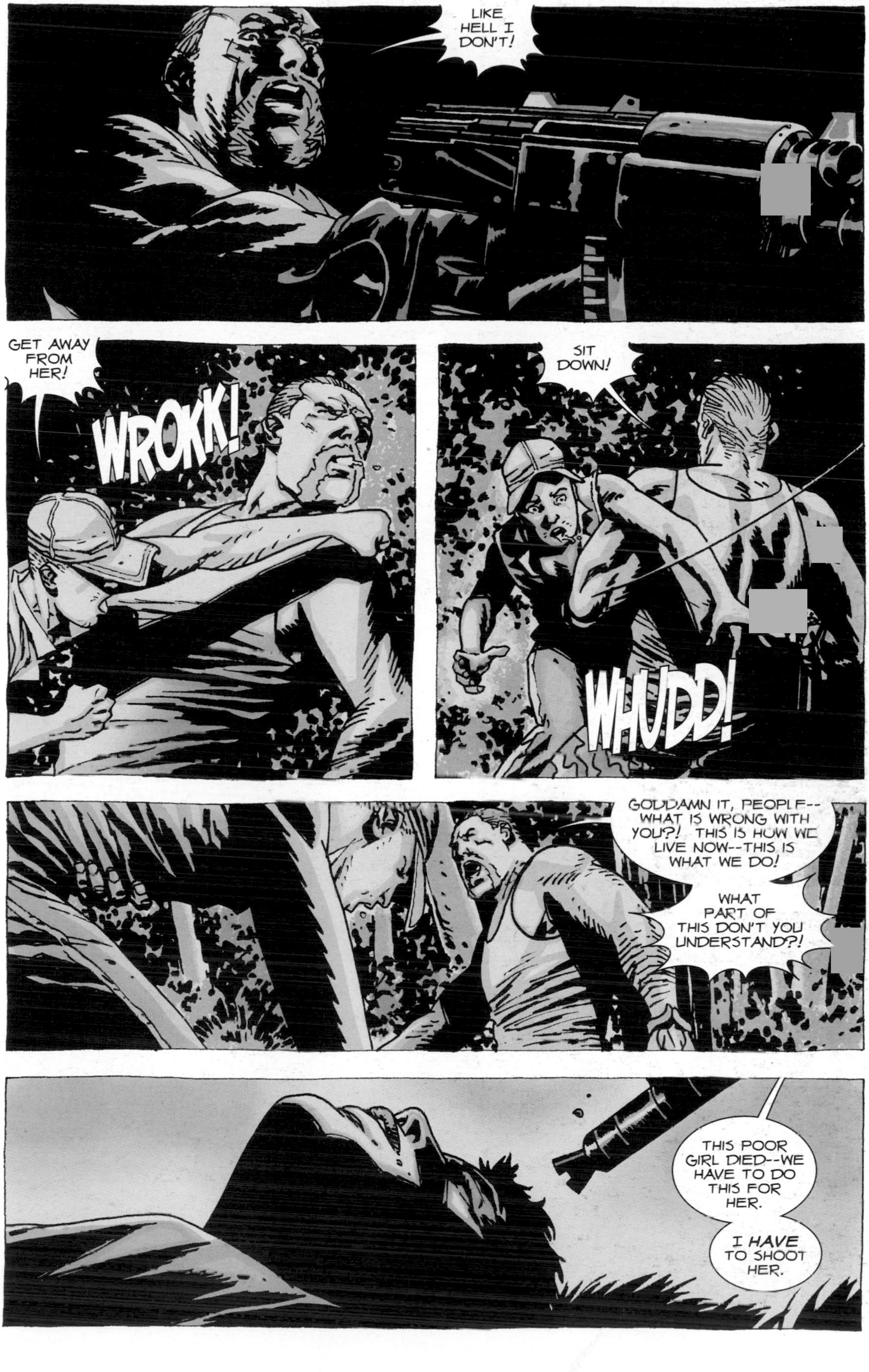
LIKE HELL I DON'T!
GET AWAY FROM HER!
WROKK!
SIT DOWN!
WHUDD!
GODDAMN IT, PEOPLE-- WHAT IS WRONG WITH YOU?! THIS IS HOW WE LIVE NOW--THIS IS WHAT WE DO!
WHAT PART OF THIS DON'T YOU UNDERSTAND?!
THIS POOR GIRL DIED--WE HAVE TO DO THIS FOR HER.
I *HAVE* TO SHOOT HER.

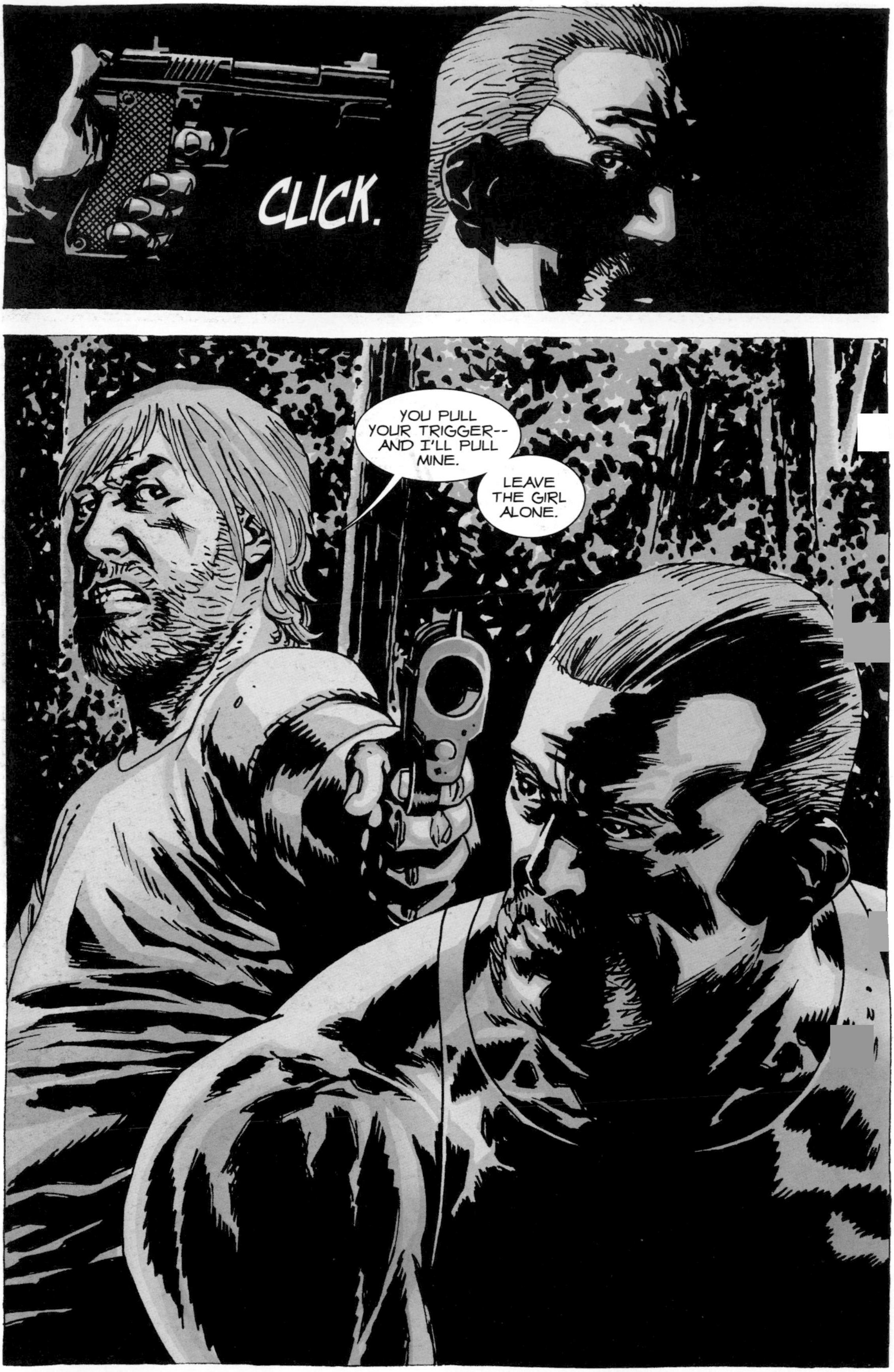
CLICK.
YOU PULL YOUR TRIGGER-- AND I'LL PULL MINE.
LEAVE THE GIRL ALONE.

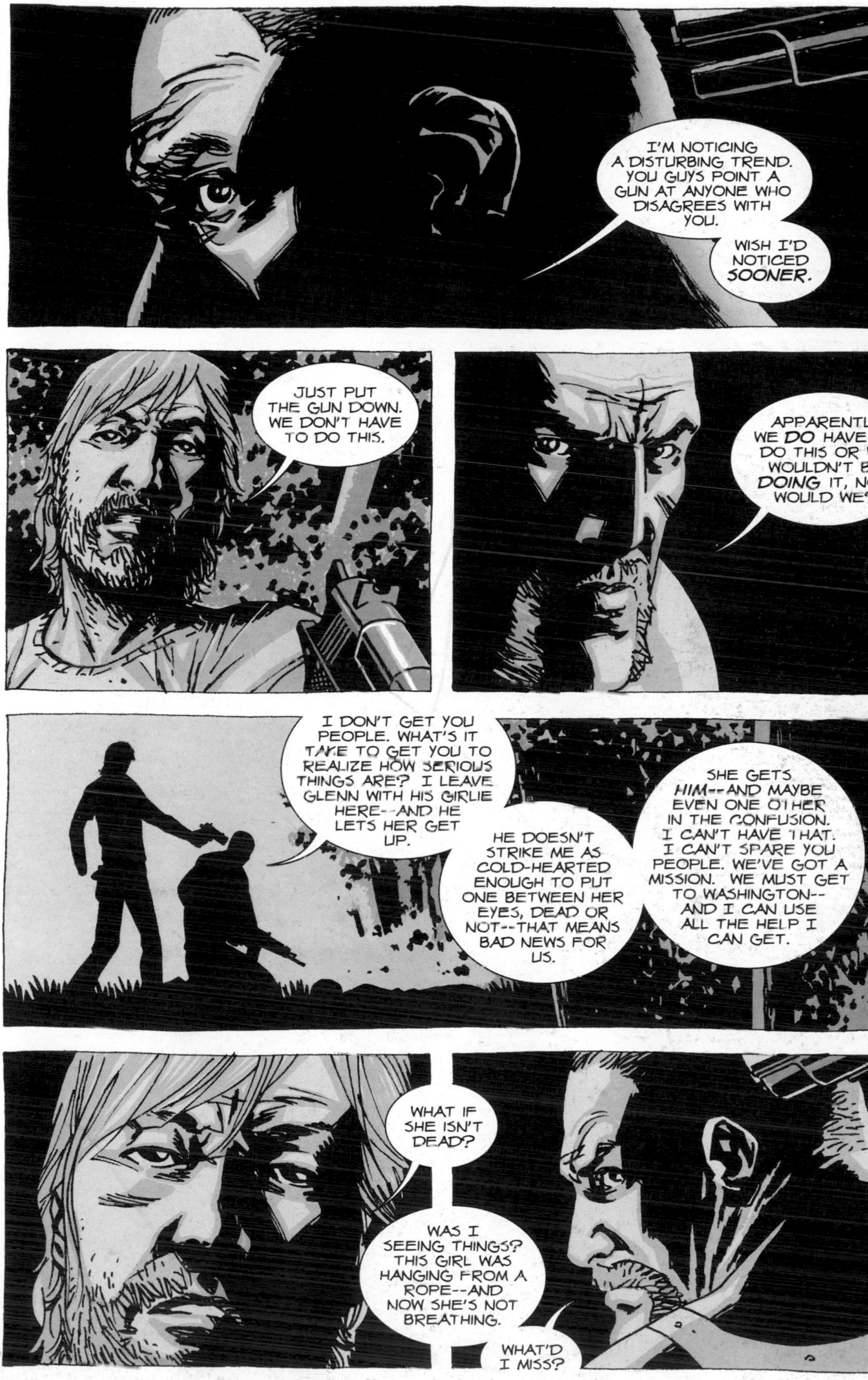
I'M NOTICING A DISTURBING TREND. YOU GUYS POINT A GUN AT ANYONE WHO DISAGREES WITH YOU.
WISH I'D NOTICED SOONER.
JUST PUT THE GUN DOWN. WE DON'T HAVE TO DO THIS.
APPARENTLY WE DO HAVE TO DO THIS OR WE WOULDN'T BE DOING IT, NOW WOULD WE?
I DON'T GET YOU PEOPLE. WHAT'S IT TAKE TO GET YOU TO REALIZE HOW SERIOUS THINGS ARE? I LEAVE GLENN WITH HIS GIRLIE HERE--AND HE LETS HER GET UP.
HE DOESN'T STRIKE ME AS COLD-HEARTED ENOUGH TO PUT ONE BETWEEN HER EYES, DEAD OR NOT--THAT MEANS BAD NEWS FOR US.
SHE GETS HIM--AND MAYBE EVEN ONE OTHER IN THE CONFUSION. I CAN'T HAVE THAT. I CAN'T SPARE YOU PEOPLE. WE'VE GOT A MISSION. WE MUST GET TO WASHINGTON--AND I CAN USE ALL THE HELP I CAN GET.
WHAT IF SHE ISN'T DEAD?
WAS I SEEING THINGS? THIS GIRL WAS HANGING FROM A ROPE--AND NOW SHE'S NOT BREATHING.
WHAT'D I MISS?

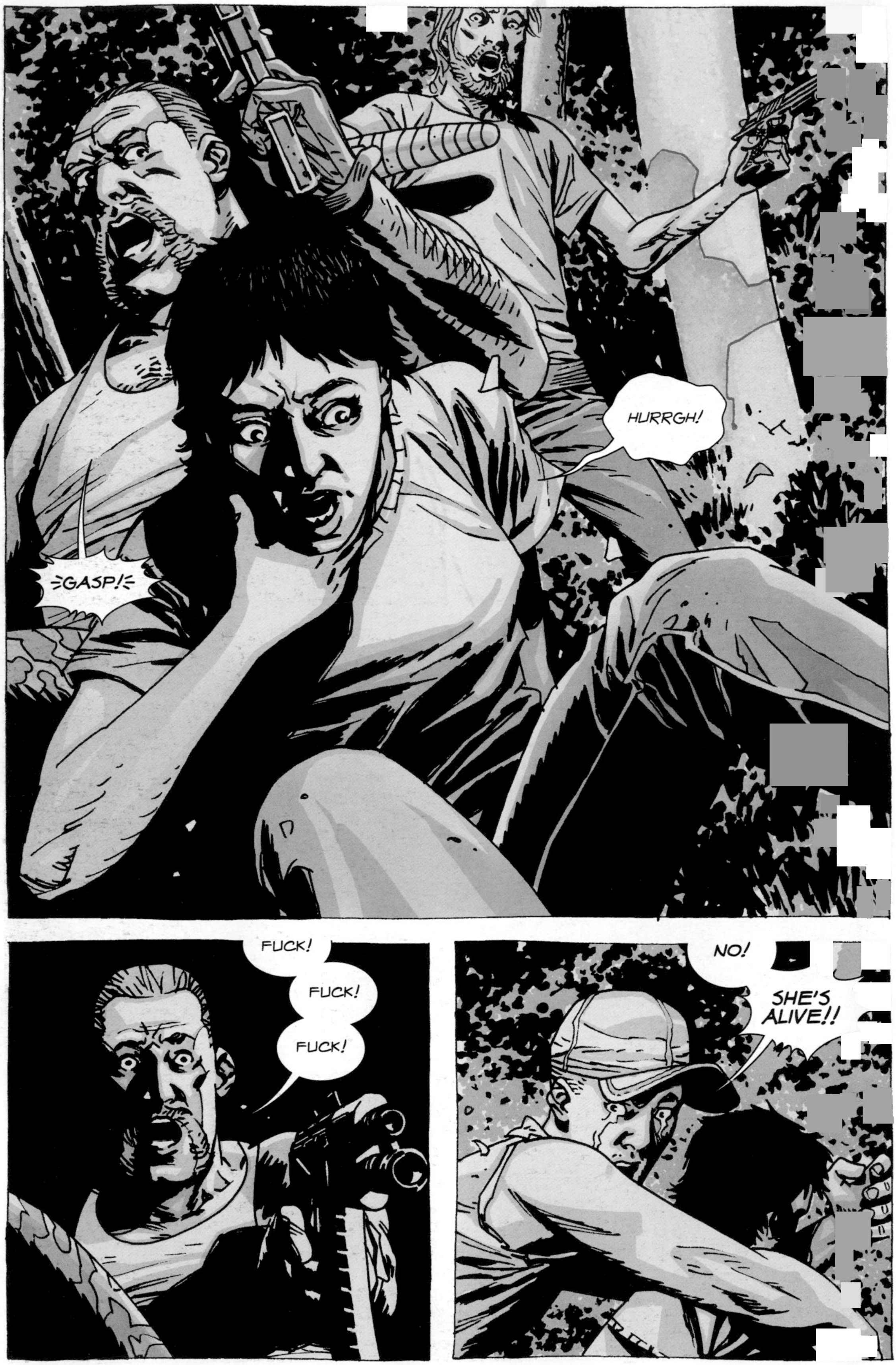
HURRGH!
GASP!
FUCK!
FUCK!
FUCK!
NO!
SHE'S ALIVE!!

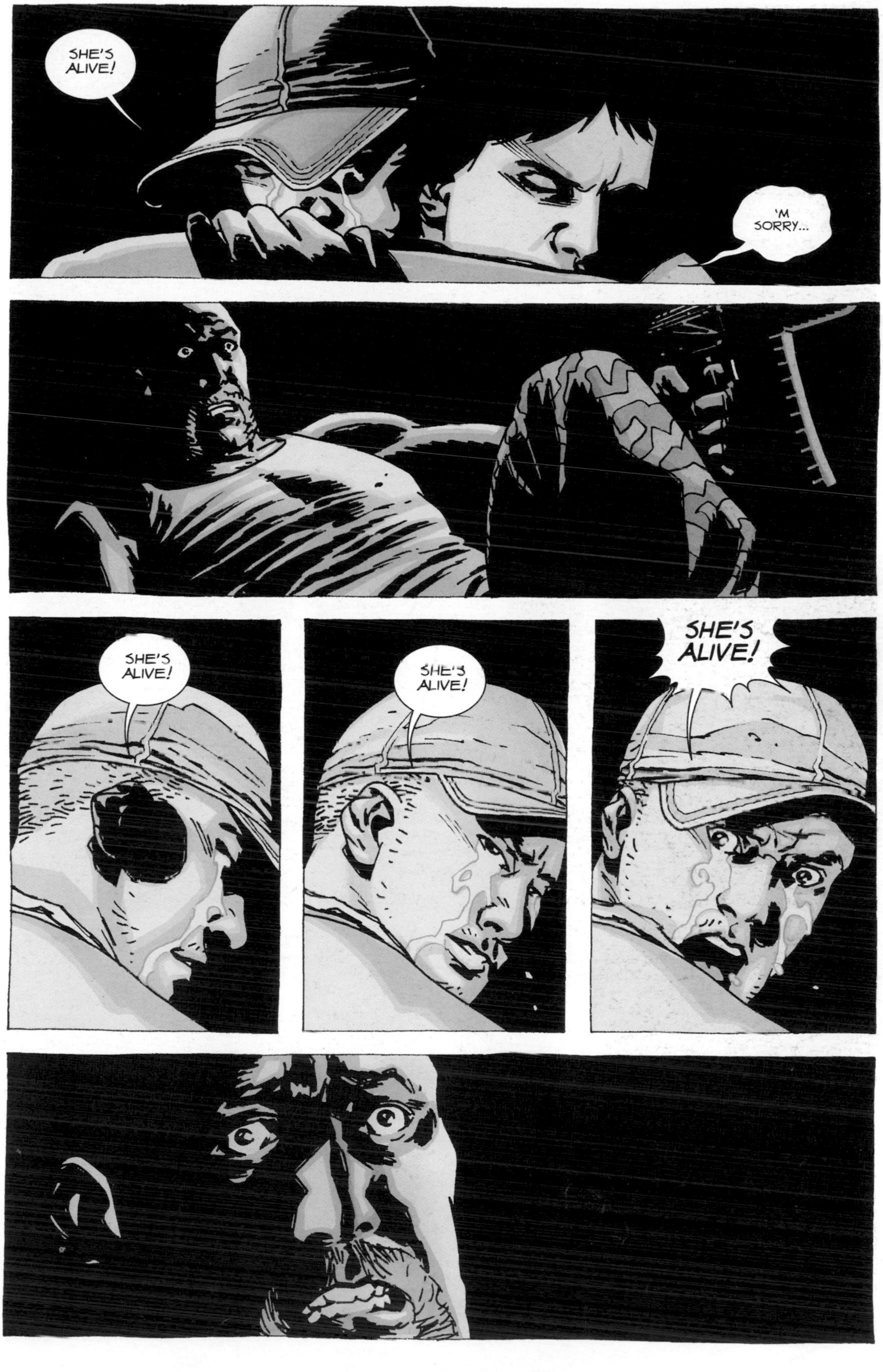
SHE'S ALIVE!
'M SORRY...
SHE'S ALIVE!
SHE'S ALIVE!
SHE'S ALIVE!

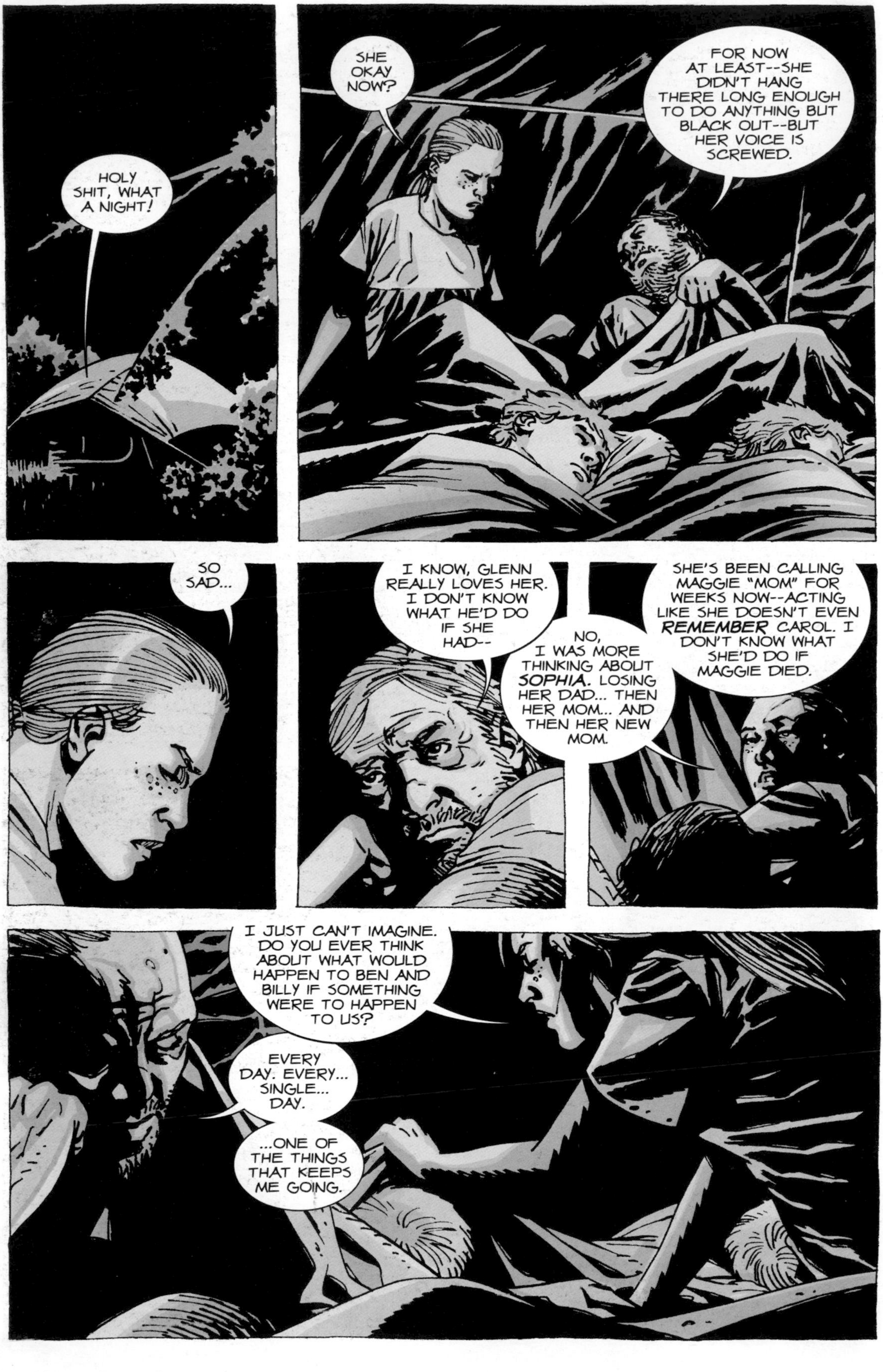
HOLY SHIT, WHAT A NIGHT!
SHE OKAY NOW?
FOR NOW AT LEAST--SHE DIDN'T HANG THERE LONG ENOUGH TO DO ANYTHING BUT BLACK OUT--BUT HER VOICE IS SCREWED.
SO SAD...
I KNOW, GLENN REALLY LOVES HER. I DON'T KNOW WHAT HE'D DO IF SHE HAD--
NO, I WAS MORE THINKING ABOUT SOPHIA. LOSING HER DAD... THEN HER MOM... AND THEN HER NEW MOM.
SHE'S BEEN CALLING MAGGIE "MOM" FOR WEEKS NOW--ACTING LIKE SHE DOESN'T EVEN REMEMBER CAROL. I DON'T KNOW WHAT SHE'D DO IF MAGGIE DIED.
I JUST CAN'T IMAGINE. DO YOU EVER THINK ABOUT WHAT WOULD HAPPEN TO BEN AND BILLY IF SOMETHING WERE TO HAPPEN TO US?
EVERY DAY. EVERY... SINGLE... DAY.
...ONE OF THE THINGS THAT KEEPS ME GOING.

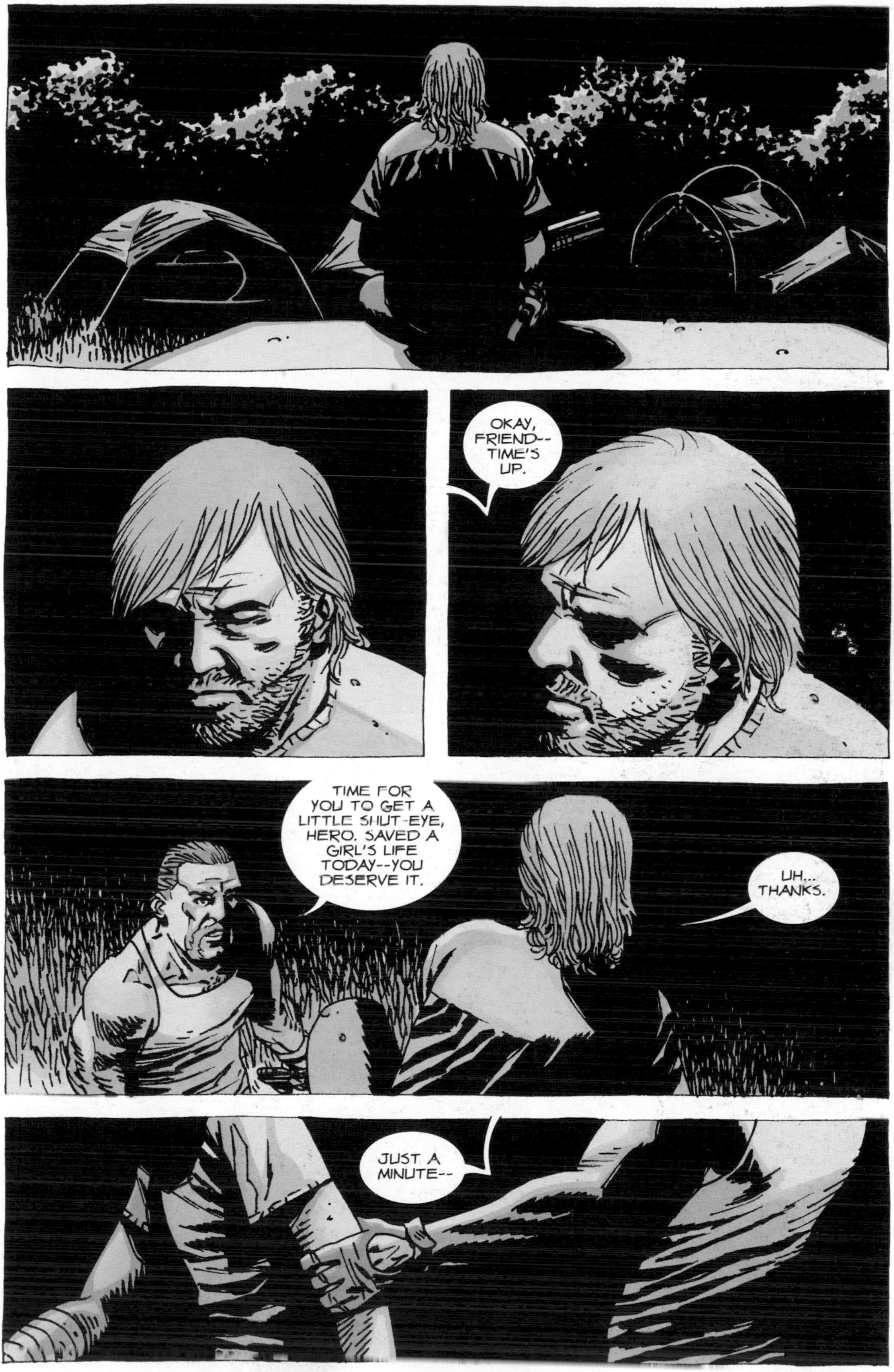
OKAY, FRIEND-- TIME'S UP.
TIME FOR YOU TO GET A LITTLE SHUT-EYE, HERO. SAVED A GIRL'S LIFE TODAY--YOU DESERVE IT.
UH... THANKS.
JUST A MINUTE--

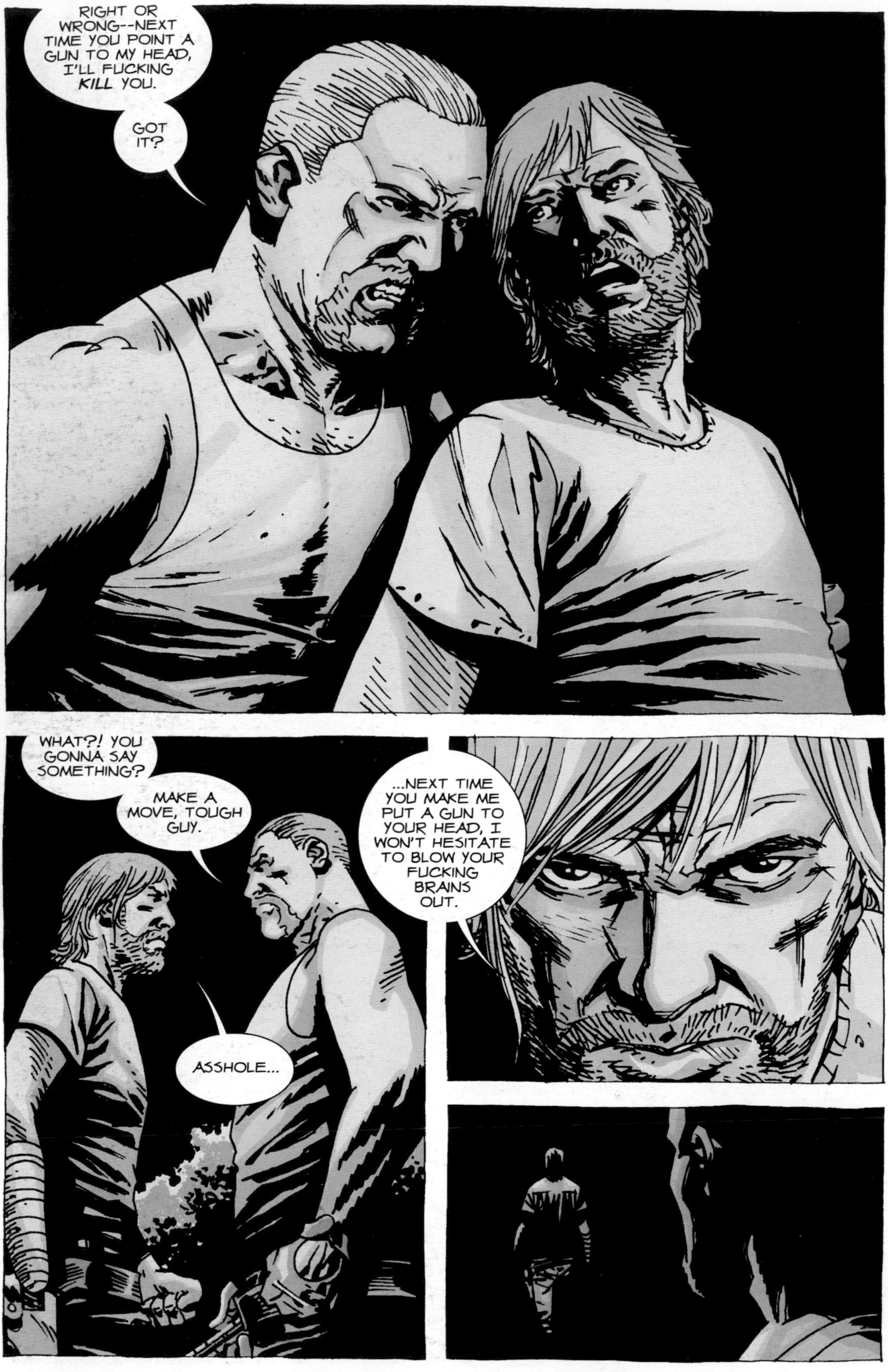
RIGHT OR WRONG--NEXT TIME YOU POINT A GUN TO MY HEAD, I'LL FUCKING KILL YOU.
GOT IT?
WHAT?! YOU GONNA SAY SOMETHING?
MAKE A MOVE, TOUGH GUY.
ASSHOLE...
...NEXT TIME YOU MAKE ME PUT A GUN TO YOUR HEAD, I WON'T HESITATE TO BLOW YOUR FUCKING BRAINS OUT.

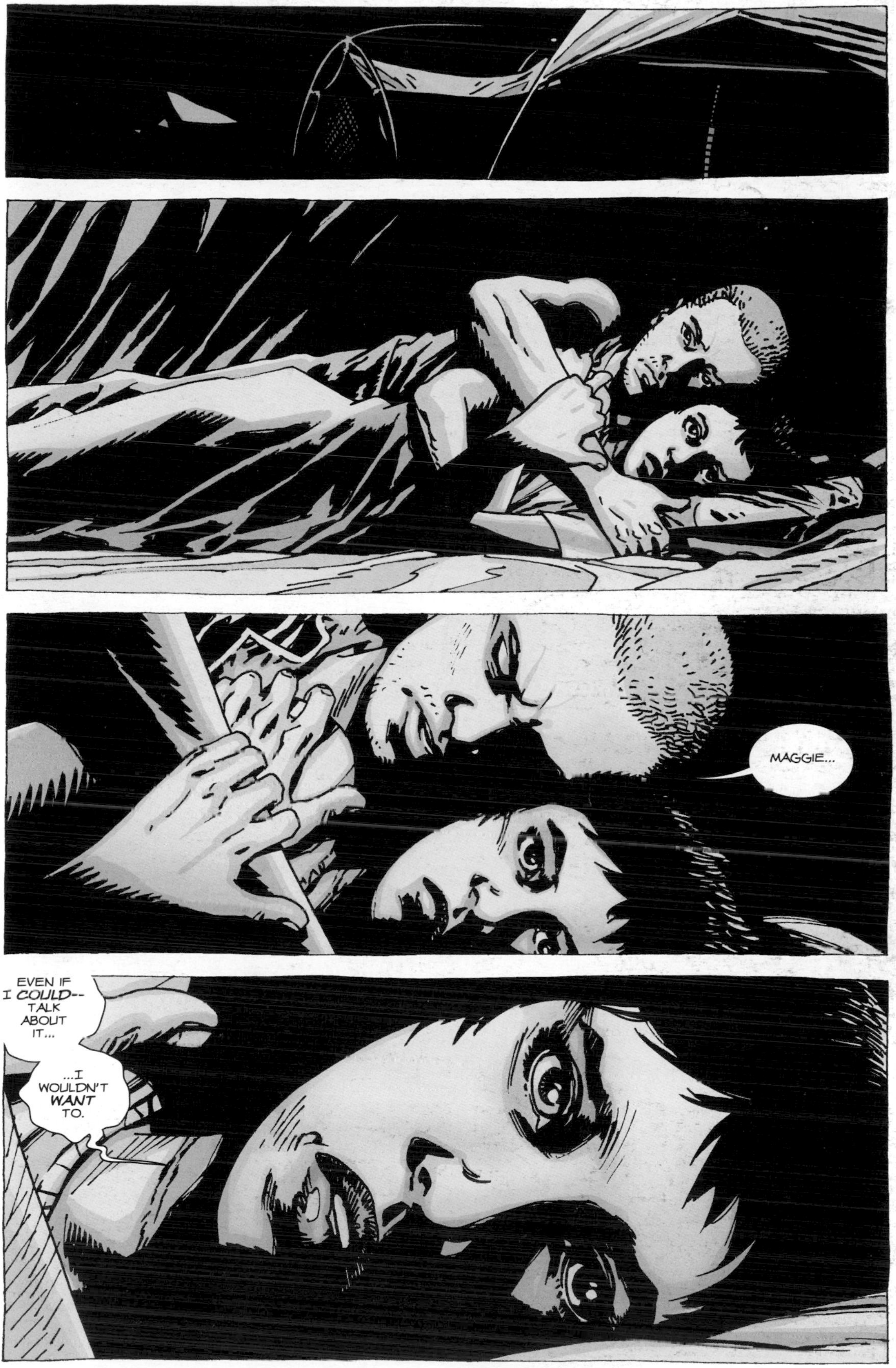
MAGGIE...
EVEN IF I COULD-- TALK ABOUT IT...
...I WOULDN'T WANT TO.

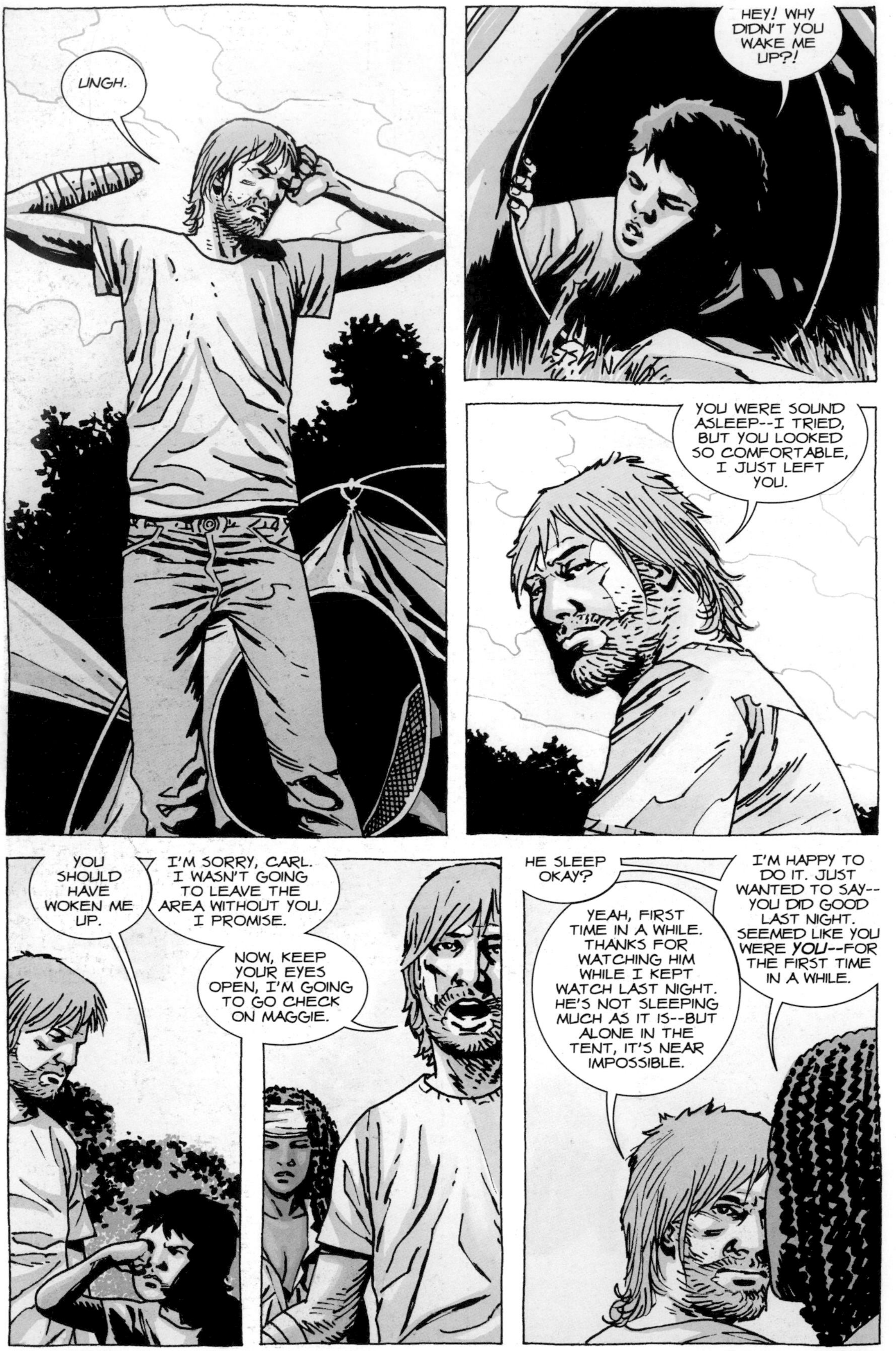
UNGH.
HEY! WHY DIDN'T YOU WAKE ME UP?!
YOU WERE SOUND ASLEEP--I TRIED, BUT YOU LOOKED SO COMFORTABLE, I JUST LEFT YOU.
YOU SHOULD HAVE WOKEN ME UP.
I'M SORRY, CARL. I WASN'T GOING TO LEAVE THE AREA WITHOUT YOU. I PROMISE.
NOW, KEEP YOUR EYES OPEN, I'M GOING TO GO CHECK ON MAGGIE.
HE SLEEP OKAY?
YEAH, FIRST TIME IN A WHILE. THANKS FOR WATCHING HIM WHILE I KEPT WATCH LAST NIGHT. HE'S NOT SLEEPING MUCH AS IT IS--BUT ALONE IN THE TENT, IT'S NEAR IMPOSSIBLE.
I'M HAPPY TO DO IT. JUST WANTED TO SAY-- YOU DID GOOD LAST NIGHT. SEEMED LIKE YOU WERE *YOU*--FOR THE FIRST TIME IN A WHILE.

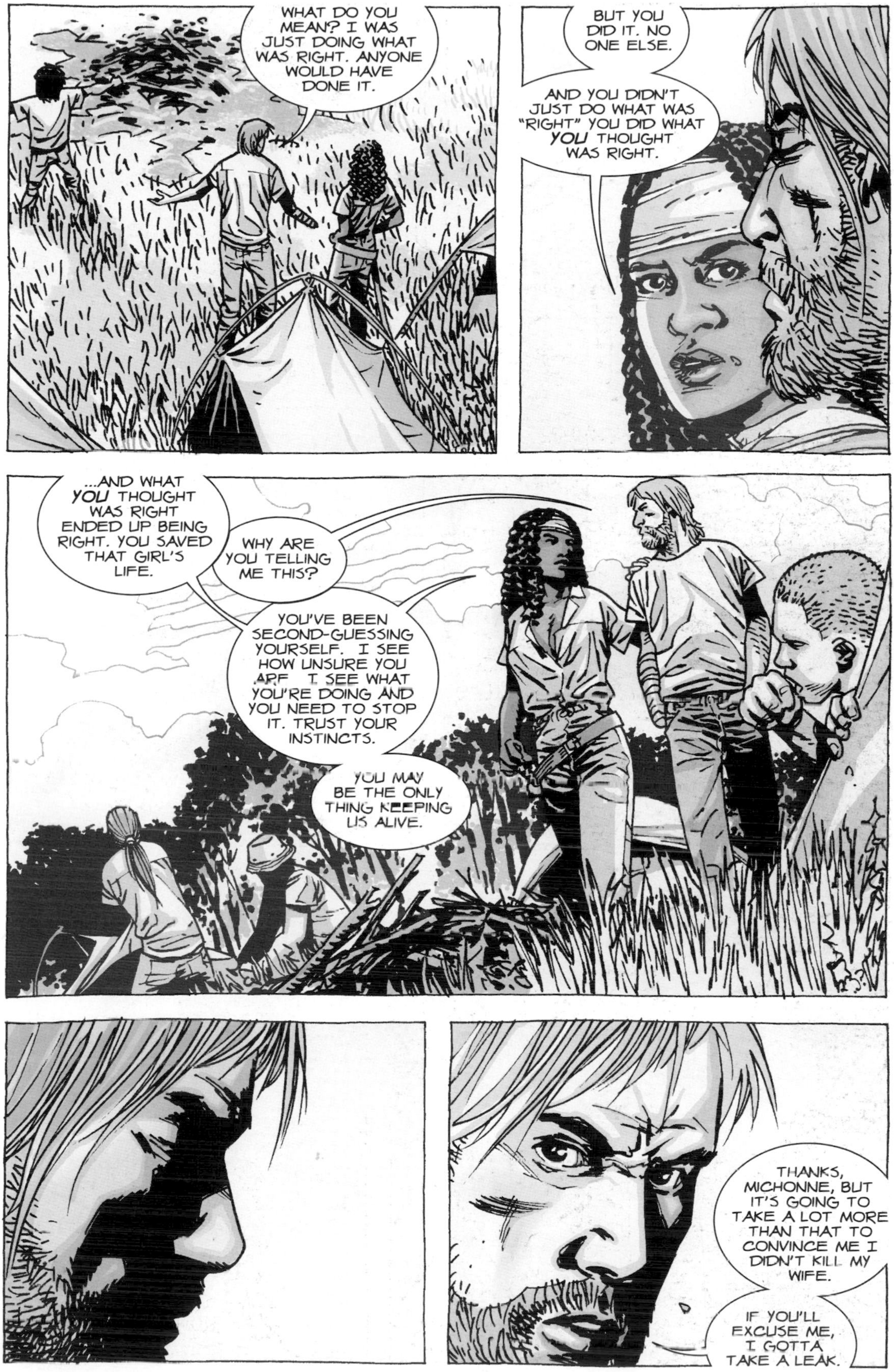
WHAT DO YOU MEAN? I WAS JUST DOING WHAT WAS RIGHT. ANYONE WOULD HAVE DONE IT.
BUT YOU DID IT. NO ONE ELSE.
AND YOU DIDN'T JUST DO WHAT WAS "RIGHT" YOU DID WHAT YOU THOUGHT WAS RIGHT.
...AND WHAT YOU THOUGHT WAS RIGHT ENDED UP BEING RIGHT. YOU SAVED THAT GIRL'S LIFE.
WHY ARE YOU TELLING ME THIS?
YOU'VE BEEN SECOND-GUESSING YOURSELF. I SEE HOW UNSURE YOU ARE. I SEE WHAT YOU'RE DOING AND YOU NEED TO STOP IT. TRUST YOUR INSTINCTS.
YOU MAY BE THE ONLY THING KEEPING US ALIVE.
THANKS, MICHONNE, BUT IT'S GOING TO TAKE A LOT MORE THAN THAT TO CONVINCE ME I DIDN'T KILL MY WIFE.
IF YOU'LL EXCUSE ME, I GOTTA TAKE A LEAK.

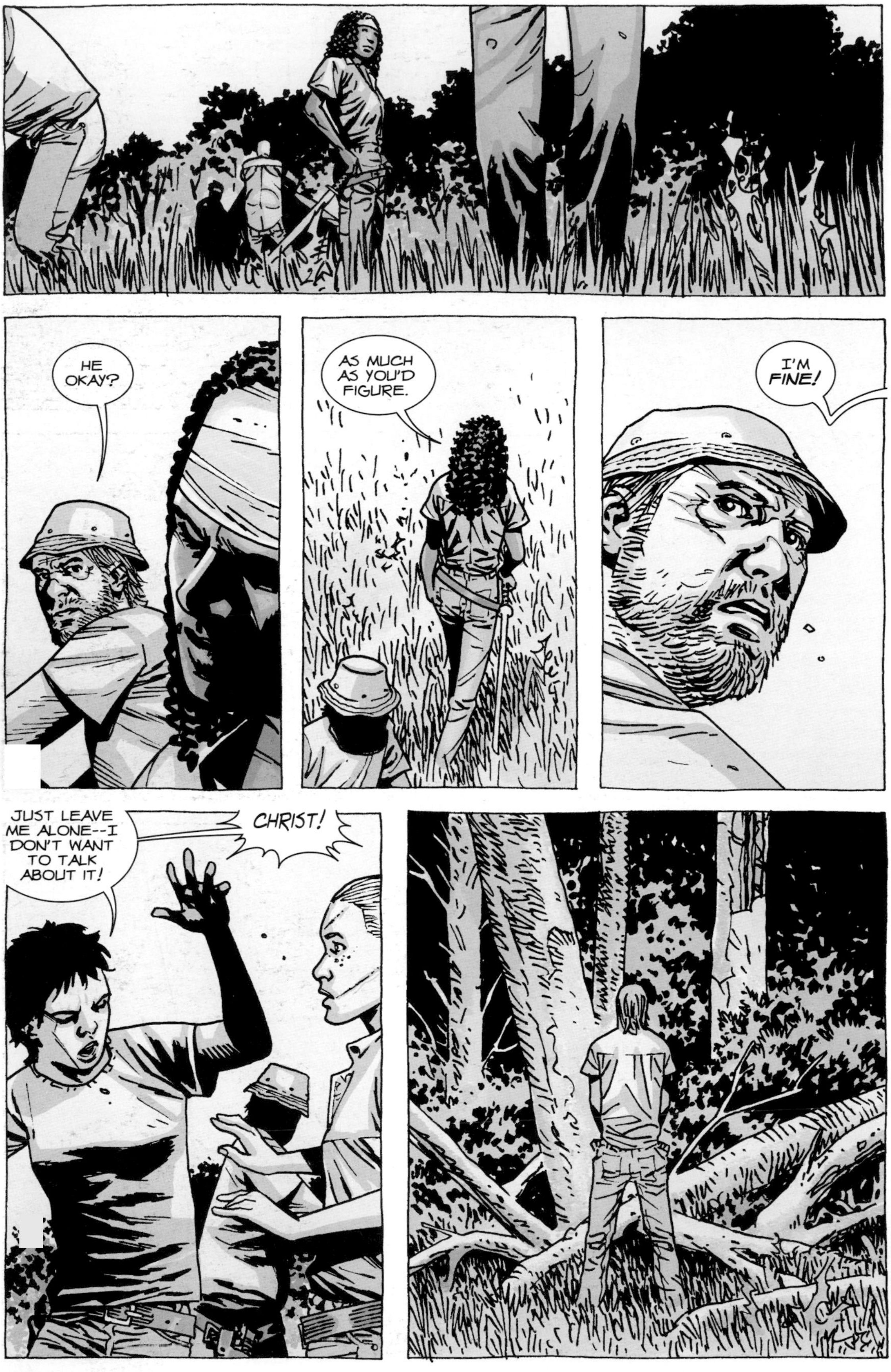
HE OKAY?
AS MUCH AS YOU'D FIGURE.
I'M FINE!
CHRIST!
JUST LEAVE ME ALONE--I DON'T WANT TO TALK ABOUT IT!

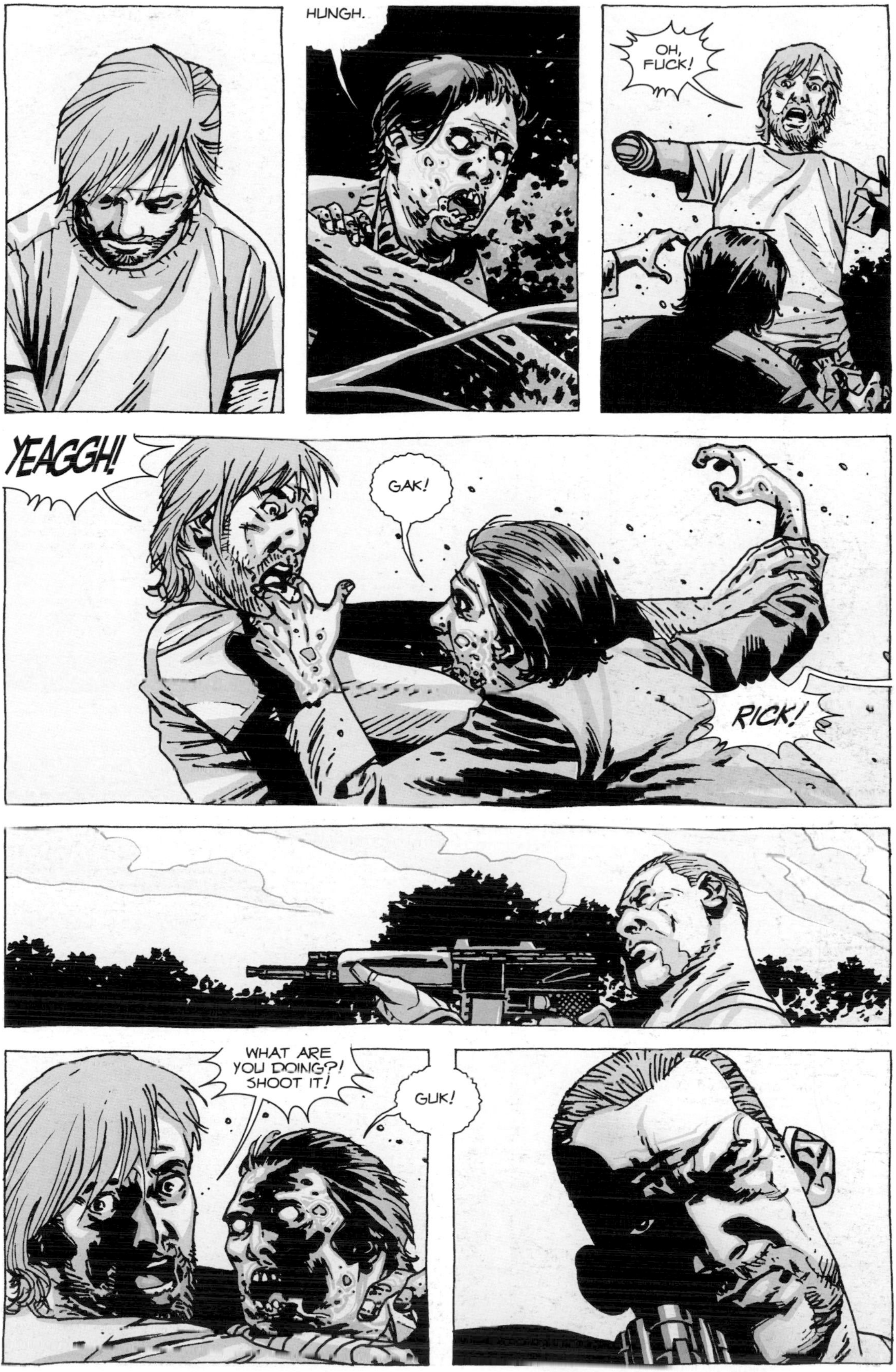
HUNGH.
OH, FUCK!
YEAGGH!
GAK!
RICK!
WHAT ARE YOU DOING?! SHOOT IT!
GUK!

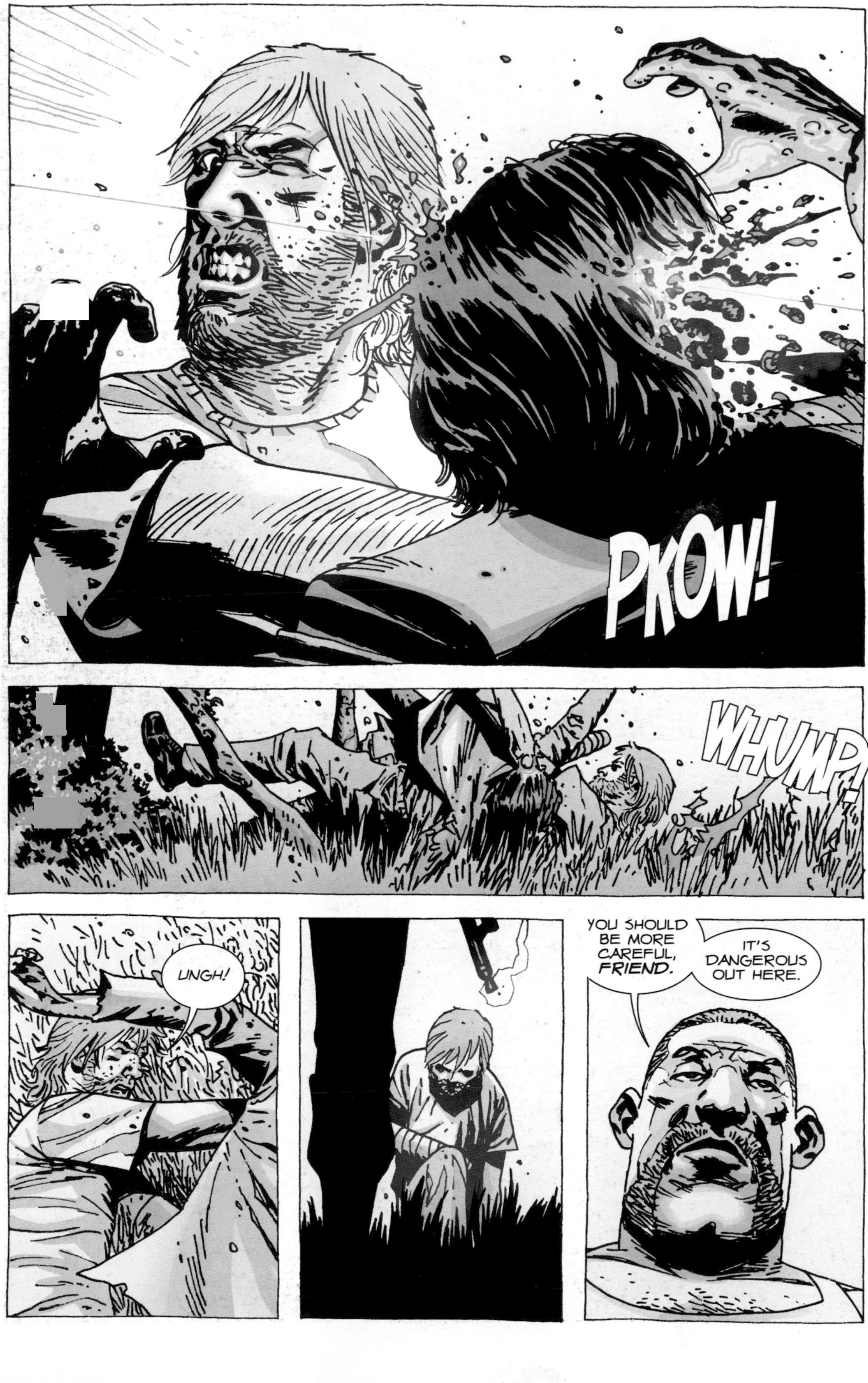
PKOW!
WHUMP!
UNGH!
YOU SHOULD BE MORE CAREFUL, FRIEND.
IT'S DANGEROUS OUT HERE.

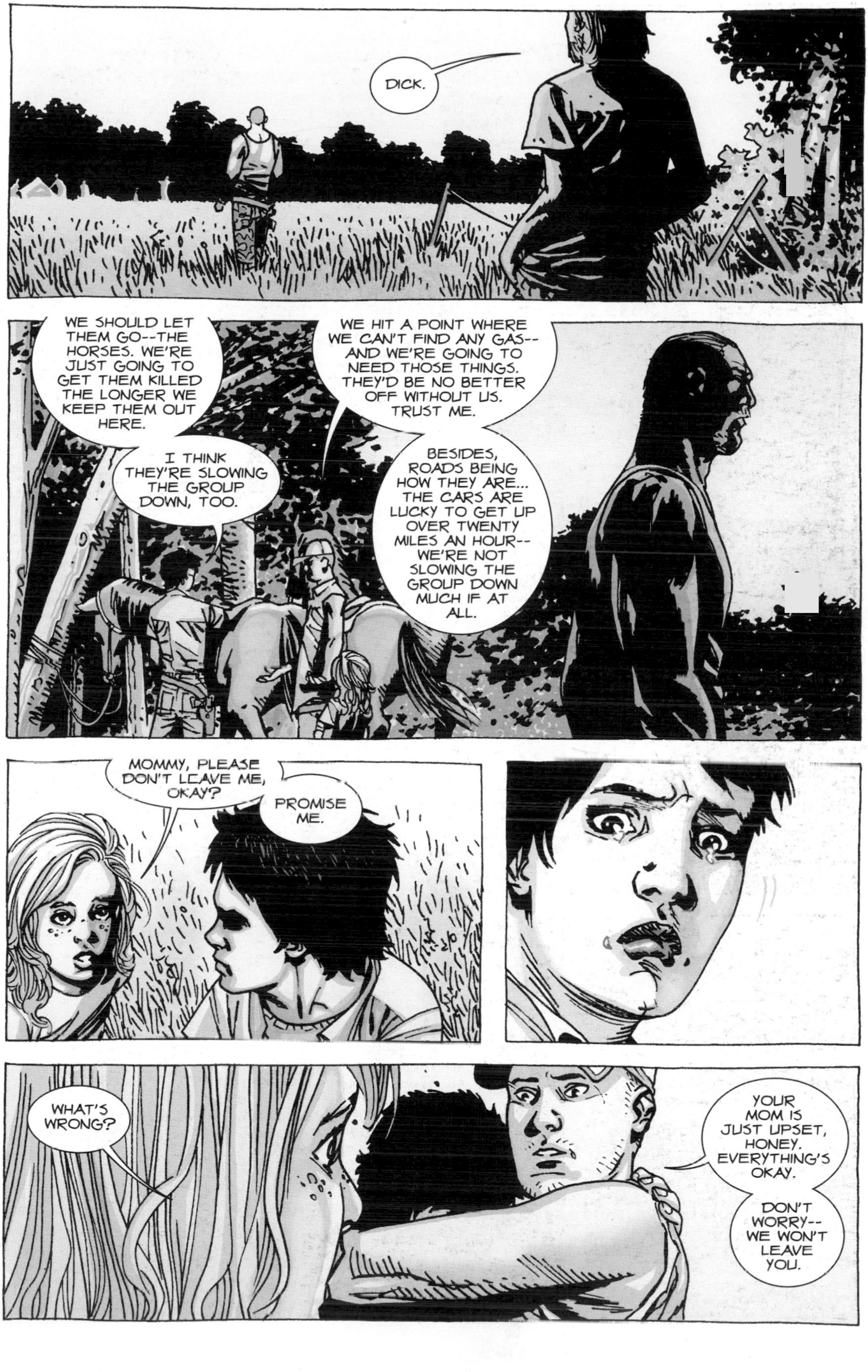
DICK.
WE SHOULD LET THEM GO--THE HORSES. WE'RE JUST GOING TO GET THEM KILLED THE LONGER WE KEEP THEM OUT HERE.
I THINK THEY'RE SLOWING THE GROUP DOWN, TOO.
WE HIT A POINT WHERE WE CAN'T FIND ANY GAS--AND WE'RE GOING TO NEED THOSE THINGS. THEY'D BE NO BETTER OFF WITHOUT US. TRUST ME.
BESIDES, ROADS BEING HOW THEY ARE... THE CARS ARE LUCKY TO GET UP OVER TWENTY MILES AN HOUR--WE'RE NOT SLOWING THE GROUP DOWN MUCH IF AT ALL.
MOMMY, PLEASE DON'T LEAVE ME, OKAY?
PROMISE ME.
WHAT'S WRONG?
YOUR MOM IS JUST UPSET, HONEY. EVERYTHING'S OKAY.
DON'T WORRY--WE WON'T LEAVE YOU.

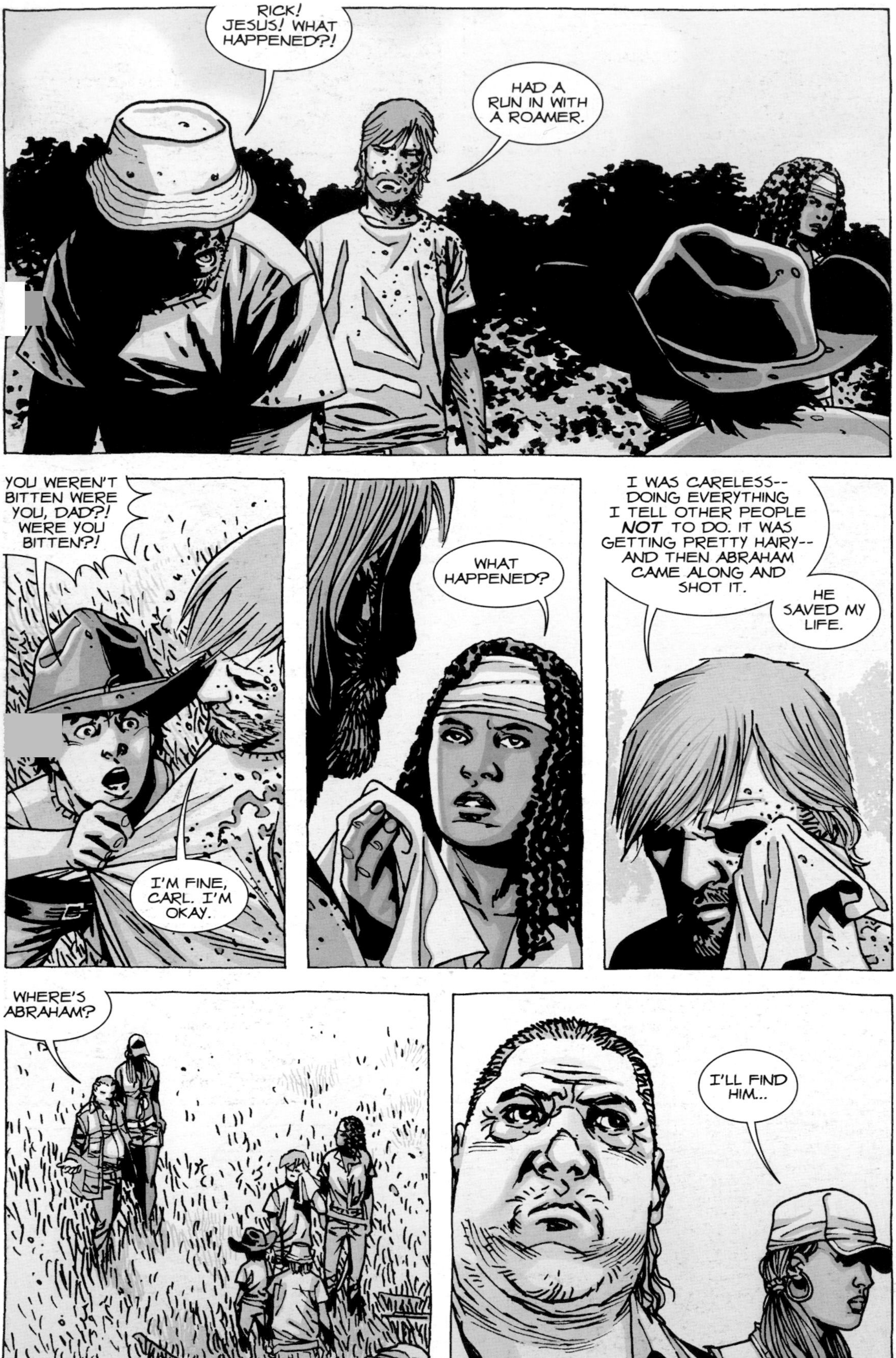
RICK! JESUS! WHAT HAPPENED?!
HAD A RUN IN WITH A ROAMER.
YOU WEREN'T BITTEN WERE YOU, DAD?! WERE YOU BITTEN?!
I'M FINE, CARL. I'M OKAY.
WHAT HAPPENED?
I WAS CARELESS-- DOING EVERYTHING I TELL OTHER PEOPLE NOT TO DO. IT WAS GETTING PRETTY HAIRY-- AND THEN ABRAHAM CAME ALONG AND SHOT IT.
HE SAVED MY LIFE.
WHERE'S ABRAHAM?
I'LL FIND HIM...

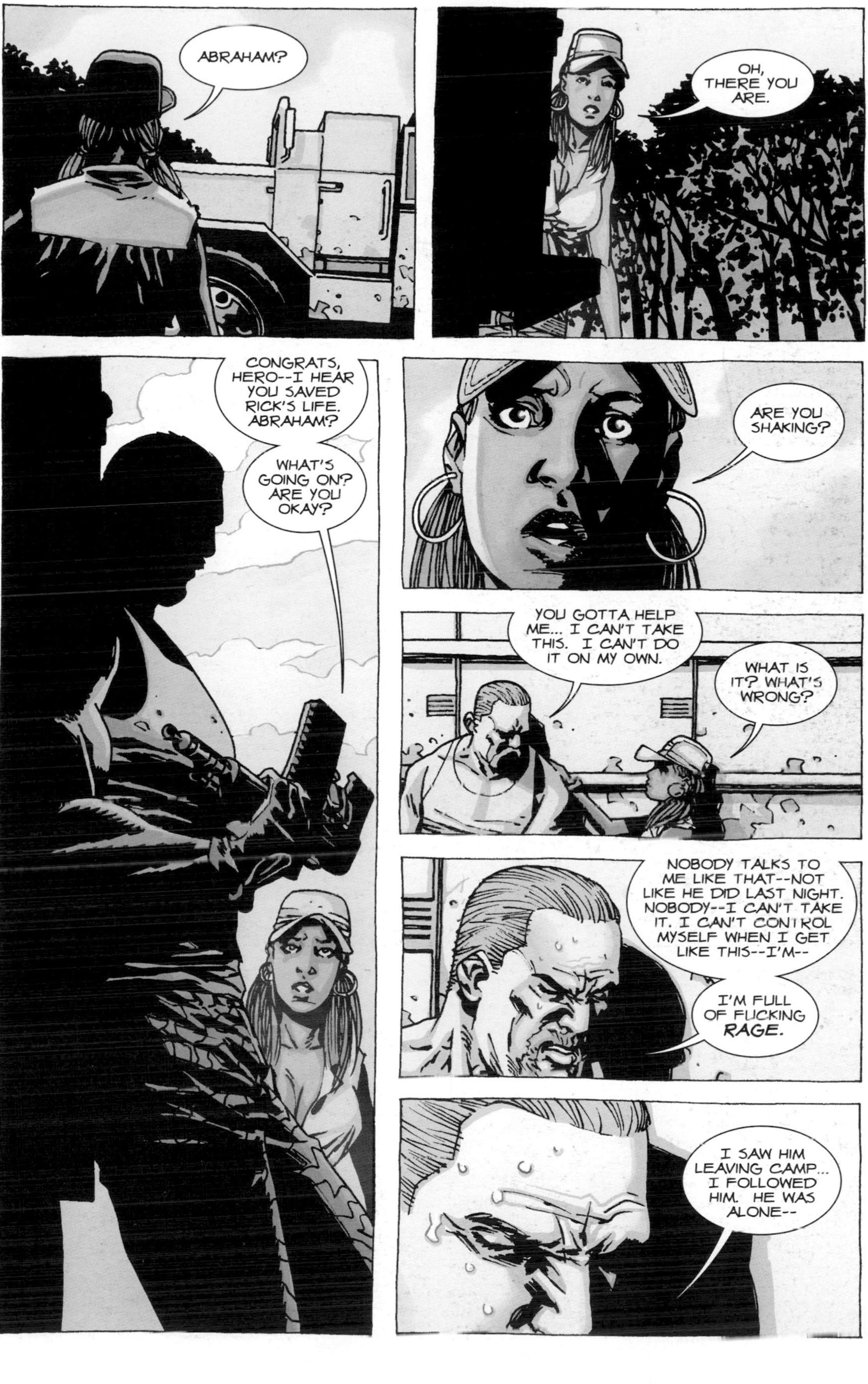
ABRAHAM?
OH, THERE YOU ARE.
CONGRATS, HERO--I HEAR YOU SAVED RICK'S LIFE. ABRAHAM?
WHAT'S GOING ON? ARE YOU OKAY?
ARE YOU SHAKING?
YOU GOTTA HELP ME... I CAN'T TAKE THIS. I CAN'T DO IT ON MY OWN.
WHAT IS IT? WHAT'S WRONG?
NOBODY TALKS TO ME LIKE THAT--NOT LIKE HE DID LAST NIGHT. NOBODY--I CAN'T TAKE IT. I CAN'T CONTROL MYSELF WHEN I GET LIKE THIS--I'M--
I'M FULL OF FUCKING *RAGE.*
I SAW HIM LEAVING CAMP... I FOLLOWED HIM. HE WAS ALONE--

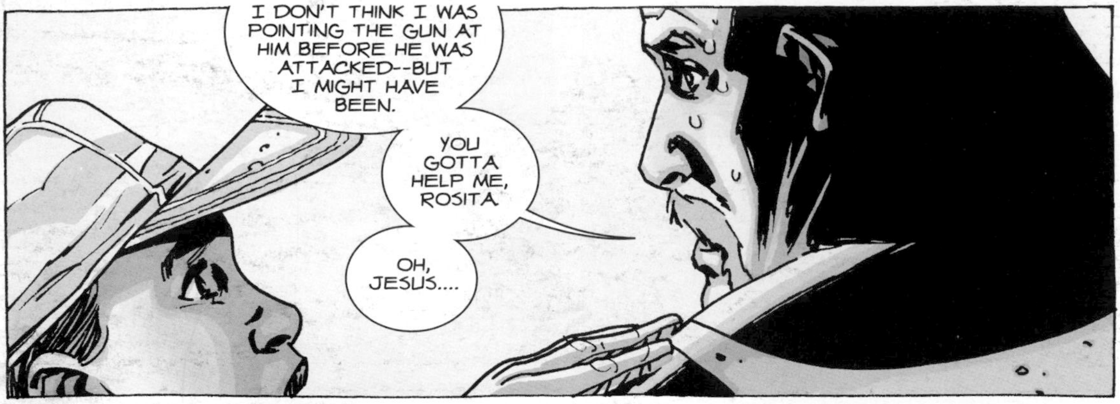
I DON'T THINK I WAS POINTING THE GUN AT HIM BEFORE HE WAS ATTACKED--BUT I MIGHT HAVE BEEN.
YOU GOTTA HELP ME, ROSITA.
OH, JESUS....

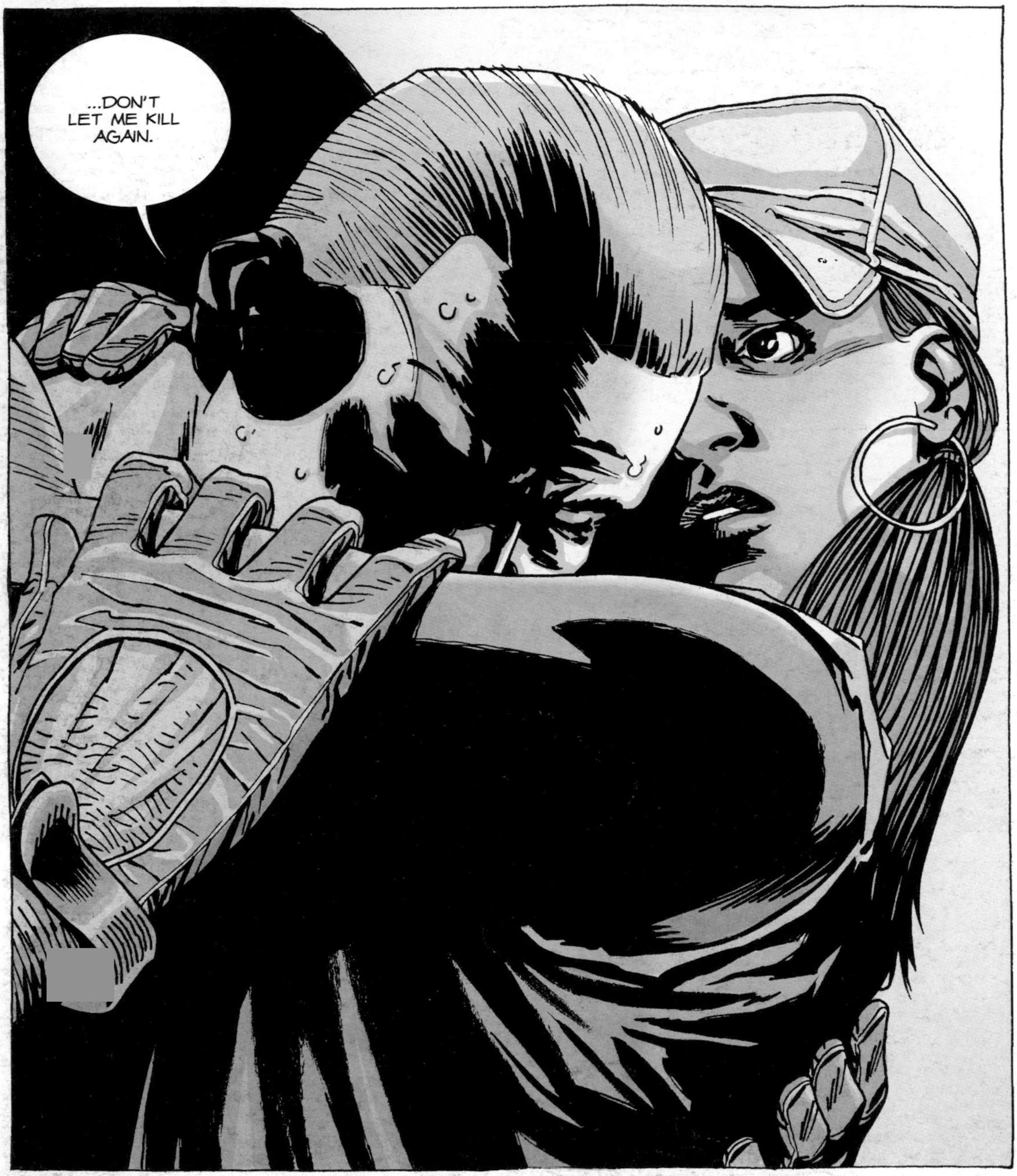
...DON'T LET ME KILL AGAIN.

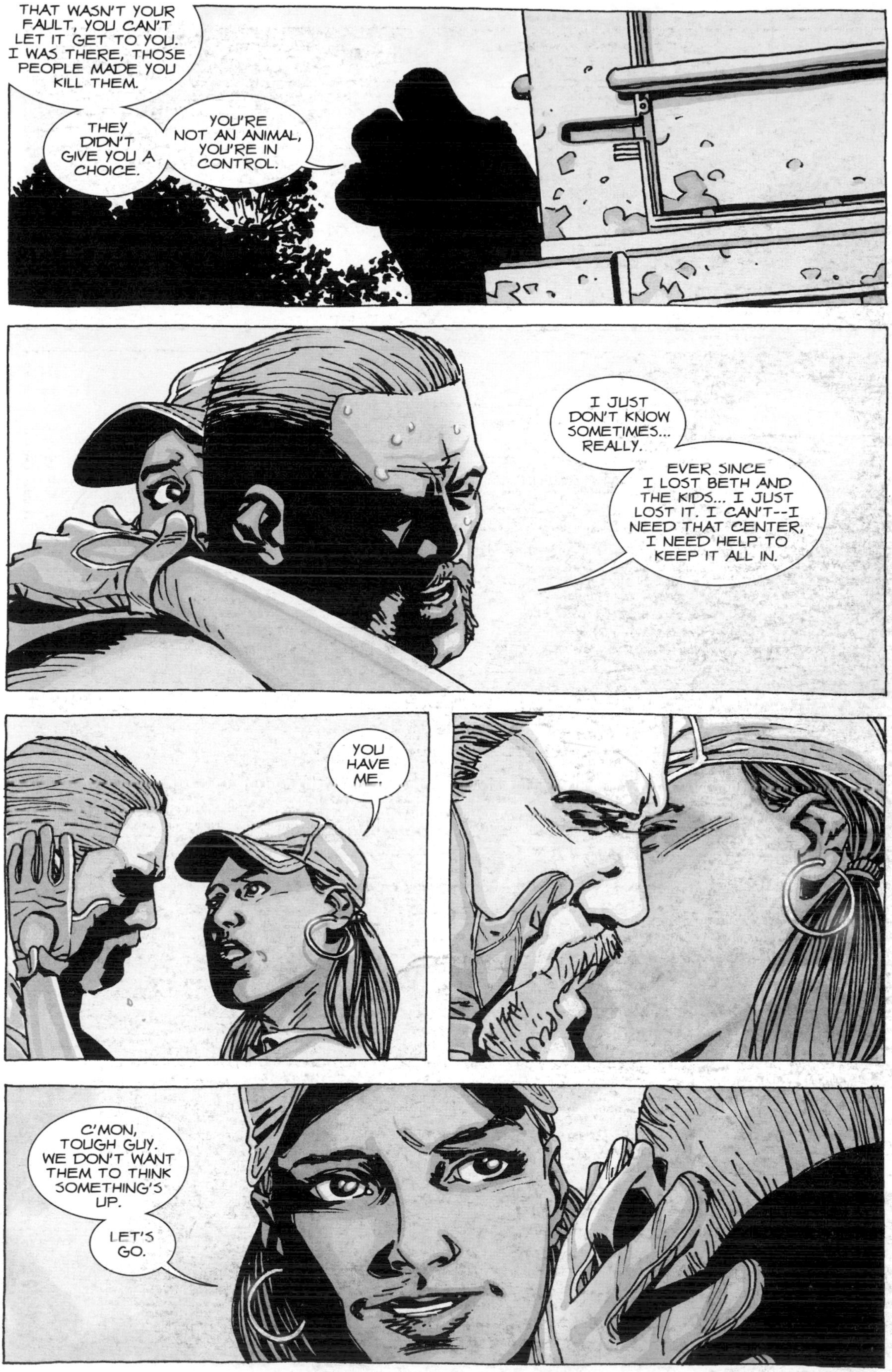
THAT WASN'T YOUR FAULT, YOU CAN'T LET IT GET TO YOU. I WAS THERE, THOSE PEOPLE MADE YOU KILL THEM.
THEY DIDN'T GIVE YOU A CHOICE.
YOU'RE NOT AN ANIMAL, YOU'RE IN CONTROL.
I JUST DON'T KNOW SOMETIMES... REALLY.
EVER SINCE I LOST BETH AND THE KIDS... I JUST LOST IT. I CAN'T--I NEED THAT CENTER, I NEED HELP TO KEEP IT ALL IN.
YOU HAVE ME.
C'MON, TOUGH GUY. WE DON'T WANT THEM TO THINK SOMETHING'S UP.
LET'S GO.

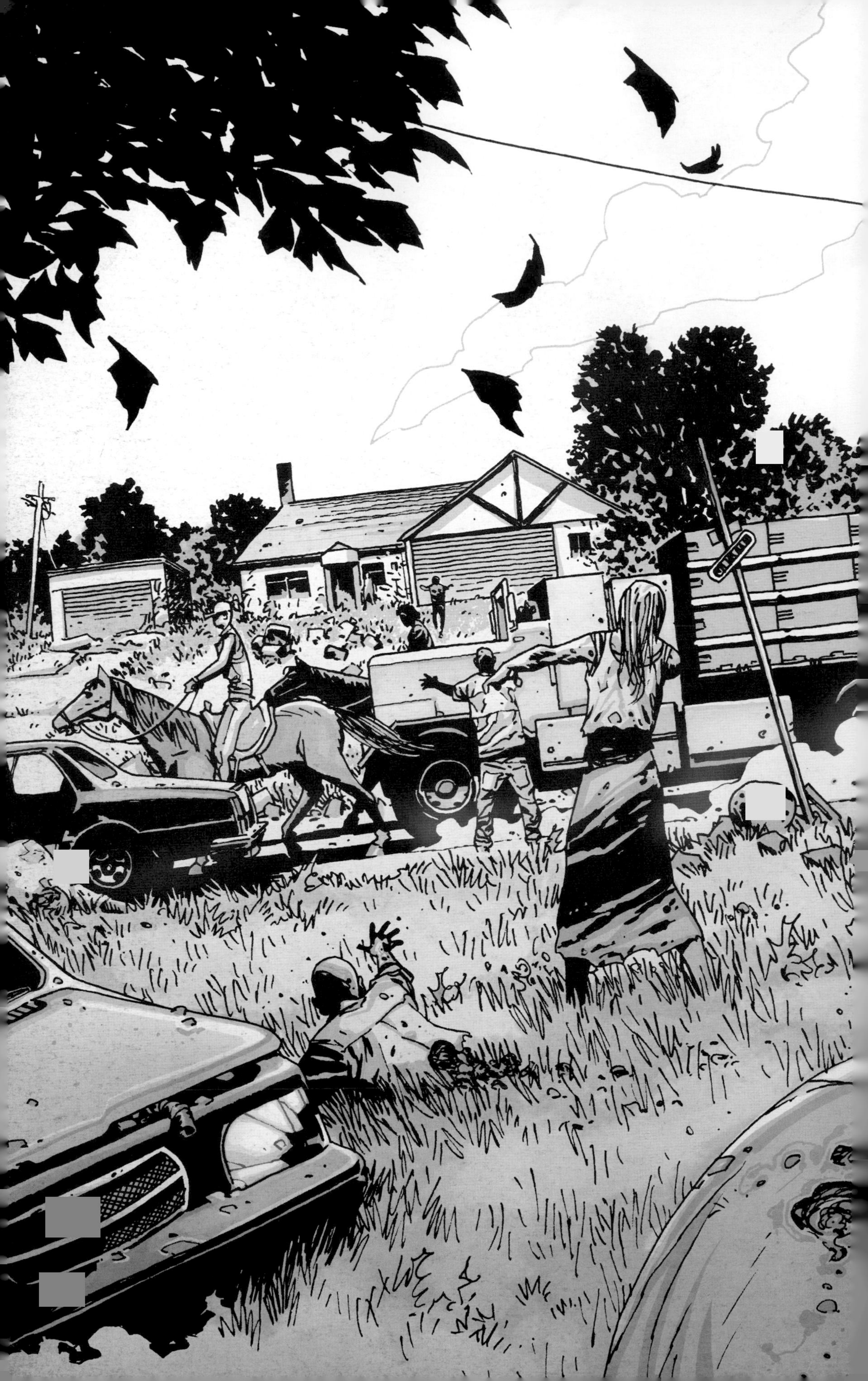

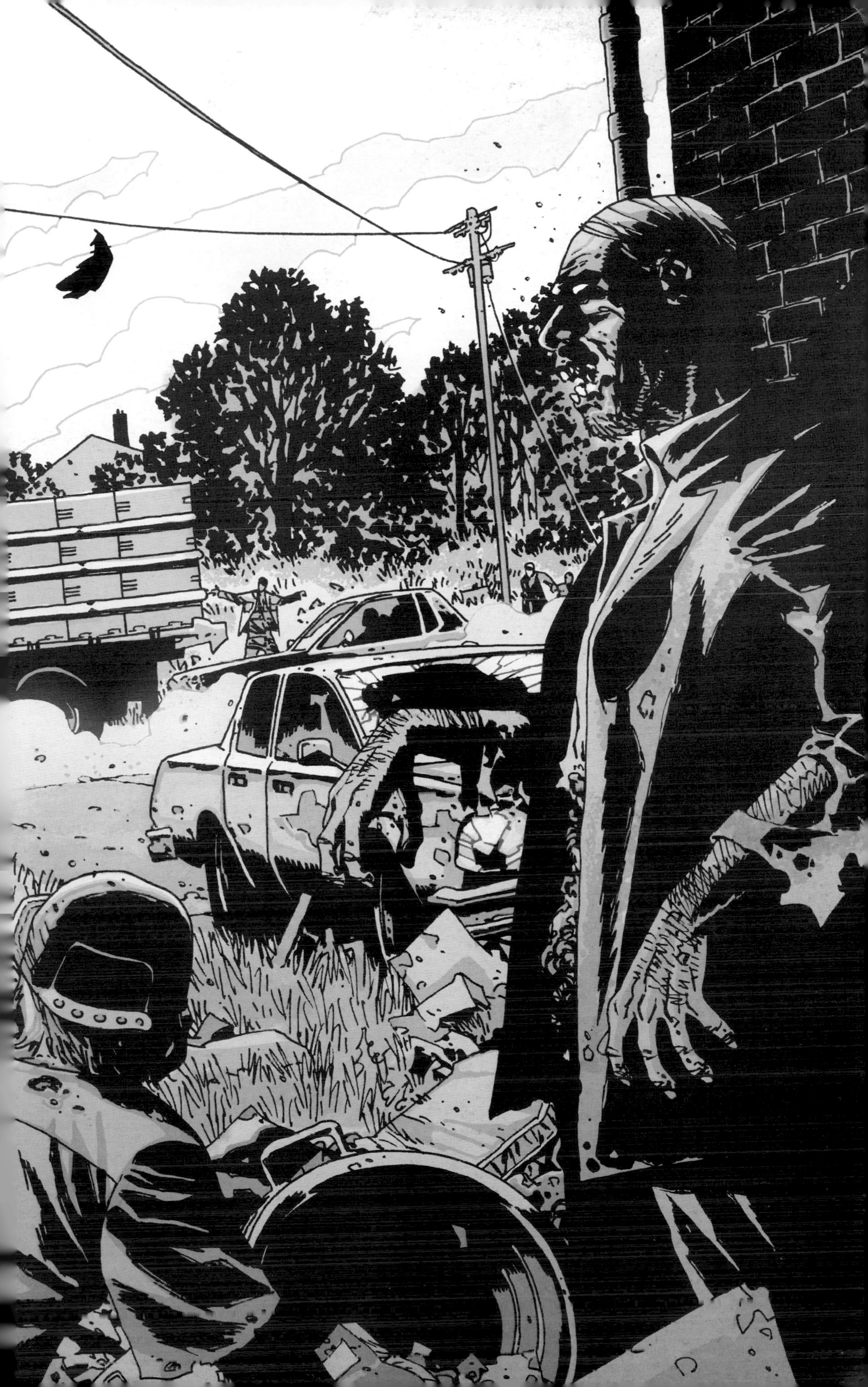

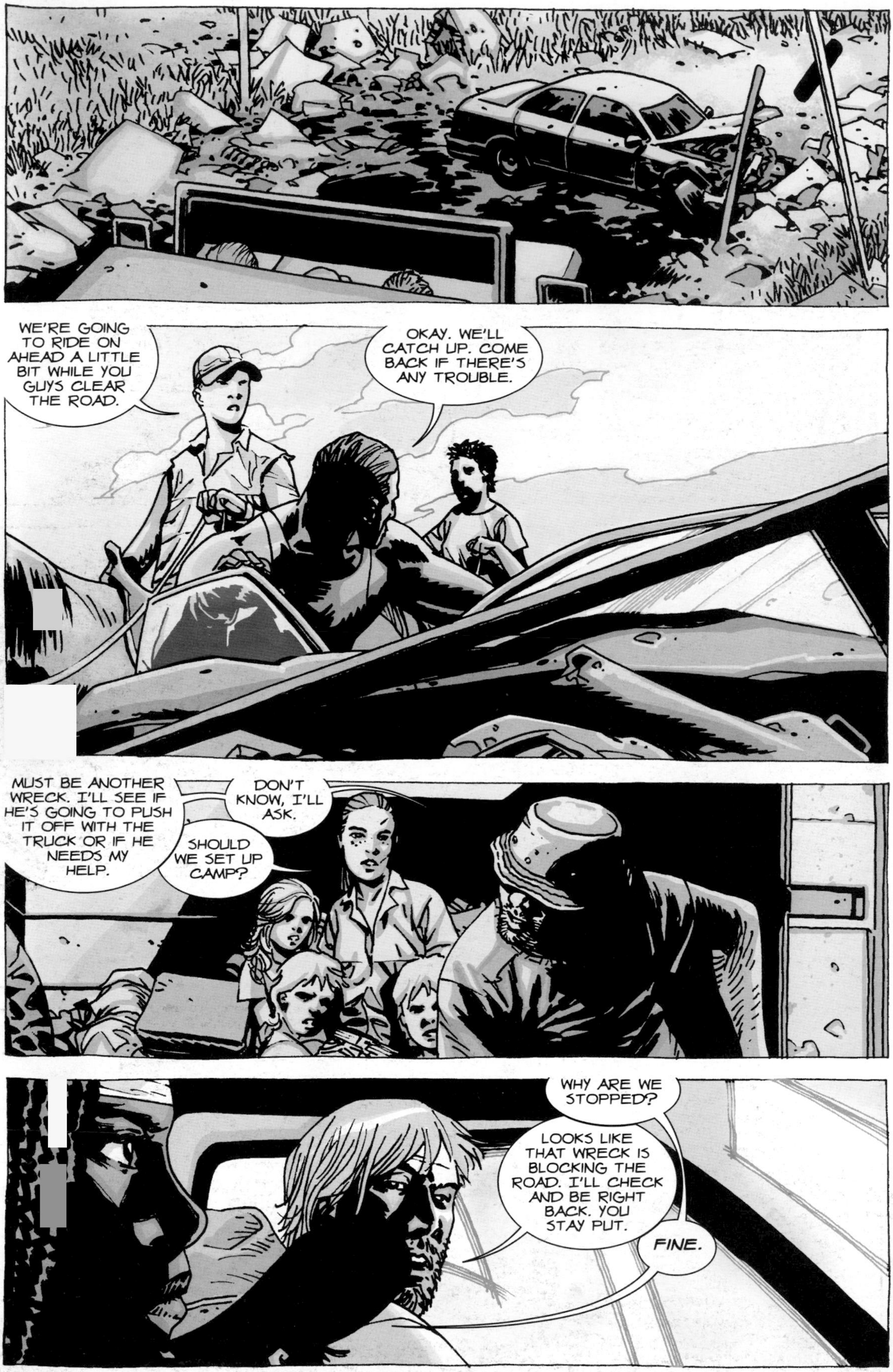
WE'RE GOING TO RIDE ON AHEAD A LITTLE BIT WHILE YOU GUYS CLEAR THE ROAD.
OKAY. WE'LL CATCH UP. COME BACK IF THERE'S ANY TROUBLE.
MUST BE ANOTHER WRECK. I'LL SEE IF HE'S GOING TO PUSH IT OFF WITH THE TRUCK OR IF HE NEEDS MY HELP.
SHOULD WE SET UP CAMP?
DON'T KNOW, I'LL ASK.
WHY ARE WE STOPPED?
LOOKS LIKE THAT WRECK IS BLOCKING THE ROAD. I'LL CHECK AND BE RIGHT BACK. YOU STAY PUT.
FINE.

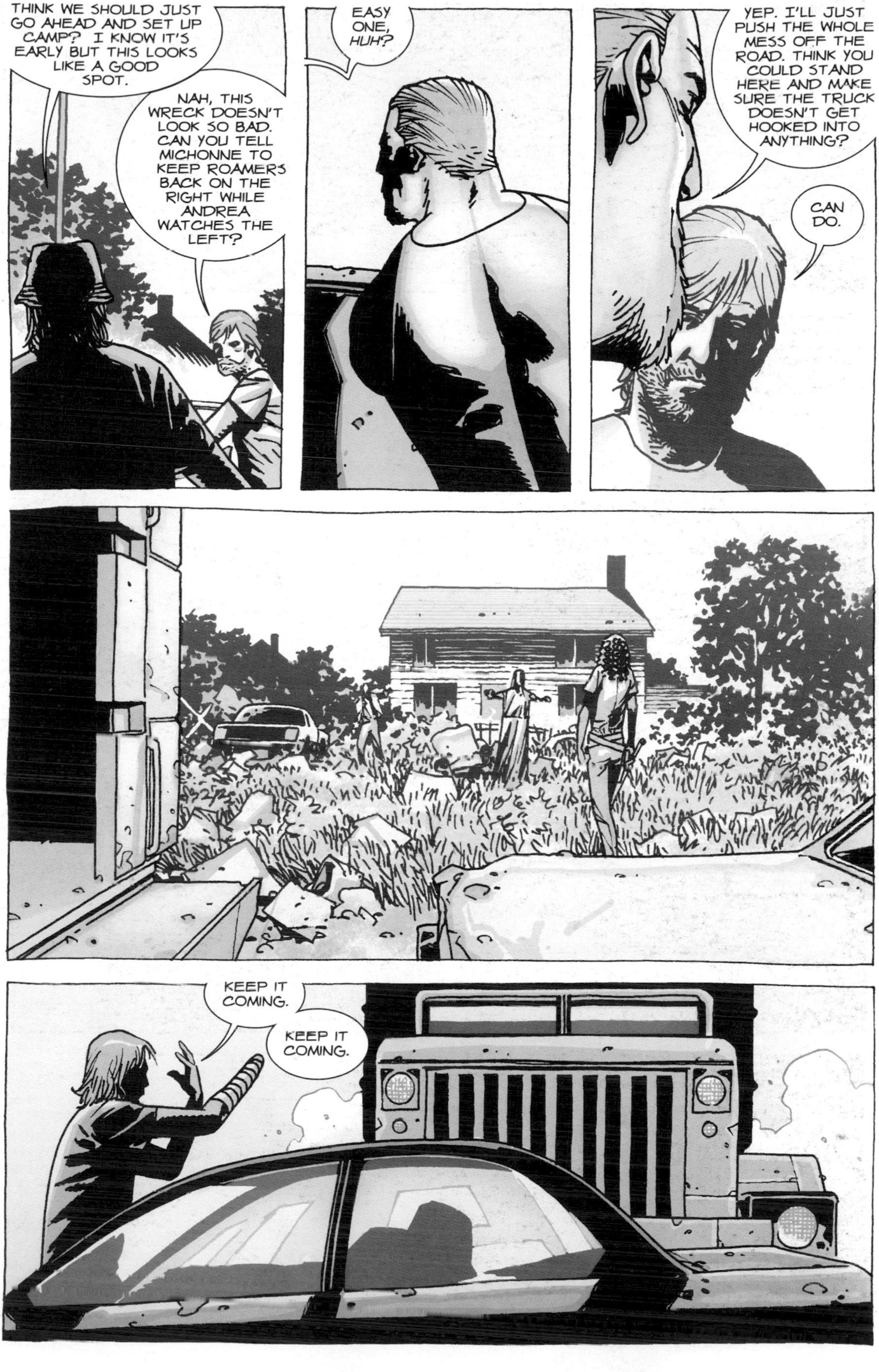
THINK WE SHOULD JUST GO AHEAD AND SET UP CAMP? I KNOW IT'S EARLY BUT THIS LOOKS LIKE A GOOD SPOT.
NAH, THIS WRECK DOESN'T LOOK SO BAD. CAN YOU TELL MICHONNE TO KEEP ROAMERS BACK ON THE RIGHT WHILE ANDREA WATCHES THE LEFT?
EASY ONE, HUH?
YEP. I'LL JUST PUSH THE WHOLE MESS OFF THE ROAD. THINK YOU COULD STAND HERE AND MAKE SURE THE TRUCK DOESN'T GET HOOKED INTO ANYTHING?
CAN DO.
KEEP IT COMING.
KEEP IT COMING.

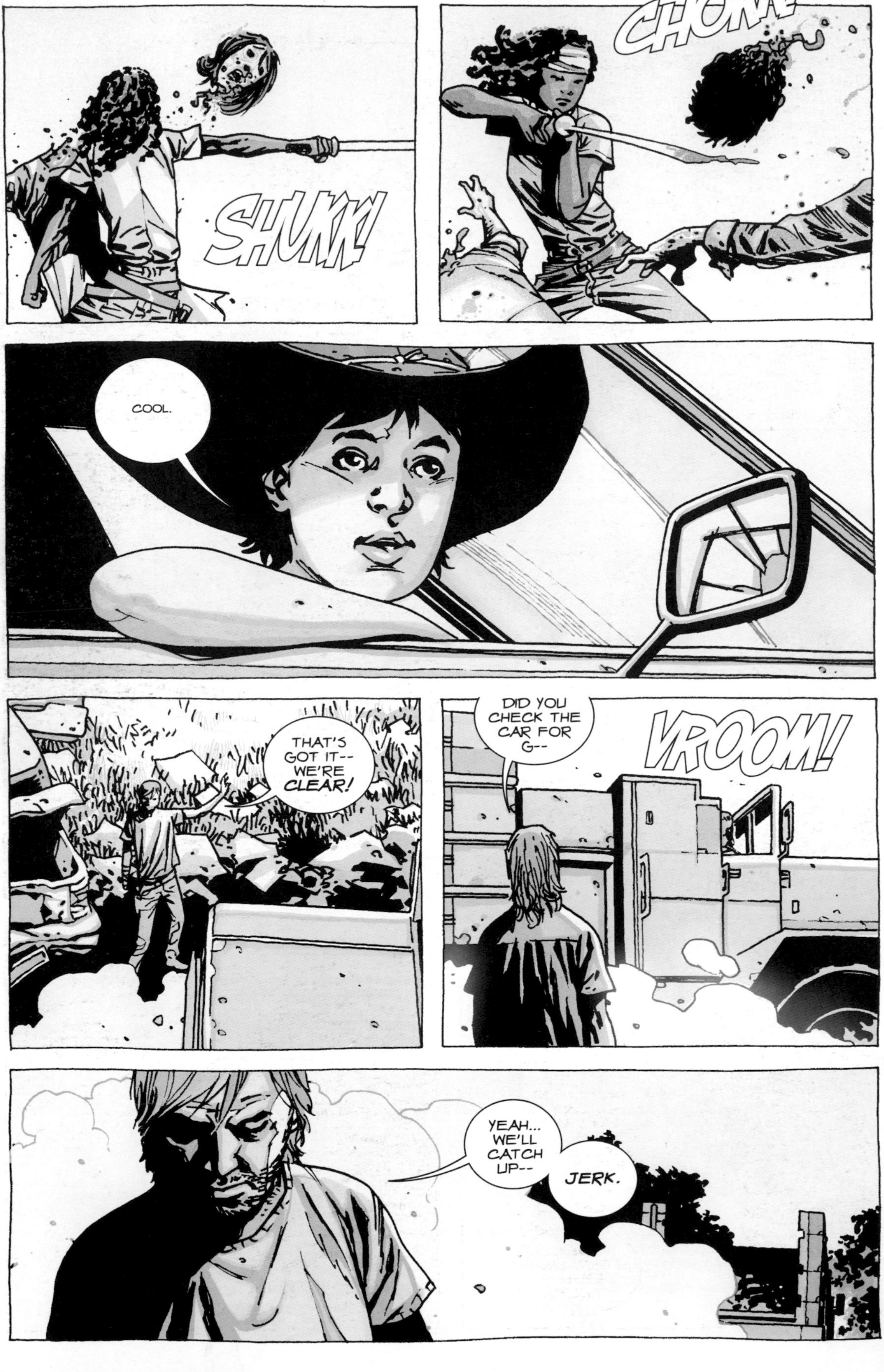
SHUKK!
CHOKK!
COOL.
THAT'S GOT IT-- WE'RE CLEAR!
DID YOU CHECK THE CAR FOR G--
VROOM!
YEAH... WE'LL CATCH UP--
JERK.

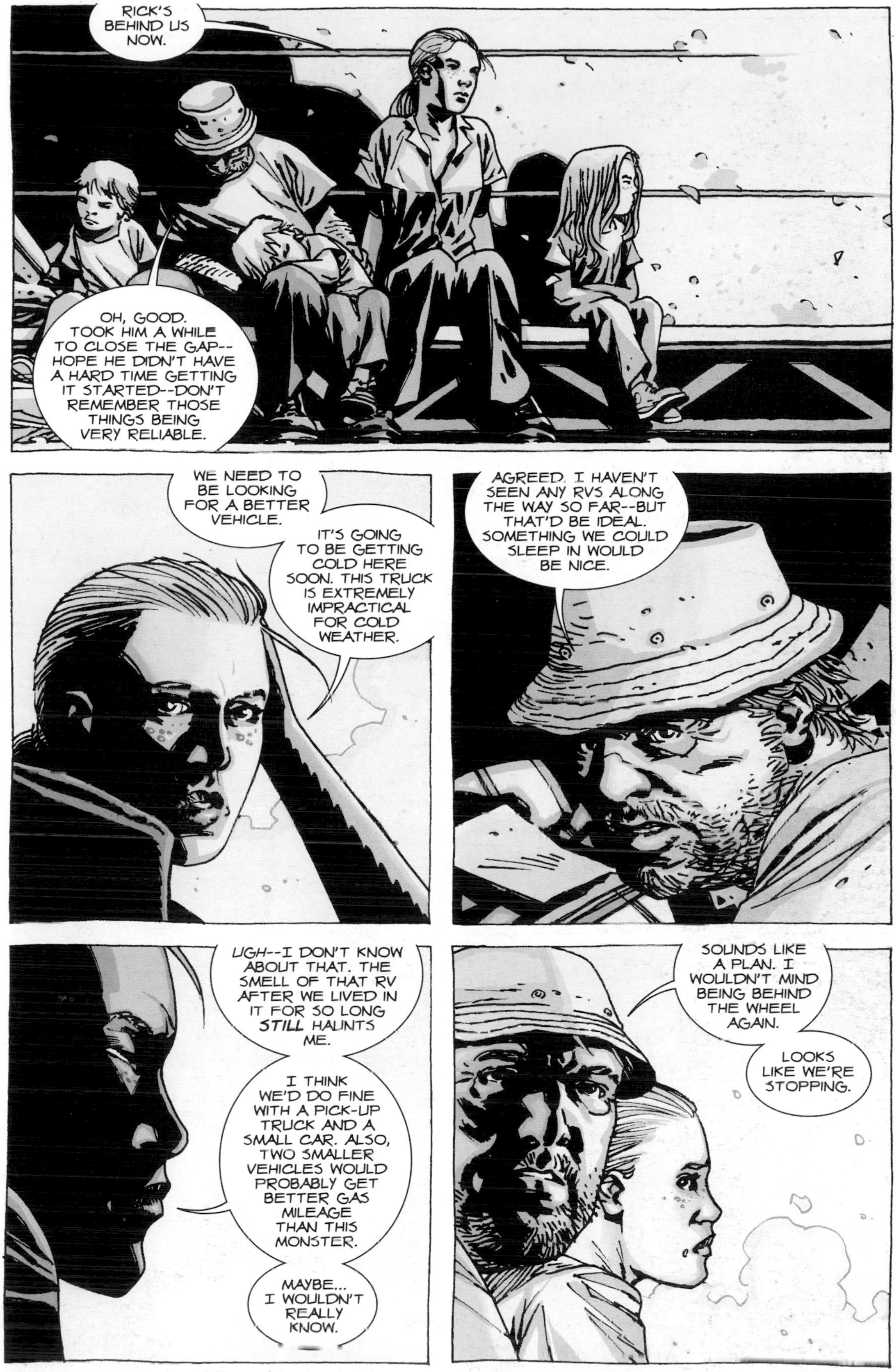
RICK'S BEHIND US NOW.
OH, GOOD. TOOK HIM A WHILE TO CLOSE THE GAP-- HOPE HE DIDN'T HAVE A HARD TIME GETTING IT STARTED--DON'T REMEMBER THOSE THINGS BEING VERY RELIABLE.
WE NEED TO BE LOOKING FOR A BETTER VEHICLE.
IT'S GOING TO BE GETTING COLD HERE SOON. THIS TRUCK IS EXTREMELY IMPRACTICAL FOR COLD WEATHER.
AGREED. I HAVEN'T SEEN ANY RVS ALONG THE WAY SO FAR--BUT THAT'D BE IDEAL. SOMETHING WE COULD SLEEP IN WOULD BE NICE.
UGH--I DON'T KNOW ABOUT THAT. THE SMELL OF THAT RV AFTER WE LIVED IN IT FOR SO LONG STILL HAUNTS ME.
I THINK WE'D DO FINE WITH A PICK-UP TRUCK AND A SMALL CAR. ALSO, TWO SMALLER VEHICLES WOULD PROBABLY GET BETTER GAS MILEAGE THAN THIS MONSTER.
MAYBE... I WOULDN'T REALLY KNOW.
SOUNDS LIKE A PLAN. I WOULDN'T MIND BEING BEHIND THE WHEEL AGAIN.
LOOKS LIKE WE'RE STOPPING.

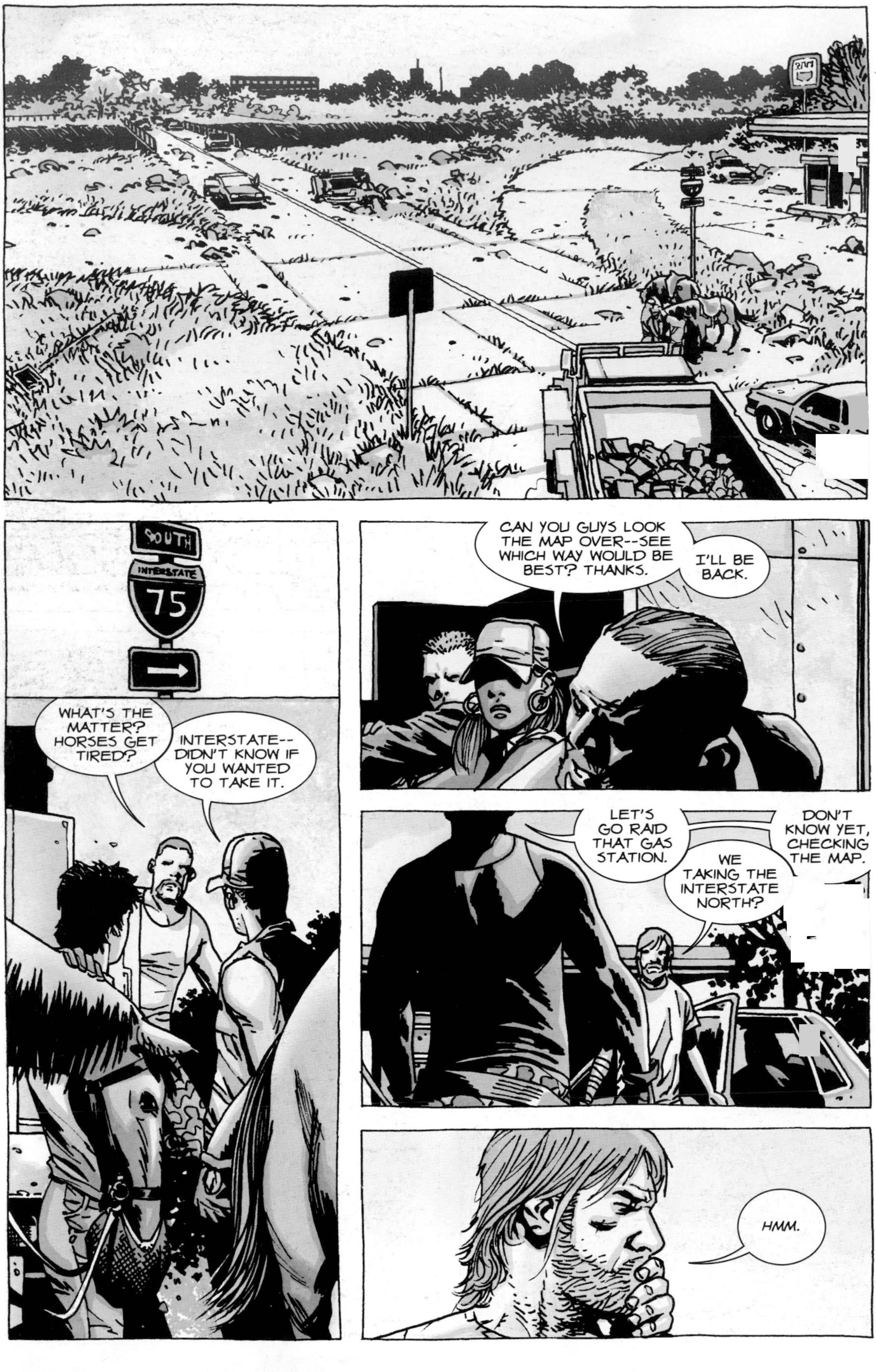
SOUTH
INTERSTATE
75
WHAT'S THE MATTER? HORSES GET TIRED?
INTERSTATE-- DIDN'T KNOW IF YOU WANTED TO TAKE IT.
CAN YOU GUYS LOOK THE MAP OVER--SEE WHICH WAY WOULD BE BEST? THANKS.
I'LL BE BACK.
LET'S GO RAID THAT GAS STATION.
WE TAKING THE INTERSTATE NORTH?
DON'T KNOW YET, CHECKING THE MAP.
HMM.

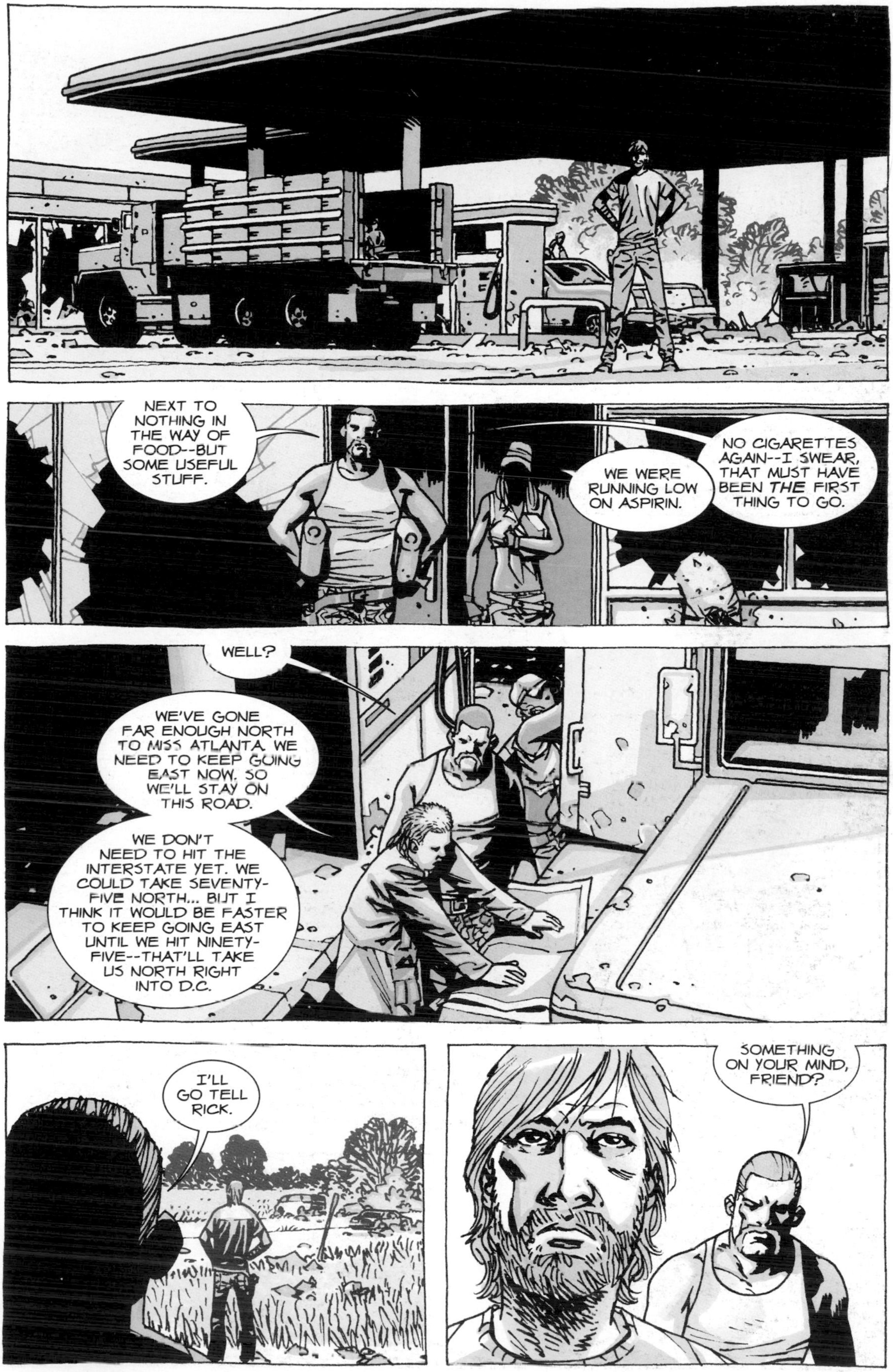
NEXT TO NOTHING IN THE WAY OF FOOD--BUT SOME USEFUL STUFF.
WE WERE RUNNING LOW ON ASPIRIN.
NO CIGARETTES AGAIN--I SWEAR, THAT MUST HAVE BEEN THE FIRST THING TO GO.
WELL?
WE'VE GONE FAR ENOUGH NORTH TO MISS ATLANTA. WE NEED TO KEEP GOING EAST NOW. SO WE'LL STAY ON THIS ROAD.
WE DON'T NEED TO HIT THE INTERSTATE YET. WE COULD TAKE SEVENTY-FIVE NORTH... BUT I THINK IT WOULD BE FASTER TO KEEP GOING EAST UNTIL WE HIT NINETY-FIVE--THAT'LL TAKE US NORTH RIGHT INTO D.C.
I'LL GO TELL RICK.
SOMETHING ON YOUR MIND, FRIEND?

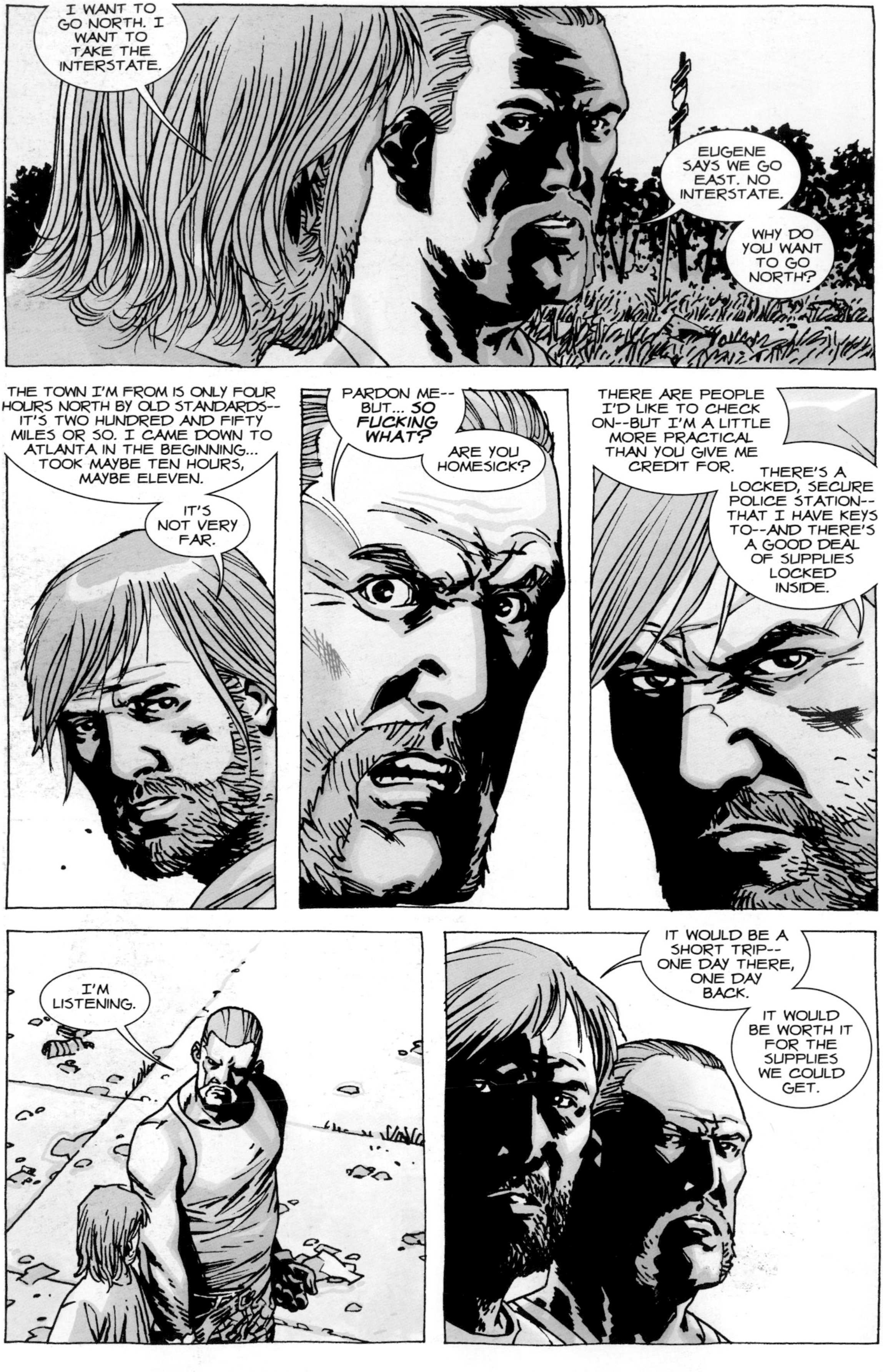
I WANT TO GO NORTH. I WANT TO TAKE THE INTERSTATE.
EUGENE SAYS WE GO EAST. NO INTERSTATE.
WHY DO YOU WANT TO GO NORTH?
THE TOWN I'M FROM IS ONLY FOUR HOURS NORTH BY OLD STANDARDS-- IT'S TWO HUNDRED AND FIFTY MILES OR SO. I CAME DOWN TO ATLANTA IN THE BEGINNING... TOOK MAYBE TEN HOURS, MAYBE ELEVEN.
IT'S NOT VERY FAR.
PARDON ME-- BUT... SO FUCKING WHAT?
ARE YOU HOMESICK?
THERE ARE PEOPLE I'D LIKE TO CHECK ON--BUT I'M A LITTLE MORE PRACTICAL THAN YOU GIVE ME CREDIT FOR.
THERE'S A LOCKED, SECURE POLICE STATION-- THAT I HAVE KEYS TO--AND THERE'S A GOOD DEAL OF SUPPLIES LOCKED INSIDE.
I'M LISTENING.
IT WOULD BE A SHORT TRIP-- ONE DAY THERE, ONE DAY BACK.
IT WOULD BE WORTH IT FOR THE SUPPLIES WE COULD GET.

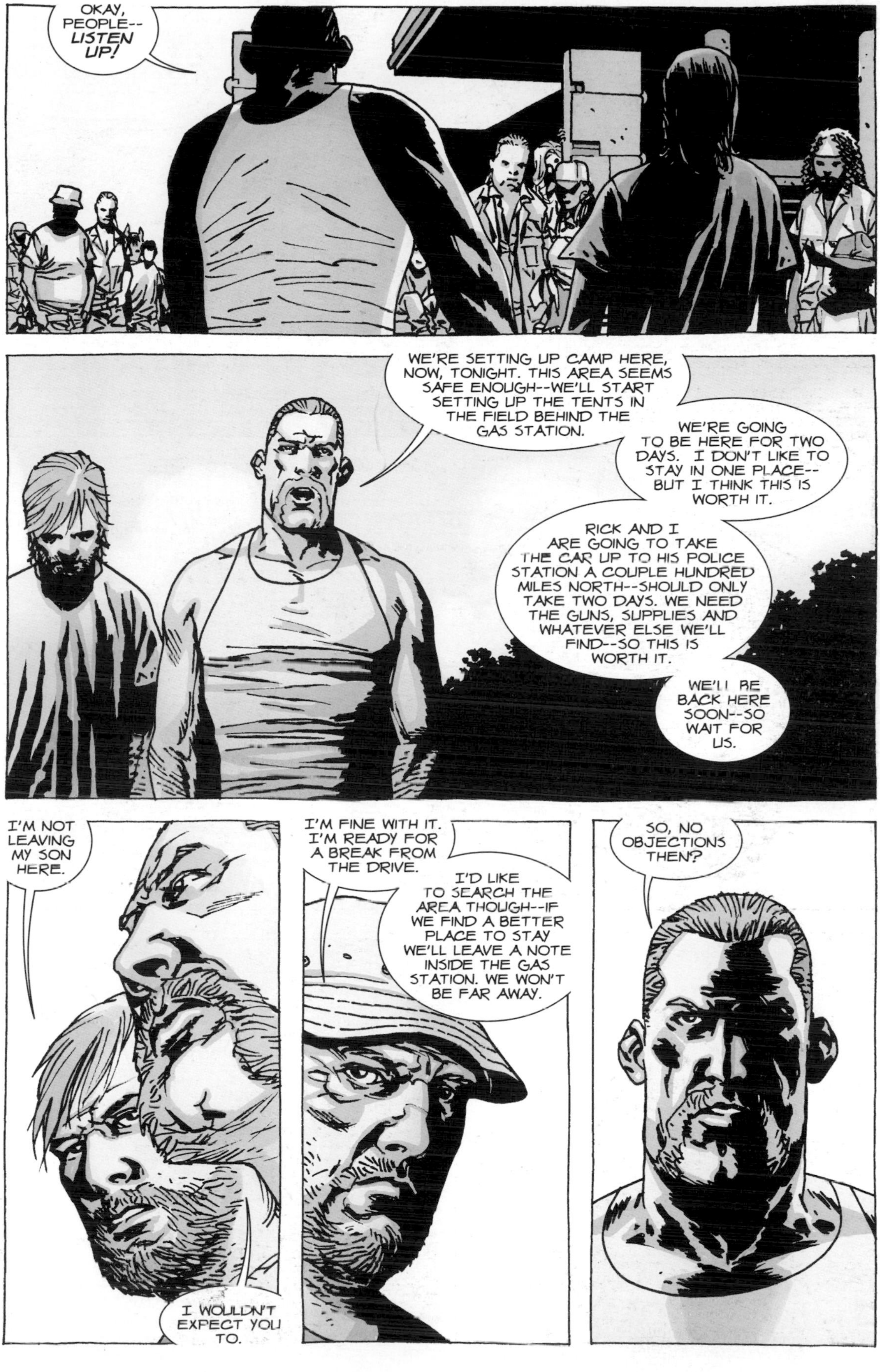
OKAY, PEOPLE-- LISTEN UP!
WE'RE SETTING UP CAMP HERE, NOW, TONIGHT. THIS AREA SEEMS SAFE ENOUGH--WE'LL START SETTING UP THE TENTS IN THE FIELD BEHIND THE GAS STATION.
WE'RE GOING TO BE HERE FOR TWO DAYS. I DON'T LIKE TO STAY IN ONE PLACE-- BUT I THINK THIS IS WORTH IT.
RICK AND I ARE GOING TO TAKE THE CAR UP TO HIS POLICE STATION A COUPLE HUNDRED MILES NORTH--SHOULD ONLY TAKE TWO DAYS. WE NEED THE GUNS, SUPPLIES AND WHATEVER ELSE WE'LL FIND--SO THIS IS WORTH IT.
WE'LL BE BACK HERE SOON--SO WAIT FOR US.
I'M NOT LEAVING MY SON HERE.
I WOULDN'T EXPECT YOU TO.
I'M FINE WITH IT. I'M READY FOR A BREAK FROM THE DRIVE.
I'D LIKE TO SEARCH THE AREA THOUGH--IF WE FIND A BETTER PLACE TO STAY WE'LL LEAVE A NOTE INSIDE THE GAS STATION. WE WON'T BE FAR AWAY.
SO, NO OBJECTIONS THEN?

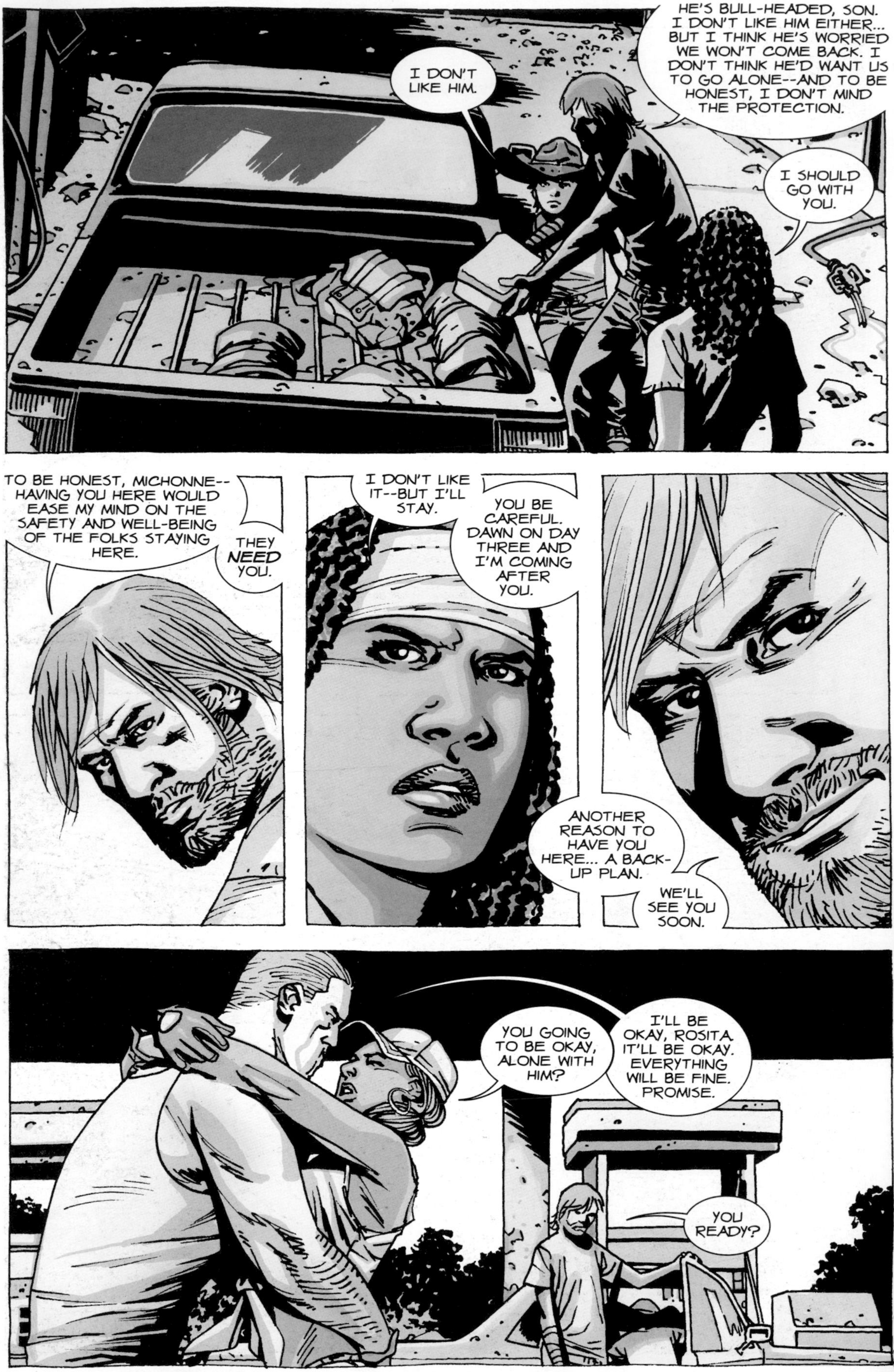
I DON'T LIKE HIM.
HE'S BULL-HEADED, SON. I DON'T LIKE HIM EITHER... BUT I THINK HE'S WORRIED WE WON'T COME BACK. I DON'T THINK HE'D WANT US TO GO ALONE--AND TO BE HONEST, I DON'T MIND THE PROTECTION.
I SHOULD GO WITH YOU.
TO BE HONEST, MICHONNE-- HAVING YOU HERE WOULD EASE MY MIND ON THE SAFETY AND WELL-BEING OF THE FOLKS STAYING HERE.
THEY **NEED** YOU.
I DON'T LIKE IT--BUT I'LL STAY.
YOU BE CAREFUL. DAWN ON DAY THREE AND I'M COMING AFTER YOU.
ANOTHER REASON TO HAVE YOU HERE... A BACK-UP PLAN.
WE'LL SEE YOU SOON.
YOU GOING TO BE OKAY, ALONE WITH HIM?
I'LL BE OKAY, ROSITA. IT'LL BE OKAY. EVERYTHING WILL BE FINE. PROMISE.
YOU READY?

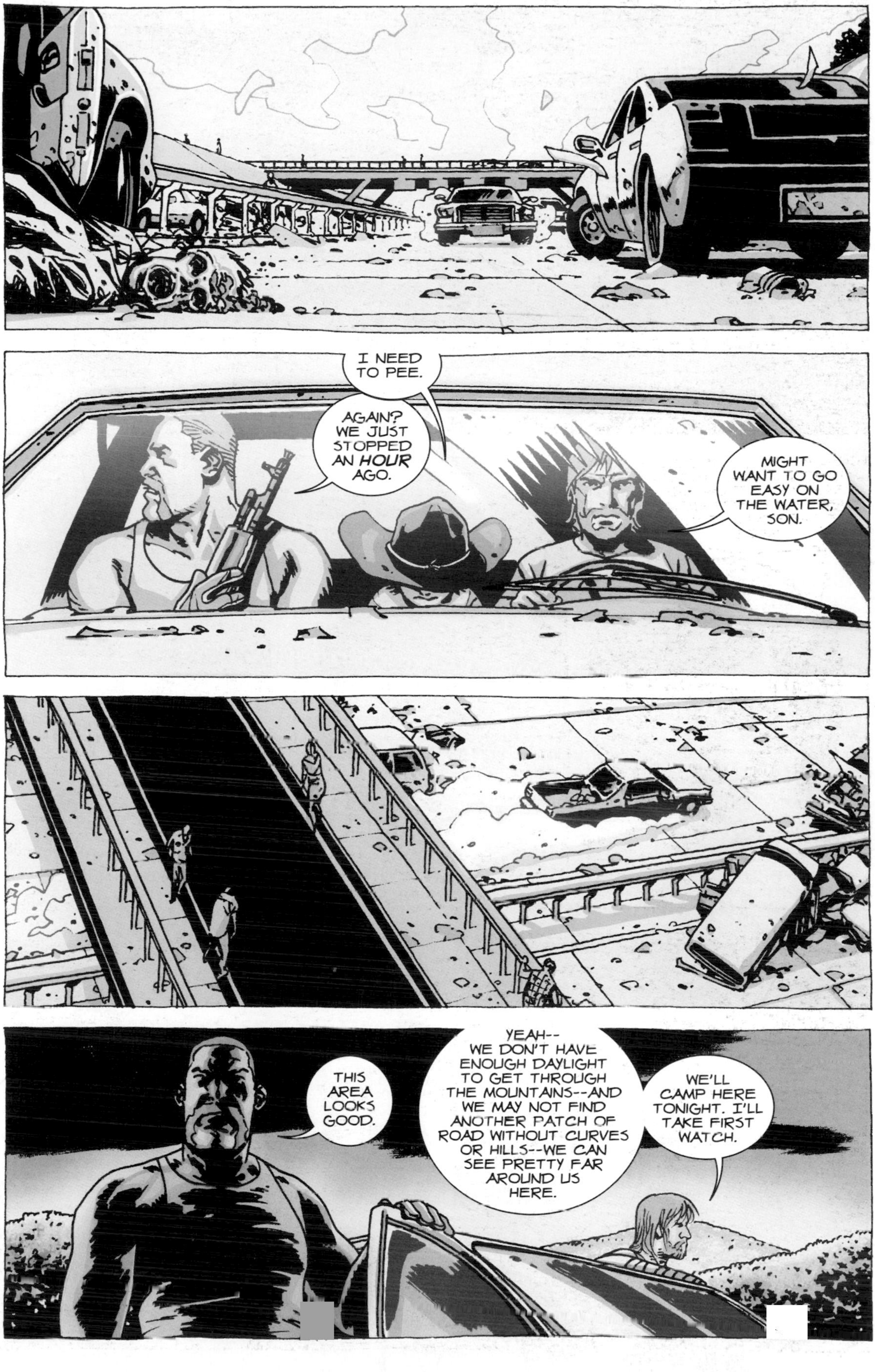

I NEED TO PEE.
AGAIN? WE JUST STOPPED AN *HOUR* AGO.
MIGHT WANT TO GO EASY ON THE WATER, SON.
THIS AREA LOOKS GOOD.
YEAH-- WE DON'T HAVE ENOUGH DAYLIGHT TO GET THROUGH THE MOUNTAINS--AND WE MAY NOT FIND ANOTHER PATCH OF ROAD WITHOUT CURVES OR HILLS--WE CAN SEE PRETTY FAR AROUND US HERE.
WE'LL CAMP HERE TONIGHT. I'LL TAKE FIRST WATCH.

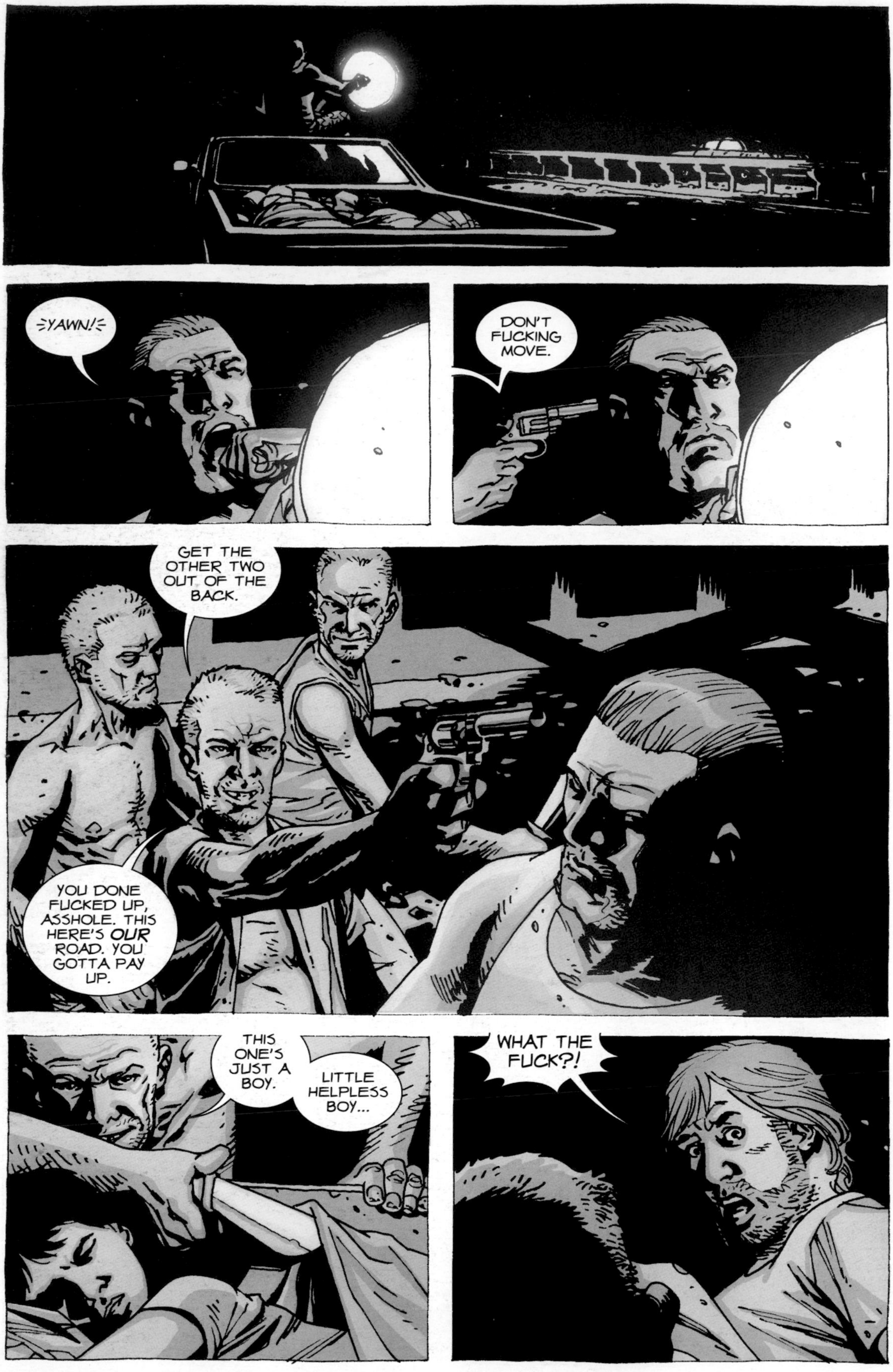

=YAWN!=
DON'T FUCKING MOVE.
GET THE OTHER TWO OUT OF THE BACK.
YOU DONE FUCKED UP, ASSHOLE. THIS HERE'S OUR ROAD. YOU GOTTA PAY UP.
THIS ONE'S JUST A BOY.
LITTLE HELPLESS BOY...
WHAT THE FUCK?!

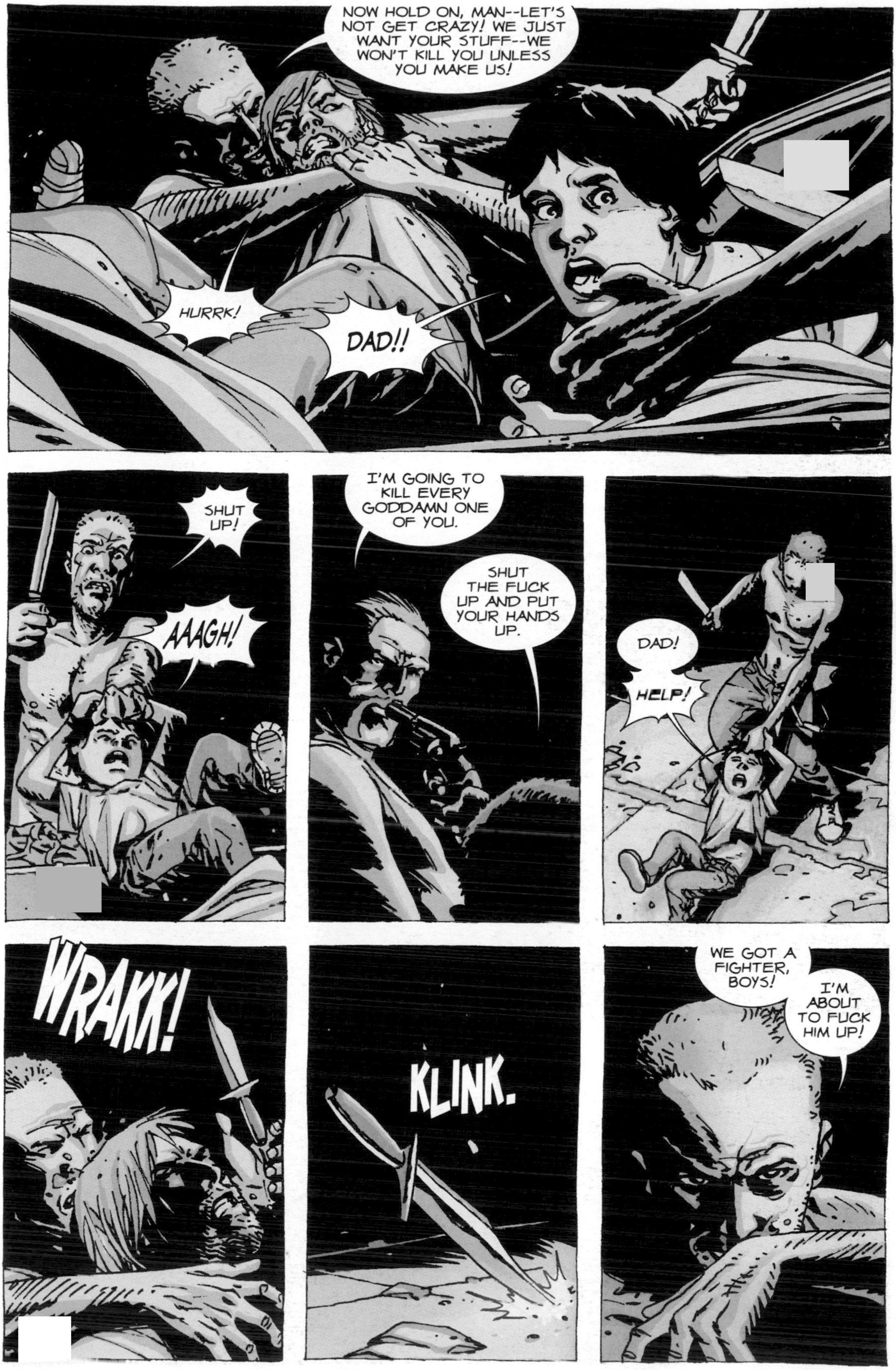
NOW HOLD ON, MAN--LET'S NOT GET CRAZY! WE JUST WANT YOUR STUFF--WE WON'T KILL YOU UNLESS YOU MAKE US!
HURRK!
DAD!!
SHUT UP!
AAAGH!
I'M GOING TO KILL EVERY GODDAMN ONE OF YOU.
SHUT THE FUCK UP AND PUT YOUR HANDS UP.
DAD!
HELP!
WRAKK!
KLINK.
WE GOT A FIGHTER, BOYS!
I'M ABOUT TO FUCK HIM UP!

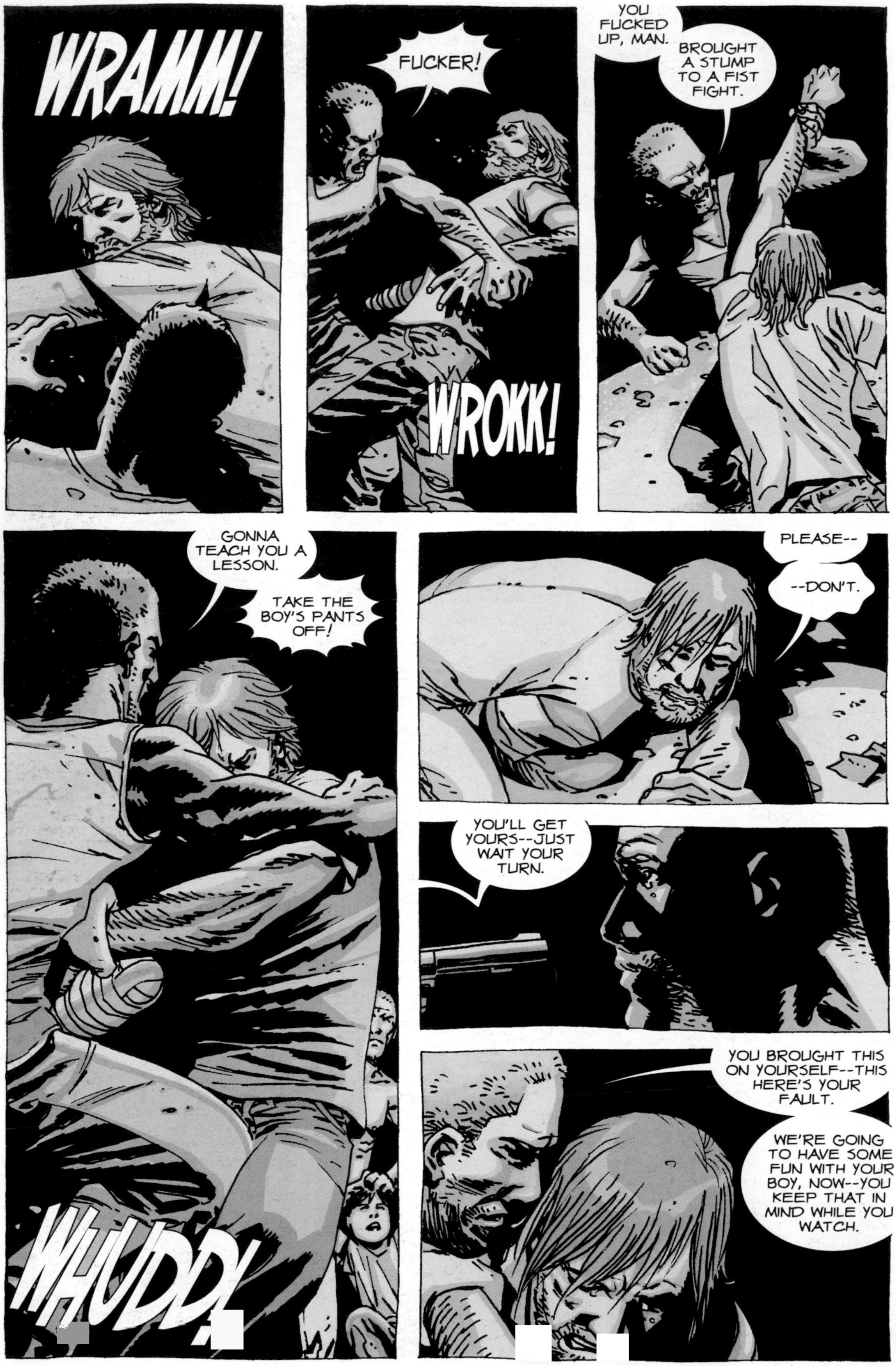
WRAMM!
FUCKER!
WROKK!
YOU FUCKED UP, MAN.
BROUGHT A STUMP TO A FIST FIGHT.
GONNA TEACH YOU A LESSON.
TAKE THE BOY'S PANTS OFF!
WHUDD!
PLEASE--
--DON'T.
YOU'LL GET YOURS--JUST WAIT YOUR TURN.
YOU BROUGHT THIS ON YOURSELF--THIS HERE'S YOUR FAULT.
WE'RE GOING TO HAVE SOME FUN WITH YOUR BOY, NOW--YOU KEEP THAT IN MIND WHILE YOU WATCH.

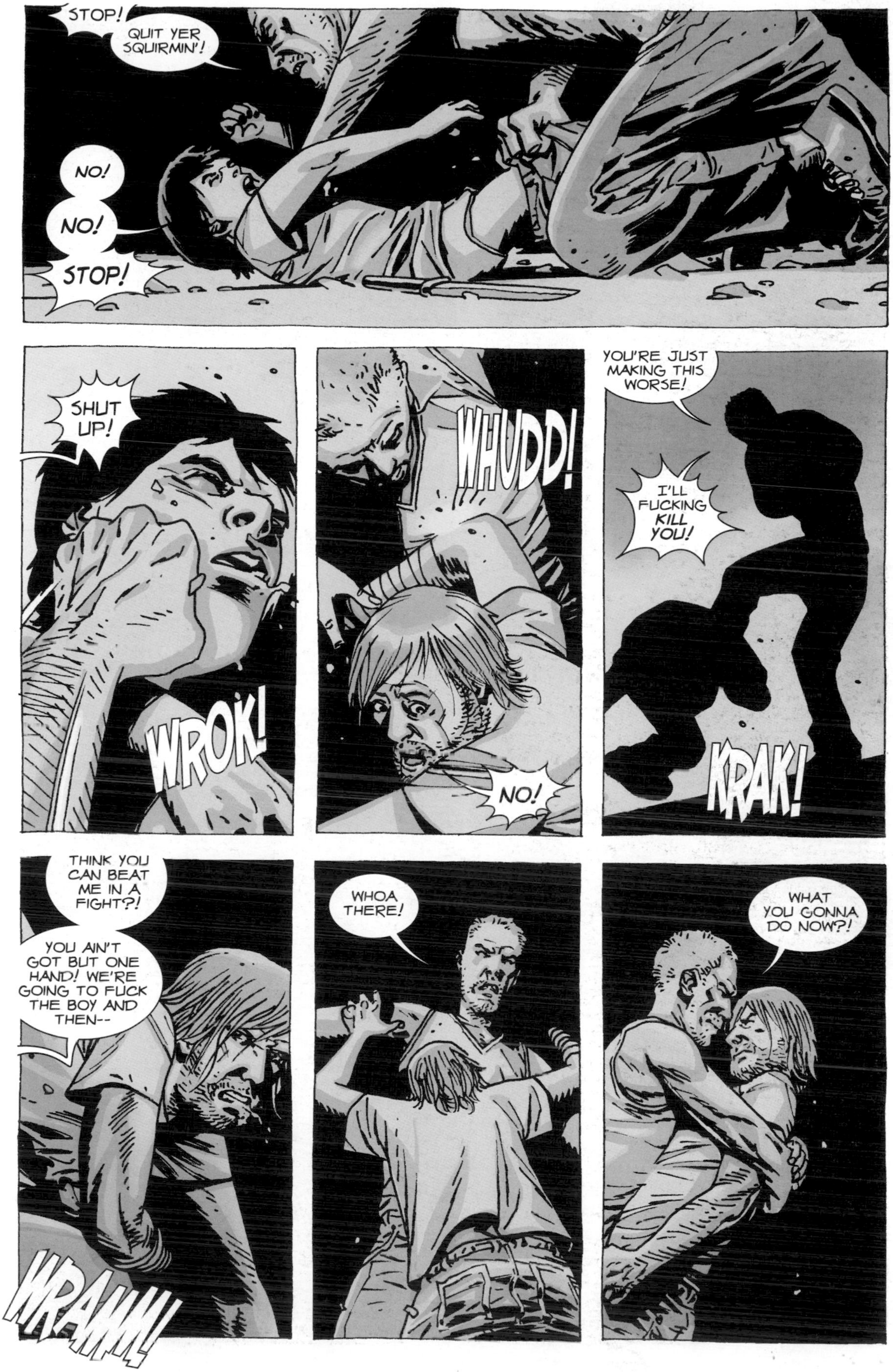

STOP!
QUIT YER SQUIRMIN'!
NO!
NO!
STOP!
SHUT UP!
WROK!
WHUDD!
NO!
YOU'RE JUST MAKING THIS WORSE!
I'LL FUCKING KILL YOU!
KRAK!
THINK YOU CAN BEAT ME IN A FIGHT?!
YOU AIN'T GOT BUT ONE HAND! WE'RE GOING TO FUCK THE BOY AND THEN--
WRAMM!
WHOA THERE!
WHAT YOU GONNA DO NOW?!

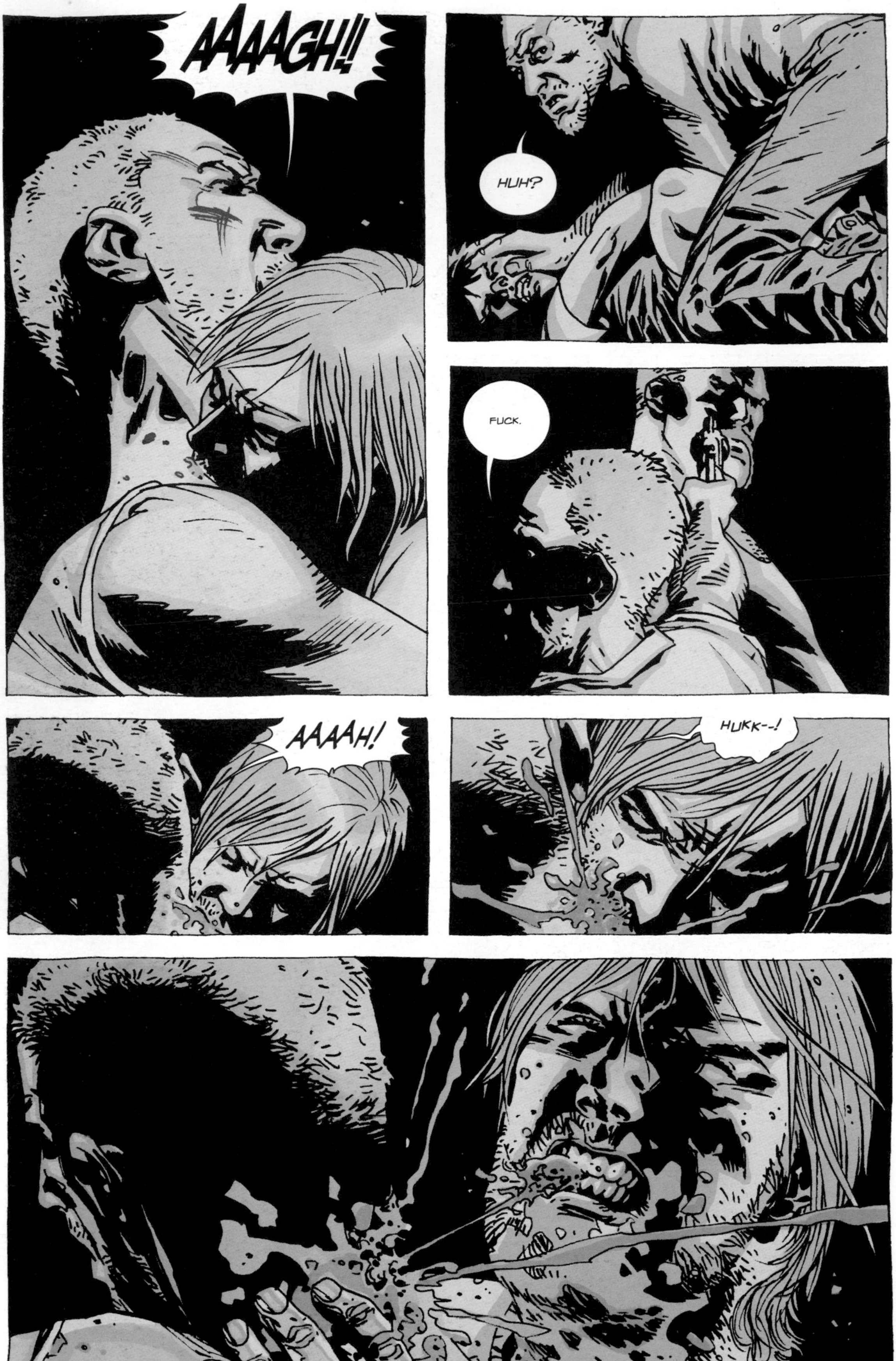
AAAAGH!!
HUH?
FUCK.
AAAAH!
HUKK--!

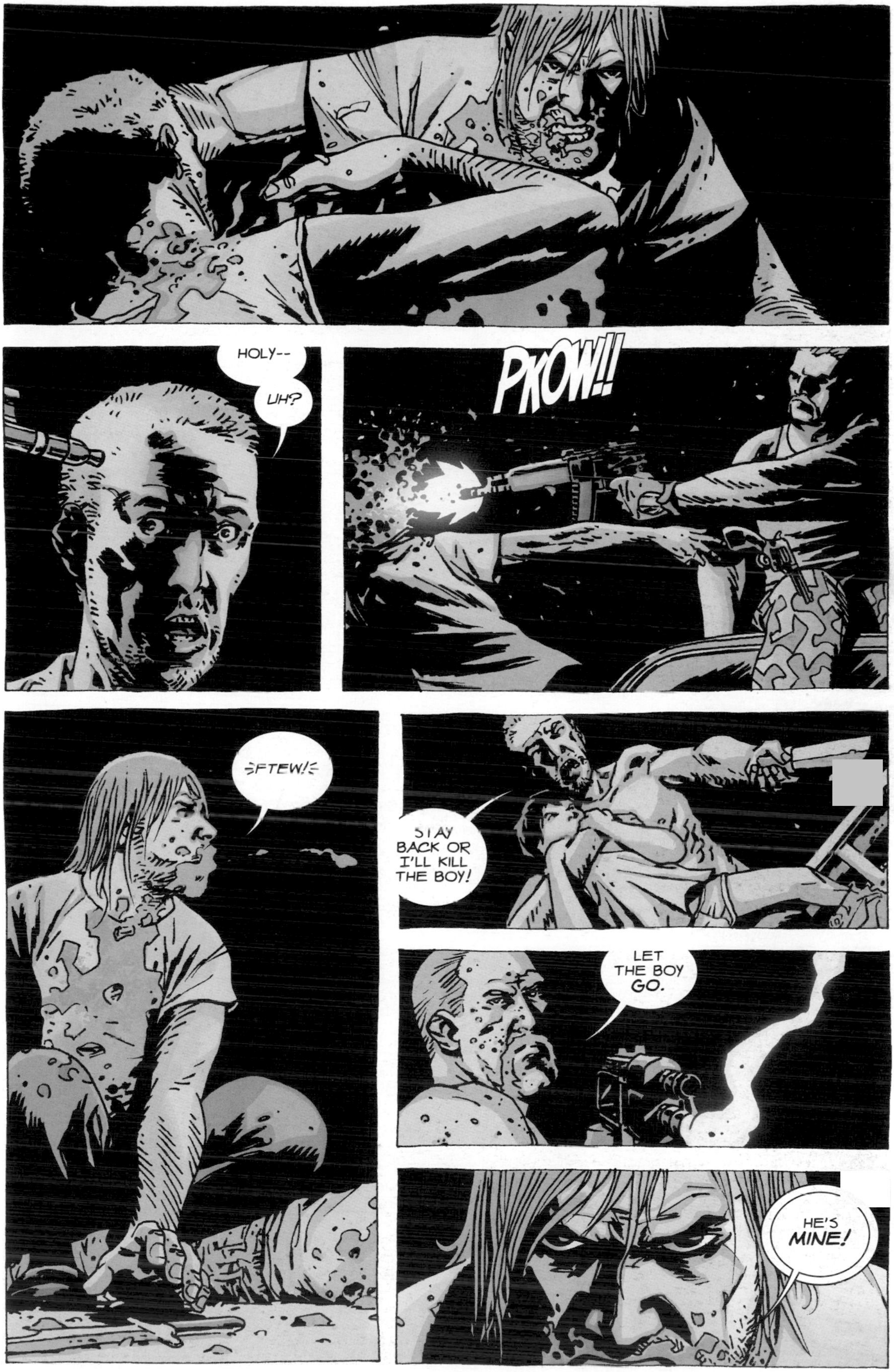
HOLY--
UH?
PKOW!!
FTEW!
STAY BACK OR I'LL KILL THE BOY!
LET THE BOY GO.
HE'S MINE!

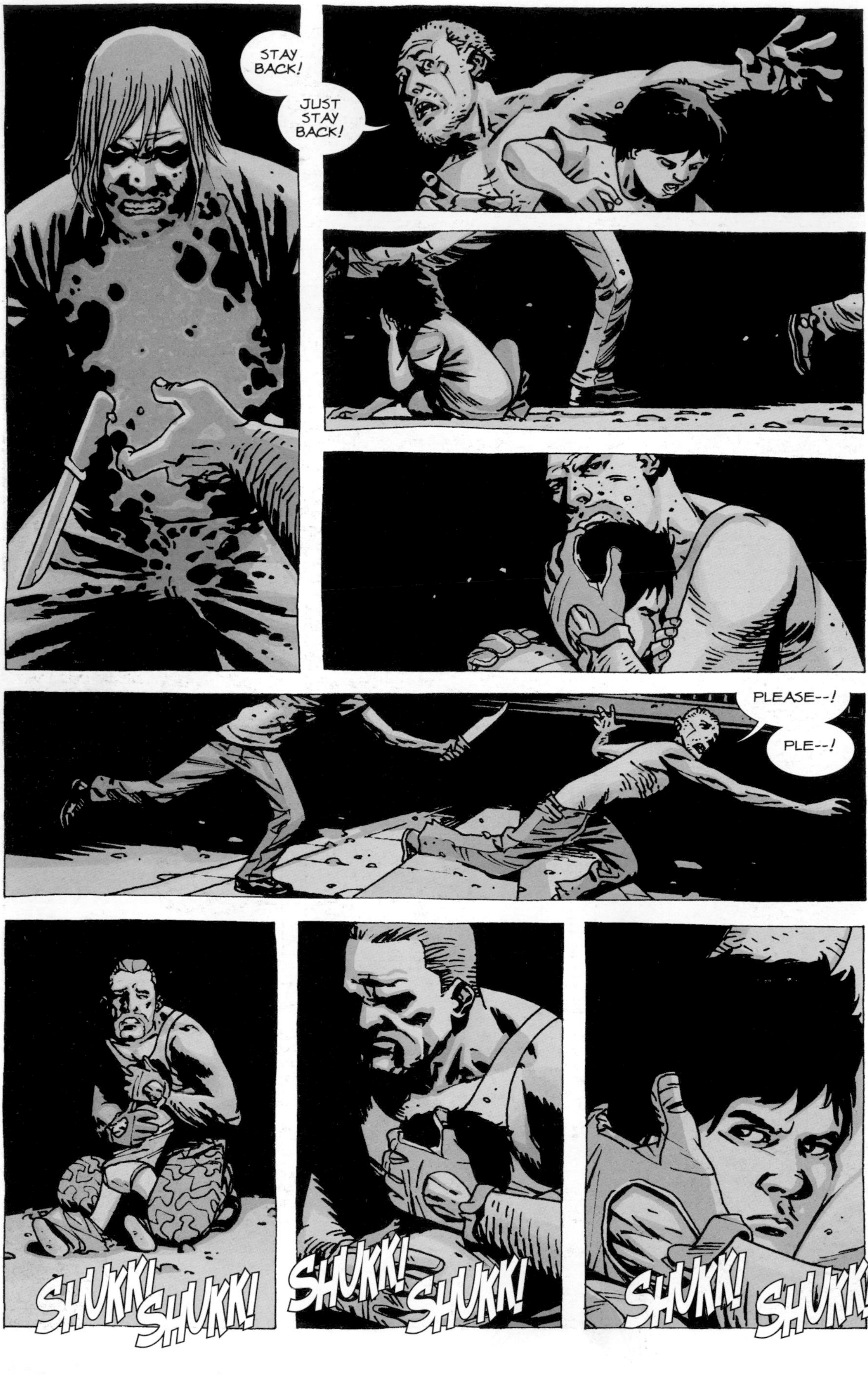
STAY BACK!
JUST STAY BACK!
PLEASE--!
PLE--!
SHUKK! SHUKK!
SHUKK! SHUKK!
SHUKK! SHUKK!

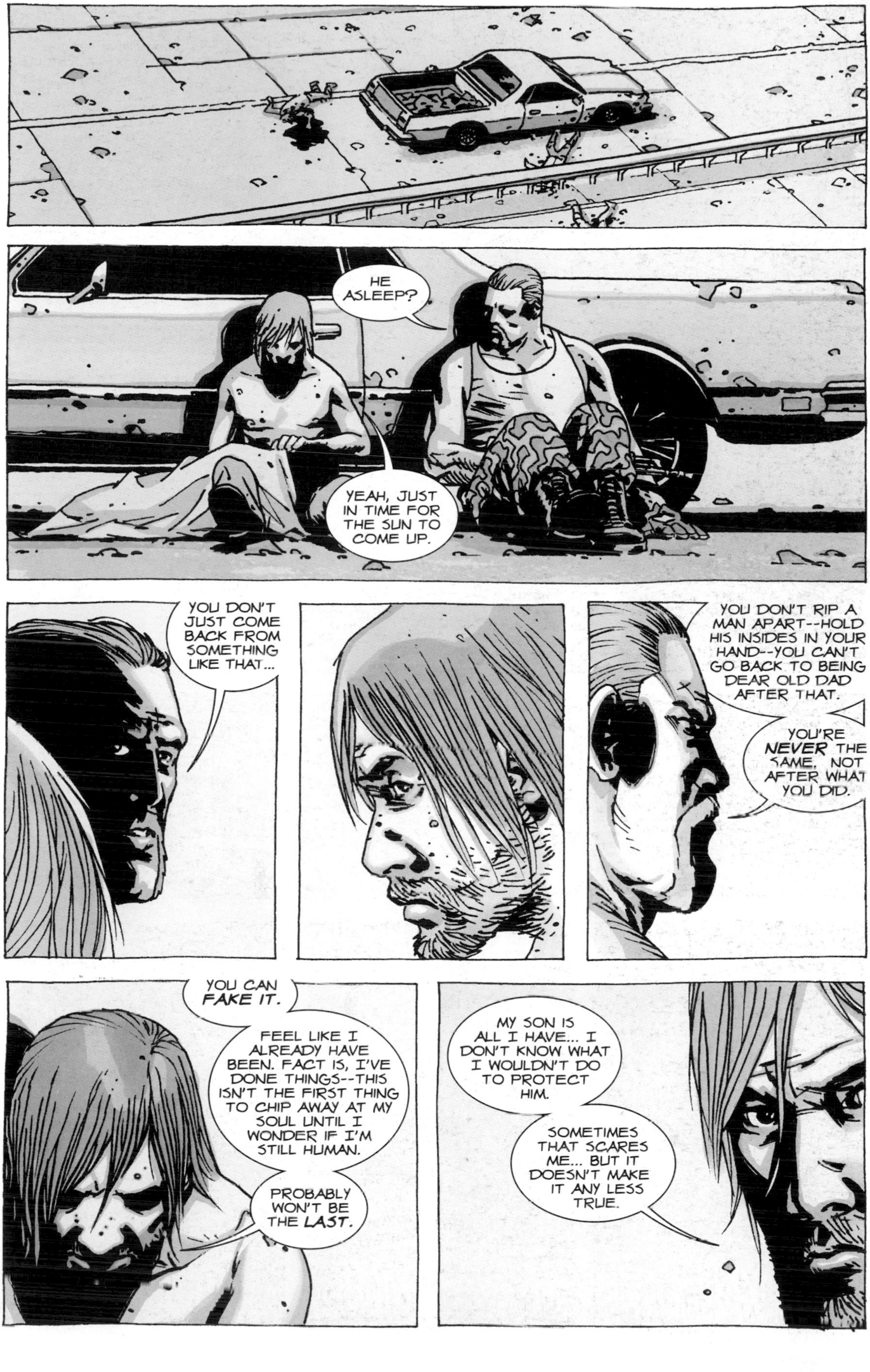
HE ASLEEP?
YEAH, JUST IN TIME FOR THE SUN TO COME UP.
YOU DON'T JUST COME BACK FROM SOMETHING LIKE THAT...
YOU DON'T RIP A MAN APART--HOLD HIS INSIDES IN YOUR HAND--YOU CAN'T GO BACK TO BEING DEAR OLD DAD AFTER THAT.
YOU'RE ***NEVER*** THE SAME. NOT AFTER WHAT YOU DID.
YOU CAN ***FAKE IT.***
FEEL LIKE I ALREADY HAVE BEEN. FACT IS, I'VE DONE THINGS--THIS ISN'T THE FIRST THING TO CHIP AWAY AT MY SOUL UNTIL I WONDER IF I'M STILL HUMAN.
PROBABLY WON'T BE THE ***LAST.***
MY SON IS ALL I HAVE... I DON'T KNOW WHAT I WOULDN'T DO TO PROTECT HIM.
SOMETIMES THAT SCARES ME... BUT IT DOESN'T MAKE IT ANY LESS TRUE.

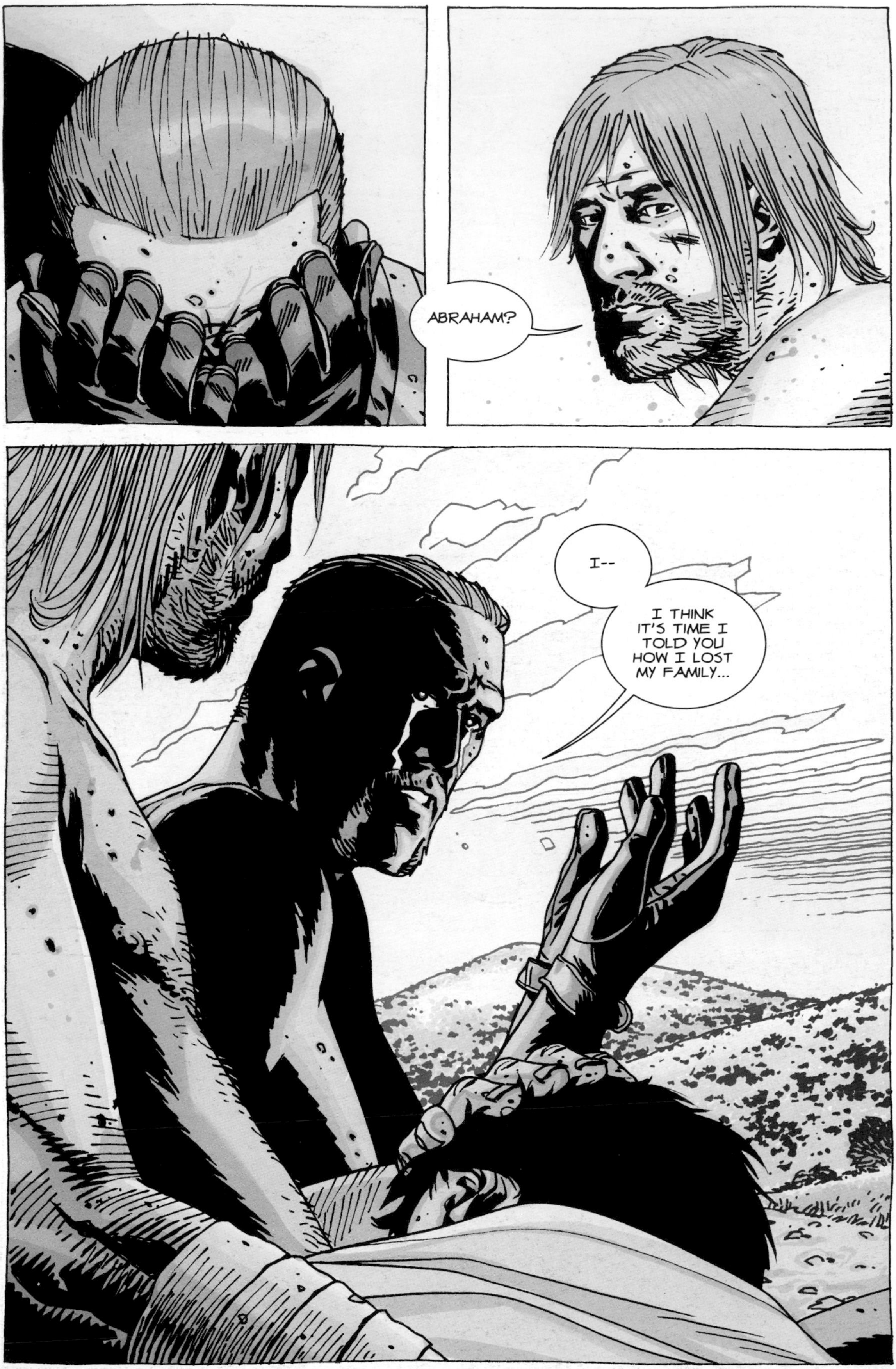
ABRAHAM?
I--
I THINK IT'S TIME I TOLD YOU HOW I LOST MY FAMILY...

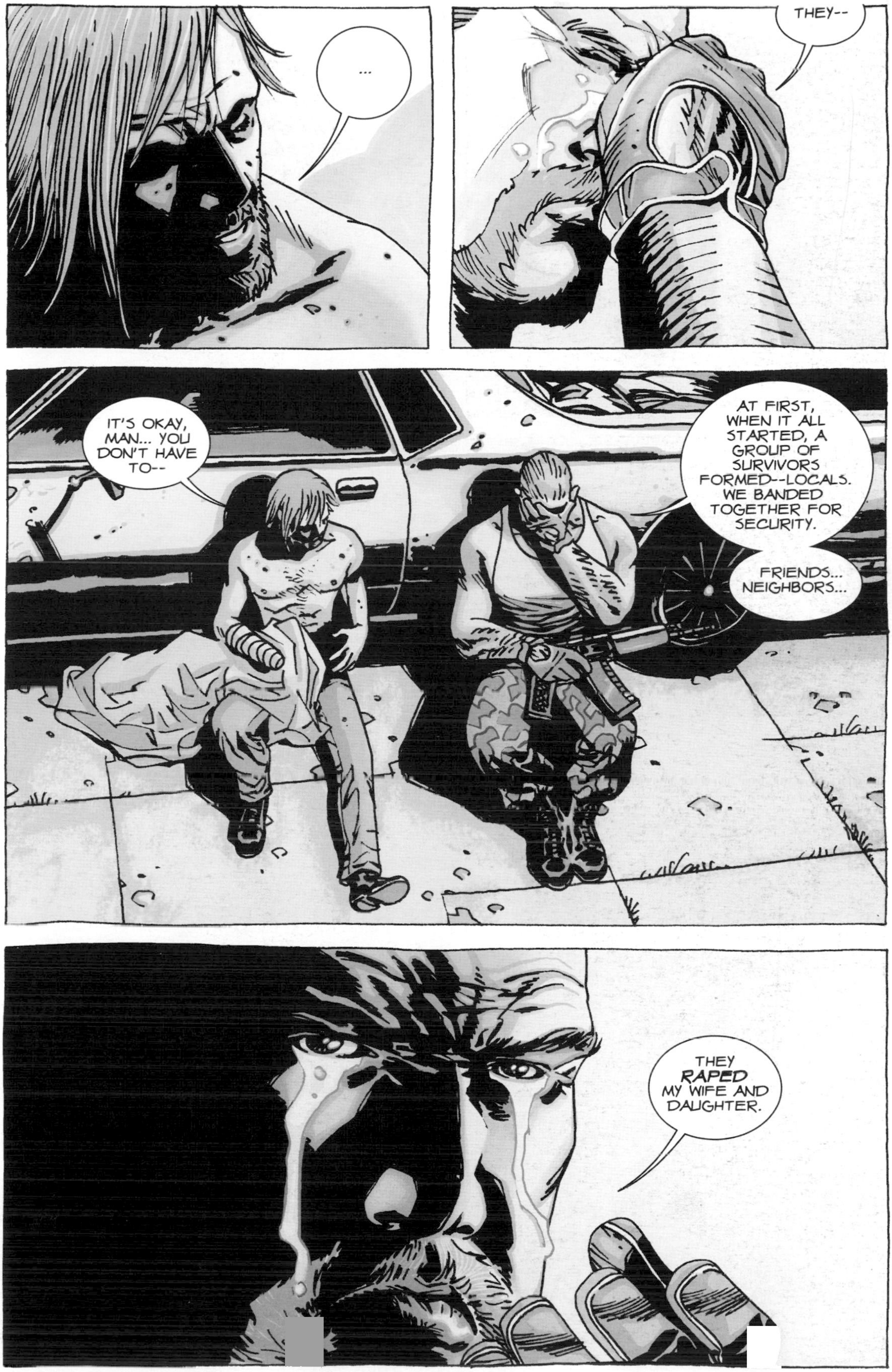
...
THEY--
IT'S OKAY, MAN... YOU DON'T HAVE TO--
AT FIRST, WHEN IT ALL STARTED, A GROUP OF SURVIVORS FORMED--LOCALS. WE BANDED TOGETHER FOR SECURITY.
FRIENDS... NEIGHBORS...
THEY RAPED MY WIFE AND DAUGHTER.

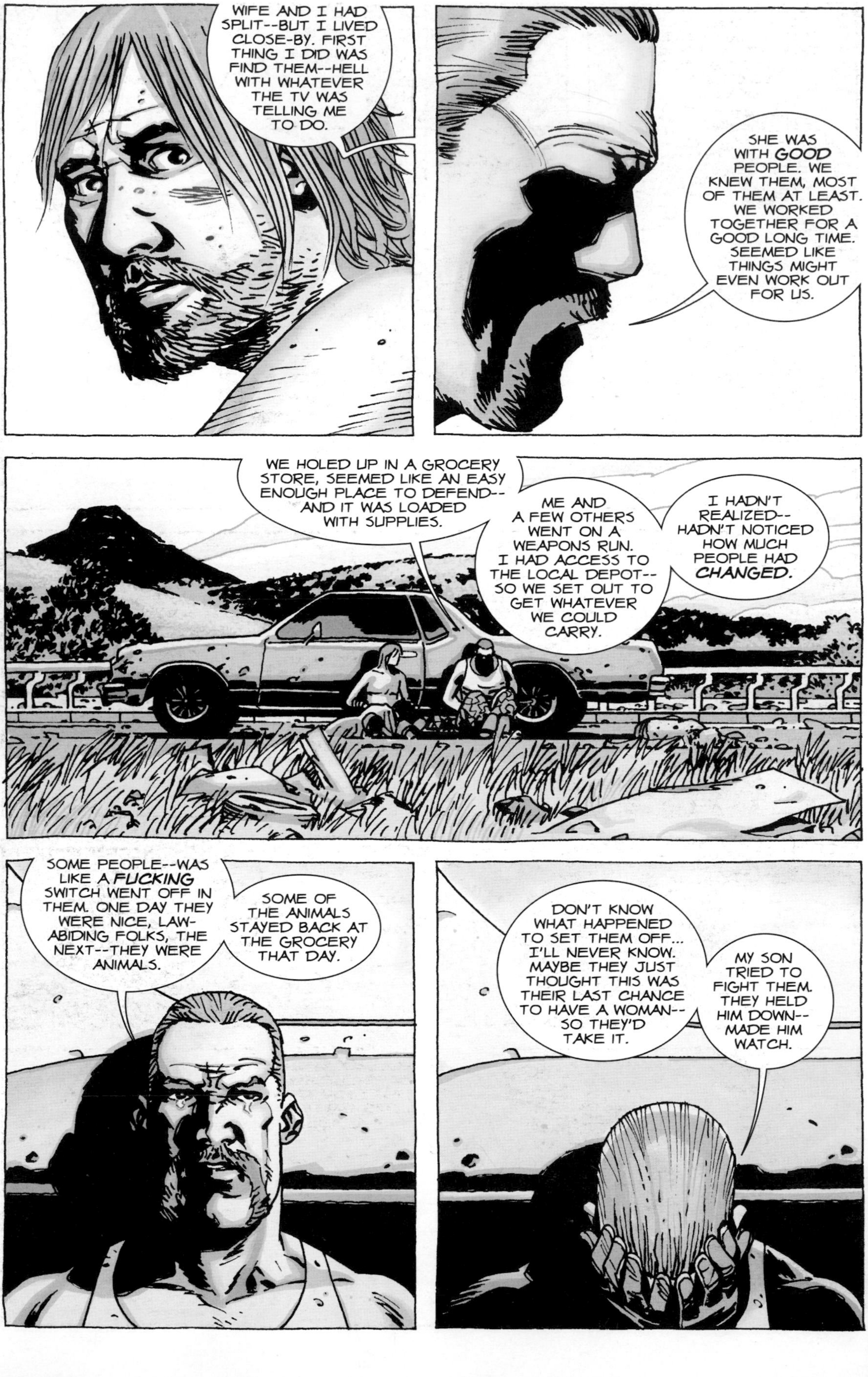
WIFE AND I HAD SPLIT--BUT I LIVED CLOSE-BY. FIRST THING I DID WAS FIND THEM--HELL WITH WHATEVER THE TV WAS TELLING ME TO DO.
SHE WAS WITH GOOD PEOPLE. WE KNEW THEM, MOST OF THEM AT LEAST. WE WORKED TOGETHER FOR A GOOD LONG TIME. SEEMED LIKE THINGS MIGHT EVEN WORK OUT FOR US.
WE HOLED UP IN A GROCERY STORE, SEEMED LIKE AN EASY ENOUGH PLACE TO DEFEND--AND IT WAS LOADED WITH SUPPLIES.
ME AND A FEW OTHERS WENT ON A WEAPONS RUN. I HAD ACCESS TO THE LOCAL DEPOT--SO WE SET OUT TO GET WHATEVER WE COULD CARRY.
I HADN'T REALIZED--HADN'T NOTICED HOW MUCH PEOPLE HAD CHANGED.
SOME PEOPLE--WAS LIKE A FUCKING SWITCH WENT OFF IN THEM. ONE DAY THEY WERE NICE, LAW-ABIDING FOLKS, THE NEXT--THEY WERE ANIMALS.
SOME OF THE ANIMALS STAYED BACK AT THE GROCERY THAT DAY.
DON'T KNOW WHAT HAPPENED TO SET THEM OFF... I'LL NEVER KNOW. MAYBE THEY JUST THOUGHT THIS WAS THEIR LAST CHANCE TO HAVE A WOMAN--SO THEY'D TAKE IT.
MY SON TRIED TO FIGHT THEM. THEY HELD HIM DOWN--MADE HIM WATCH.

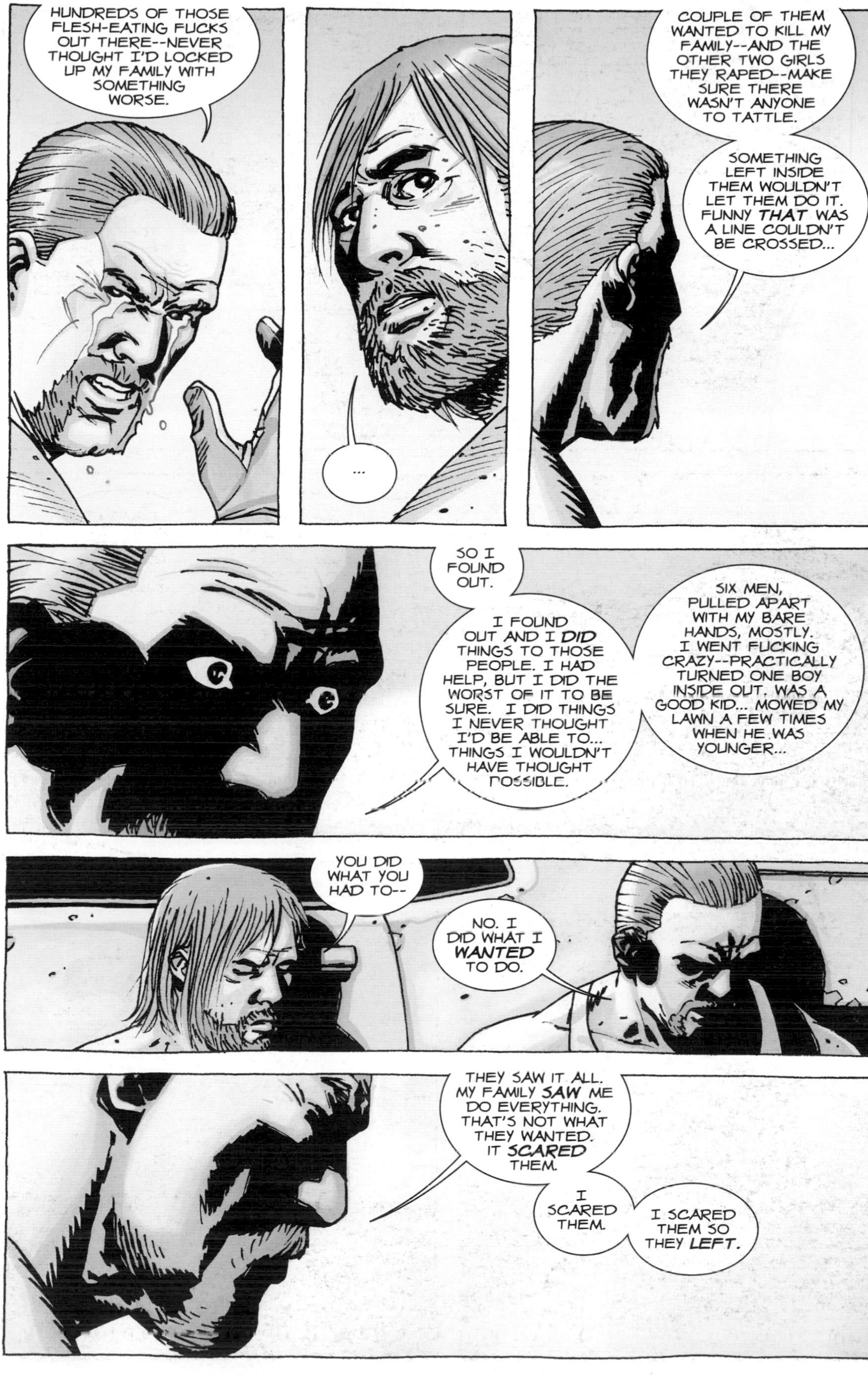

HUNDREDS OF THOSE FLESH-EATING FUCKS OUT THERE--NEVER THOUGHT I'D LOCKED UP MY FAMILY WITH SOMETHING WORSE.
...
COUPLE OF THEM WANTED TO KILL MY FAMILY--AND THE OTHER TWO GIRLS THEY RAPED--MAKE SURE THERE WASN'T ANYONE TO TATTLE.
SOMETHING LEFT INSIDE THEM WOULDN'T LET THEM DO IT. FUNNY THAT WAS A LINE COULDN'T BE CROSSED...
SO I FOUND OUT.
I FOUND OUT AND I DID THINGS TO THOSE PEOPLE. I HAD HELP, BUT I DID THE WORST OF IT TO BE SURE. I DID THINGS I NEVER THOUGHT I'D BE ABLE TO... THINGS I WOULDN'T HAVE THOUGHT POSSIBLE.
SIX MEN, PULLED APART WITH MY BARE HANDS, MOSTLY. I WENT FUCKING CRAZY--PRACTICALLY TURNED ONE BOY INSIDE OUT. WAS A GOOD KID... MOWED MY LAWN A FEW TIMES WHEN HE WAS YOUNGER...
YOU DID WHAT YOU HAD TO--
NO. I DID WHAT I WANTED TO DO.
THEY SAW IT ALL. MY FAMILY SAW ME DO EVERYTHING. THAT'S NOT WHAT THEY WANTED. IT SCARED THEM.
I SCARED THEM.
I SCARED THEM SO THEY LEFT.

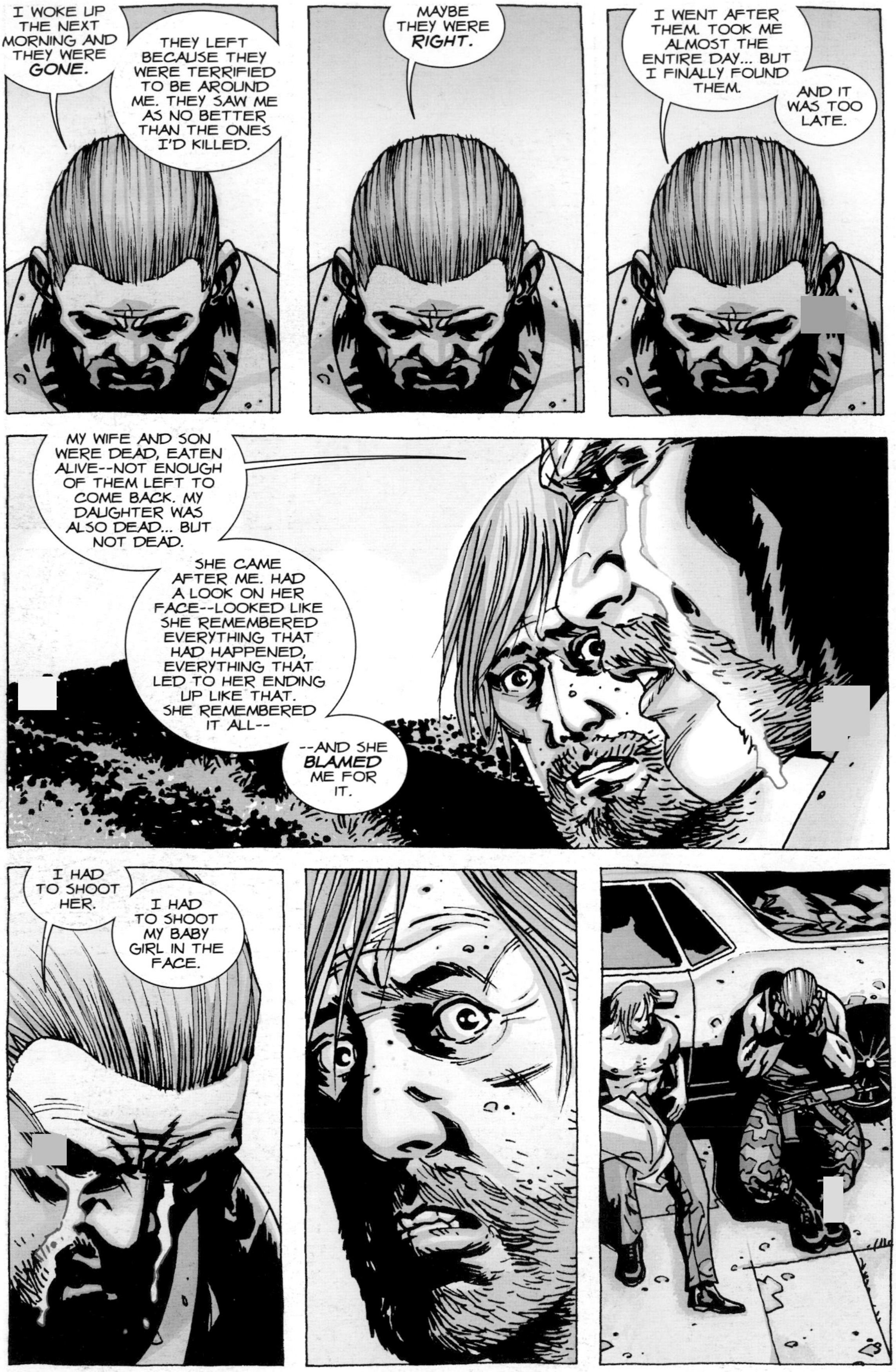
I WOKE UP THE NEXT MORNING AND THEY WERE GONE.
THEY LEFT BECAUSE THEY WERE TERRIFIED TO BE AROUND ME. THEY SAW ME AS NO BETTER THAN THE ONES I'D KILLED.
MAYBE THEY WERE RIGHT.
I WENT AFTER THEM. TOOK ME ALMOST THE ENTIRE DAY... BUT I FINALLY FOUND THEM.
AND IT WAS TOO LATE.
MY WIFE AND SON WERE DEAD, EATEN ALIVE--NOT ENOUGH OF THEM LEFT TO COME BACK. MY DAUGHTER WAS ALSO DEAD... BUT NOT DEAD.
SHE CAME AFTER ME. HAD A LOOK ON HER FACE--LOOKED LIKE SHE REMEMBERED EVERYTHING THAT HAD HAPPENED, EVERYTHING THAT LED TO HER ENDING UP LIKE THAT. SHE REMEMBERED IT ALL--
--AND SHE BLAMED ME FOR IT.
I HAD TO SHOOT HER.
I HAD TO SHOOT MY BABY GIRL IN THE FACE.

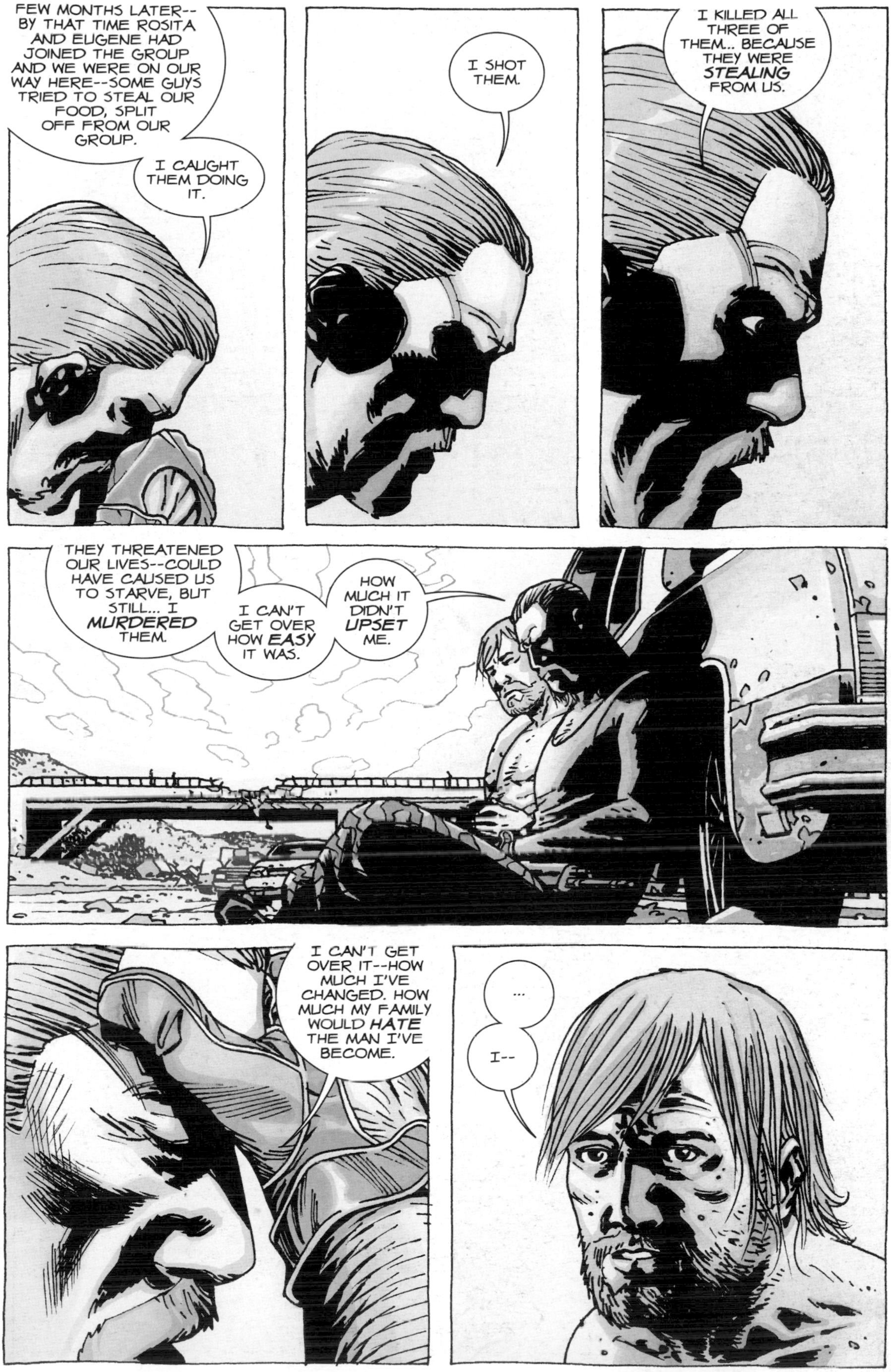
FEW MONTHS LATER-- BY THAT TIME ROSITA AND EUGENE HAD JOINED THE GROUP AND WE WERE ON OUR WAY HERE--SOME GUYS TRIED TO STEAL OUR FOOD, SPLIT OFF FROM OUR GROUP.
I CAUGHT THEM DOING IT.
I SHOT THEM.
I KILLED ALL THREE OF THEM... BECAUSE THEY WERE STEALING FROM US.
THEY THREATENED OUR LIVES--COULD HAVE CAUSED US TO STARVE, BUT STILL... I MURDERED THEM.
I CAN'T GET OVER HOW EASY IT WAS.
HOW MUCH IT DIDN'T UPSET ME.
I CAN'T GET OVER IT--HOW MUCH I'VE CHANGED. HOW MUCH MY FAMILY WOULD HATE THE MAN I'VE BECOME.
...
I--

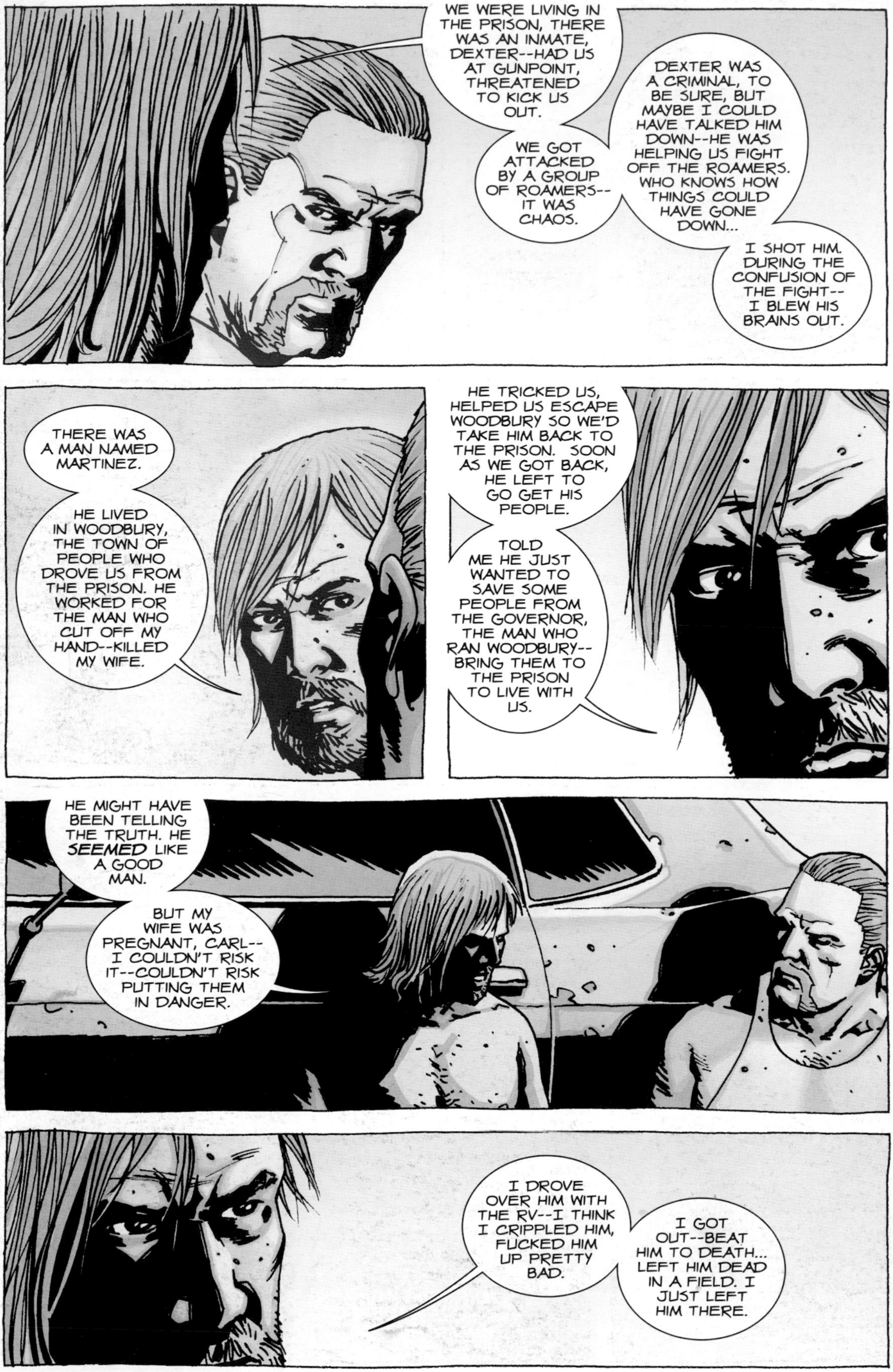
WE WERE LIVING IN THE PRISON, THERE WAS AN INMATE, DEXTER--HAD US AT GUNPOINT, THREATENED TO KICK US OUT.
WE GOT ATTACKED BY A GROUP OF ROAMERS-- IT WAS CHAOS.
DEXTER WAS A CRIMINAL, TO BE SURE, BUT MAYBE I COULD HAVE TALKED HIM DOWN--HE WAS HELPING US FIGHT OFF THE ROAMERS. WHO KNOWS HOW THINGS COULD HAVE GONE DOWN...
I SHOT HIM. DURING THE CONFUSION OF THE FIGHT-- I BLEW HIS BRAINS OUT.
THERE WAS A MAN NAMED MARTINEZ.
HE LIVED IN WOODBURY, THE TOWN OF PEOPLE WHO DROVE US FROM THE PRISON. HE WORKED FOR THE MAN WHO CUT OFF MY HAND--KILLED MY WIFE.
HE TRICKED US, HELPED US ESCAPE WOODBURY SO WE'D TAKE HIM BACK TO THE PRISON. SOON AS WE GOT BACK, HE LEFT TO GO GET HIS PEOPLE.
TOLD ME HE JUST WANTED TO SAVE SOME PEOPLE FROM THE GOVERNOR, THE MAN WHO RAN WOODBURY-- BRING THEM TO THE PRISON TO LIVE WITH US.
HE MIGHT HAVE BEEN TELLING THE TRUTH. HE SEEMED LIKE A GOOD MAN.
BUT MY WIFE WAS PREGNANT, CARL-- I COULDN'T RISK IT--COULDN'T RISK PUTTING THEM IN DANGER.
I DROVE OVER HIM WITH THE RV--I THINK I CRIPPLED HIM, FUCKED HIM UP PRETTY BAD.
I GOT OUT--BEAT HIM TO DEATH... LEFT HIM DEAD IN A FIELD. I JUST LEFT HIM THERE.

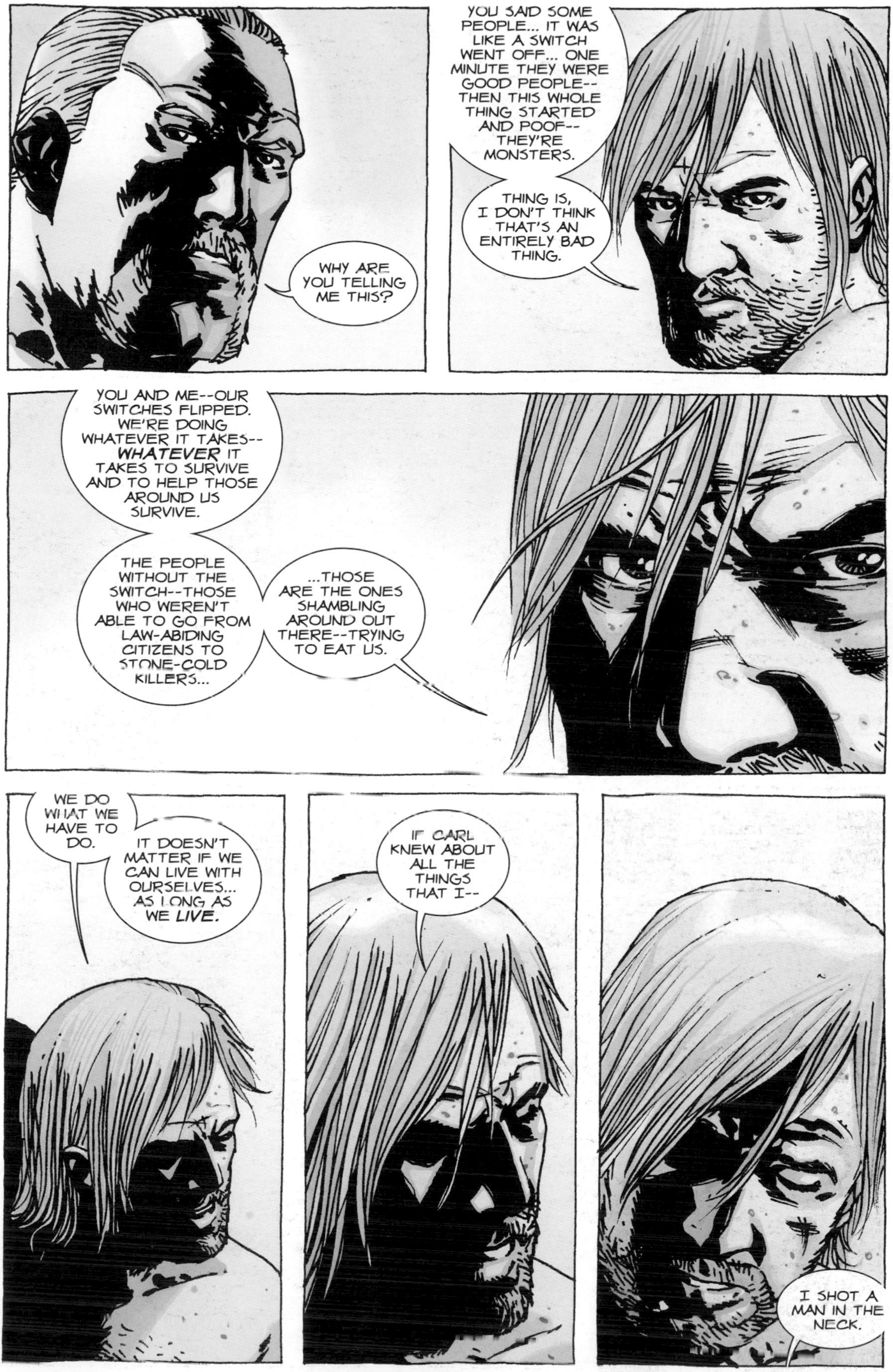
WHY ARE YOU TELLING ME THIS?
YOU SAID SOME PEOPLE... IT WAS LIKE A SWITCH WENT OFF... ONE MINUTE THEY WERE GOOD PEOPLE-- THEN THIS WHOLE THING STARTED AND POOF-- THEY'RE MONSTERS.
THING IS, I DON'T THINK THAT'S AN ENTIRELY BAD THING.
YOU AND ME--OUR SWITCHES FLIPPED. WE'RE DOING WHATEVER IT TAKES-- *WHATEVER* IT TAKES TO SURVIVE AND TO HELP THOSE AROUND US SURVIVE.
THE PEOPLE WITHOUT THE SWITCH--THOSE WHO WEREN'T ABLE TO GO FROM LAW-ABIDING CITIZENS TO STONE-COLD KILLERS...
...THOSE ARE THE ONES SHAMBLING AROUND OUT THERE--TRYING TO EAT US.
WE DO WHAT WE HAVE TO DO.
IT DOESN'T MATTER IF WE CAN LIVE WITH OURSELVES... AS LONG AS WE *LIVE.*
IF CARL KNEW ABOUT ALL THE THINGS THAT I--
I SHOT A MAN IN THE NECK.

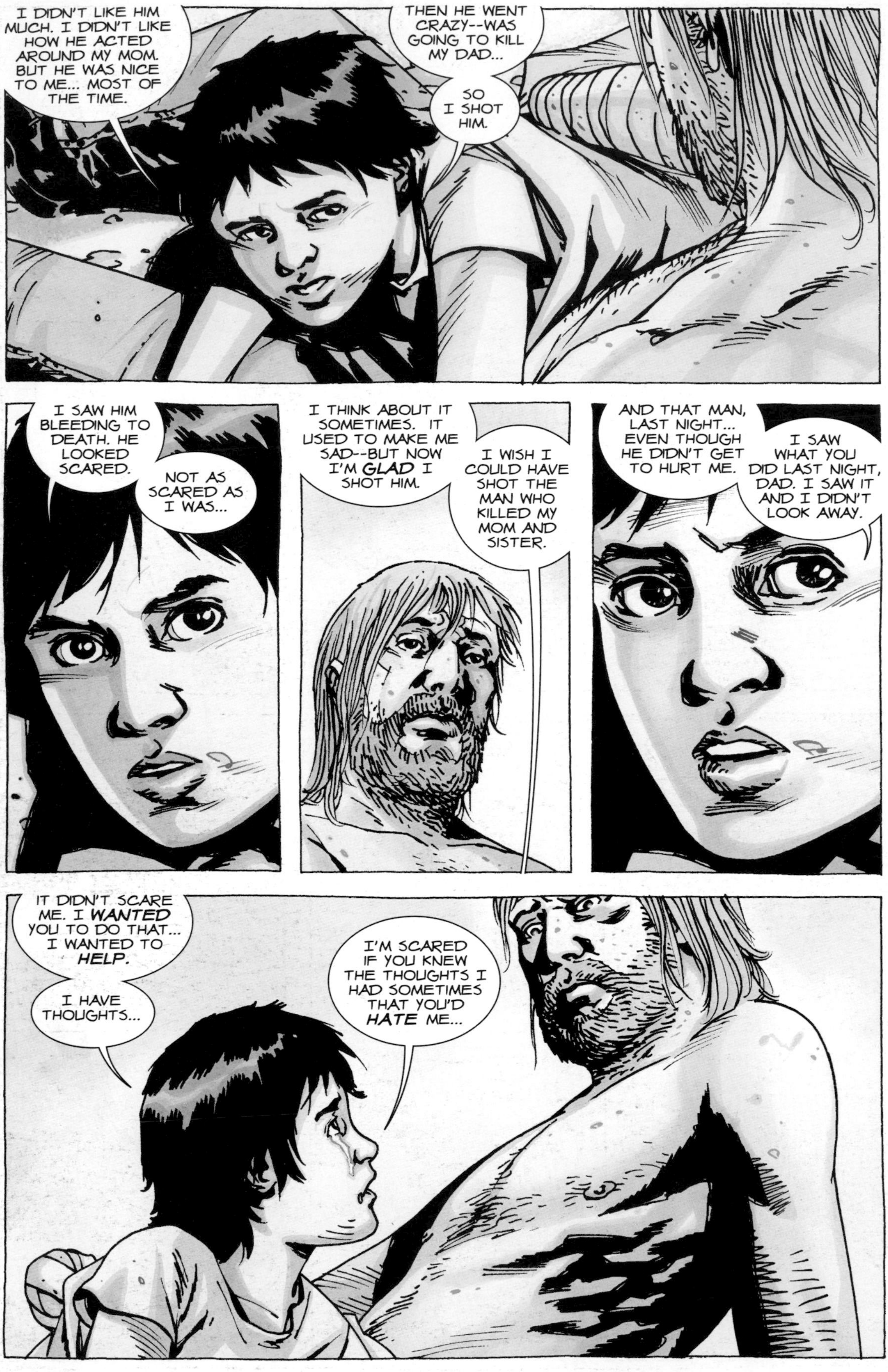
I DIDN'T LIKE HIM MUCH. I DIDN'T LIKE HOW HE ACTED AROUND MY MOM. BUT HE WAS NICE TO ME... MOST OF THE TIME.
THEN HE WENT CRAZY--WAS GOING TO KILL MY DAD...
SO I SHOT HIM.
I SAW HIM BLEEDING TO DEATH. HE LOOKED SCARED.
NOT AS SCARED AS I WAS...
I THINK ABOUT IT SOMETIMES. IT USED TO MAKE ME SAD--BUT NOW I'M GLAD I SHOT HIM.
I WISH I COULD HAVE SHOT THE MAN WHO KILLED MY MOM AND SISTER.
AND THAT MAN, LAST NIGHT... EVEN THOUGH HE DIDN'T GET TO HURT ME.
I SAW WHAT YOU DID LAST NIGHT, DAD. I SAW IT AND I DIDN'T LOOK AWAY.
IT DIDN'T SCARE ME. I WANTED YOU TO DO THAT... I WANTED TO HELP.
I HAVE THOUGHTS...
I'M SCARED IF YOU KNEW THE THOUGHTS I HAD SOMETIMES THAT YOU'D HATE ME...

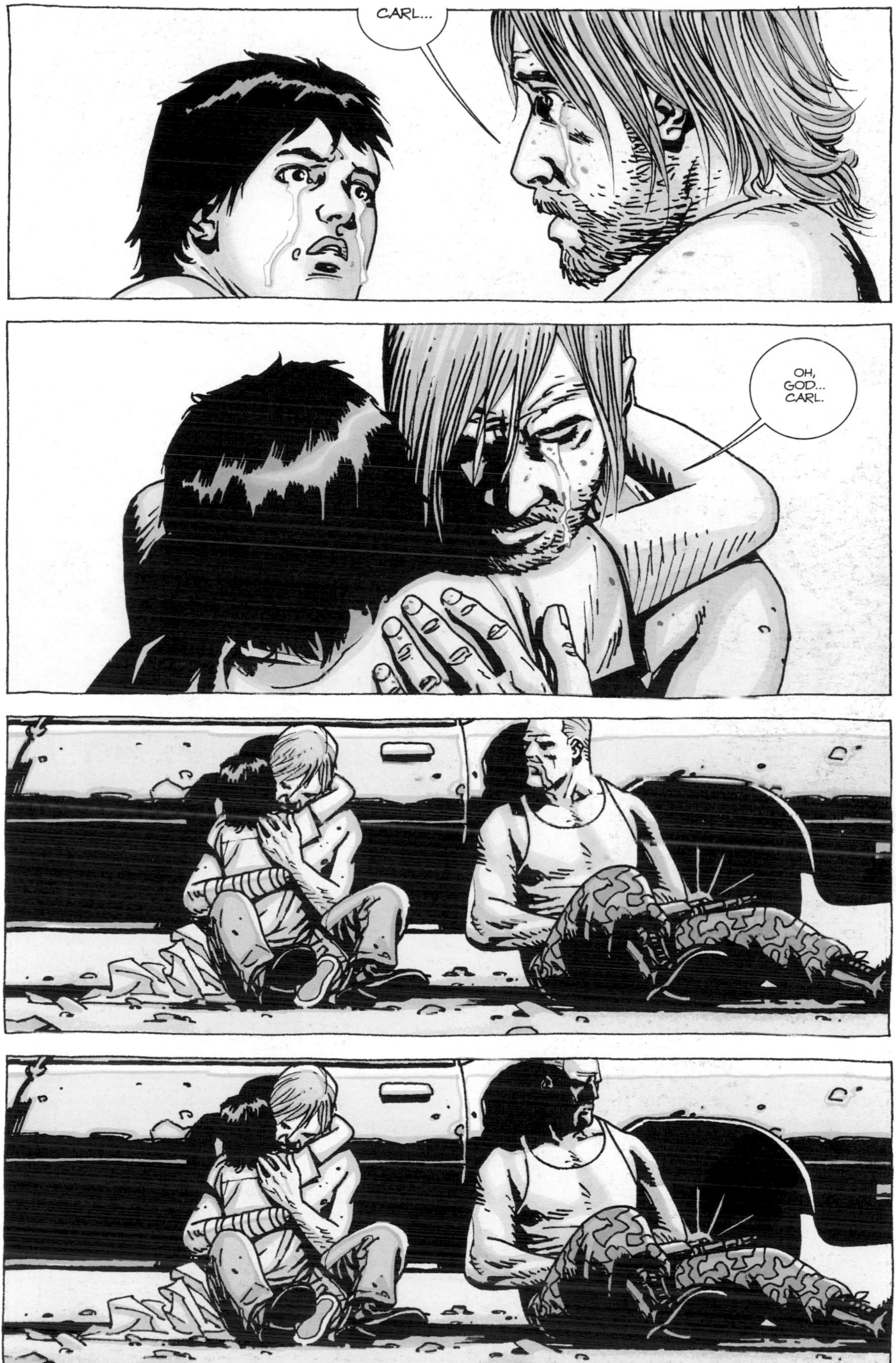
CARL...
OH, GOD... CARL.

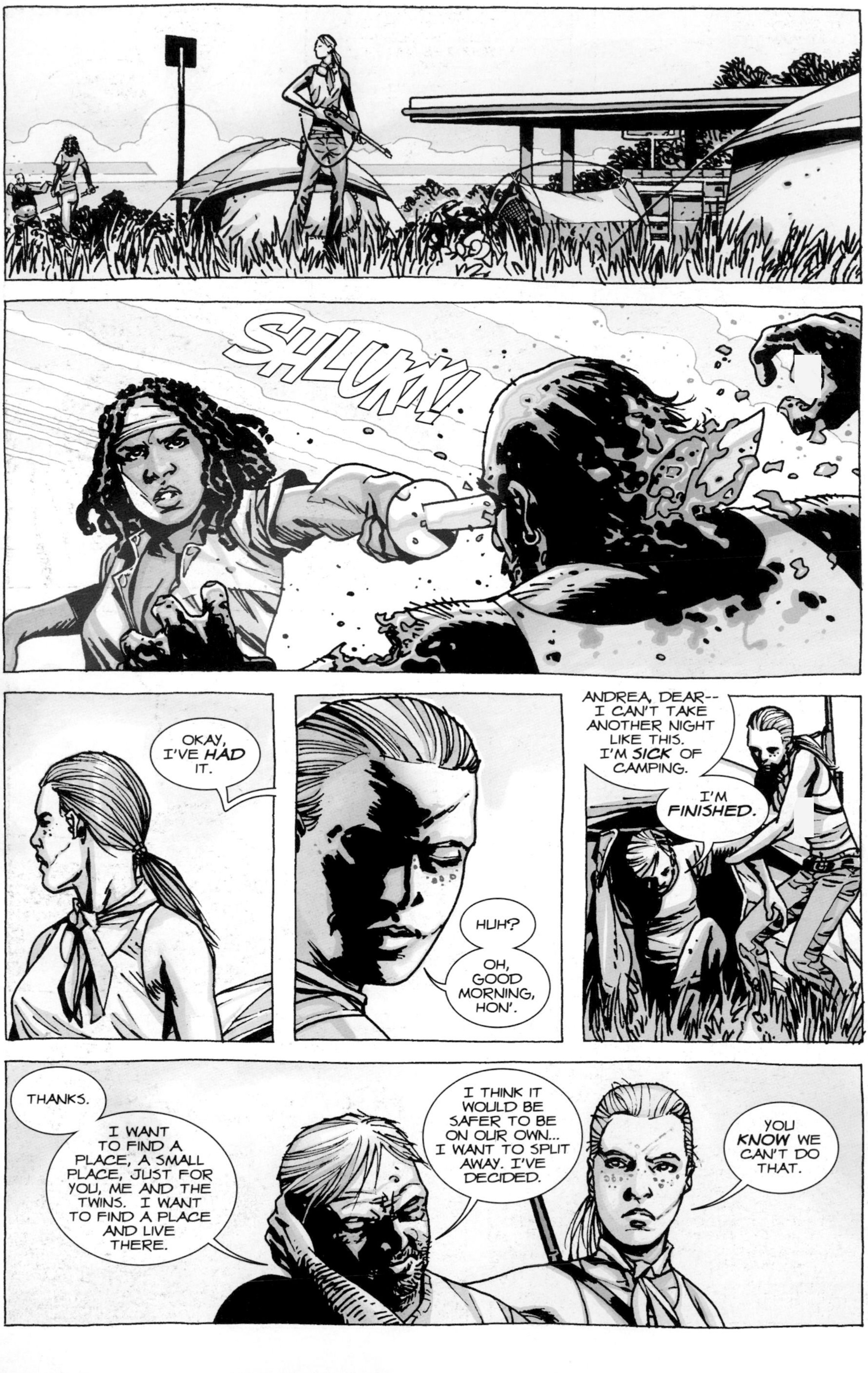
SHLUKK!
OKAY, I'VE HAD IT.
HUH?
OH, GOOD MORNING, HON'.
ANDREA, DEAR-- I CAN'T TAKE ANOTHER NIGHT LIKE THIS. I'M SICK OF CAMPING.
I'M FINISHED.
THANKS.
I WANT TO FIND A PLACE, A SMALL PLACE, JUST FOR YOU, ME AND THE TWINS. I WANT TO FIND A PLACE AND LIVE THERE.
I THINK IT WOULD BE SAFER TO BE ON OUR OWN... I WANT TO SPLIT AWAY. I'VE DECIDED.
YOU KNOW WE CAN'T DO THAT.

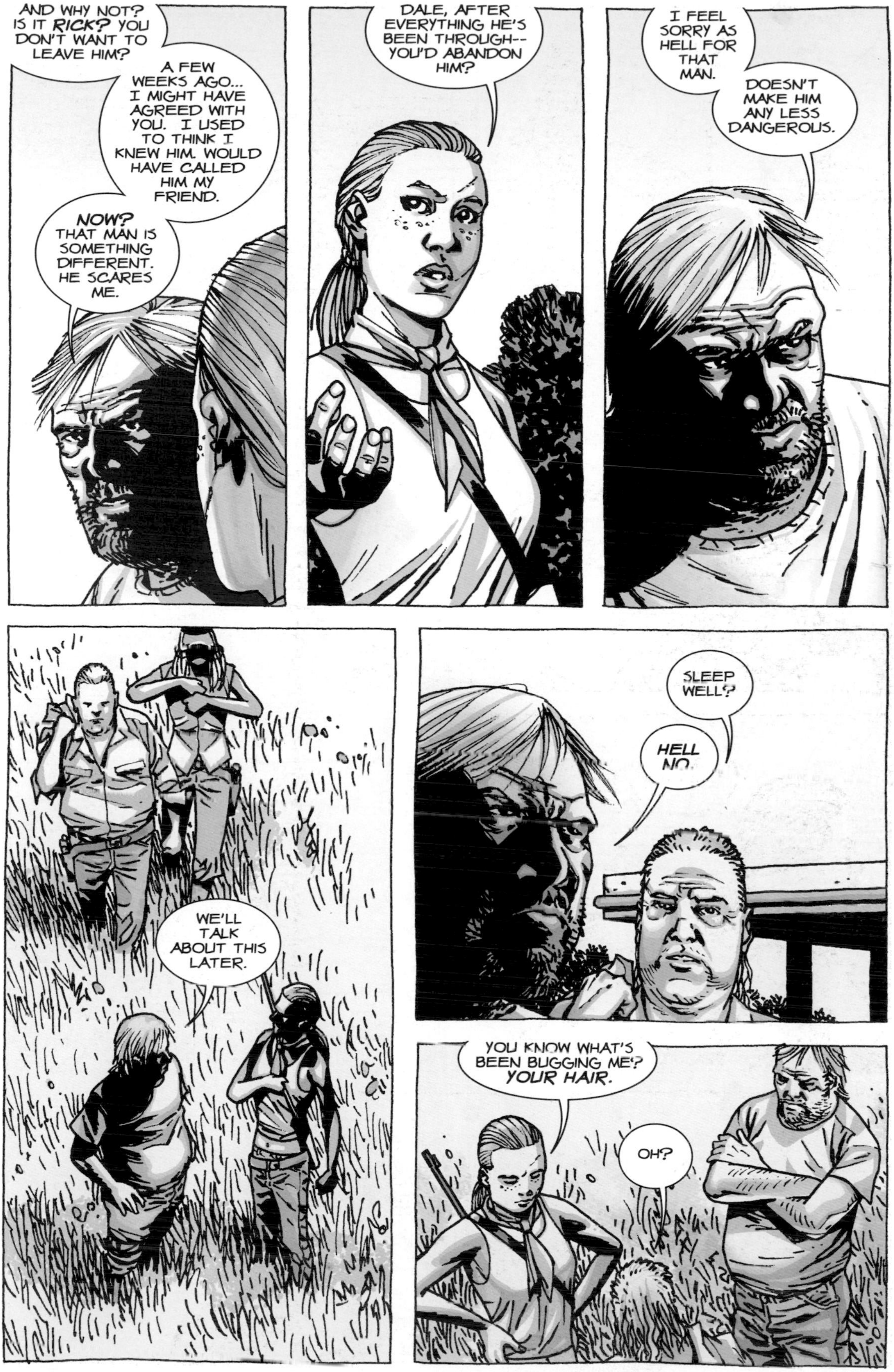
AND WHY NOT? IS IT RICK? YOU DON'T WANT TO LEAVE HIM?
A FEW WEEKS AGO... I MIGHT HAVE AGREED WITH YOU. I USED TO THINK I KNEW HIM. WOULD HAVE CALLED HIM MY FRIEND.
NOW? THAT MAN IS SOMETHING DIFFERENT. HE SCARES ME.
DALE, AFTER EVERYTHING HE'S BEEN THROUGH-- YOU'D ABANDON HIM?
I FEEL SORRY AS HELL FOR THAT MAN.
DOESN'T MAKE HIM ANY LESS DANGEROUS.
WE'LL TALK ABOUT THIS LATER.
SLEEP WELL?
HELL NO.
YOU KNOW WHAT'S BEEN BUGGING ME? YOUR HAIR.
OH?

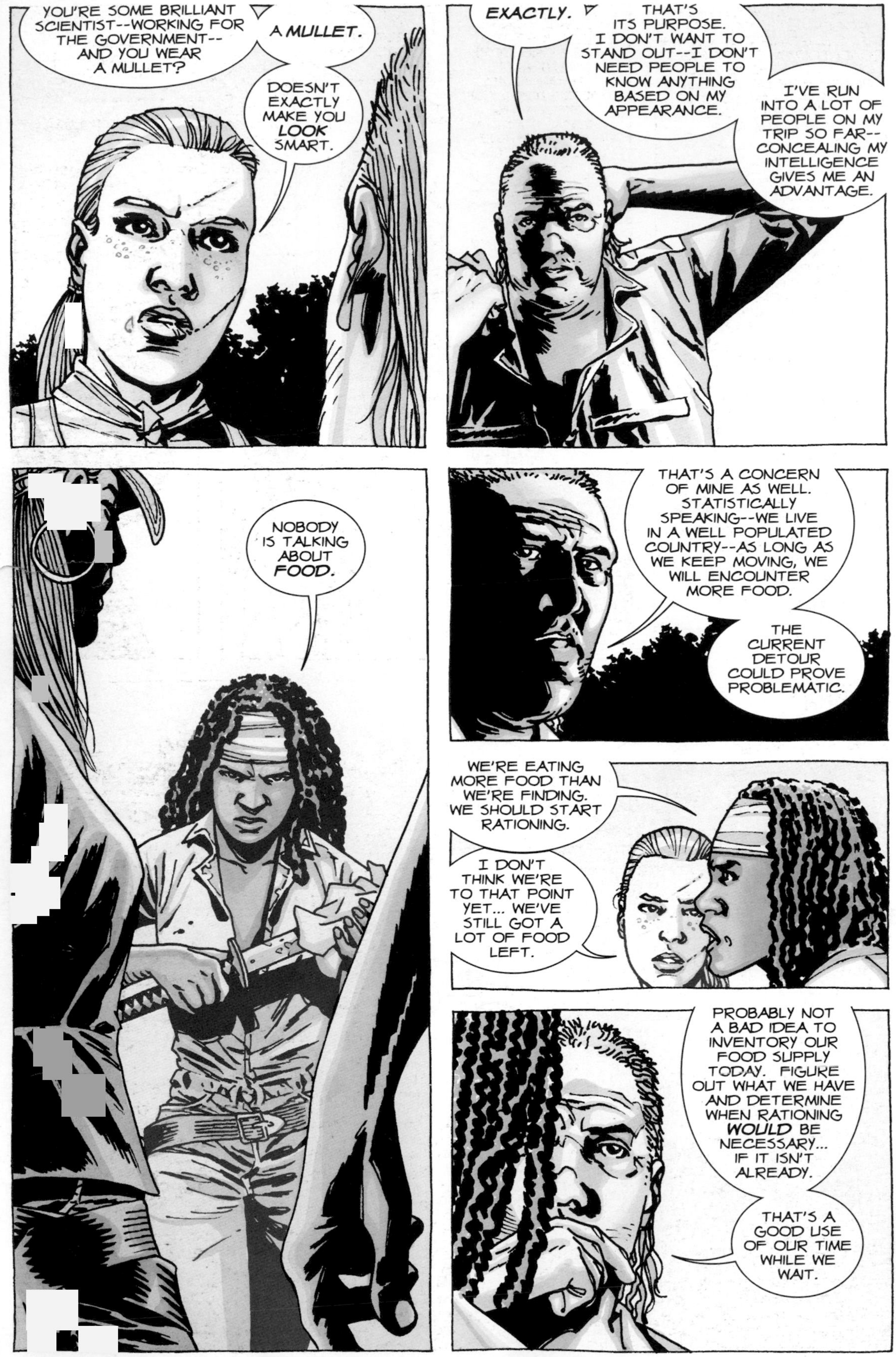
YOU'RE SOME BRILLIANT SCIENTIST--WORKING FOR THE GOVERNMENT-- AND YOU WEAR A MULLET?
A MULLET.
DOESN'T EXACTLY MAKE YOU LOOK SMART.
EXACTLY.
THAT'S ITS PURPOSE. I DON'T WANT TO STAND OUT--I DON'T NEED PEOPLE TO KNOW ANYTHING BASED ON MY APPEARANCE.
I'VE RUN INTO A LOT OF PEOPLE ON MY TRIP SO FAR-- CONCEALING MY INTELLIGENCE GIVES ME AN ADVANTAGE.
NOBODY IS TALKING ABOUT FOOD.
THAT'S A CONCERN OF MINE AS WELL. STATISTICALLY SPEAKING--WE LIVE IN A WELL POPULATED COUNTRY--AS LONG AS WE KEEP MOVING, WE WILL ENCOUNTER MORE FOOD.
THE CURRENT DETOUR COULD PROVE PROBLEMATIC.
WE'RE EATING MORE FOOD THAN WE'RE FINDING. WE SHOULD START RATIONING.
I DON'T THINK WE'RE TO THAT POINT YET... WE'VE STILL GOT A LOT OF FOOD LEFT.
PROBABLY NOT A BAD IDEA TO INVENTORY OUR FOOD SUPPLY TODAY. FIGURE OUT WHAT WE HAVE AND DETERMINE WHEN RATIONING WOULD BE NECESSARY... IF IT ISN'T ALREADY.
THAT'S A GOOD USE OF OUR TIME WHILE WE WAIT.

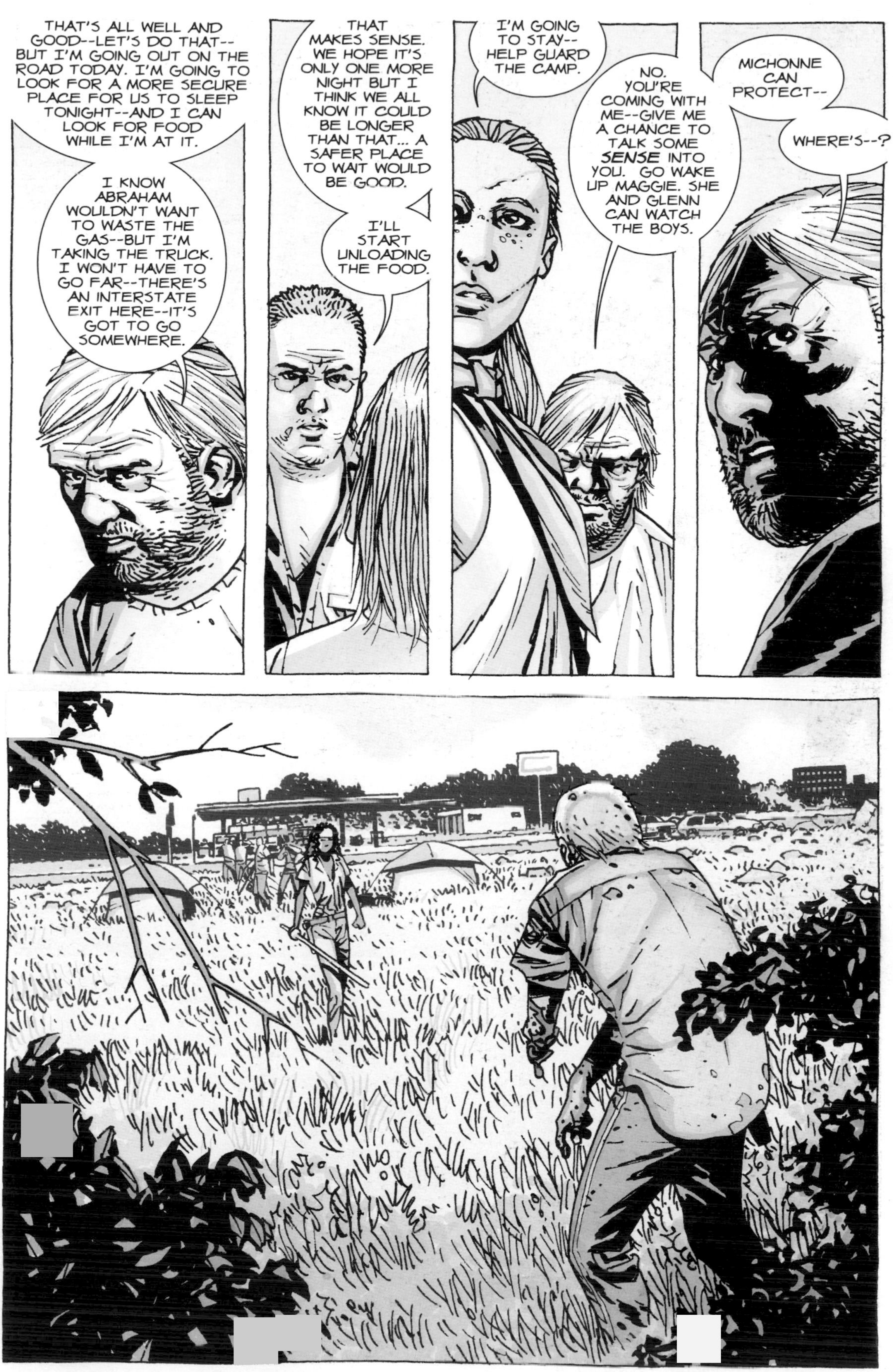
THAT'S ALL WELL AND GOOD--LET'S DO THAT--BUT I'M GOING OUT ON THE ROAD TODAY. I'M GOING TO LOOK FOR A MORE SECURE PLACE FOR US TO SLEEP TONIGHT--AND I CAN LOOK FOR FOOD WHILE I'M AT IT.
I KNOW ABRAHAM WOULDN'T WANT TO WASTE THE GAS--BUT I'M TAKING THE TRUCK. I WON'T HAVE TO GO FAR--THERE'S AN INTERSTATE EXIT HERE--IT'S GOT TO GO SOMEWHERE.
THAT MAKES SENSE. WE HOPE IT'S ONLY ONE MORE NIGHT BUT I THINK WE ALL KNOW IT COULD BE LONGER THAN THAT... A SAFER PLACE TO WAIT WOULD BE GOOD.
I'LL START UNLOADING THE FOOD.
I'M GOING TO STAY--HELP GUARD THE CAMP.
NO. YOU'RE COMING WITH ME--GIVE ME A CHANCE TO TALK SOME SENSE INTO YOU. GO WAKE UP MAGGIE. SHE AND GLENN CAN WATCH THE BOYS.
MICHONNE CAN PROTECT--
WHERE'S--?

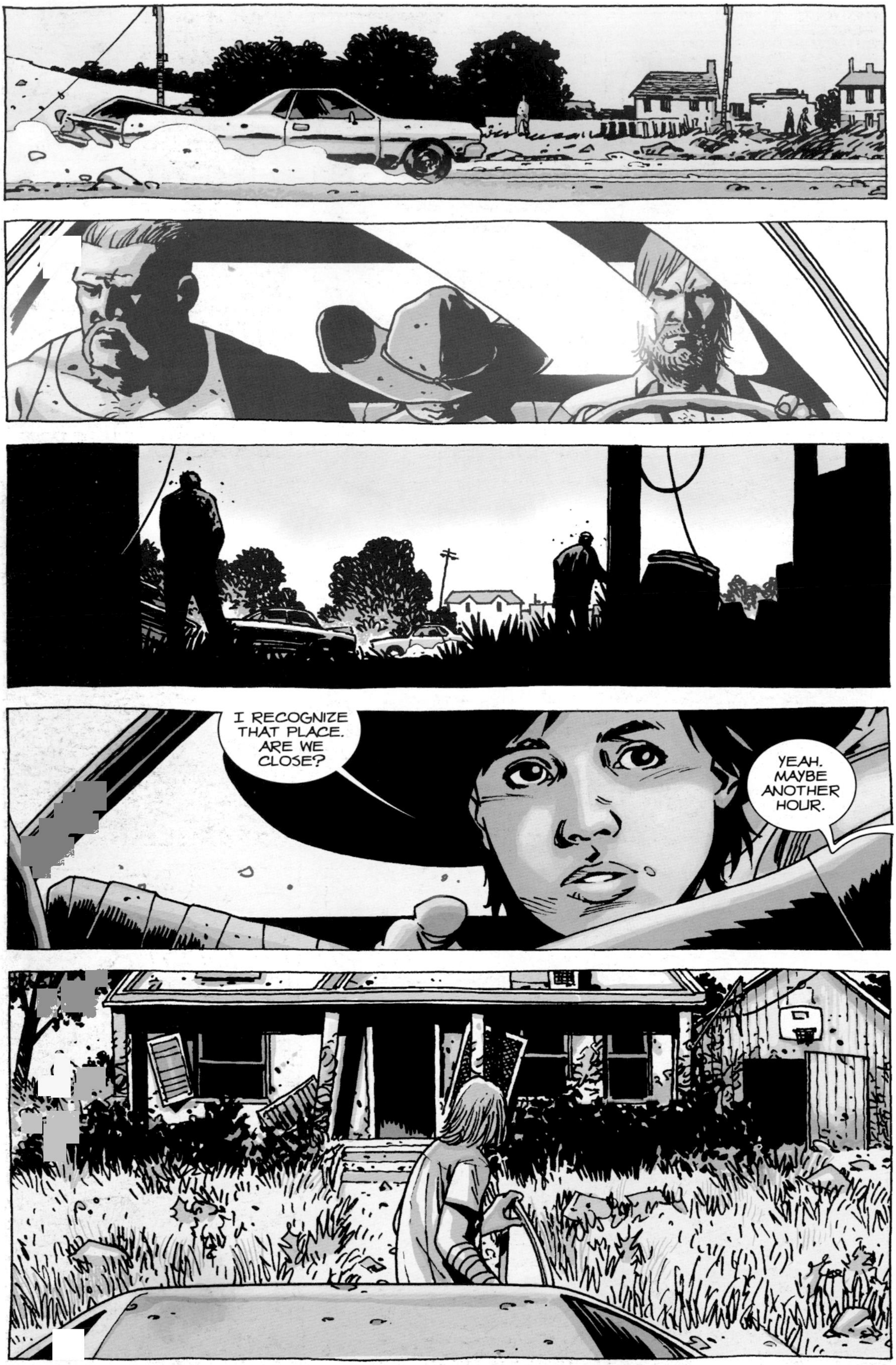
I RECOGNIZE THAT PLACE. ARE WE CLOSE?
YEAH. MAYBE ANOTHER HOUR.

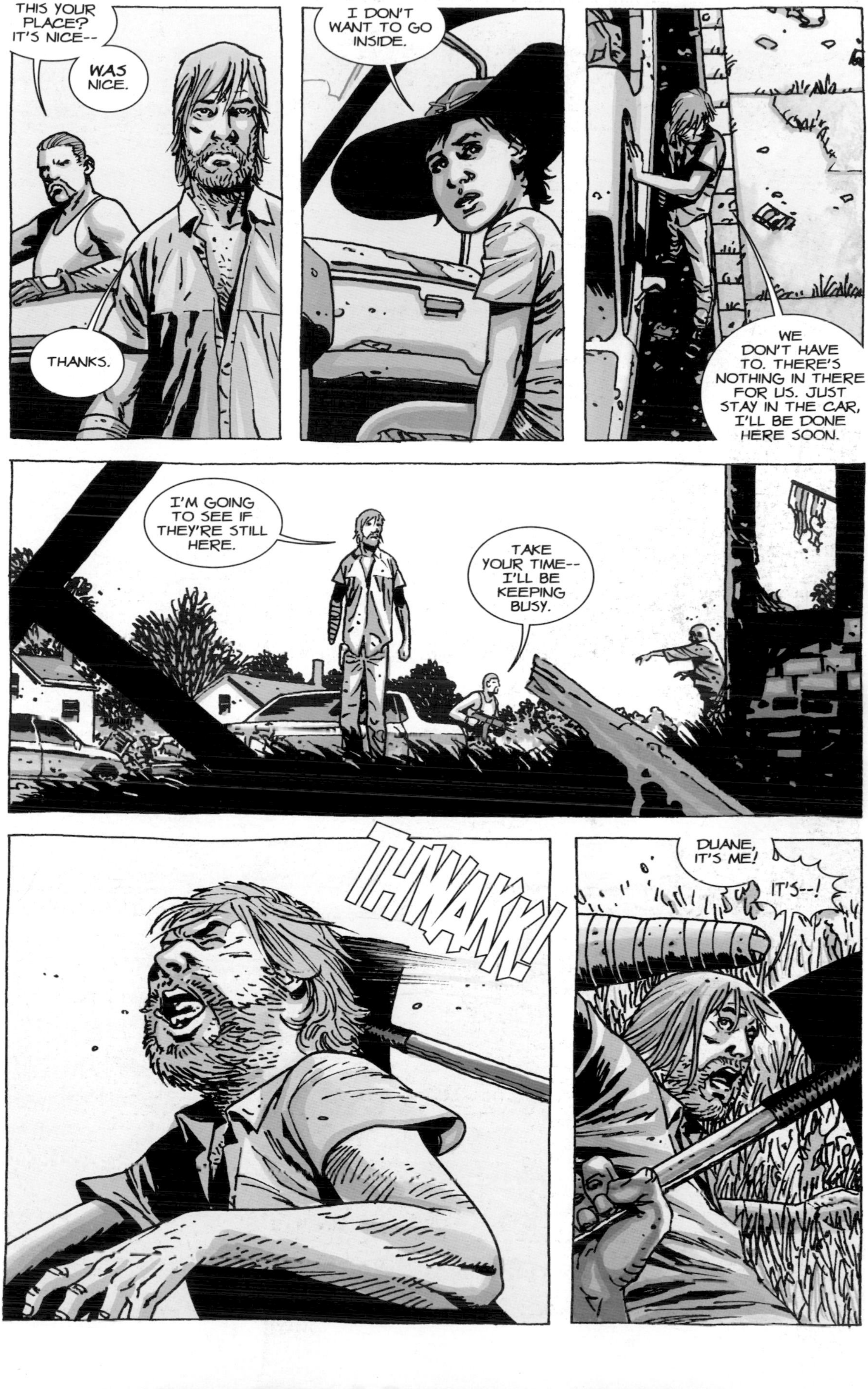
THIS YOUR PLACE? IT'S NICE--
WAS NICE.
THANKS.
I DON'T WANT TO GO INSIDE.
WE DON'T HAVE TO. THERE'S NOTHING IN THERE FOR US. JUST STAY IN THE CAR, I'LL BE DONE HERE SOON.
I'M GOING TO SEE IF THEY'RE STILL HERE.
TAKE YOUR TIME-- I'LL BE KEEPING BUSY.
THWAKK!
DUANE, IT'S ME!
IT'S--!

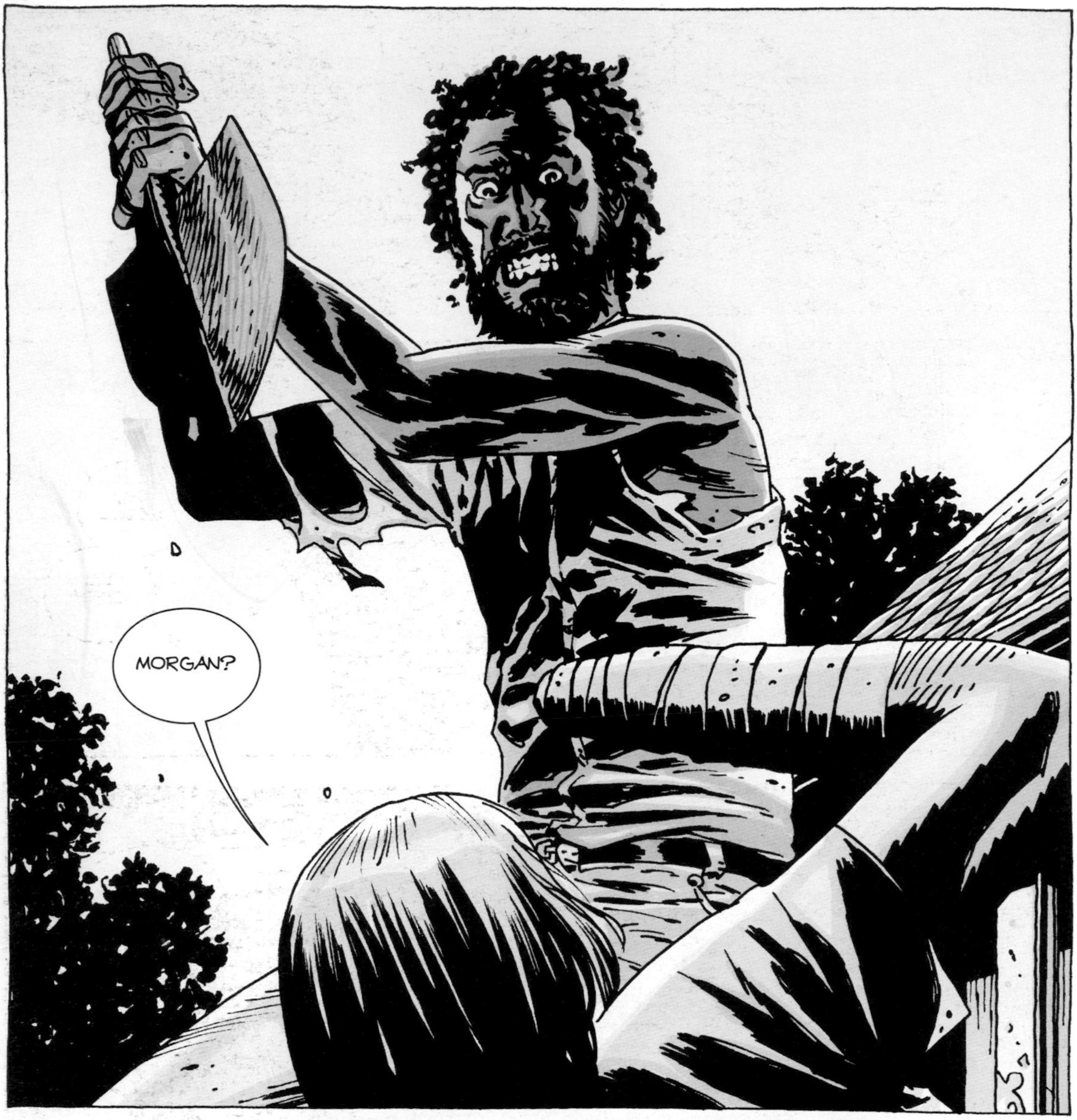
MORGAN?

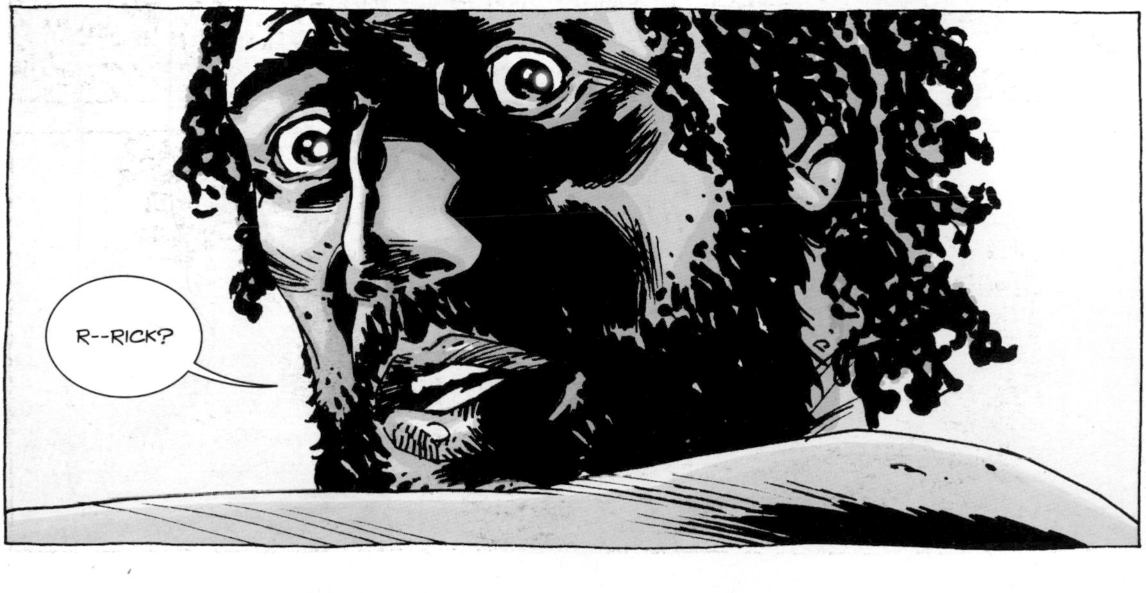
R--RICK?

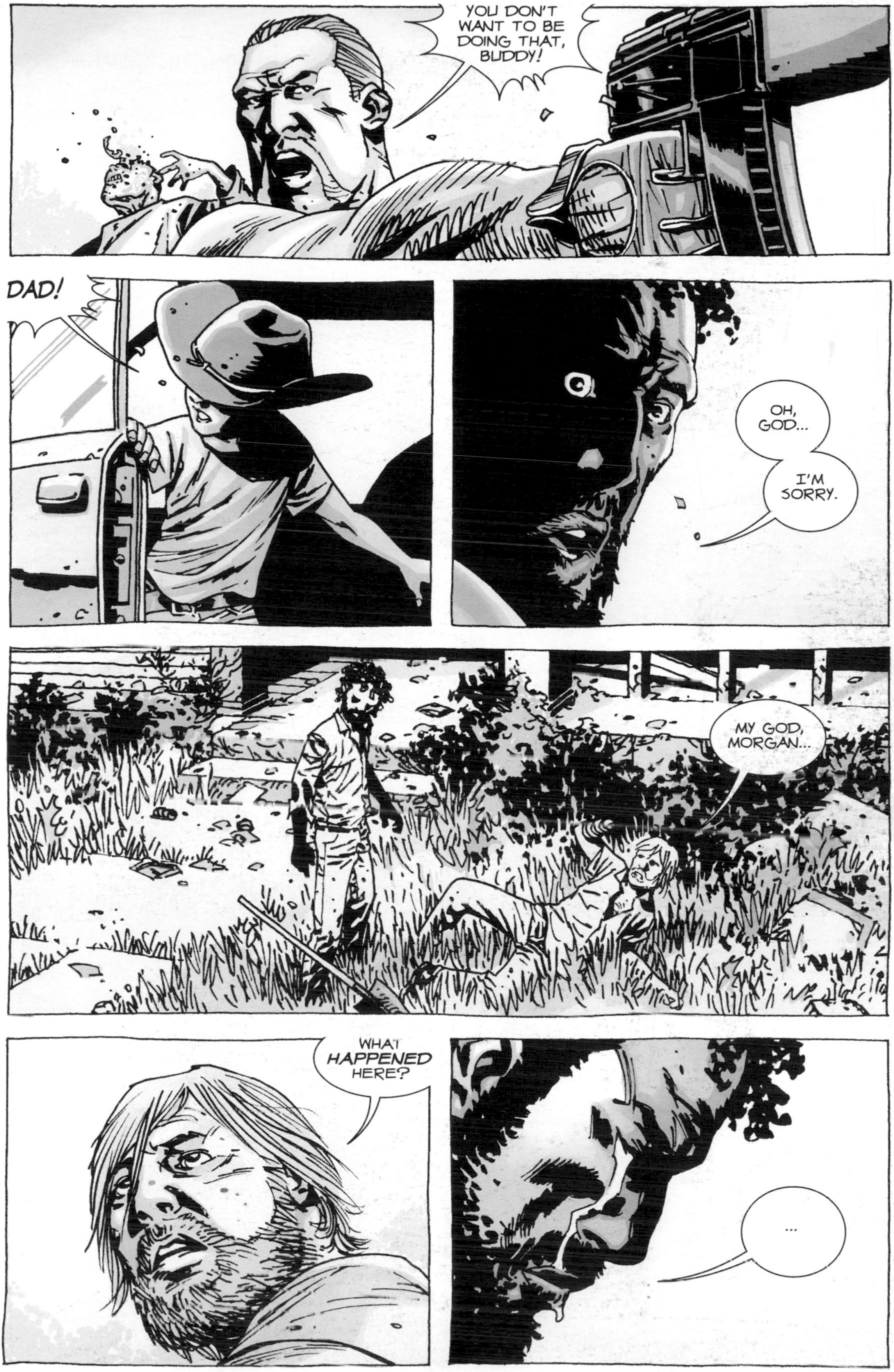
YOU DON'T WANT TO BE DOING THAT, BUDDY!
DAD!
OH, GOD...
I'M SORRY.
MY GOD, MORGAN...
WHAT HAPPENED HERE?
...

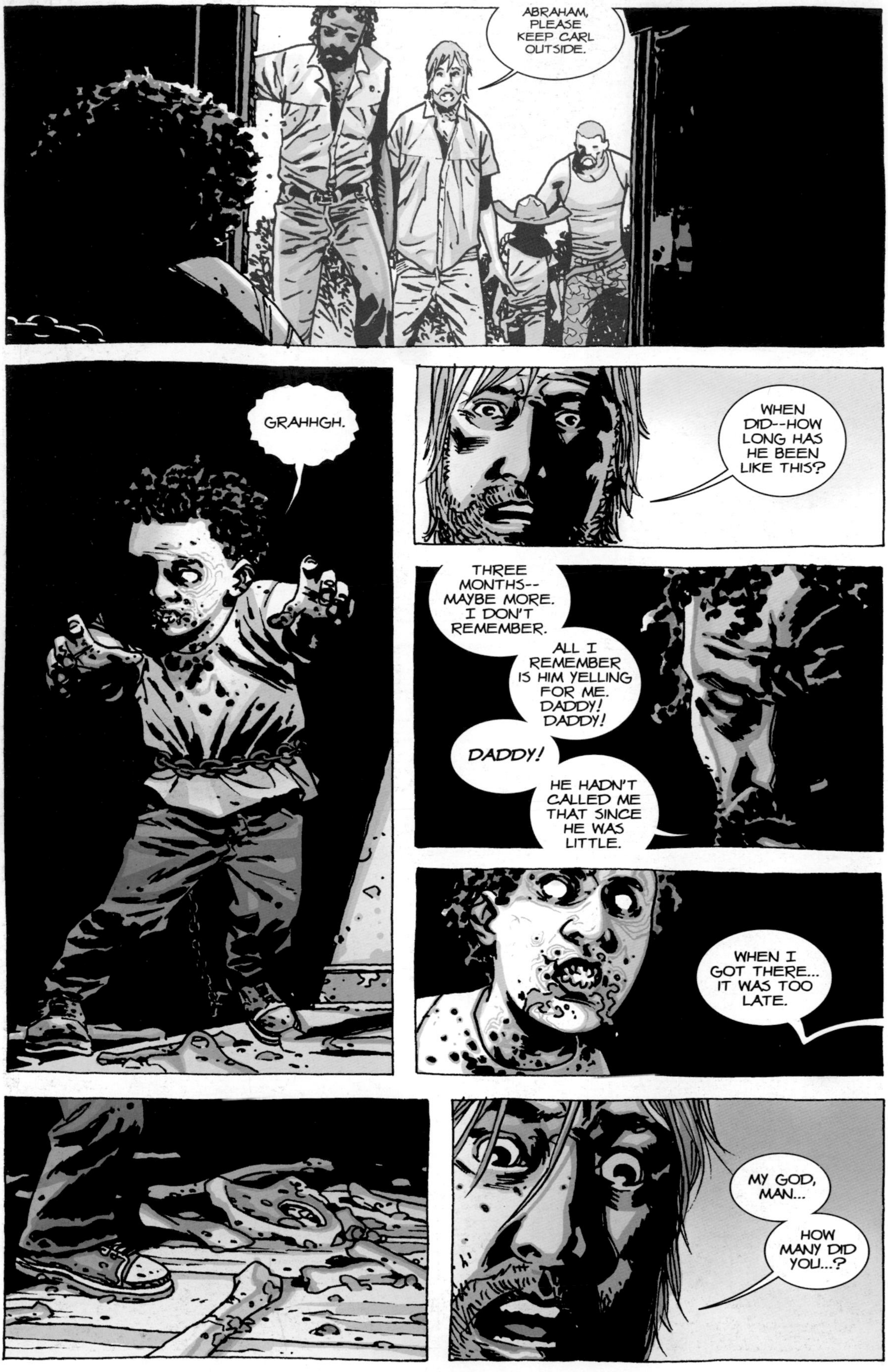
ABRAHAM, PLEASE KEEP CARL OUTSIDE.
GRAHHGH.
WHEN DID--HOW LONG HAS HE BEEN LIKE THIS?
THREE MONTHS-- MAYBE MORE. I DON'T REMEMBER.
ALL I REMEMBER IS HIM YELLING FOR ME. DADDY! DADDY!
DADDY!
HE HADN'T CALLED ME THAT SINCE HE WAS LITTLE.
WHEN I GOT THERE... IT WAS TOO LATE.
MY GOD, MAN...
HOW MANY DID YOU...?

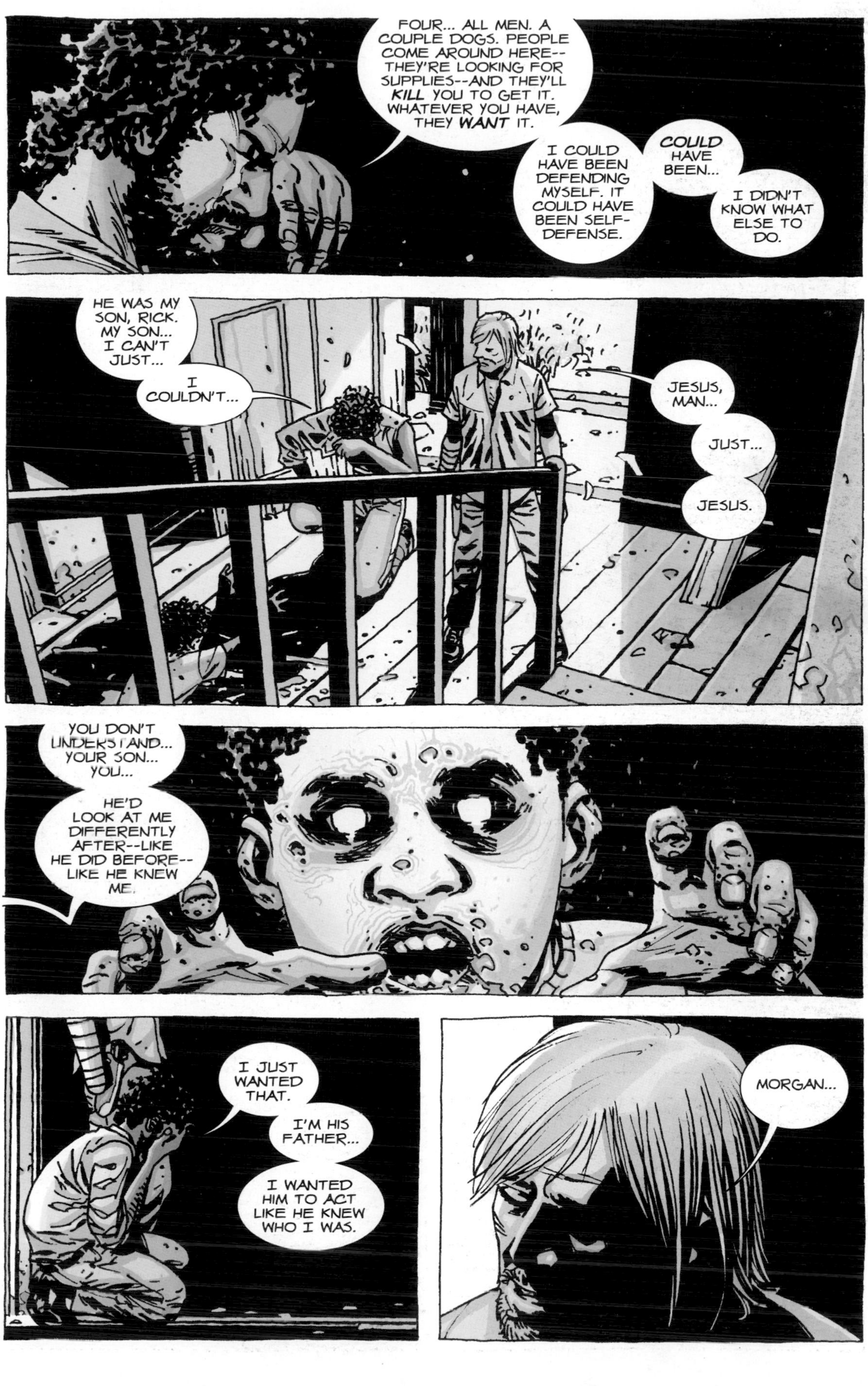
FOUR... ALL MEN. A COUPLE DOGS. PEOPLE COME AROUND HERE-- THEY'RE LOOKING FOR SUPPLIES--AND THEY'LL KILL YOU TO GET IT. WHATEVER YOU HAVE, THEY WANT IT.
I COULD HAVE BEEN DEFENDING MYSELF. IT COULD HAVE BEEN SELF-DEFENSE.
COULD HAVE BEEN...
I DIDN'T KNOW WHAT ELSE TO DO.
HE WAS MY SON, RICK. MY SON... I CAN'T JUST...
I COULDN'T...
JESUS, MAN...
JUST...
JESUS.
YOU DON'T UNDERSTAND... YOUR SON... YOU...
HE'D LOOK AT ME DIFFERENTLY AFTER--LIKE HE DID BEFORE-- LIKE HE KNEW ME.
I JUST WANTED THAT.
I'M HIS FATHER...
I WANTED HIM TO ACT LIKE HE KNEW WHO I WAS.
MORGAN...

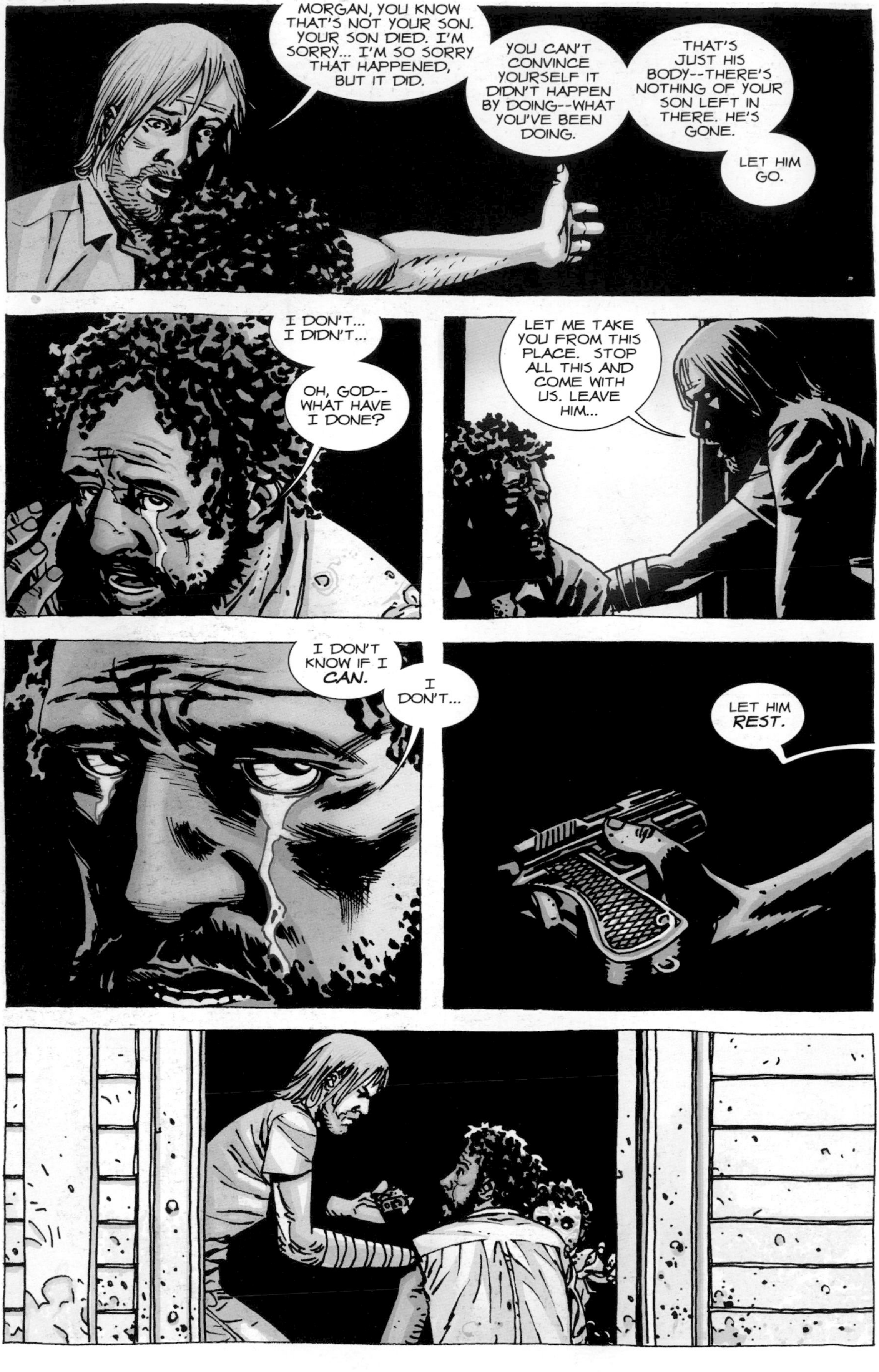

MORGAN, YOU KNOW THAT'S NOT YOUR SON. YOUR SON DIED. I'M SORRY... I'M SO SORRY THAT HAPPENED, BUT IT DID.
YOU CAN'T CONVINCE YOURSELF IT DIDN'T HAPPEN BY DOING--WHAT YOU'VE BEEN DOING.
THAT'S JUST HIS BODY--THERE'S NOTHING OF YOUR SON LEFT IN THERE. HE'S GONE.
LET HIM GO.
I DON'T... I DIDN'T...
OH, GOD--WHAT HAVE I DONE?
LET ME TAKE YOU FROM THIS PLACE. STOP ALL THIS AND COME WITH US. LEAVE HIM...
I DON'T KNOW IF I CAN.
I DON'T...
LET HIM REST.

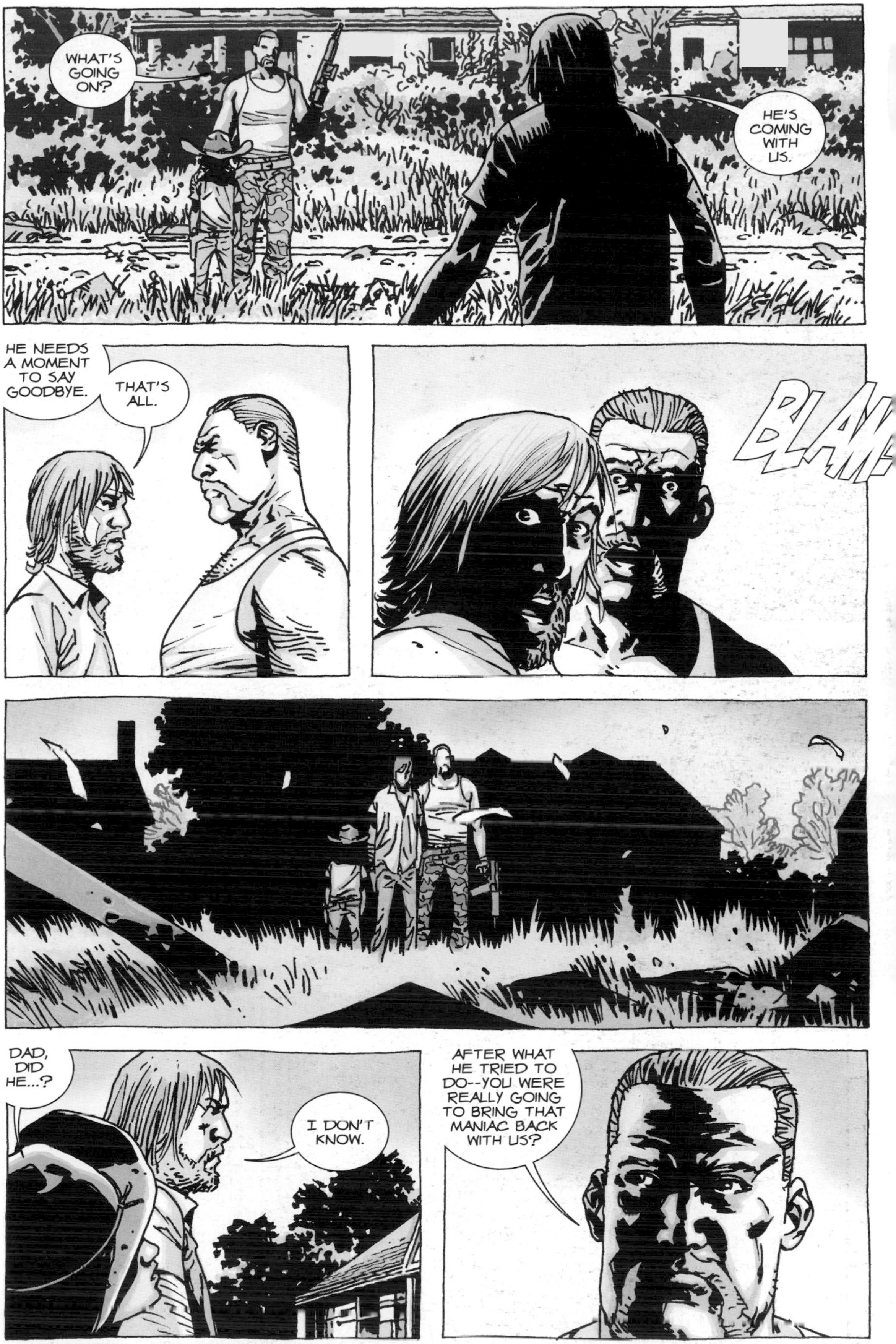
WHAT'S GOING ON?
HE'S COMING WITH US.
HE NEEDS A MOMENT TO SAY GOODBYE.
THAT'S ALL.
BLAM
DAD, DID HE...?
I DON'T KNOW.
AFTER WHAT HE TRIED TO DO--YOU WERE REALLY GOING TO BRING THAT MANIAC BACK WITH US?

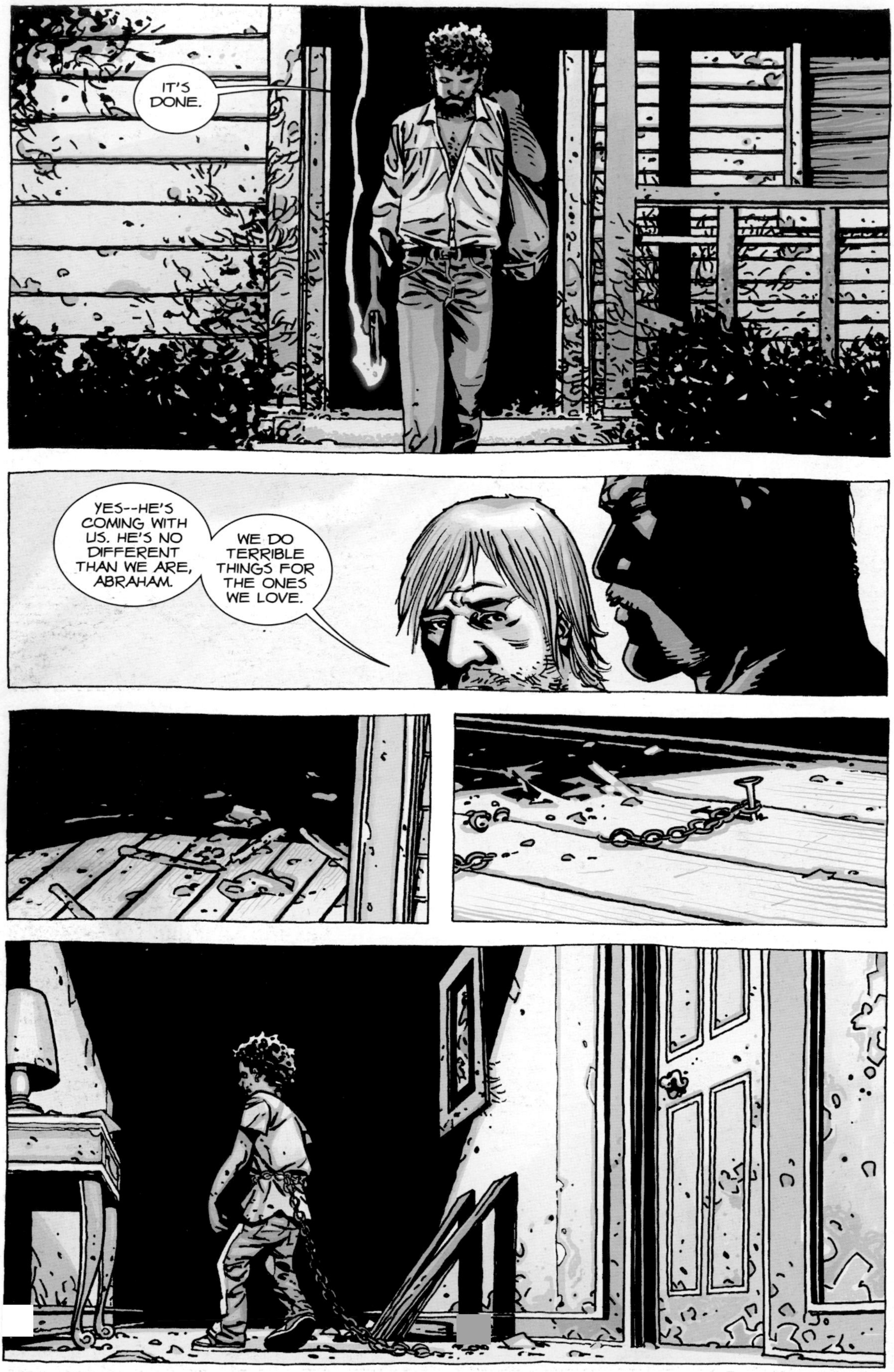
IT'S DONE.
YES--HE'S COMING WITH US. HE'S NO DIFFERENT THAN WE ARE, ABRAHAM.
WE DO TERRIBLE THINGS FOR THE ONES WE LOVE.

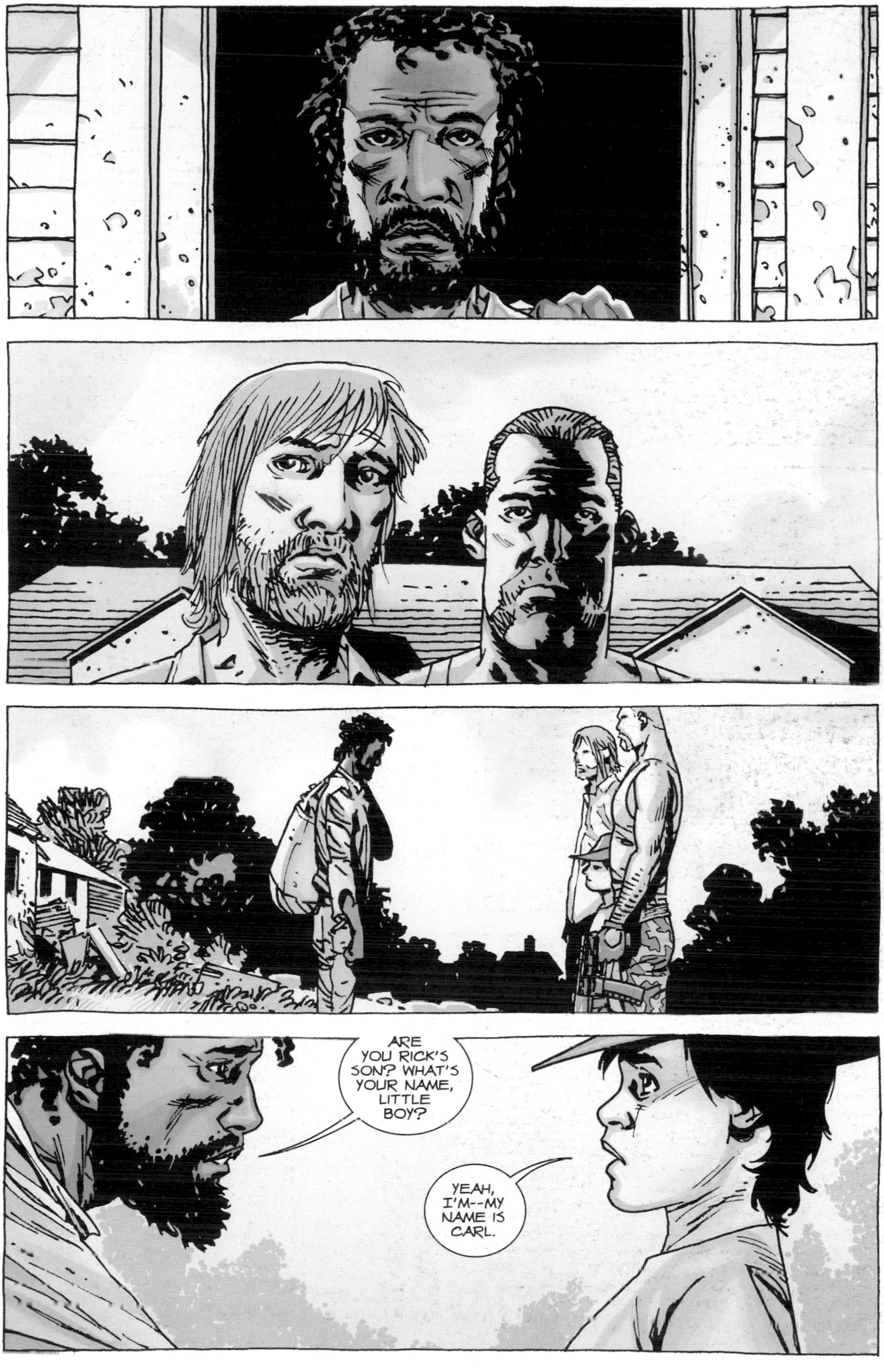
ARE YOU RICK'S SON? WHAT'S YOUR NAME, LITTLE BOY?
YEAH, I'M--MY NAME IS CARL.

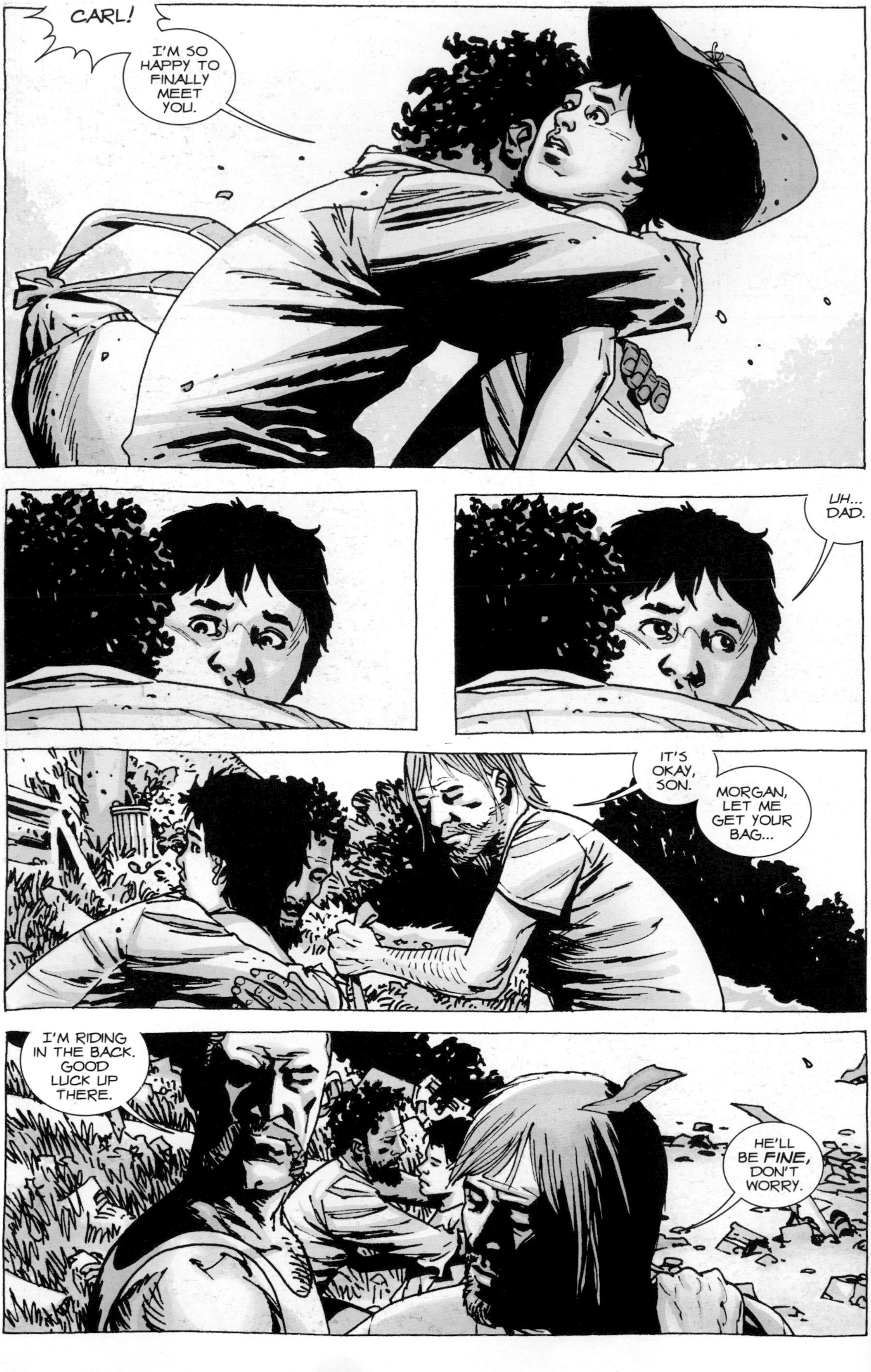
CARL!
I'M SO HAPPY TO FINALLY MEET YOU.
UH... DAD.
IT'S OKAY, SON.
MORGAN, LET ME GET YOUR BAG...
I'M RIDING IN THE BACK. GOOD LUCK UP THERE.
HE'LL BE FINE, DON'T WORRY.

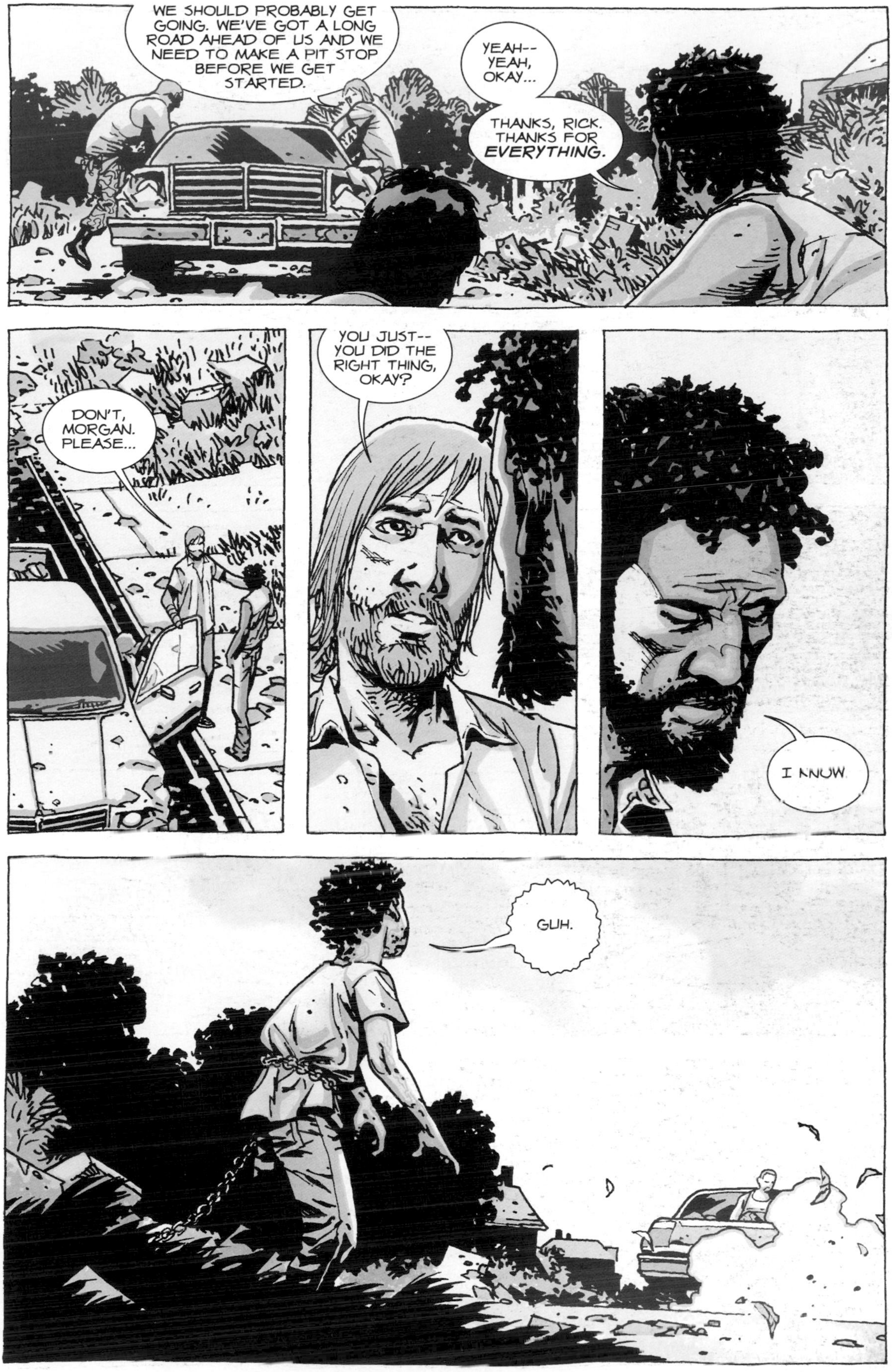
WE SHOULD PROBABLY GET GOING. WE'VE GOT A LONG ROAD AHEAD OF US AND WE NEED TO MAKE A PIT STOP BEFORE WE GET STARTED.
YEAH-- YEAH, OKAY...
THANKS, RICK. THANKS FOR EVERYTHING.
DON'T, MORGAN. PLEASE...
YOU JUST-- YOU DID THE RIGHT THING, OKAY?
I KNOW.
GUH.

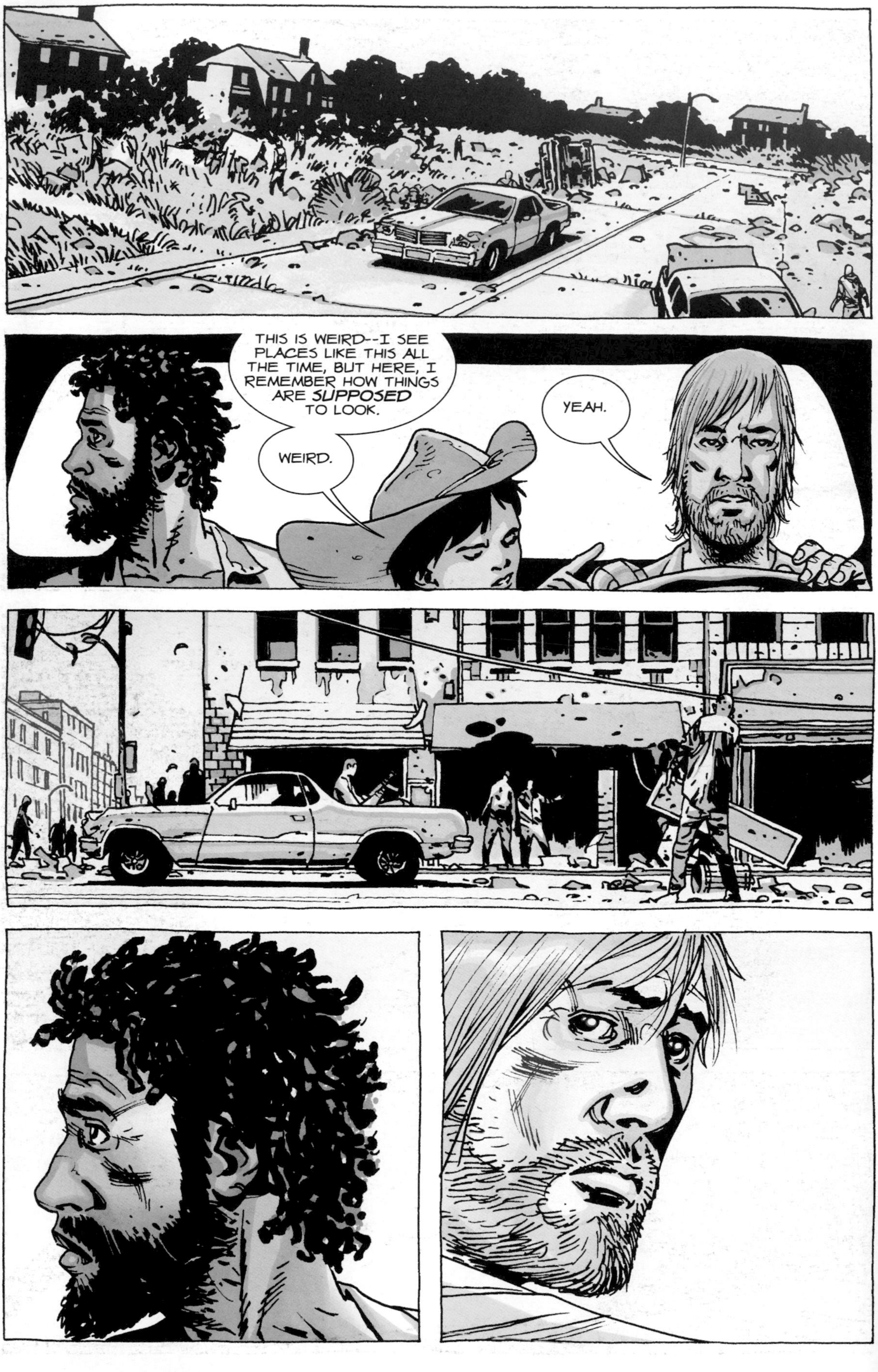
THIS IS WEIRD--I SEE PLACES LIKE THIS ALL THE TIME, BUT HERE, I REMEMBER HOW THINGS ARE *SUPPOSED* TO LOOK.
WEIRD.
YEAH.

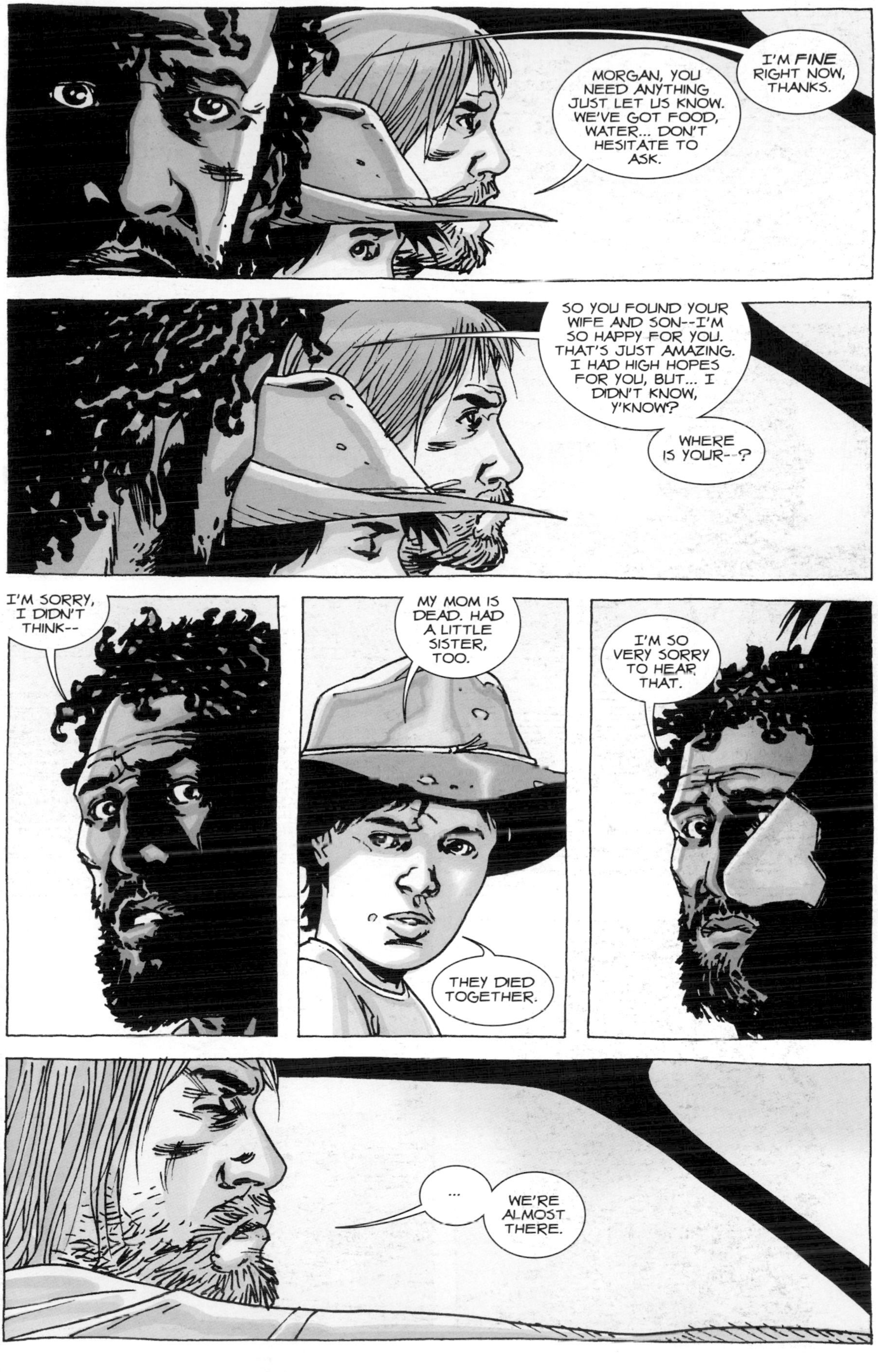
MORGAN, YOU NEED ANYTHING JUST LET US KNOW. WE'VE GOT FOOD, WATER... DON'T HESITATE TO ASK.
I'M FINE RIGHT NOW, THANKS.
SO YOU FOUND YOUR WIFE AND SON--I'M SO HAPPY FOR YOU. THAT'S JUST AMAZING. I HAD HIGH HOPES FOR YOU, BUT... I DIDN'T KNOW, Y'KNOW?
WHERE IS YOUR--?
I'M SORRY, I DIDN'T THINK--
MY MOM IS DEAD. HAD A LITTLE SISTER, TOO.
THEY DIED TOGETHER.
I'M SO VERY SORRY TO HEAR THAT.
...
WE'RE ALMOST THERE.

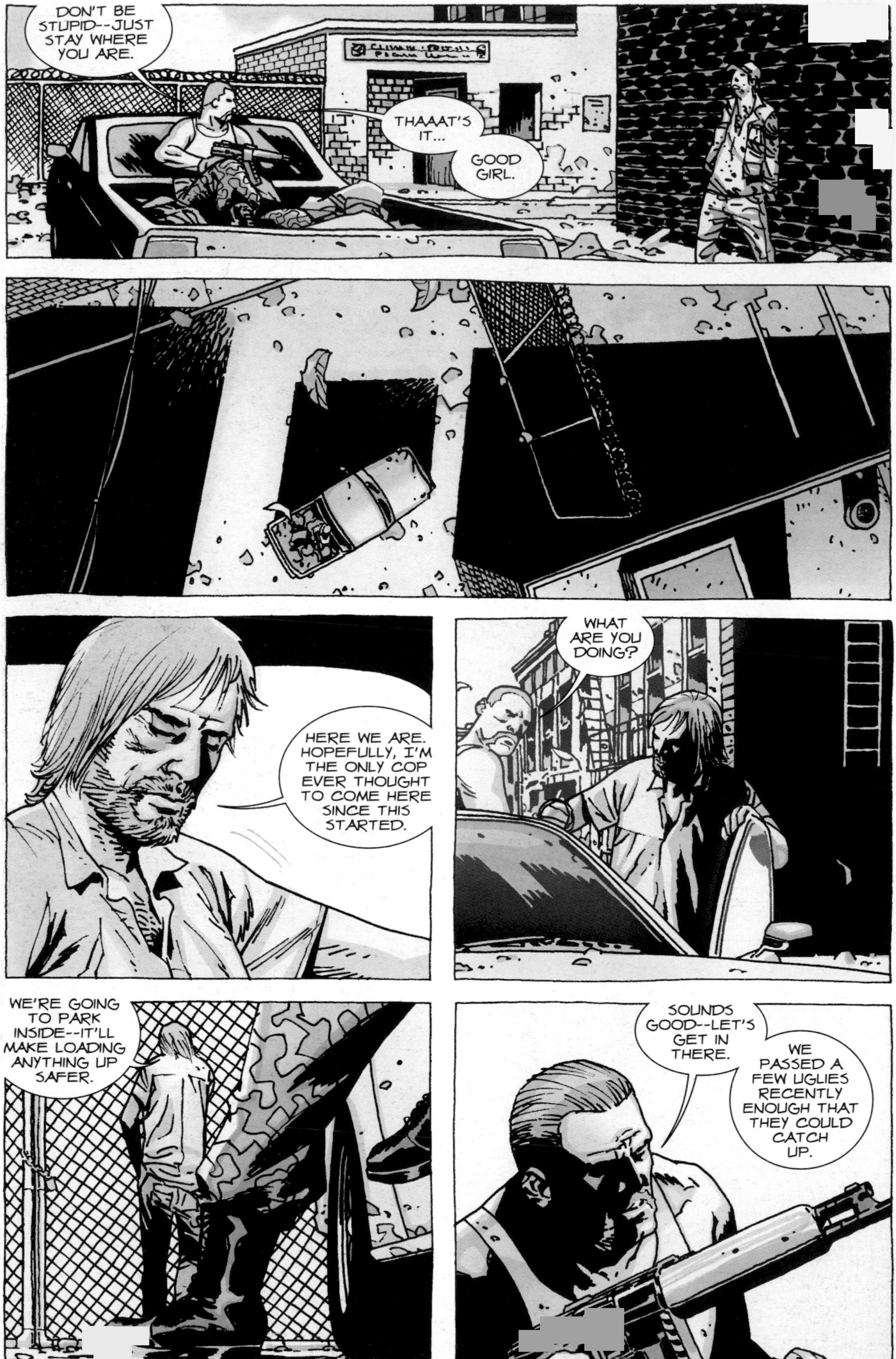
DON'T BE STUPID--JUST STAY WHERE YOU ARE.
THAAAT'S IT...
GOOD GIRL.
HERE WE ARE. HOPEFULLY, I'M THE ONLY COP EVER THOUGHT TO COME HERE SINCE THIS STARTED.
WHAT ARE YOU DOING?
WE'RE GOING TO PARK INSIDE--IT'LL MAKE LOADING ANYTHING UP SAFER.
SOUNDS GOOD--LET'S GET IN THERE.
WE PASSED A FEW UGLIES RECENTLY ENOUGH THAT THEY COULD CATCH UP.

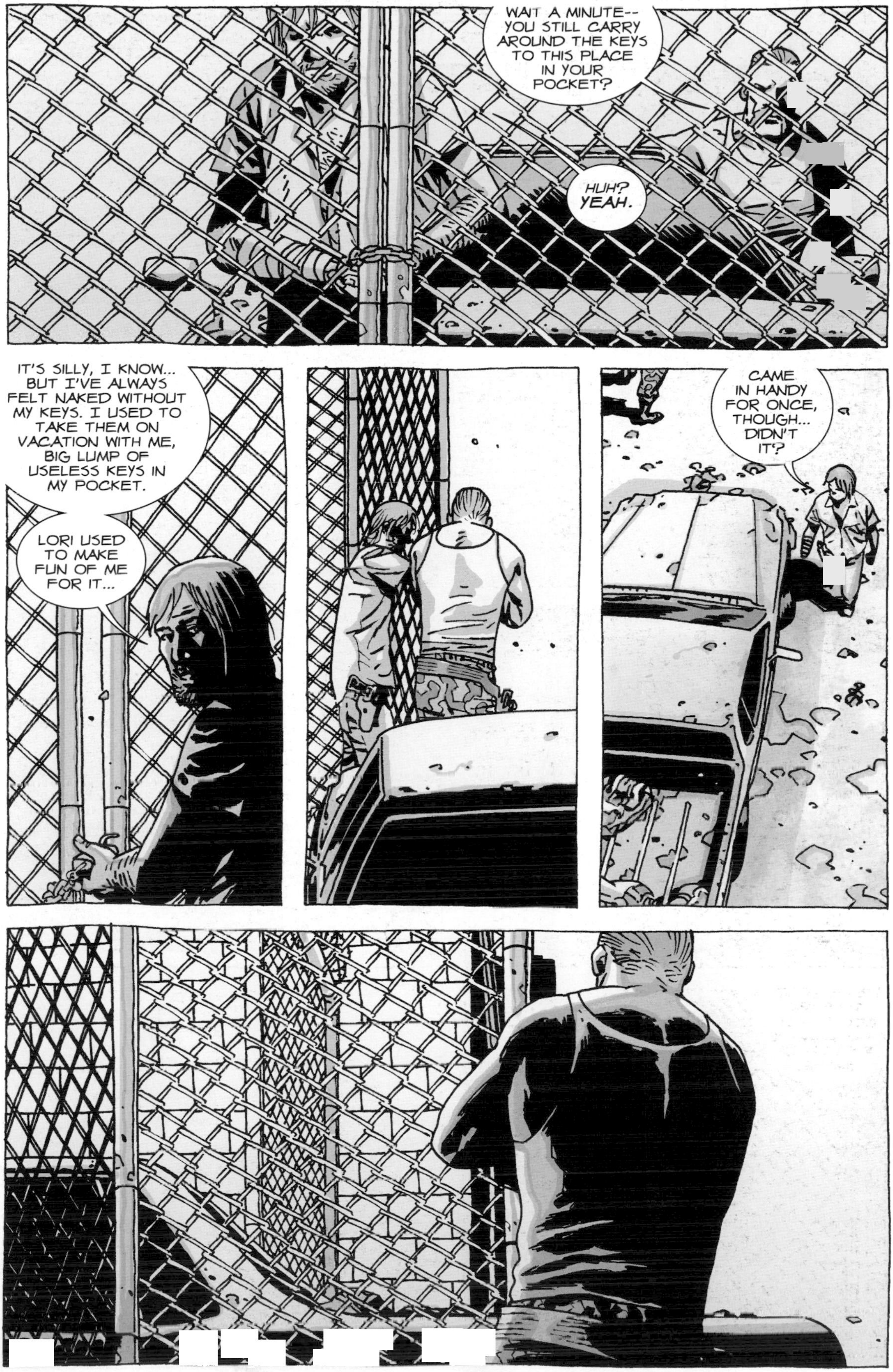
WAIT A MINUTE-- YOU STILL CARRY AROUND THE KEYS TO THIS PLACE IN YOUR POCKET?
HUH? YEAH.
IT'S SILLY, I KNOW... BUT I'VE ALWAYS FELT NAKED WITHOUT MY KEYS. I USED TO TAKE THEM ON VACATION WITH ME, BIG LUMP OF USELESS KEYS IN MY POCKET.
LORI USED TO MAKE FUN OF ME FOR IT...
CAME IN HANDY FOR ONCE, THOUGH... DIDN'T IT?

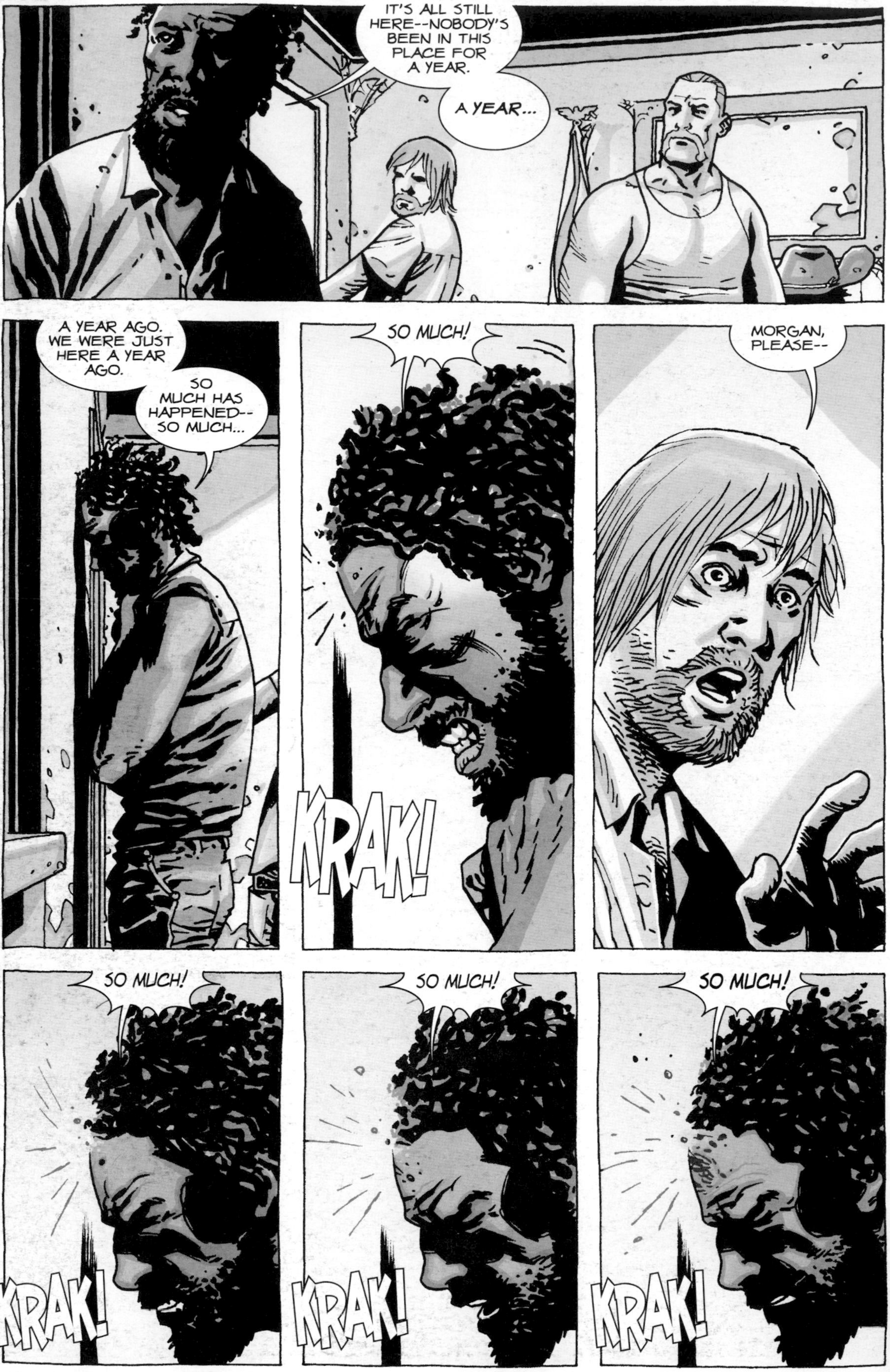
IT'S ALL STILL HERE--NOBODY'S BEEN IN THIS PLACE FOR A YEAR.
A YEAR...
A YEAR AGO. WE WERE JUST HERE A YEAR AGO.
SO MUCH HAS HAPPENED--SO MUCH...
SO MUCH!
KRAK!
MORGAN, PLEASE--
SO MUCH!
KRAK!
SO MUCH!
KRAK!
SO MUCH!
KRAK!

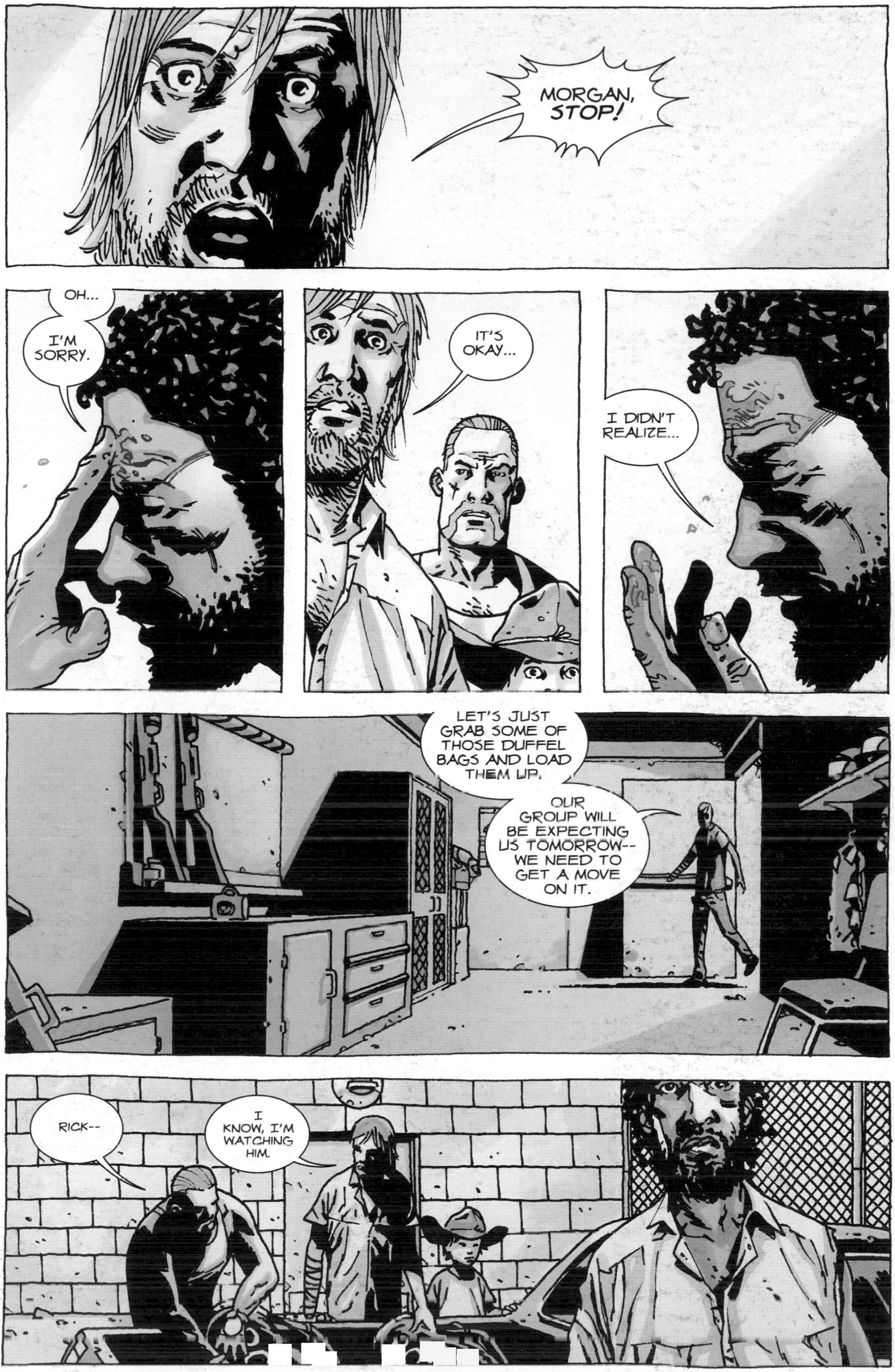
MORGAN, STOP!
OH...
I'M SORRY.
IT'S OKAY...
I DIDN'T REALIZE...
LET'S JUST GRAB SOME OF THOSE DUFFEL BAGS AND LOAD THEM UP.
OUR GROUP WILL BE EXPECTING US TOMORROW-- WE NEED TO GET A MOVE ON IT.
RICK--
I KNOW, I'M WATCHING HIM.

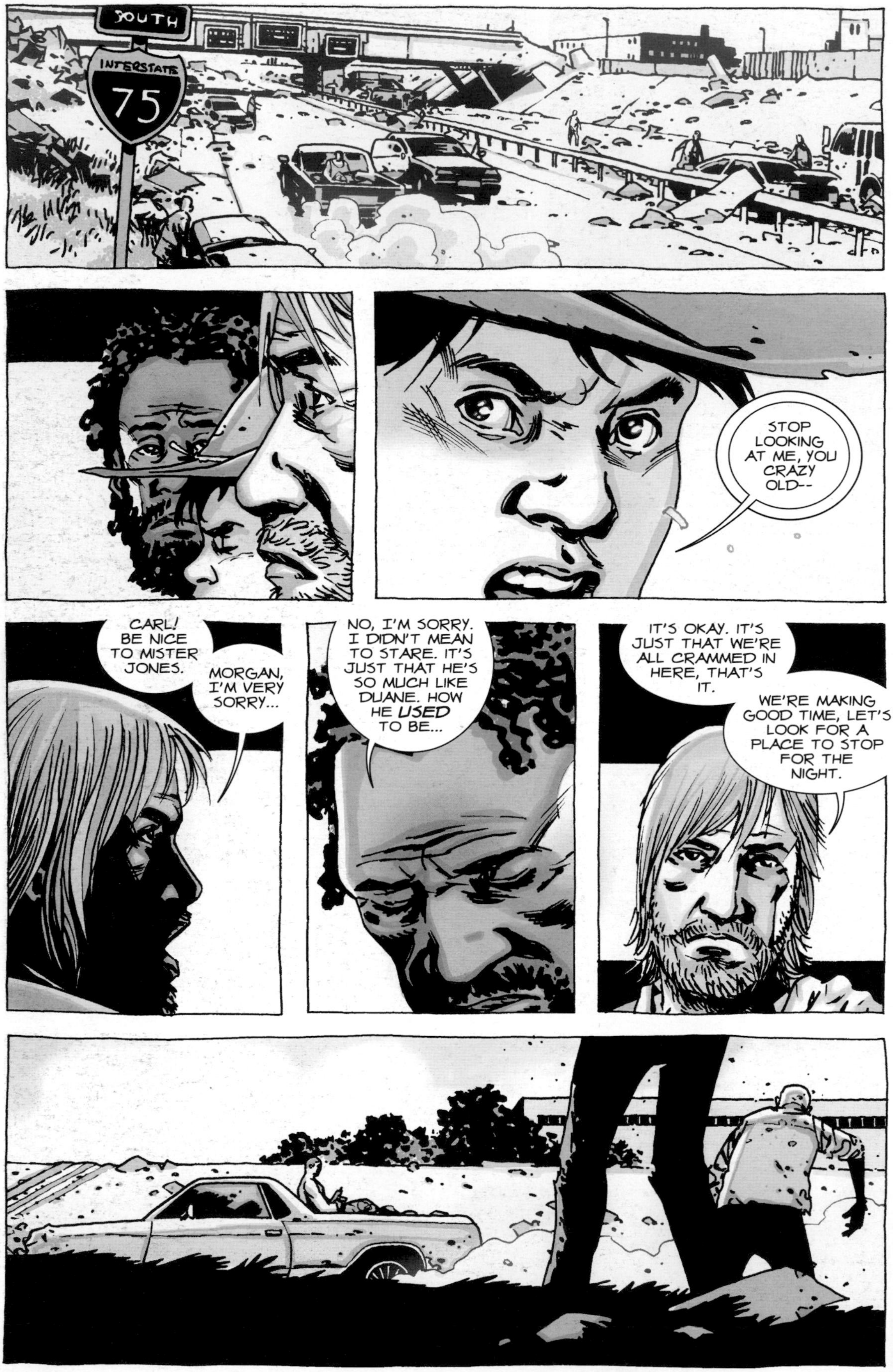
SOUTH
INTERSTATE
75
STOP LOOKING AT ME, YOU CRAZY OLD--
CARL! BE NICE TO MISTER JONES.
MORGAN, I'M VERY SORRY...
NO, I'M SORRY. I DIDN'T MEAN TO STARE. IT'S JUST THAT HE'S SO MUCH LIKE DUANE. HOW HE USED TO BE...
IT'S OKAY. IT'S JUST THAT WE'RE ALL CRAMMED IN HERE, THAT'S IT.
WE'RE MAKING GOOD TIME, LET'S LOOK FOR A PLACE TO STOP FOR THE NIGHT.

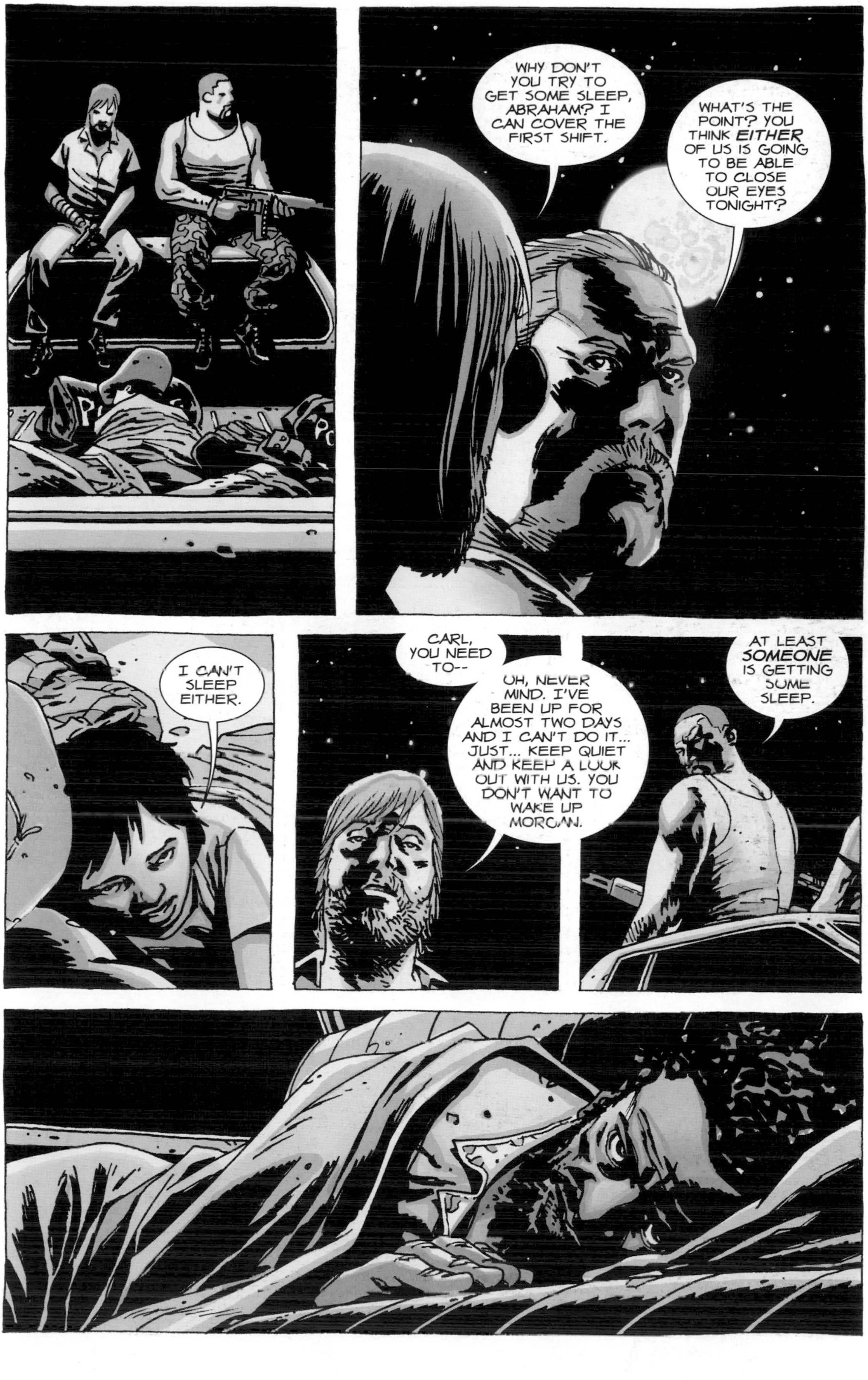
WHY DON'T YOU TRY TO GET SOME SLEEP, ABRAHAM? I CAN COVER THE FIRST SHIFT.
WHAT'S THE POINT? YOU THINK EITHER OF US IS GOING TO BE ABLE TO CLOSE OUR EYES TONIGHT?
I CAN'T SLEEP EITHER.
CARL, YOU NEED TO--
OH, NEVER MIND. I'VE BEEN UP FOR ALMOST TWO DAYS AND I CAN'T DO IT... JUST... KEEP QUIET AND KEEP A LOOK OUT WITH US. YOU DON'T WANT TO WAKE UP MORGAN.
AT LEAST SOMEONE IS GETTING SOME SLEEP.

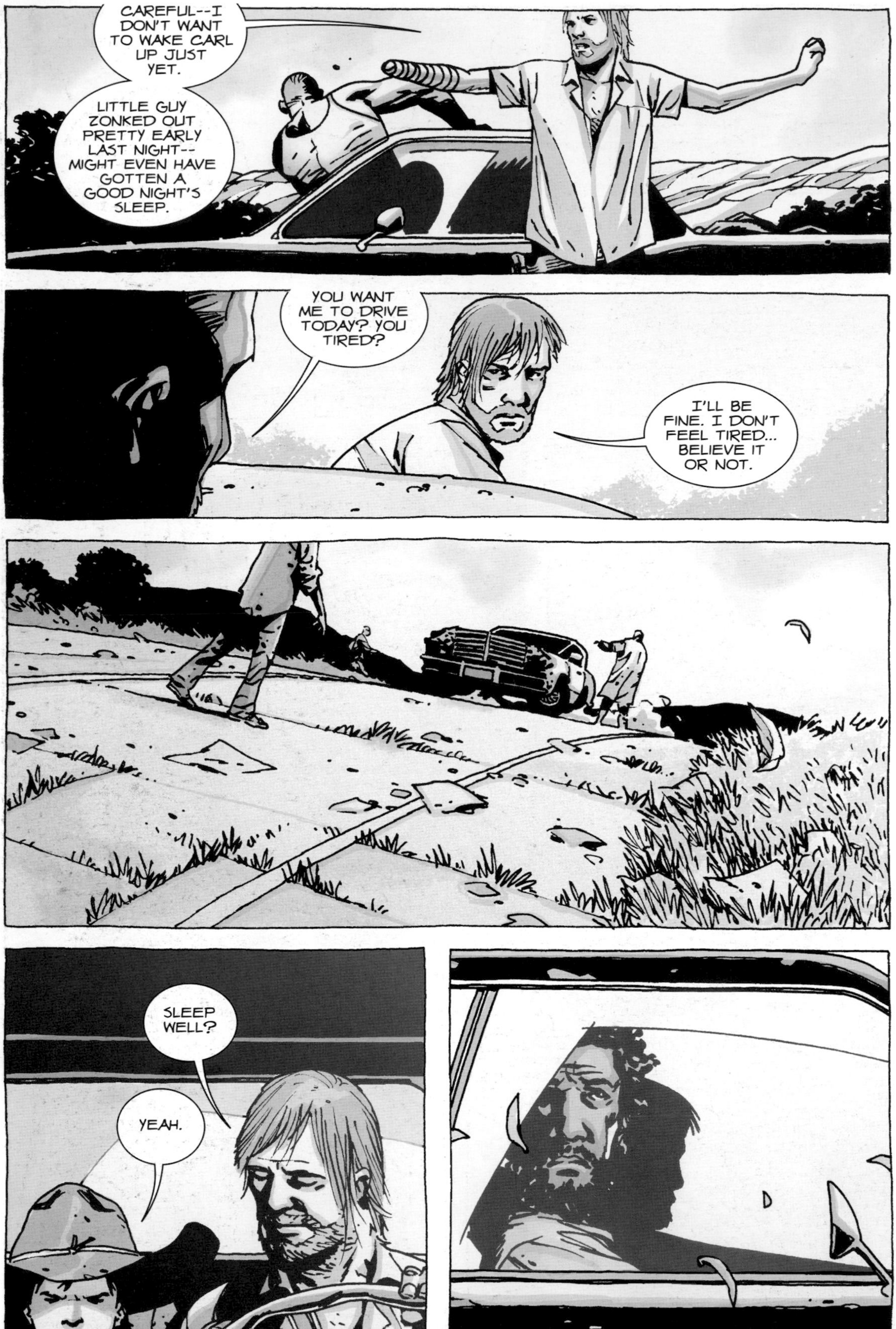
CAREFUL--I DON'T WANT TO WAKE CARL UP JUST YET.
LITTLE GUY ZONKED OUT PRETTY EARLY LAST NIGHT-- MIGHT EVEN HAVE GOTTEN A GOOD NIGHT'S SLEEP.
YOU WANT ME TO DRIVE TODAY? YOU TIRED?
I'LL BE FINE. I DON'T FEEL TIRED... BELIEVE IT OR NOT.
SLEEP WELL?
YEAH.

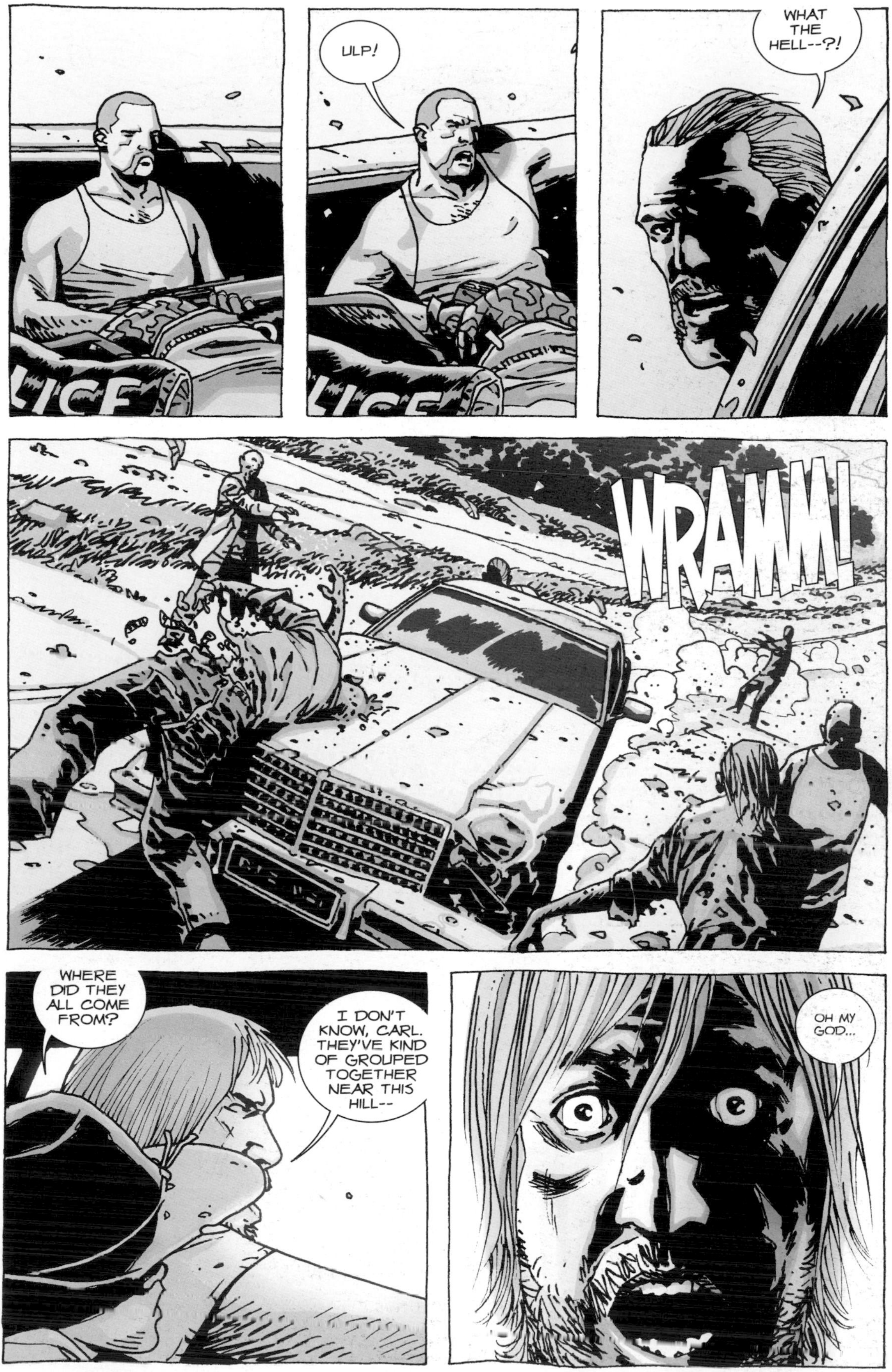
ULP!
WHAT THE HELL--?!
WRAMM!
WHERE DID THEY ALL COME FROM?
I DON'T KNOW, CARL. THEY'VE KIND OF GROUPED TOGETHER NEAR THIS HILL--
OH MY GOD...

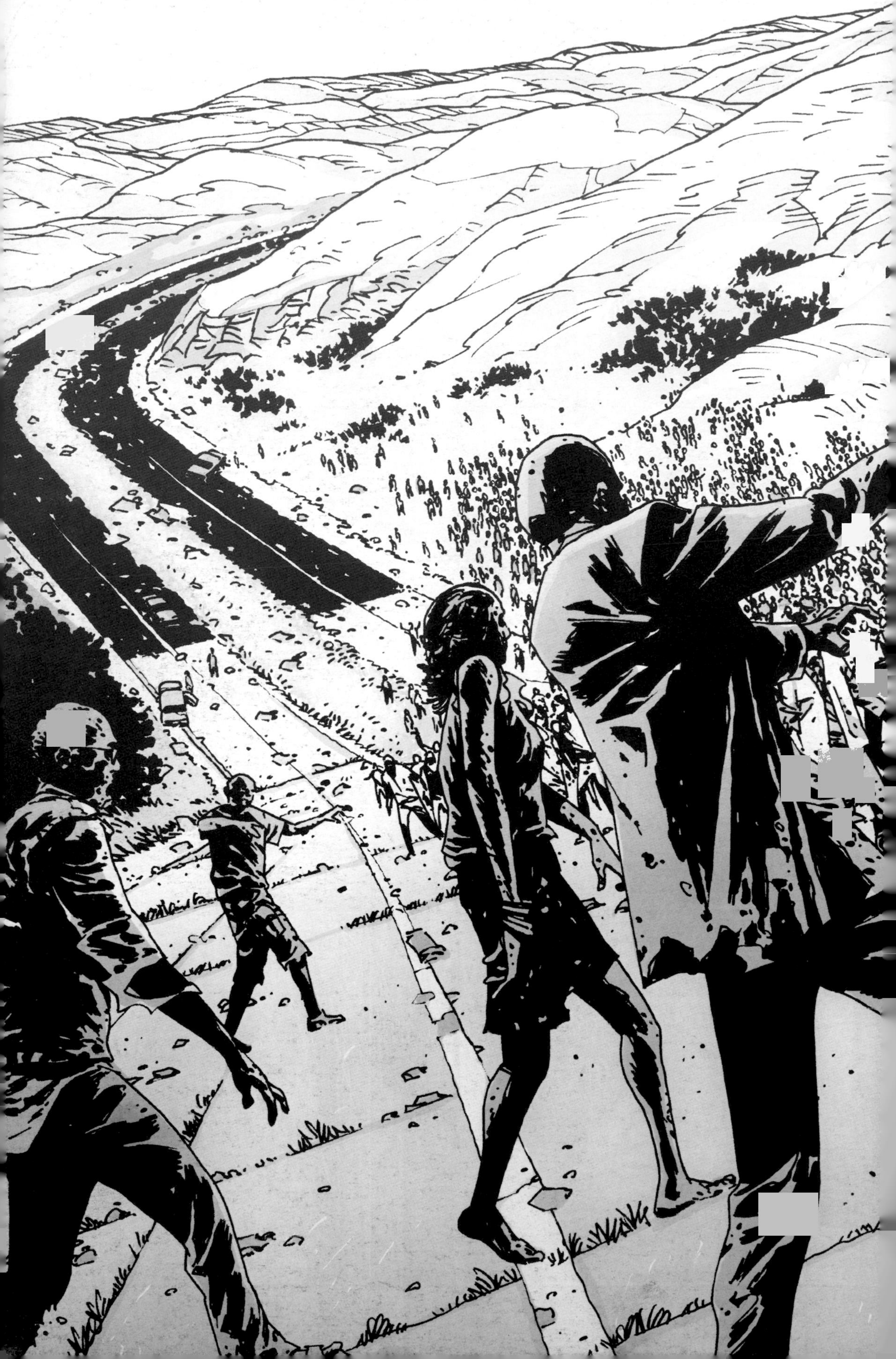

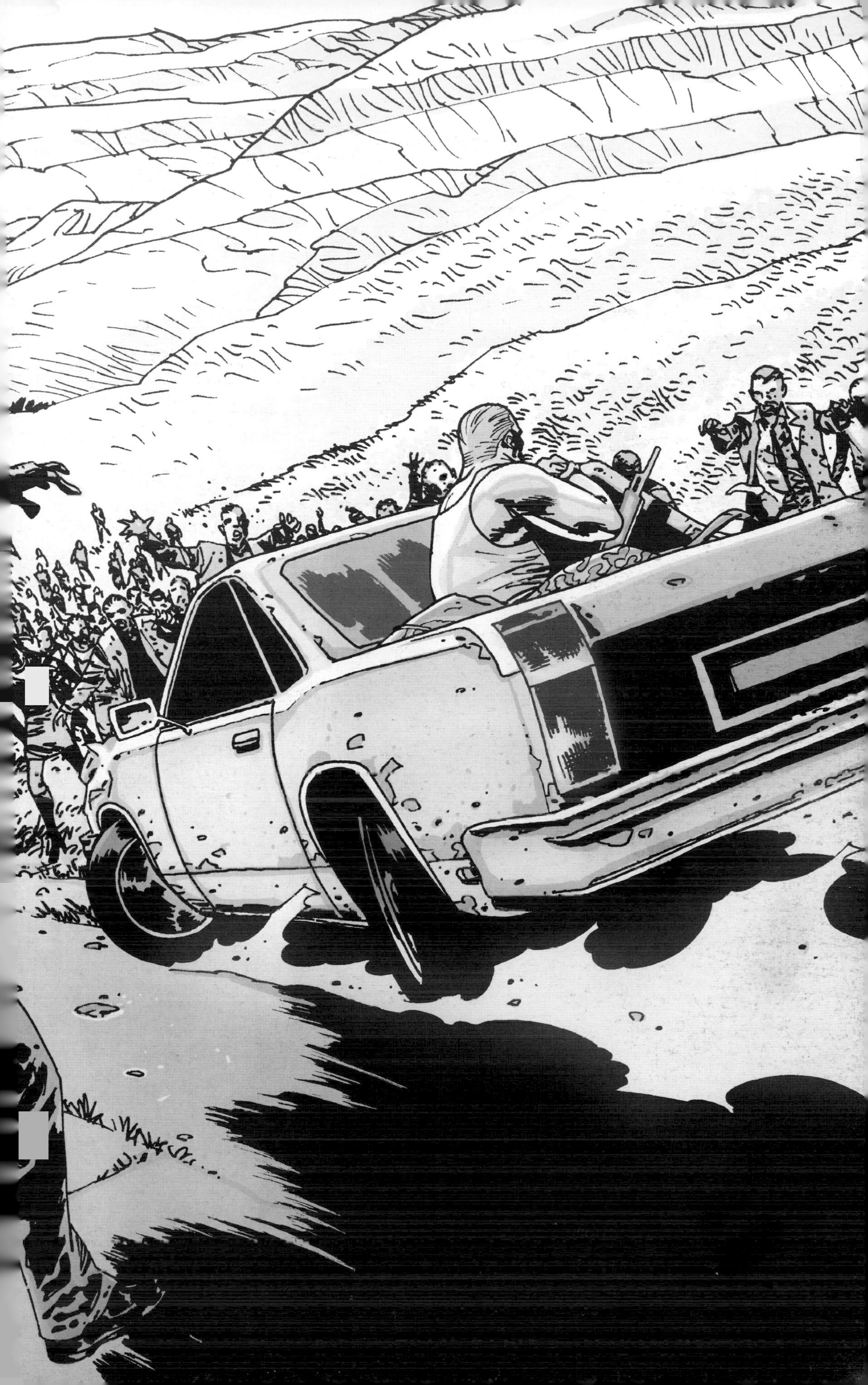

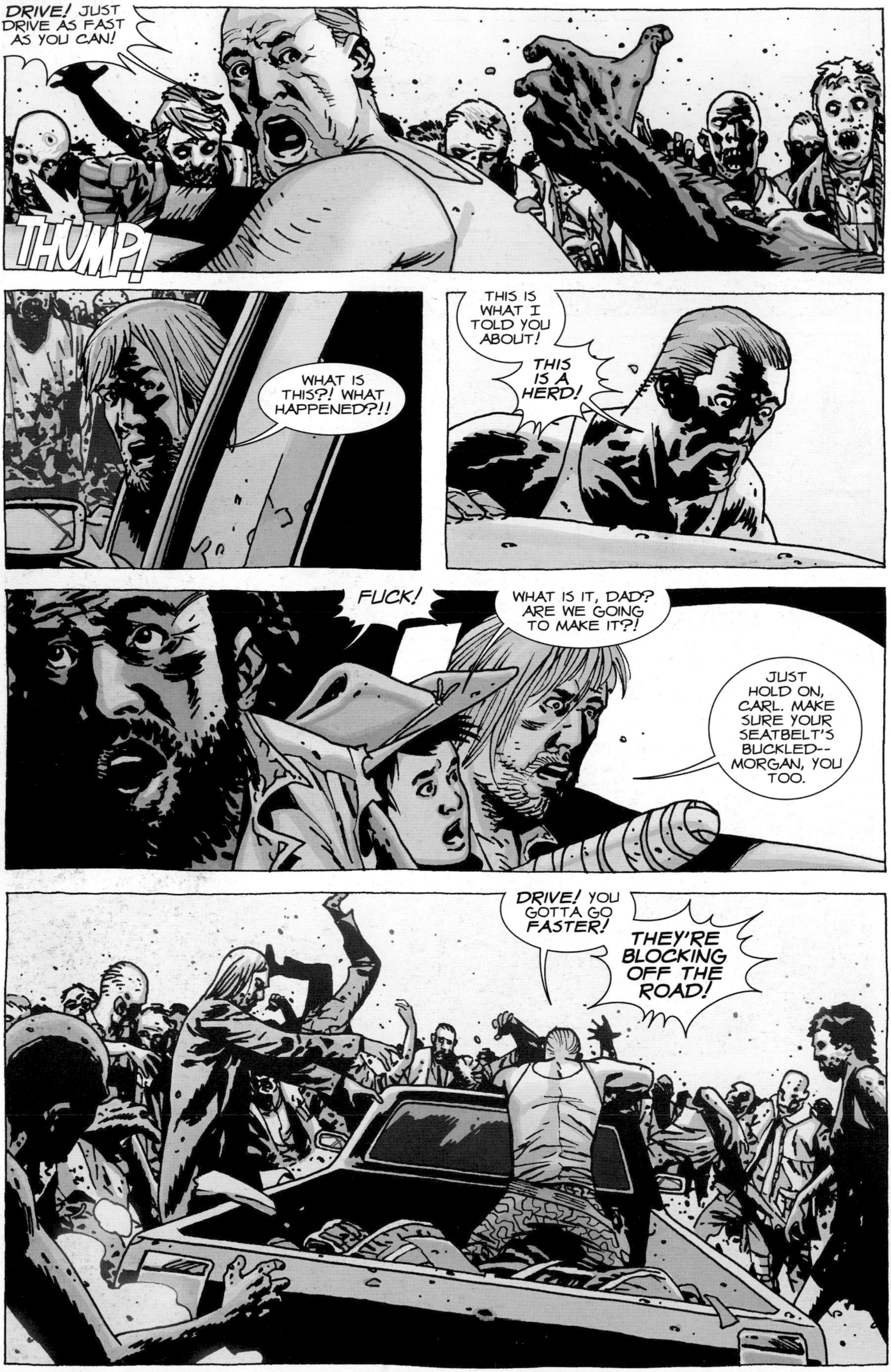
DRIVE! JUST DRIVE AS FAST AS YOU CAN!
THUMP!
WHAT IS THIS?! WHAT HAPPENED?!!
THIS IS WHAT I TOLD YOU ABOUT!
THIS IS A HERD!
FUCK!
WHAT IS IT, DAD? ARE WE GOING TO MAKE IT?!
JUST HOLD ON, CARL. MAKE SURE YOUR SEATBELT'S BUCKLED-- MORGAN, YOU TOO.
DRIVE! YOU GOTTA GO FASTER!
THEY'RE BLOCKING OFF THE ROAD!

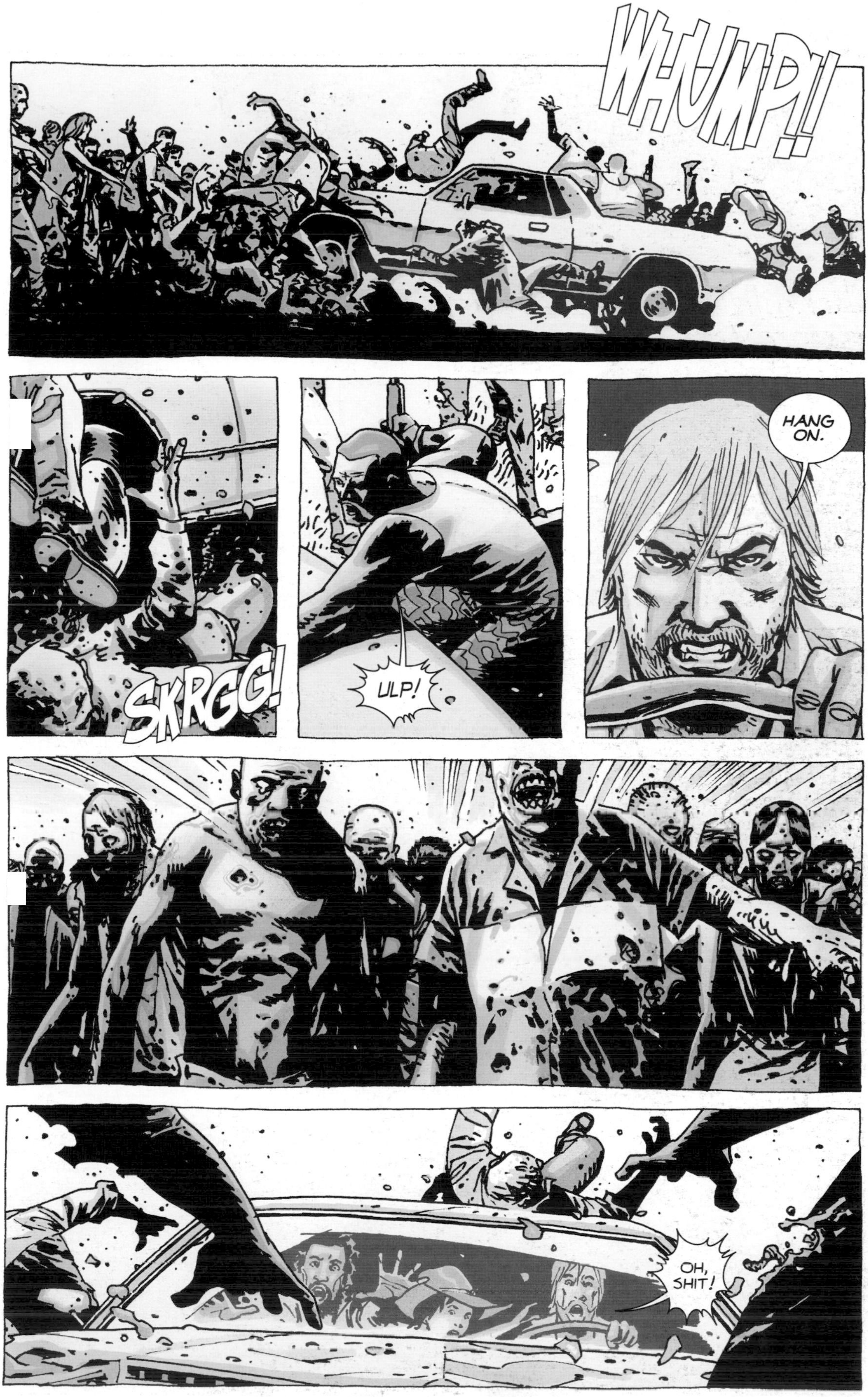
WHUMP!!
SKRGG!
ULP!
HANG ON.
OH, SHIT!

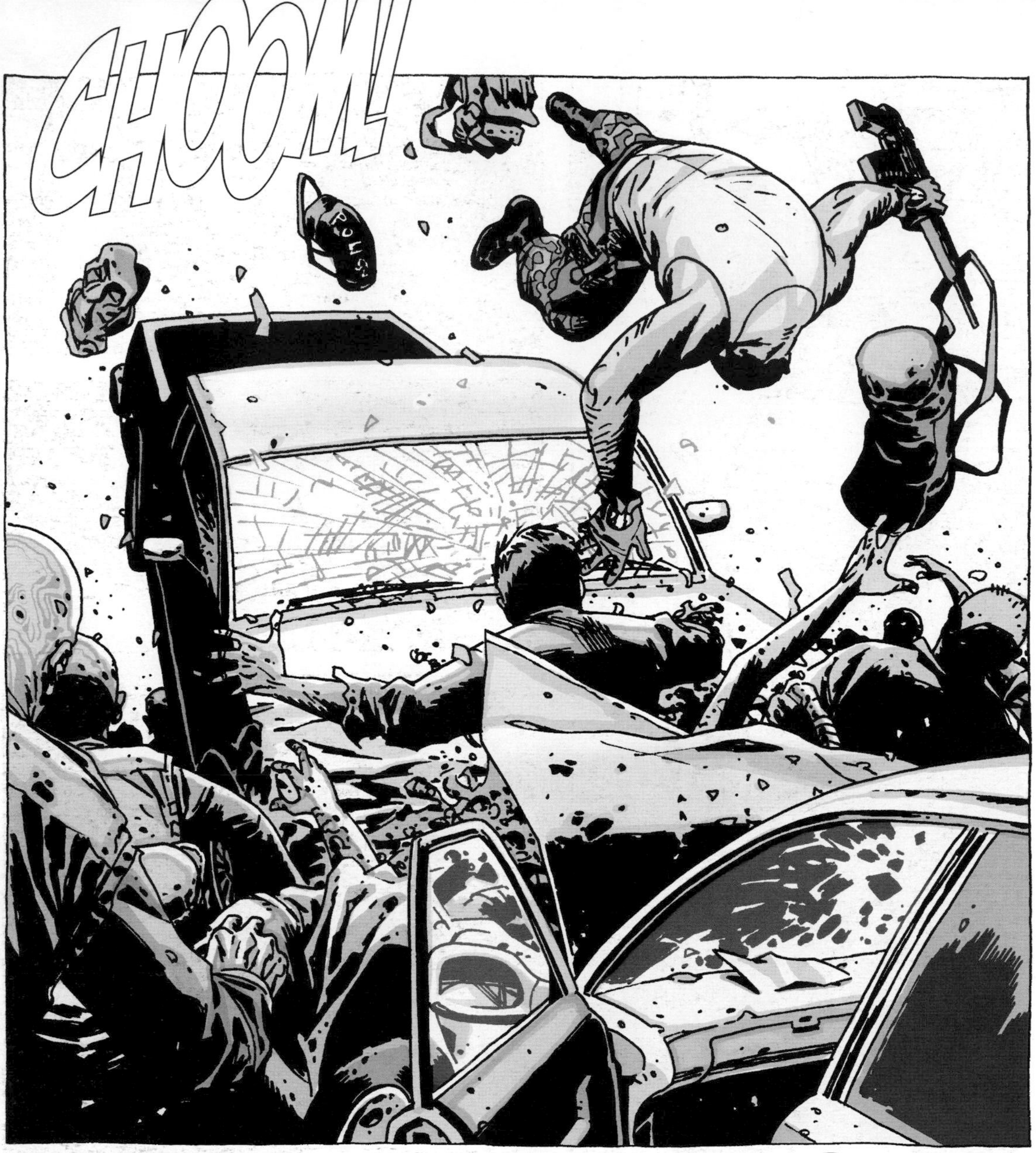
CHOOM!

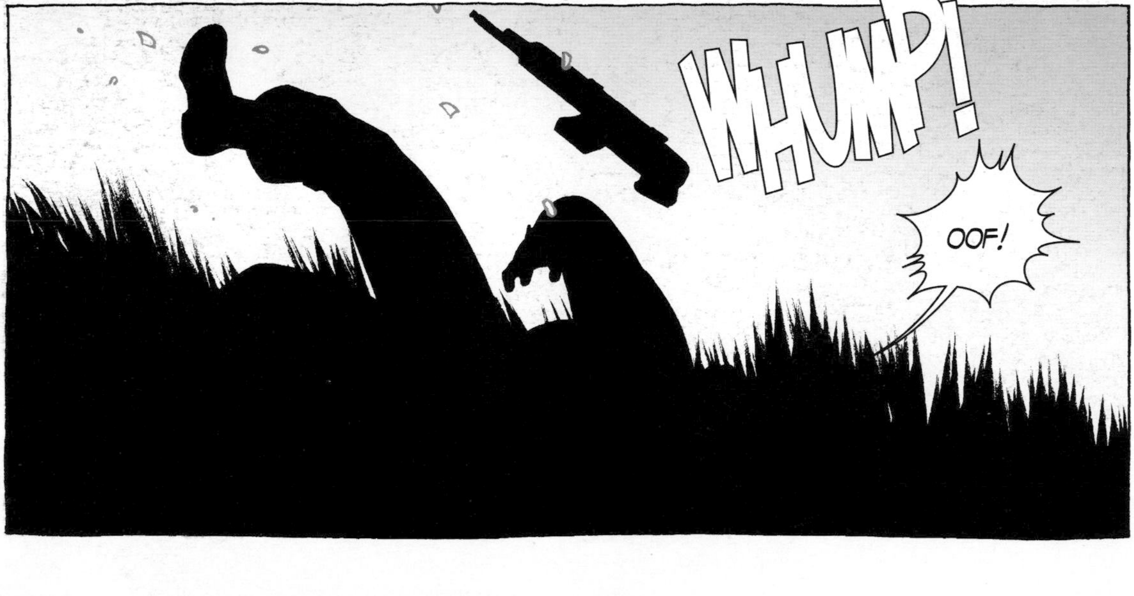
WHUMP!
OOF!

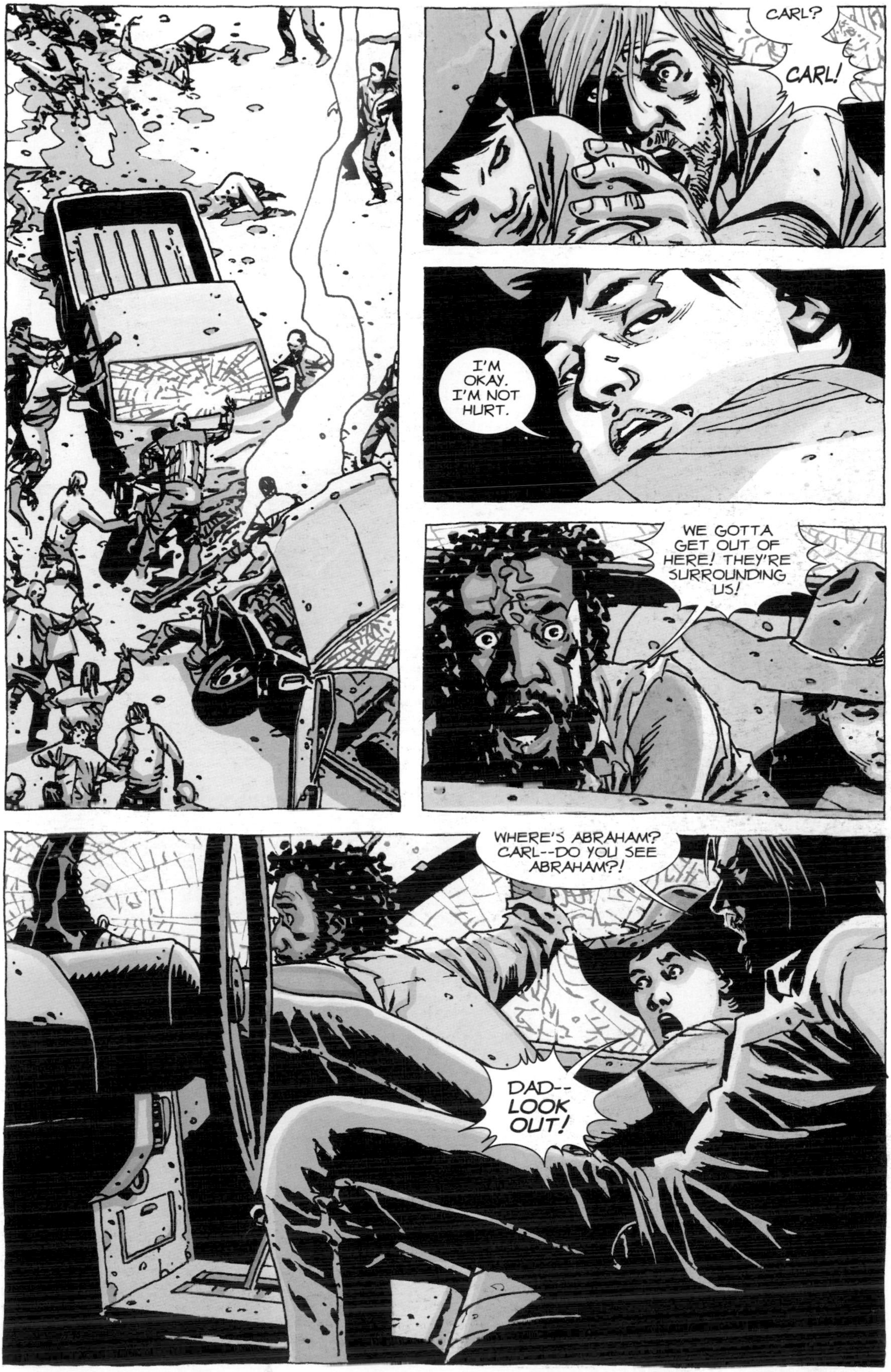
CARL?
CARL!
I'M OKAY. I'M NOT HURT.
WE GOTTA GET OUT OF HERE! THEY'RE SURROUNDING US!
WHERE'S ABRAHAM? CARL--DO YOU SEE ABRAHAM?!
DAD-- LOOK OUT!

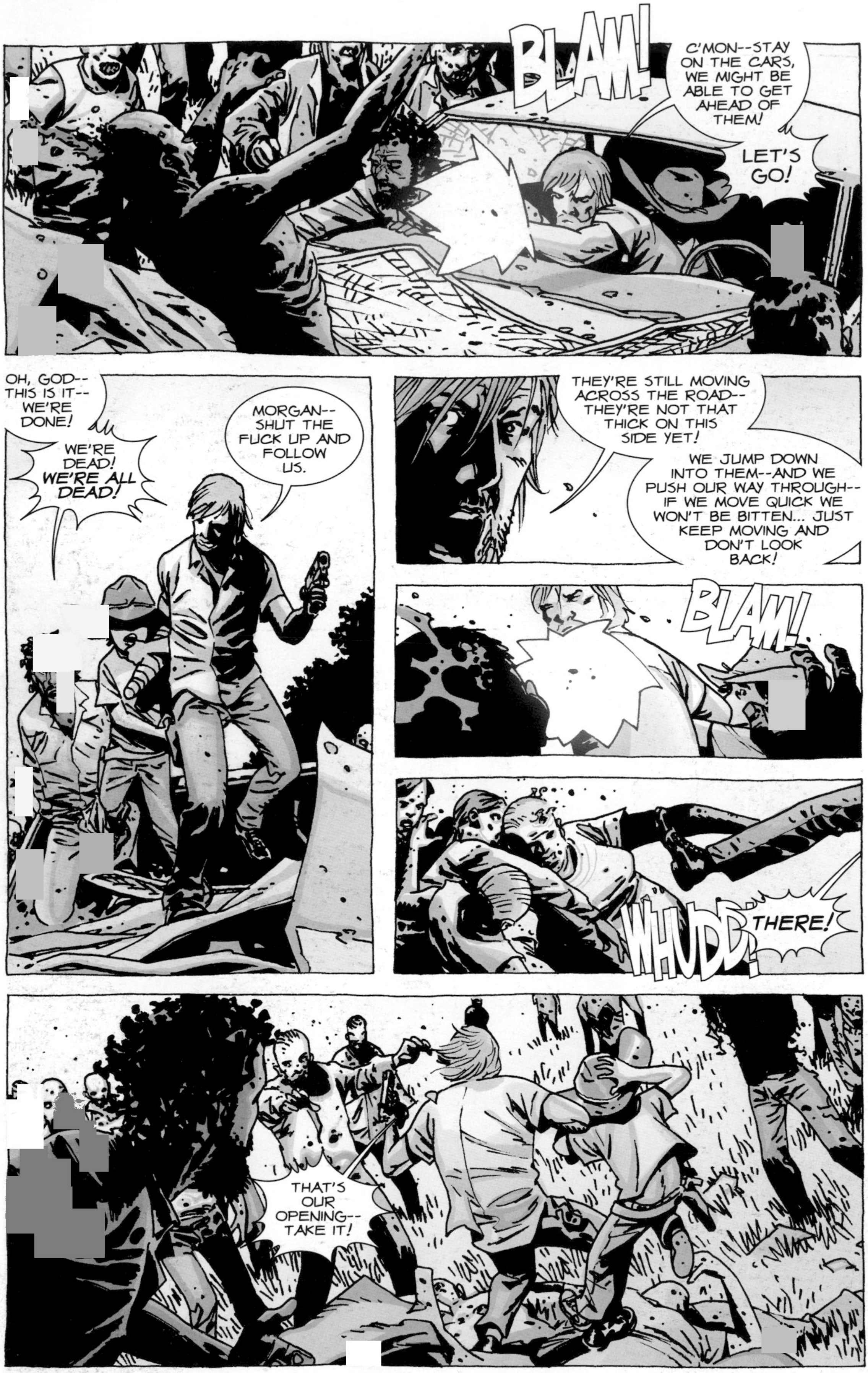
BLAM!
C'MON--STAY ON THE CARS, WE MIGHT BE ABLE TO GET AHEAD OF THEM!
LET'S GO!
OH, GOD-- THIS IS IT-- WE'RE DONE!
WE'RE DEAD! WE'RE ALL DEAD!
MORGAN-- SHUT THE FUCK UP AND FOLLOW US.
THEY'RE STILL MOVING ACROSS THE ROAD-- THEY'RE NOT THAT THICK ON THIS SIDE YET!
WE JUMP DOWN INTO THEM--AND WE PUSH OUR WAY THROUGH-- IF WE MOVE QUICK WE WON'T BE BITTEN... JUST KEEP MOVING AND DON'T LOOK BACK!
BLAM!
WHUDD!
THERE!
THAT'S OUR OPENING-- TAKE IT!

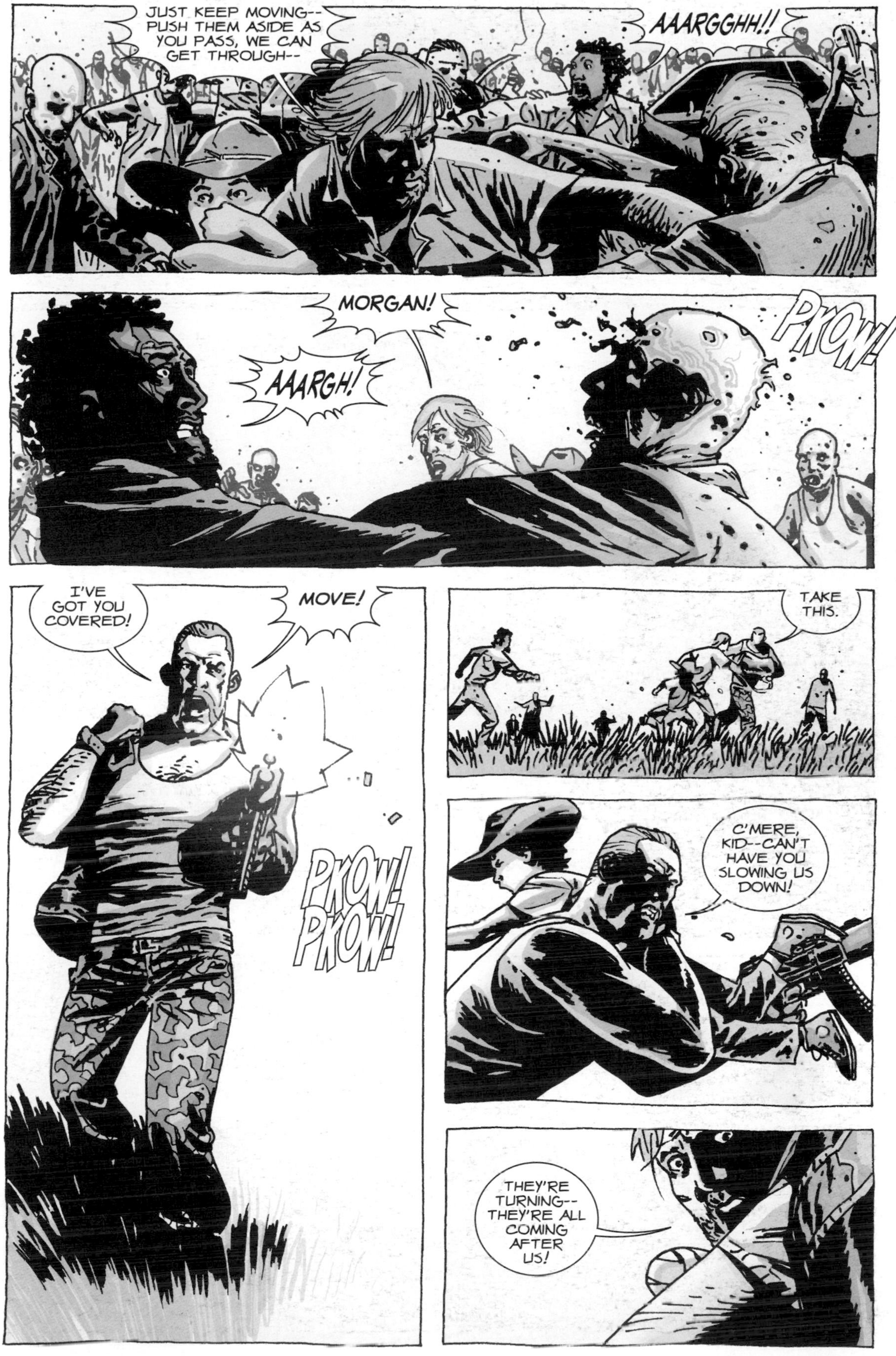
JUST KEEP MOVING-- PUSH THEM ASIDE AS YOU PASS, WE CAN GET THROUGH--
AAARGGHH!!
MORGAN!
AAARGH!
PKOW!
I'VE GOT YOU COVERED!
MOVE!
PKOW! PKOW!
TAKE THIS.
C'MERE, KID--CAN'T HAVE YOU SLOWING US DOWN!
THEY'RE TURNING-- THEY'RE ALL COMING AFTER US!

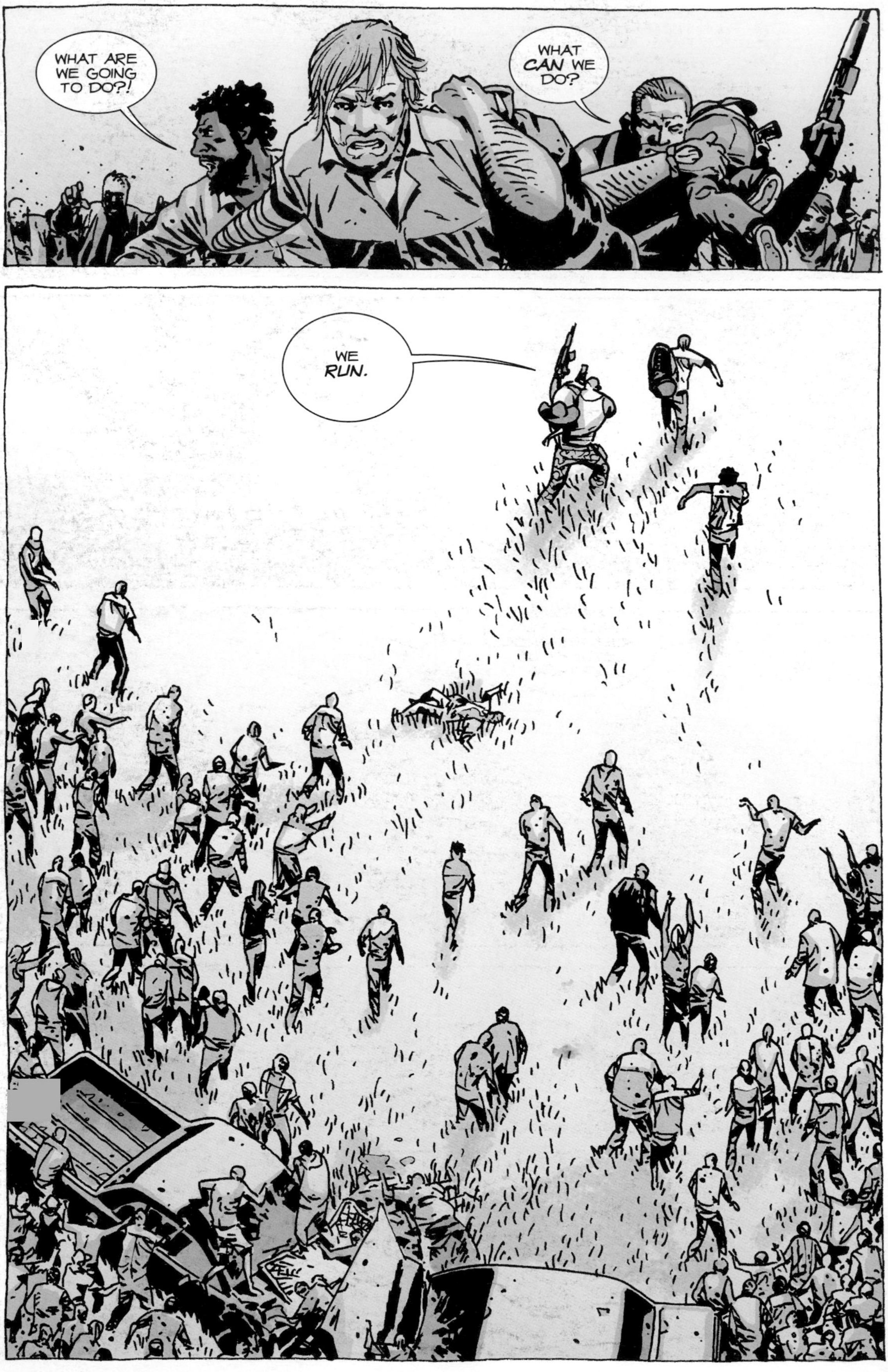
WHAT ARE WE GOING TO DO?!
WHAT CAN WE DO?
WE RUN.

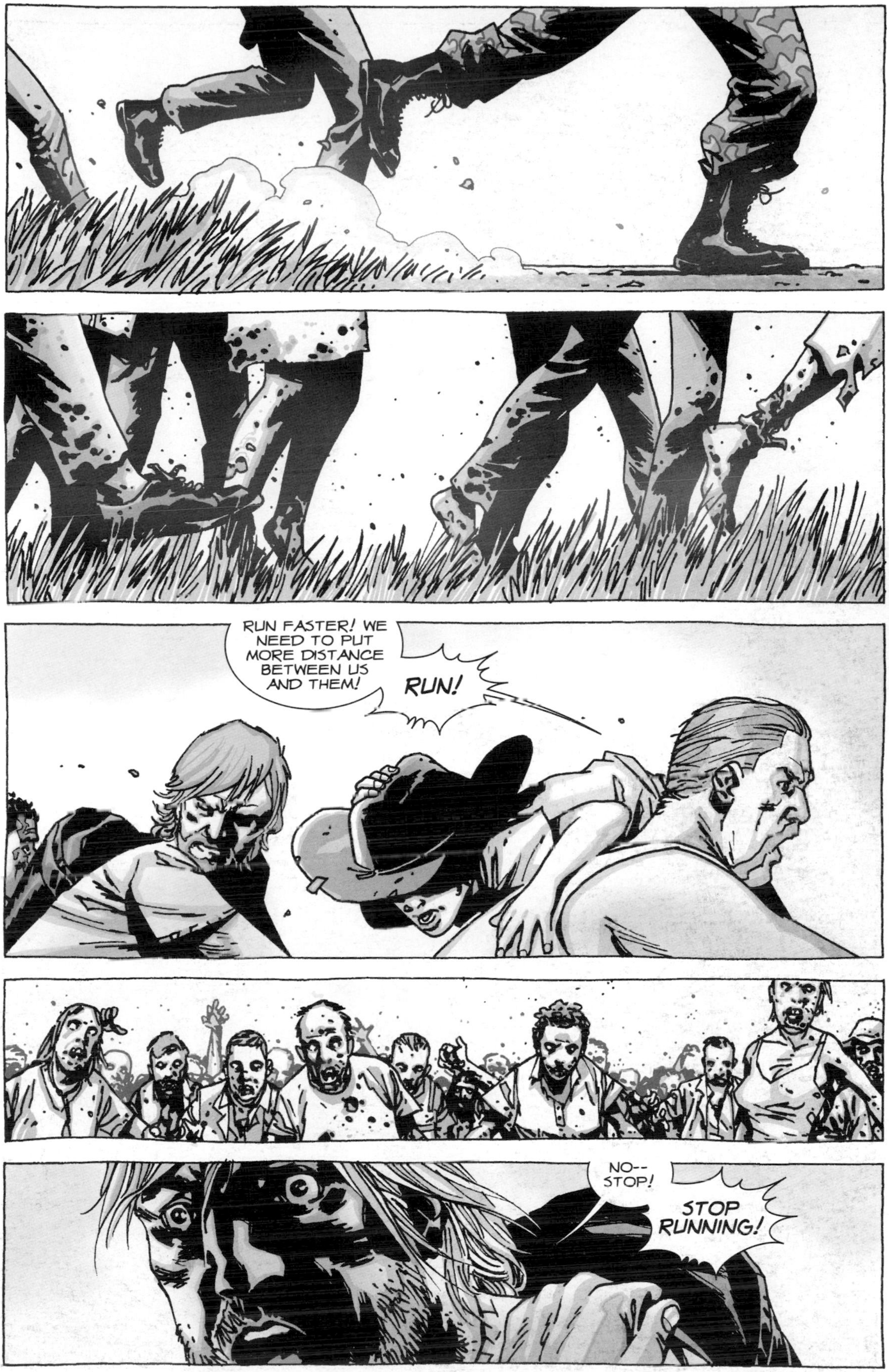
RUN FASTER! WE NEED TO PUT MORE DISTANCE BETWEEN US AND THEM!
RUN!
NO-- STOP!
STOP RUNNING!

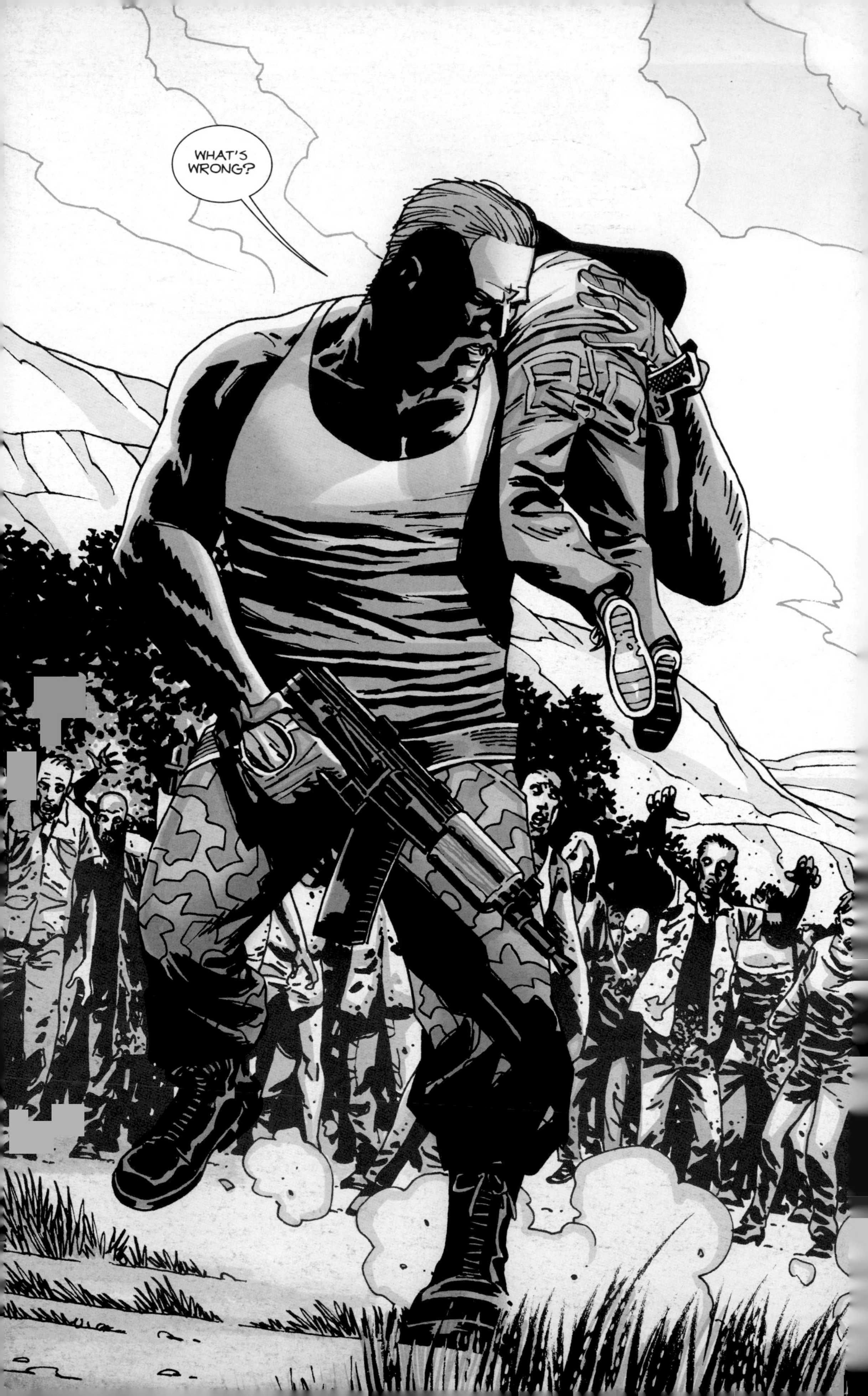
WHAT'S WRONG?

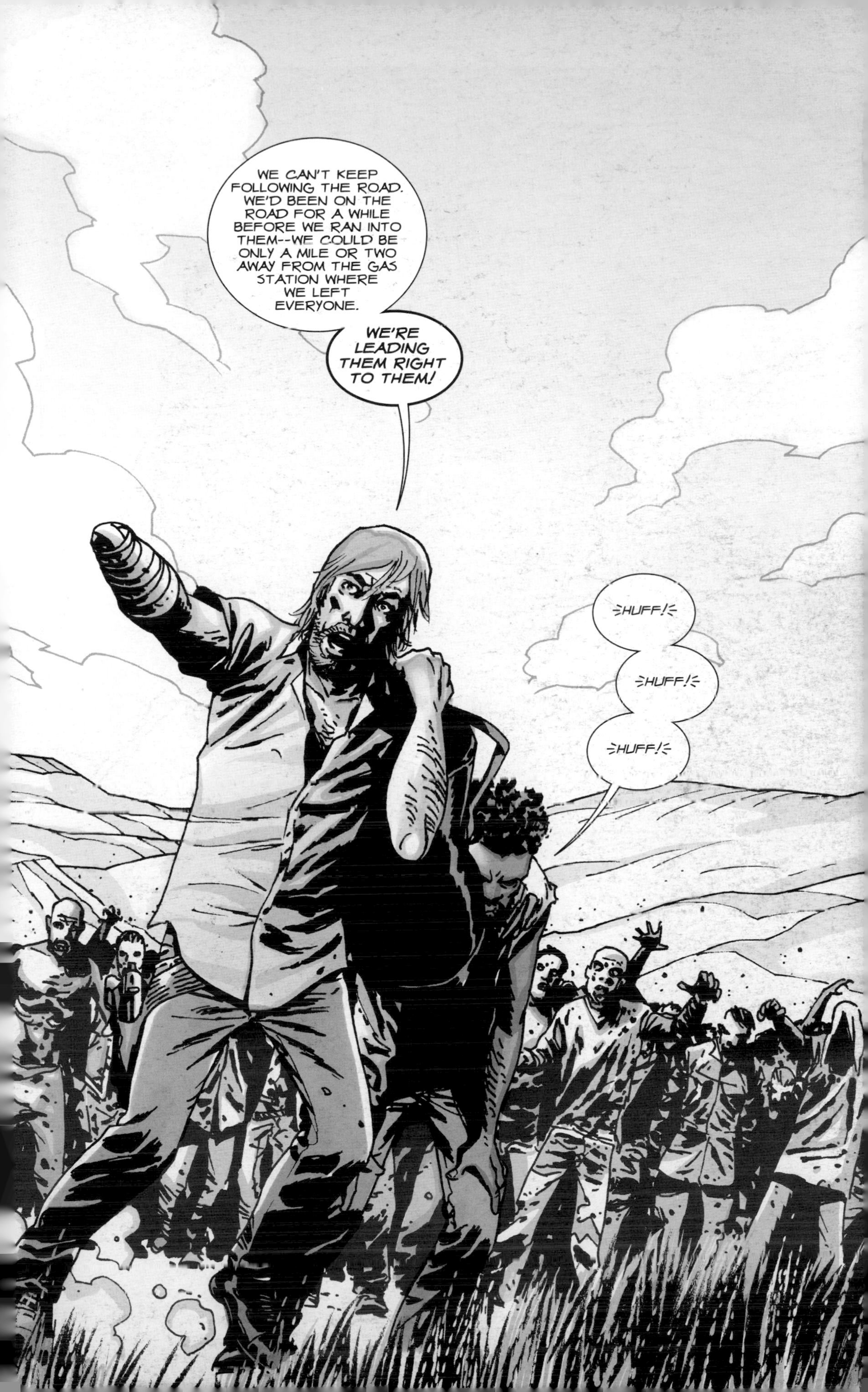
WE CAN'T KEEP FOLLOWING THE ROAD. WE'D BEEN ON THE ROAD FOR A WHILE BEFORE WE RAN INTO THEM--WE COULD BE ONLY A MILE OR TWO AWAY FROM THE GAS STATION WHERE WE LEFT EVERYONE.
WE'RE LEADING THEM RIGHT TO THEM!
HUFF!
HUFF!
HUFF!

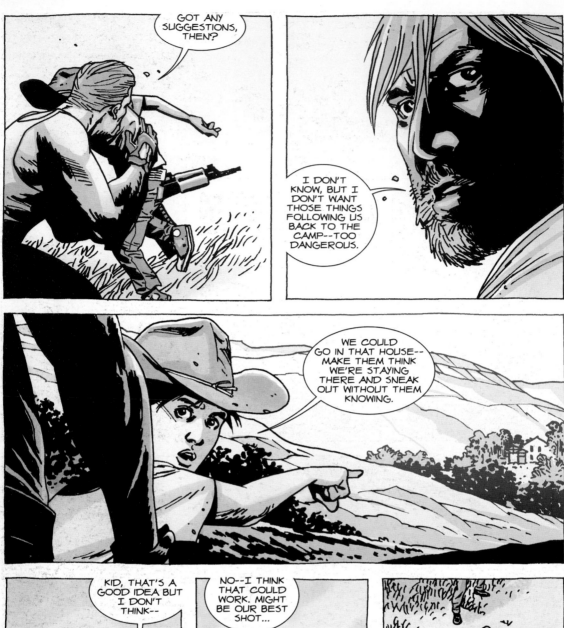

GOT ANY SUGGESTIONS, THEN?

I DON'T KNOW, BUT I DON'T WANT THOSE THINGS FOLLOWING US BACK TO THE CAMP--TOO DANGEROUS.

WE COULD GO IN THAT HOUSE-- MAKE THEM THINK WE'RE STAYING THERE AND SNEAK OUT WITHOUT THEM KNOWING.

KID, THAT'S A GOOD IDEA BUT I DON'T THINK--

NO--I THINK THAT COULD WORK. MIGHT BE OUR BEST SHOT...

THEN LET'S GO--

--C'MON!

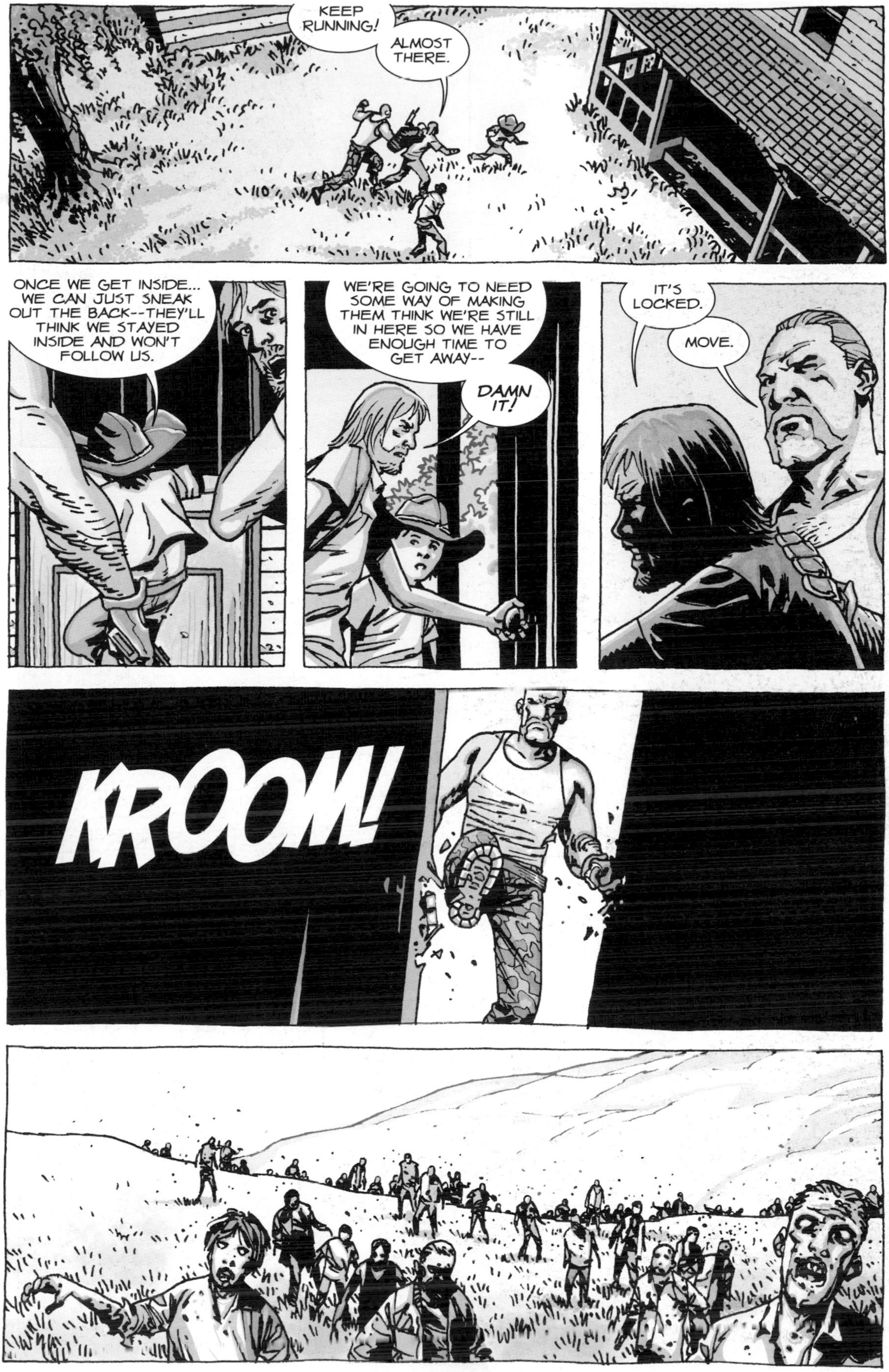
KEEP RUNNING!
ALMOST THERE.
ONCE WE GET INSIDE... WE CAN JUST SNEAK OUT THE BACK--THEY'LL THINK WE STAYED INSIDE AND WON'T FOLLOW US.
WE'RE GOING TO NEED SOME WAY OF MAKING THEM THINK WE'RE STILL IN HERE SO WE HAVE ENOUGH TIME TO GET AWAY--
DAMN IT!
IT'S LOCKED.
MOVE.
KROOM!

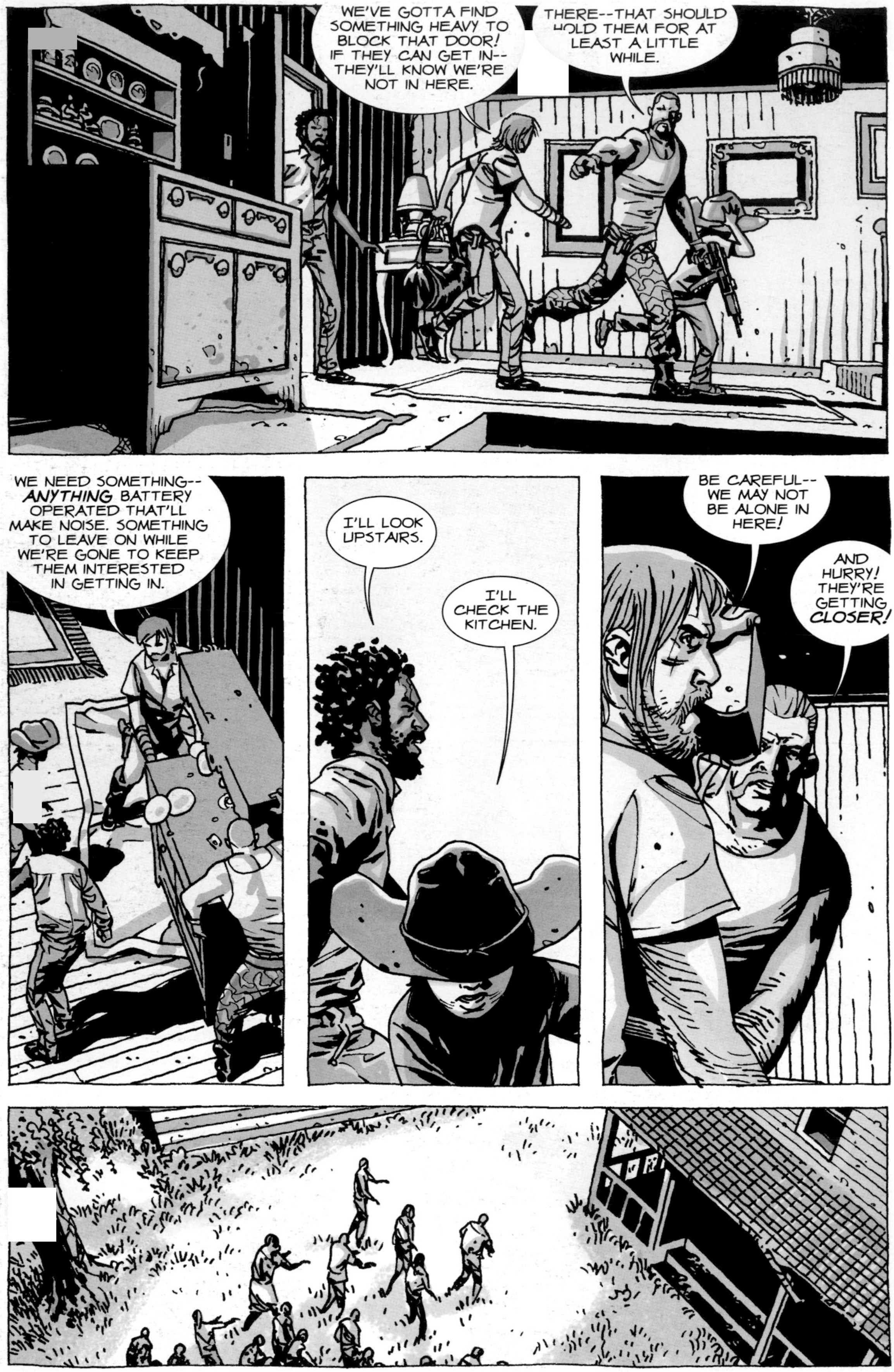
WE'VE GOTTA FIND SOMETHING HEAVY TO BLOCK THAT DOOR! IF THEY CAN GET IN-- THEY'LL KNOW WE'RE NOT IN HERE.
THERE--THAT SHOULD HOLD THEM FOR AT LEAST A LITTLE WHILE.
WE NEED SOMETHING-- ANYTHING BATTERY OPERATED THAT'LL MAKE NOISE. SOMETHING TO LEAVE ON WHILE WE'RE GONE TO KEEP THEM INTERESTED IN GETTING IN.
I'LL LOOK UPSTAIRS.
I'LL CHECK THE KITCHEN.
BE CAREFUL-- WE MAY NOT BE ALONE IN HERE!
AND HURRY! THEY'RE GETTING CLOSER!

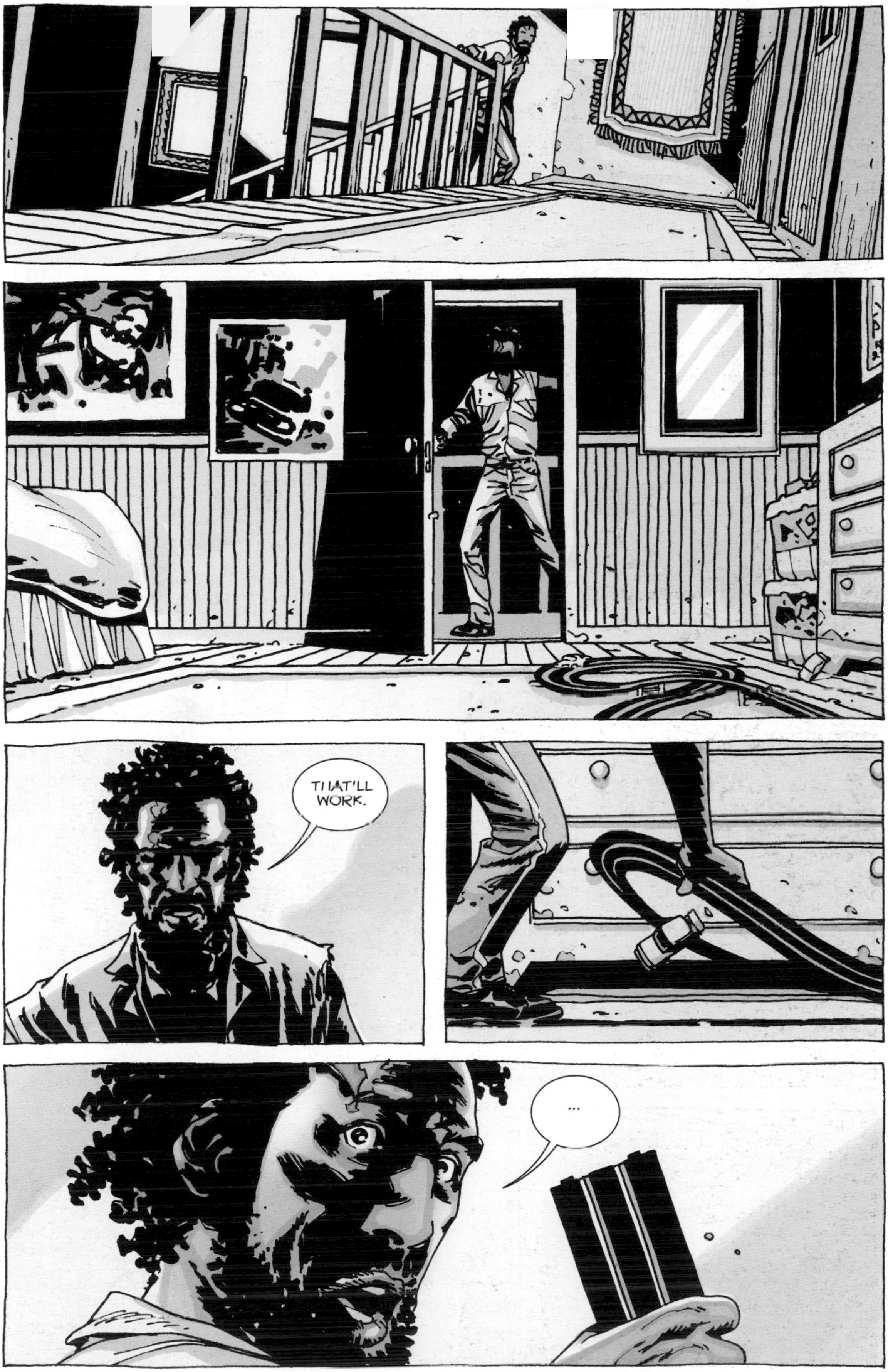
THAT'LL WORK.
...

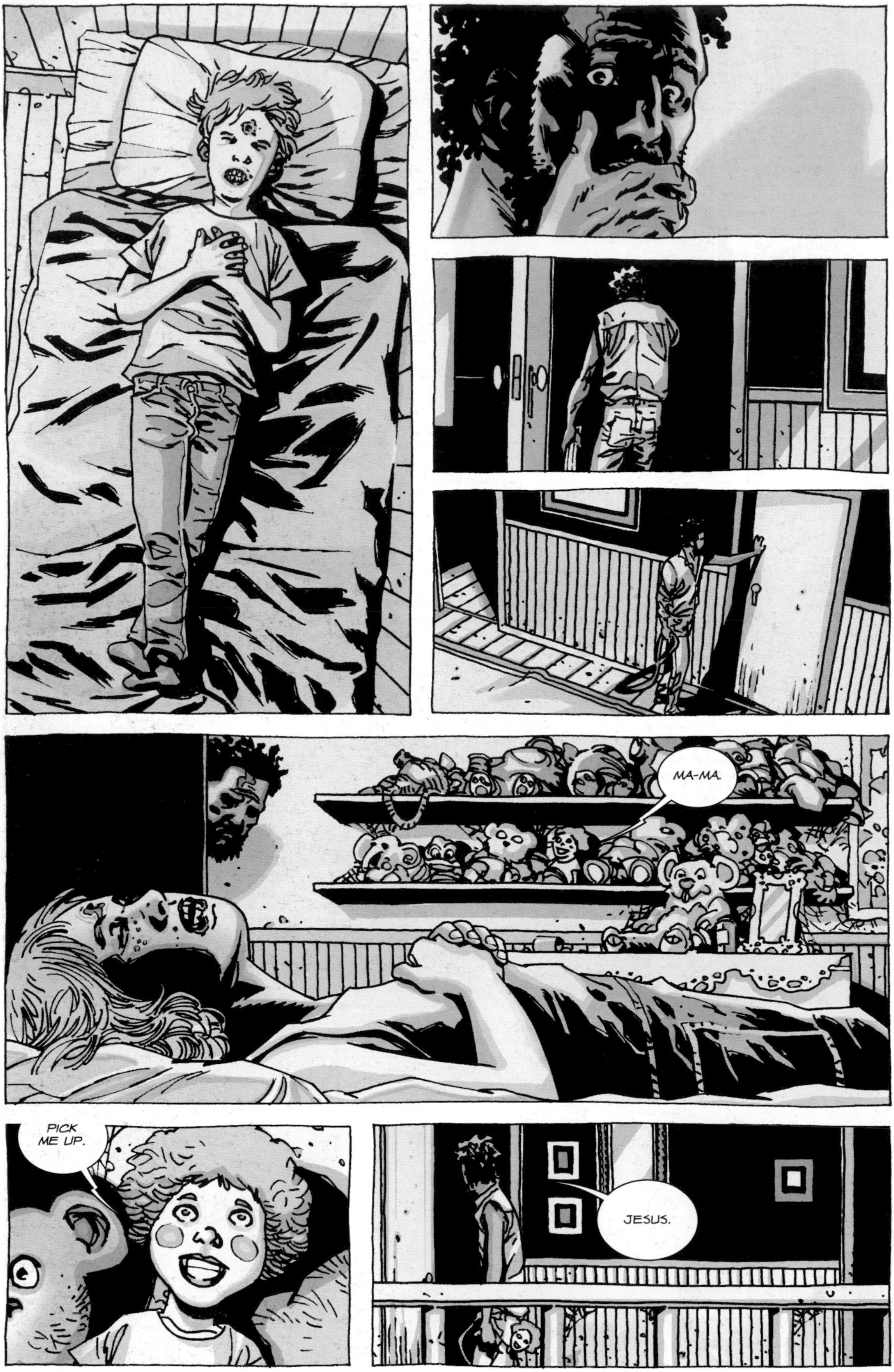
MA-MA.
PICK ME UP.
JESUS.

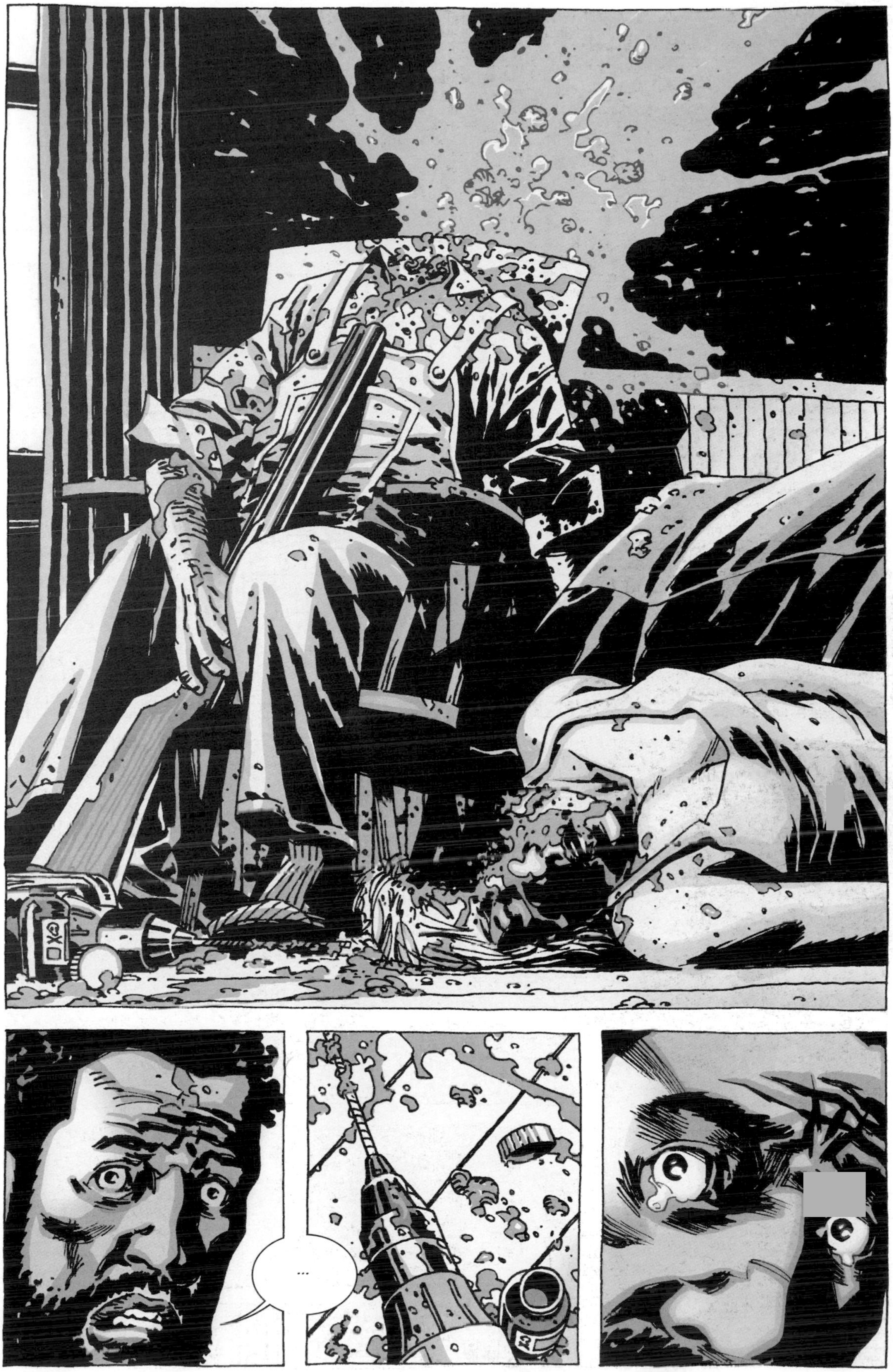
...

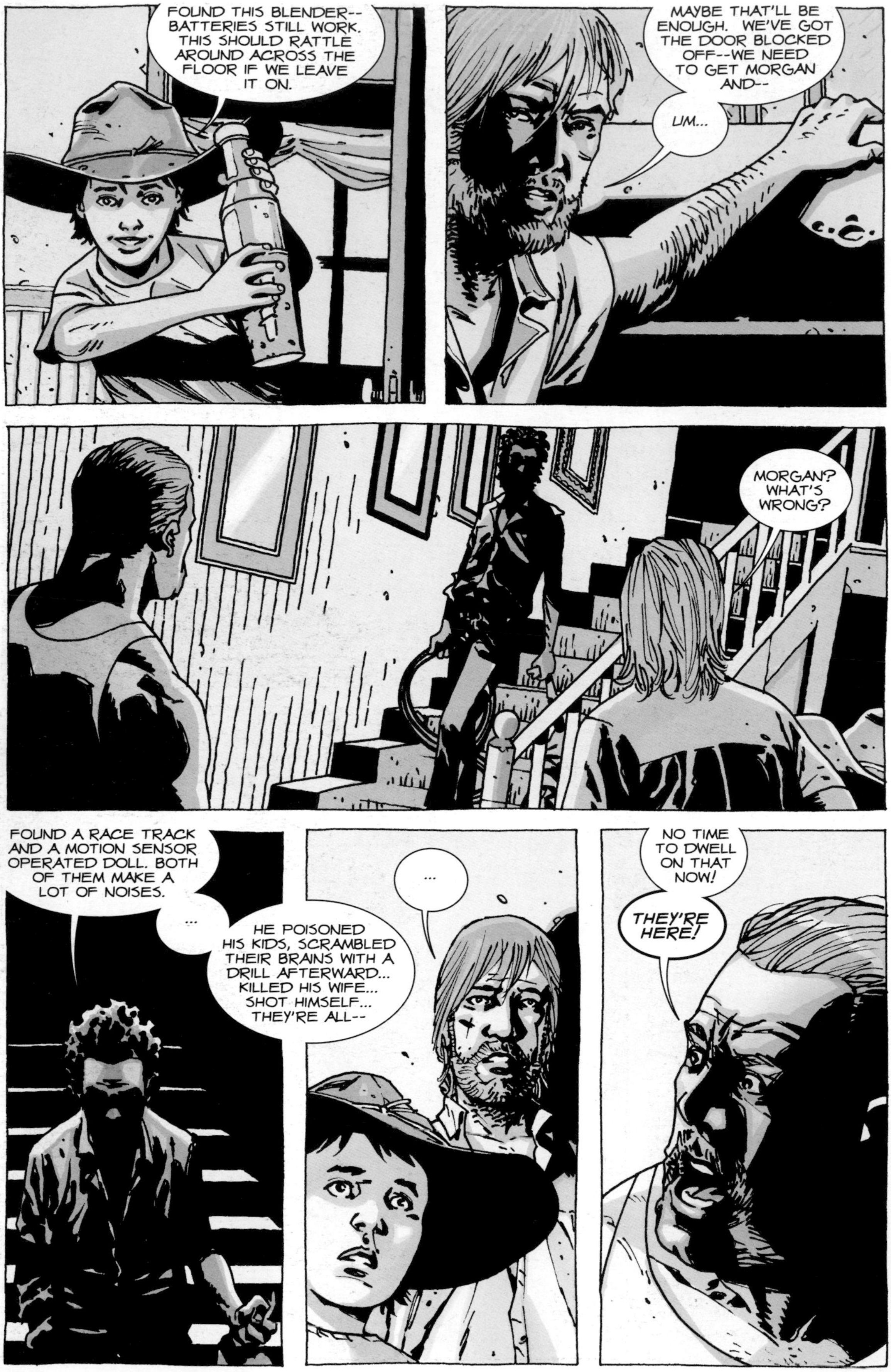
FOUND THIS BLENDER-- BATTERIES STILL WORK. THIS SHOULD RATTLE AROUND ACROSS THE FLOOR IF WE LEAVE IT ON.
MAYBE THAT'LL BE ENOUGH. WE'VE GOT THE DOOR BLOCKED OFF--WE NEED TO GET MORGAN AND--
UM...
MORGAN? WHAT'S WRONG?
FOUND A RACE TRACK AND A MOTION SENSOR OPERATED DOLL. BOTH OF THEM MAKE A LOT OF NOISES.
...
HE POISONED HIS KIDS, SCRAMBLED THEIR BRAINS WITH A DRILL AFTERWARD... KILLED HIS WIFE... SHOT HIMSELF... THEY'RE ALL--
...
NO TIME TO DWELL ON THAT NOW!
THEY'RE HERE!

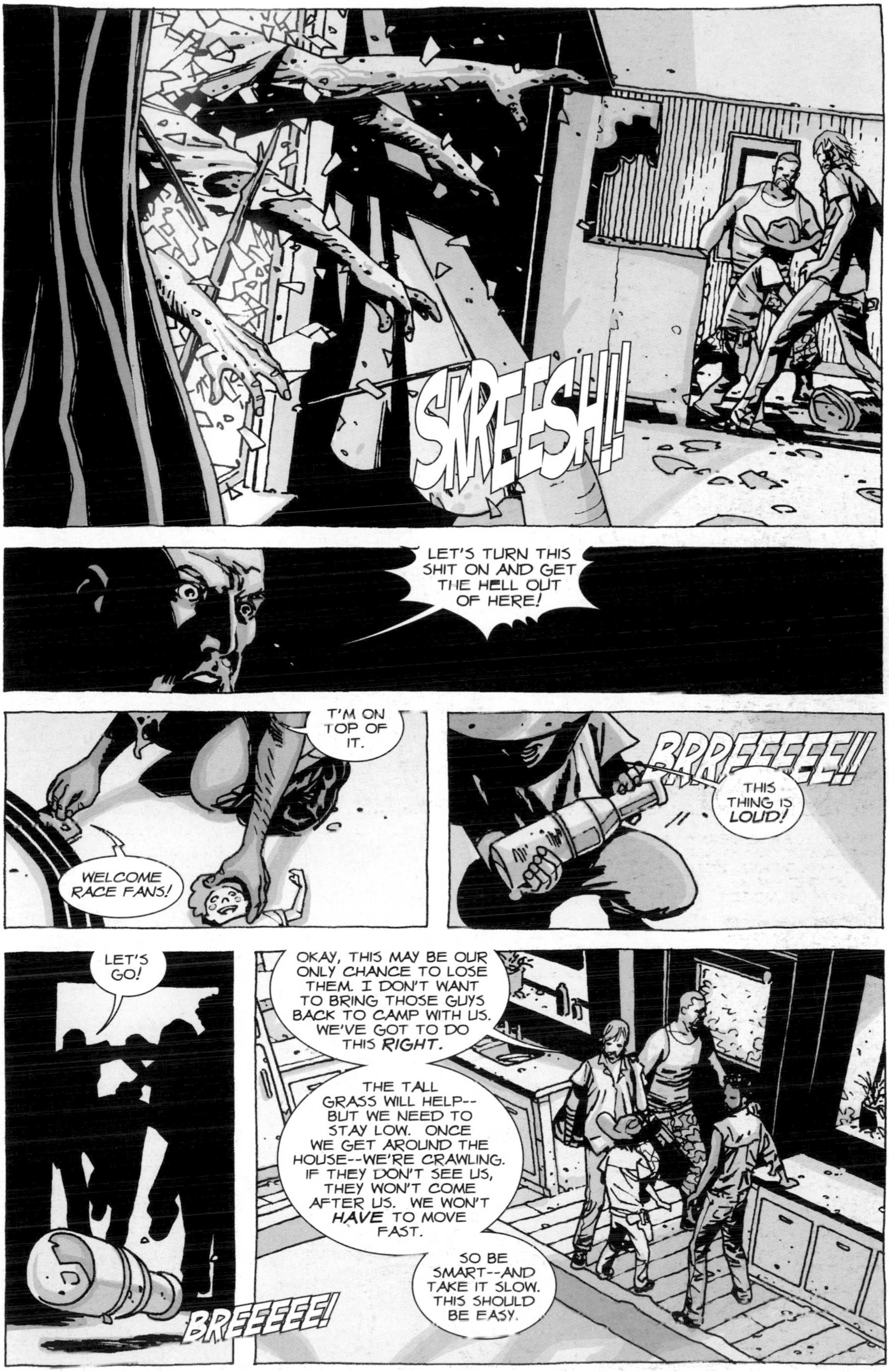
SKREESH!!
LET'S TURN THIS SHIT ON AND GET THE HELL OUT OF HERE!
I'M ON TOP OF IT.
WELCOME RACE FANS!
BRREEEEE!!
THIS THING IS LOUD!
LET'S GO!
BREEEEEE!
OKAY, THIS MAY BE OUR ONLY CHANCE TO LOSE THEM. I DON'T WANT TO BRING THOSE GUYS BACK TO CAMP WITH US. WE'VE GOT TO DO THIS RIGHT.
THE TALL GRASS WILL HELP-- BUT WE NEED TO STAY LOW. ONCE WE GET AROUND THE HOUSE--WE'RE CRAWLING. IF THEY DON'T SEE US, THEY WON'T COME AFTER US. WE WON'T HAVE TO MOVE FAST.
SO BE SMART--AND TAKE IT SLOW. THIS SHOULD BE EASY.

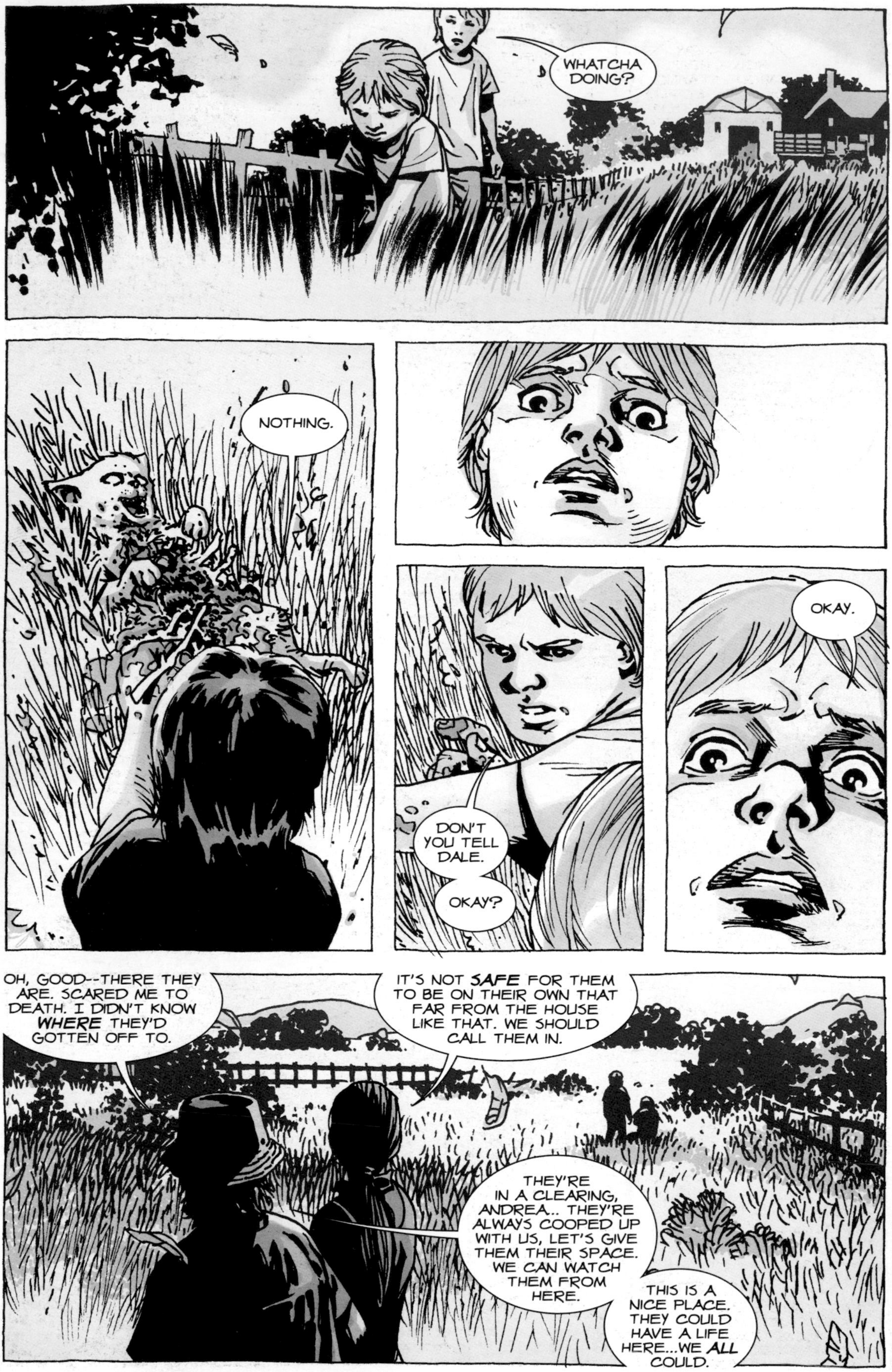
WHATCHA DOING?
NOTHING.
DON'T YOU TELL DALE.
OKAY?
OKAY.
OH, GOOD--THERE THEY ARE. SCARED ME TO DEATH. I DIDN'T KNOW WHERE THEY'D GOTTEN OFF TO.
IT'S NOT SAFE FOR THEM TO BE ON THEIR OWN THAT FAR FROM THE HOUSE LIKE THAT. WE SHOULD CALL THEM IN.
THEY'RE IN A CLEARING, ANDREA.. THEY'RE ALWAYS COOPED UP WITH US, LET'S GIVE THEM THEIR SPACE. WE CAN WATCH THEM FROM HERE.
THIS IS A NICE PLACE. THEY COULD HAVE A LIFE HERE...WE ALL COULD.

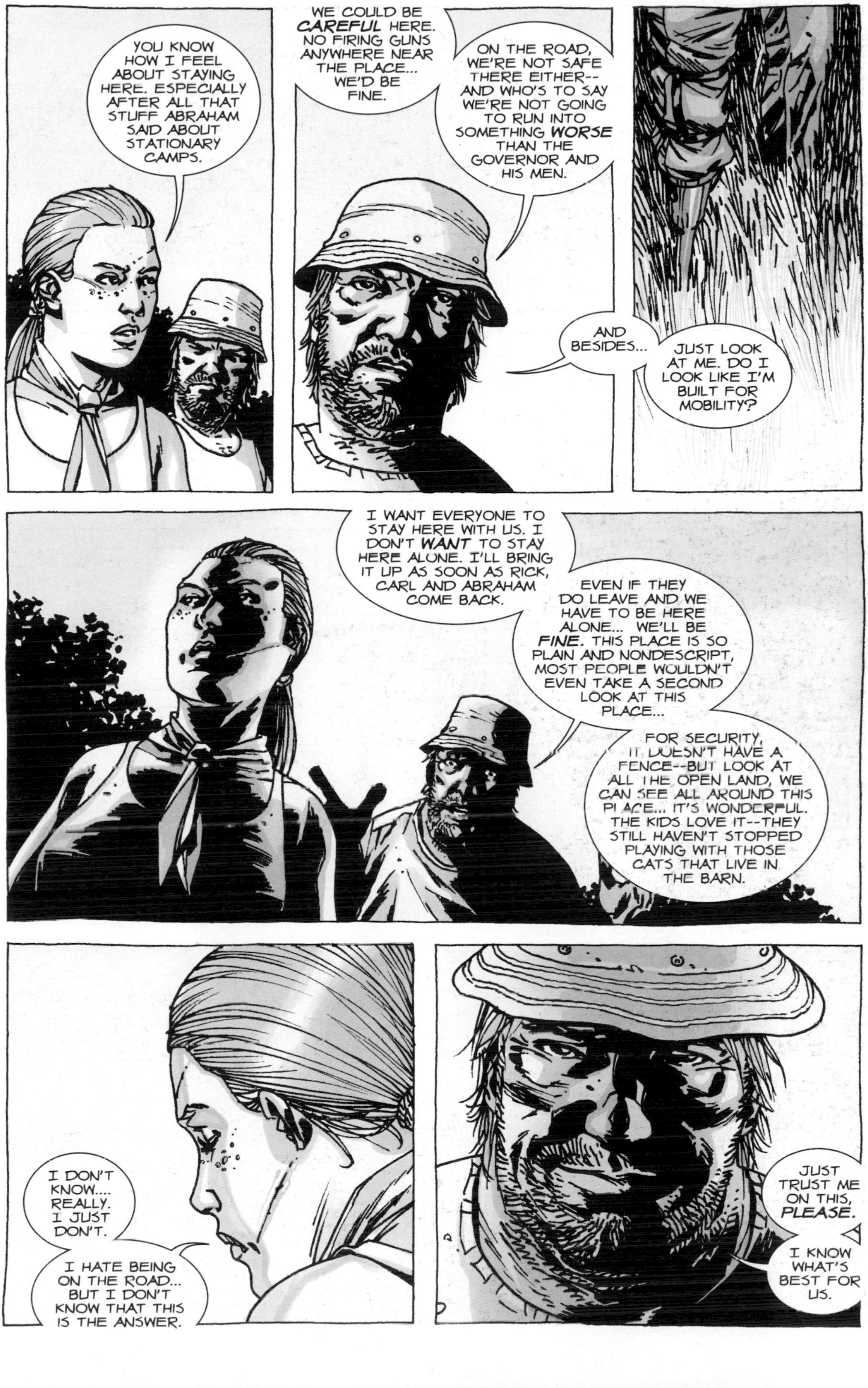
YOU KNOW HOW I FEEL ABOUT STAYING HERE. ESPECIALLY AFTER ALL THAT STUFF ABRAHAM SAID ABOUT STATIONARY CAMPS.
WE COULD BE CAREFUL HERE. NO FIRING GUNS ANYWHERE NEAR THE PLACE... WE'D BE FINE.
ON THE ROAD, WE'RE NOT SAFE THERE EITHER-- AND WHO'S TO SAY WE'RE NOT GOING TO RUN INTO SOMETHING WORSE THAN THE GOVERNOR AND HIS MEN.
AND BESIDES...
JUST LOOK AT ME. DO I LOOK LIKE I'M BUILT FOR MOBILITY?
I WANT EVERYONE TO STAY HERE WITH US. I DON'T WANT TO STAY HERE ALONE. I'LL BRING IT UP AS SOON AS RICK, CARL AND ABRAHAM COME BACK.
EVEN IF THEY DO LEAVE AND WE HAVE TO BE HERE ALONE... WE'LL BE FINE. THIS PLACE IS SO PLAIN AND NONDESCRIPT, MOST PEOPLE WOULDN'T EVEN TAKE A SECOND LOOK AT THIS PLACE...
FOR SECURITY, IT DOESN'T HAVE A FENCE--BUT LOOK AT ALL THE OPEN LAND, WE CAN SEE ALL AROUND THIS PLACE... IT'S WONDERFUL. THE KIDS LOVE IT--THEY STILL HAVEN'T STOPPED PLAYING WITH THOSE CATS THAT LIVE IN THE BARN.
I DON'T KNOW.... REALLY. I JUST DON'T.
I HATE BEING ON THE ROAD... BUT I DON'T KNOW THAT THIS IS THE ANSWER.
JUST TRUST ME ON THIS, PLEASE.
I KNOW WHAT'S BEST FOR US.

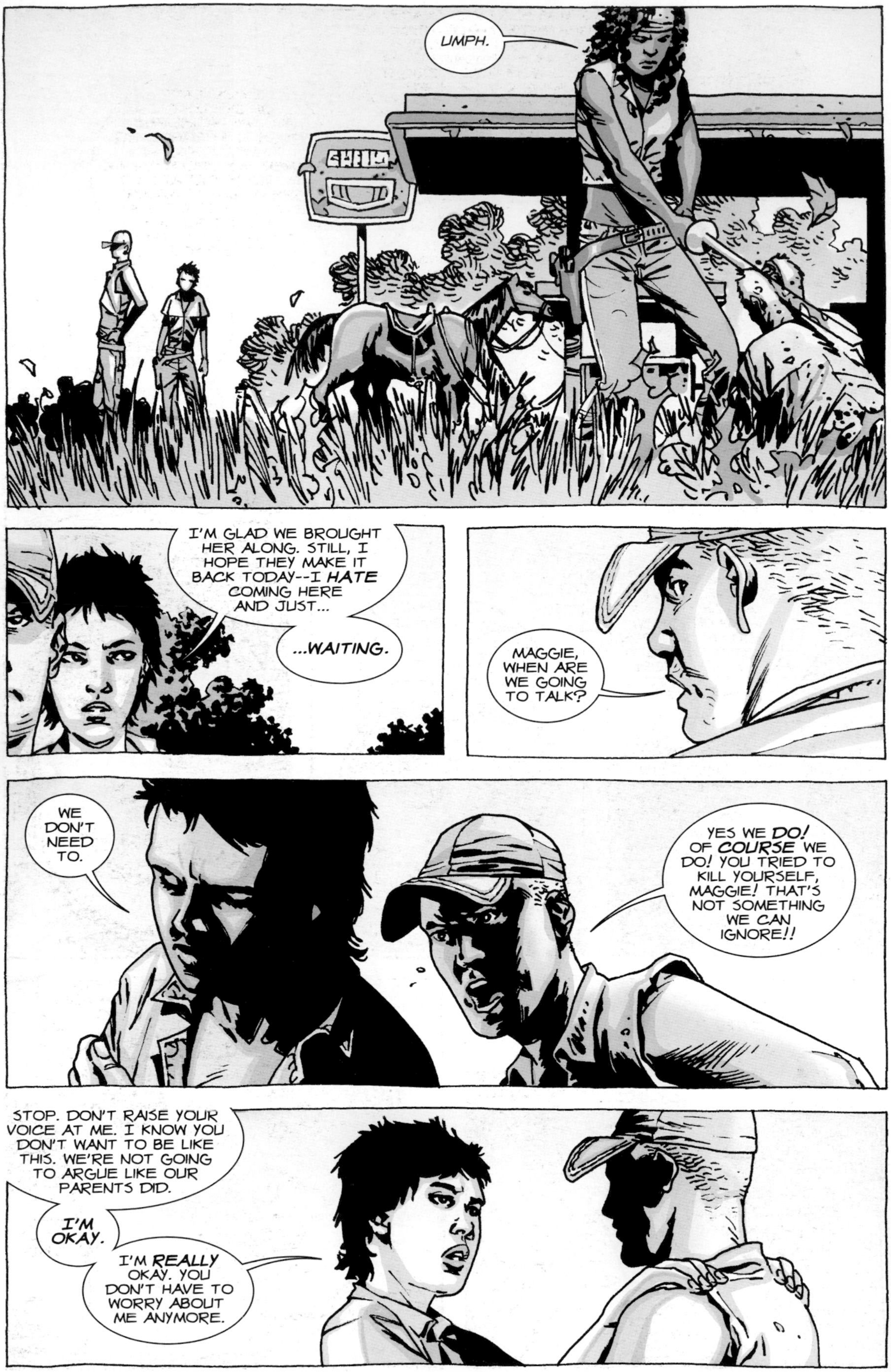
UMPH.
I'M GLAD WE BROUGHT HER ALONG. STILL, I HOPE THEY MAKE IT BACK TODAY--I HATE COMING HERE AND JUST...
...WAITING.
MAGGIE, WHEN ARE WE GOING TO TALK?
WE DON'T NEED TO.
YES WE DO! OF COURSE WE DO! YOU TRIED TO KILL YOURSELF, MAGGIE! THAT'S NOT SOMETHING WE CAN IGNORE!!
STOP. DON'T RAISE YOUR VOICE AT ME. I KNOW YOU DON'T WANT TO BE LIKE THIS. WE'RE NOT GOING TO ARGUE LIKE OUR PARENTS DID.
I'M OKAY.
I'M REALLY OKAY. YOU DON'T HAVE TO WORRY ABOUT ME ANYMORE.

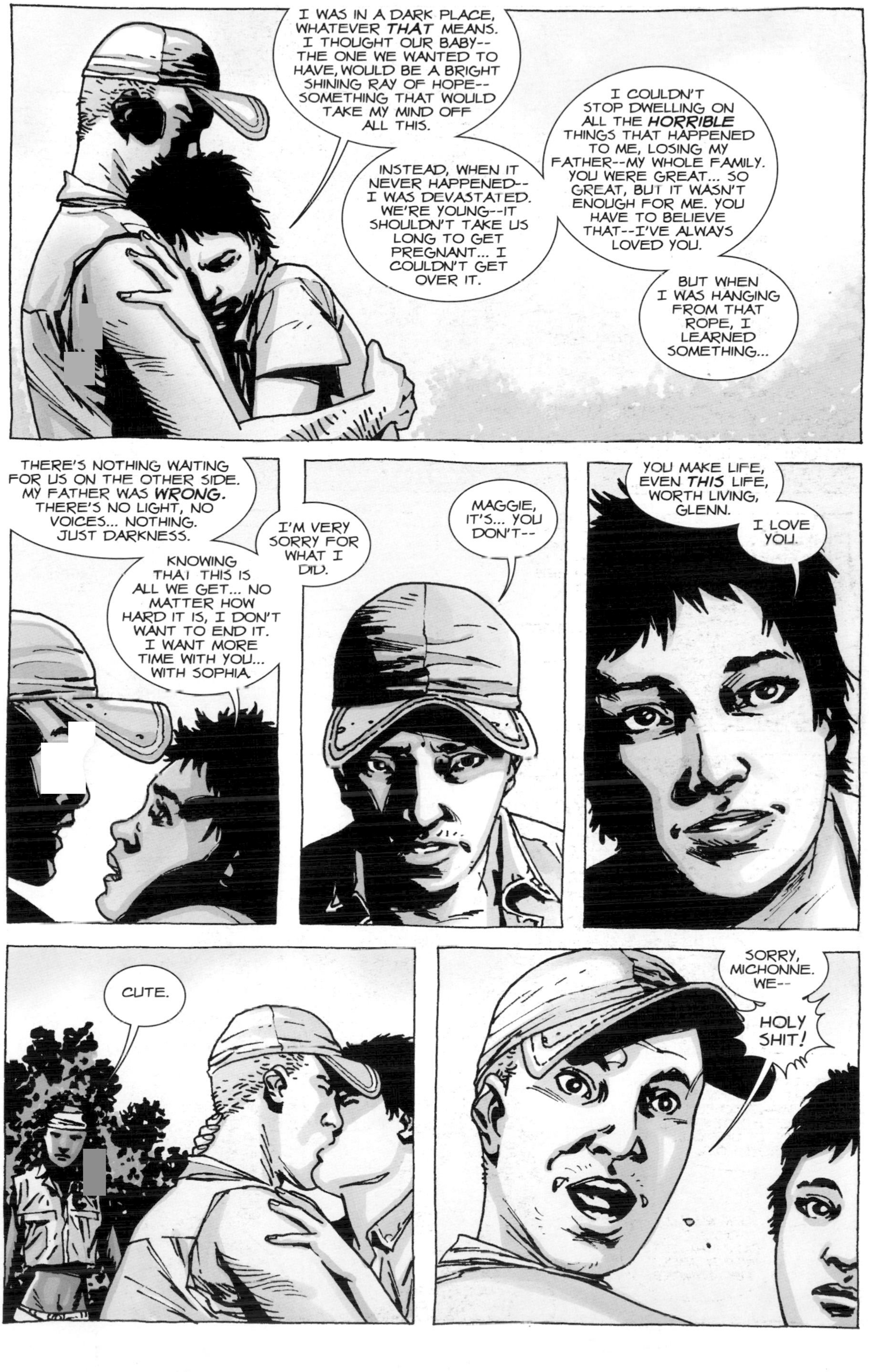
I WAS IN A DARK PLACE, WHATEVER THAT MEANS. I THOUGHT OUR BABY-- THE ONE WE WANTED TO HAVE, WOULD BE A BRIGHT SHINING RAY OF HOPE-- SOMETHING THAT WOULD TAKE MY MIND OFF ALL THIS.
INSTEAD, WHEN IT NEVER HAPPENED-- I WAS DEVASTATED. WE'RE YOUNG--IT SHOULDN'T TAKE US LONG TO GET PREGNANT... I COULDN'T GET OVER IT.
I COULDN'T STOP DWELLING ON ALL THE HORRIBLE THINGS THAT HAPPENED TO ME, LOSING MY FATHER--MY WHOLE FAMILY. YOU WERE GREAT... SO GREAT, BUT IT WASN'T ENOUGH FOR ME. YOU HAVE TO BELIEVE THAT--I'VE ALWAYS LOVED YOU.
BUT WHEN I WAS HANGING FROM THAT ROPE, I LEARNED SOMETHING...
THERE'S NOTHING WAITING FOR US ON THE OTHER SIDE. MY FATHER WAS WRONG. THERE'S NO LIGHT, NO VOICES... NOTHING. JUST DARKNESS.
KNOWING THAT THIS IS ALL WE GET... NO MATTER HOW HARD IT IS, I DON'T WANT TO END IT. I WANT MORE TIME WITH YOU... WITH SOPHIA.
I'M VERY SORRY FOR WHAT I DID.
MAGGIE, IT'S... YOU DON'T--
YOU MAKE LIFE, EVEN THIS LIFE, WORTH LIVING, GLENN.
I LOVE YOU.
CUTE.
SORRY, MICHONNE. WE--
HOLY SHIT!

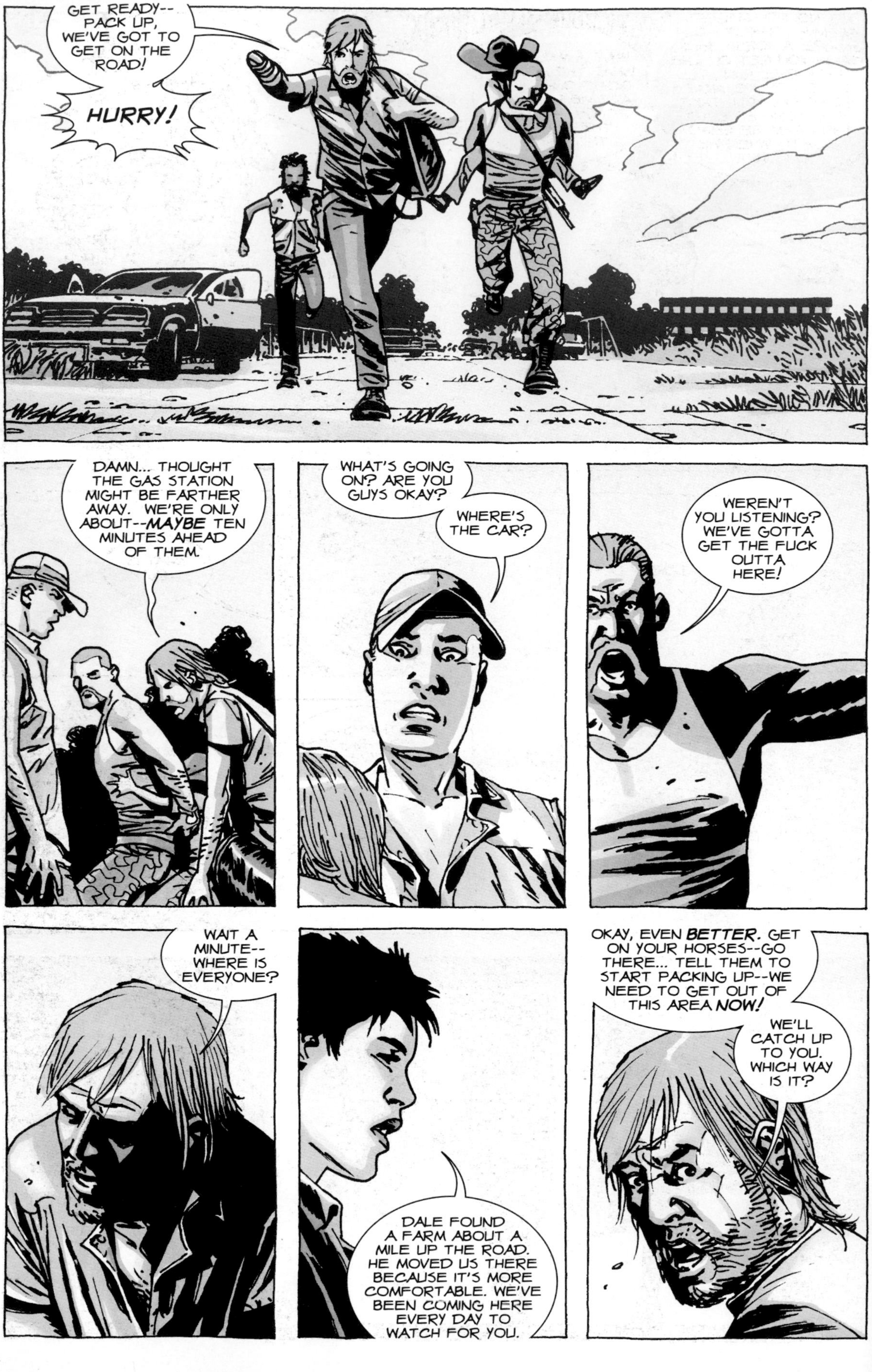
GET READY-- PACK UP, WE'VE GOT TO GET ON THE ROAD!
HURRY!
DAMN... THOUGHT THE GAS STATION MIGHT BE FARTHER AWAY. WE'RE ONLY ABOUT--MAYBE TEN MINUTES AHEAD OF THEM.
WHAT'S GOING ON? ARE YOU GUYS OKAY?
WHERE'S THE CAR?
WEREN'T YOU LISTENING? WE'VE GOTTA GET THE FUCK OUTTA HERE!
WAIT A MINUTE-- WHERE IS EVERYONE?
DALE FOUND A FARM ABOUT A MILE UP THE ROAD. HE MOVED US THERE BECAUSE IT'S MORE COMFORTABLE. WE'VE BEEN COMING HERE EVERY DAY TO WATCH FOR YOU.
OKAY, EVEN BETTER. GET ON YOUR HORSES--GO THERE... TELL THEM TO START PACKING UP--WE NEED TO GET OUT OF THIS AREA NOW!
WE'LL CATCH UP TO YOU. WHICH WAY IS IT?

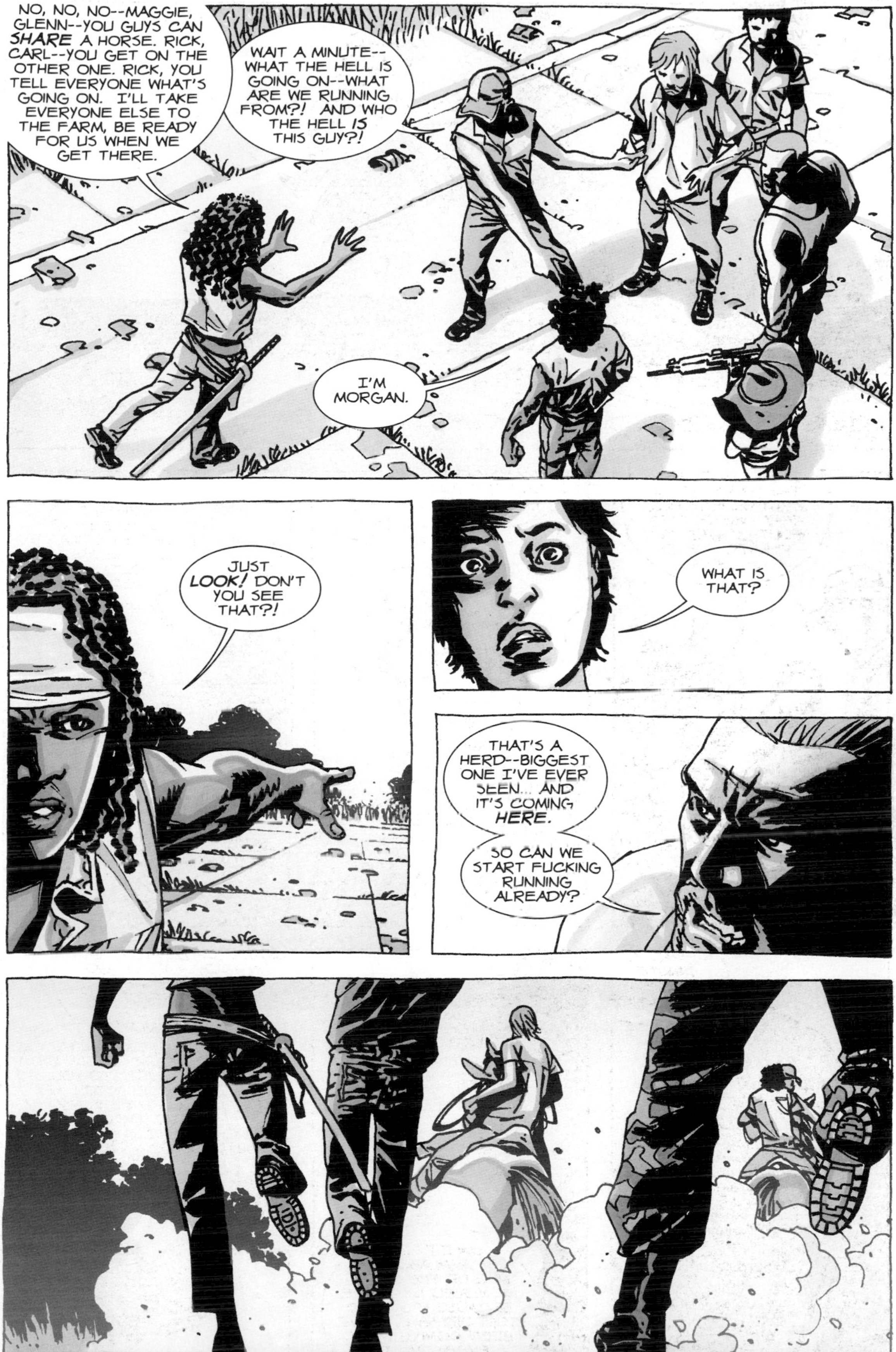

NO, NO, NO--MAGGIE, GLENN--YOU GUYS CAN SHARE A HORSE. RICK, CARL--YOU GET ON THE OTHER ONE. RICK, YOU TELL EVERYONE WHAT'S GOING ON. I'LL TAKE EVERYONE ELSE TO THE FARM, BE READY FOR US WHEN WE GET THERE.
WAIT A MINUTE--WHAT THE HELL IS GOING ON--WHAT ARE WE RUNNING FROM?! AND WHO THE HELL IS THIS GUY?!
I'M MORGAN.
JUST LOOK! DON'T YOU SEE THAT?!
WHAT IS THAT?
THAT'S A HERD--BIGGEST ONE I'VE EVER SEEN... AND IT'S COMING HERE.
SO CAN WE START FUCKING RUNNING ALREADY?

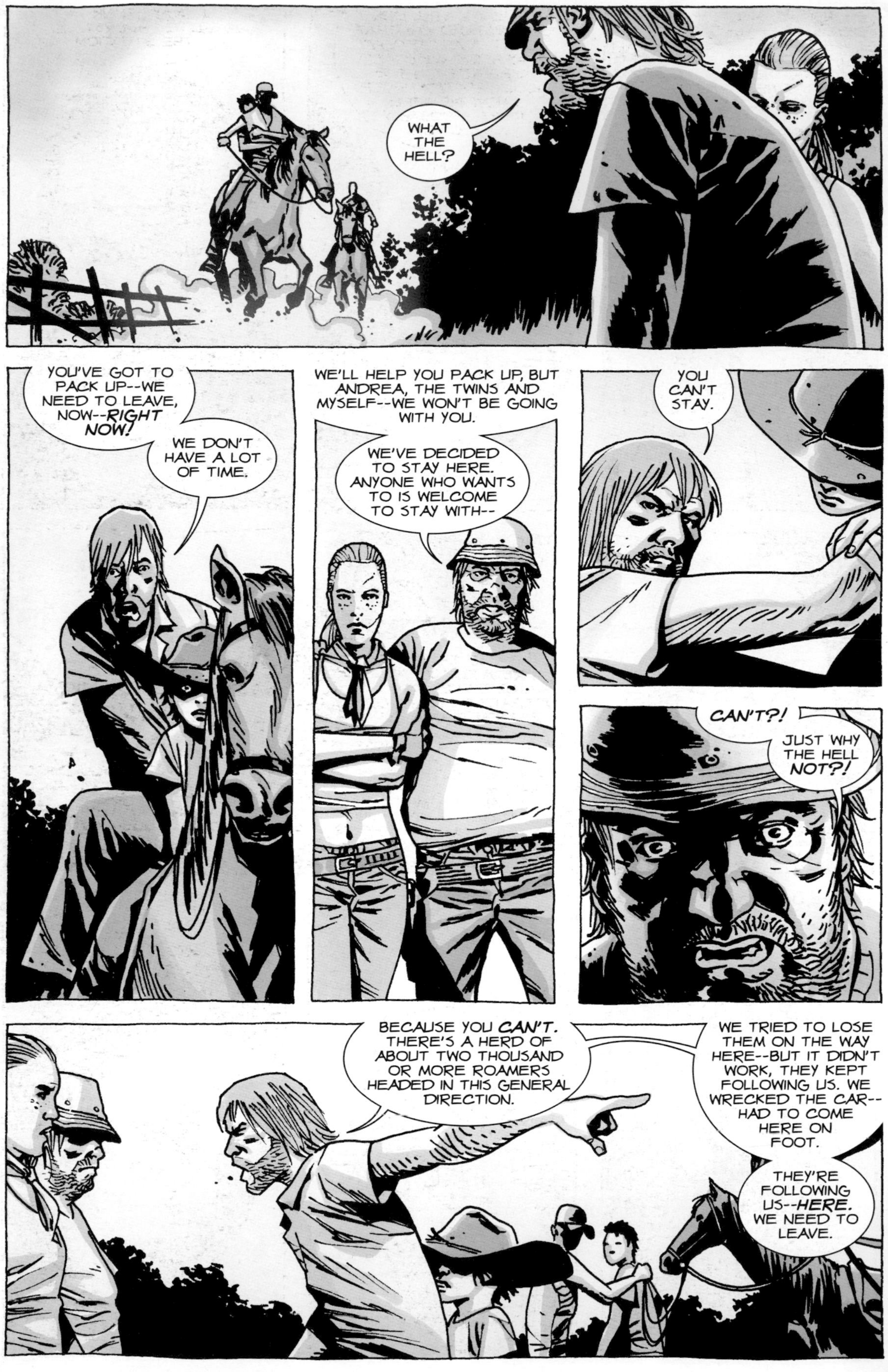

WHAT THE HELL?
YOU'VE GOT TO PACK UP--WE NEED TO LEAVE, NOW--RIGHT NOW!
WE DON'T HAVE A LOT OF TIME.
WE'LL HELP YOU PACK UP, BUT ANDREA, THE TWINS AND MYSELF--WE WON'T BE GOING WITH YOU.
WE'VE DECIDED TO STAY HERE. ANYONE WHO WANTS TO IS WELCOME TO STAY WITH--
YOU CAN'T STAY.
CAN'T?!
JUST WHY THE HELL NOT?!
BECAUSE YOU CAN'T. THERE'S A HERD OF ABOUT TWO THOUSAND OR MORE ROAMERS HEADED IN THIS GENERAL DIRECTION.
WE TRIED TO LOSE THEM ON THE WAY HERE--BUT IT DIDN'T WORK, THEY KEPT FOLLOWING US. WE WRECKED THE CAR--HAD TO COME HERE ON FOOT.
THEY'RE FOLLOWING US--HERE. WE NEED TO LEAVE.

DID YOU SAY "HERD?" DID I HEAR YOU CORRECTLY?
YES--BUT I STILL DON'T UNDERSTAND WHY THAT WOULD MEAN WE CAN'T STAY HERE. WE COULD KEEP QUIET IN THE HOUSE--THEY'D NEVER KNOW WE WERE HERE--PROBABLY WALK ON BY.
THEY CAN'T BE STOPPING AT EVERY HOUSE ALONG THE WAY.
I DON'T THINK YOU QUITE UNDERSTAND THE SITUATION.
THESE THINGS ARE A FORCE OF NATURE. THEY DON'T OPERATE ON LOGIC OR REASON. IF ONE OF THEM EVEN SO MUCH AS BRUSHES A HAND AGAINST YOUR DOOR--AND ANOTHER ONE SEES THAT, MISTAKES THAT AS AN ATTEMPT TO GET IN--IT'S ALL OVER.
THAT ONE STARTS TRYING TO GET IN--THE ONE WHO DID THE ACCIDENTAL TAP THINKS SOMETHING'S INSIDE ALL OF A SUDDEN--HE STARTS BEATING ON THE DOOR WITH HIM.
THEY WOULD KILL YOU ALL.
WE'VE GOT A LONG ROAD AHEAD OF US. WE'VE GOT TO GET ON THE ROAD BEFORE THEY GET CLOSE ENOUGH TO FOLLOW US. I DON'T WANT TO HAVE TO WORRY ABOUT STAYING AHEAD OF THAT GROUP IF WE GET STALLED OUT OR DECIDE TO SET UP CAMP FOR A WEEK.
WHAT ABOUT ME? THE TWINS?
WE CAN'T STAY HERE, DALE. IT'S NOT SAFE.

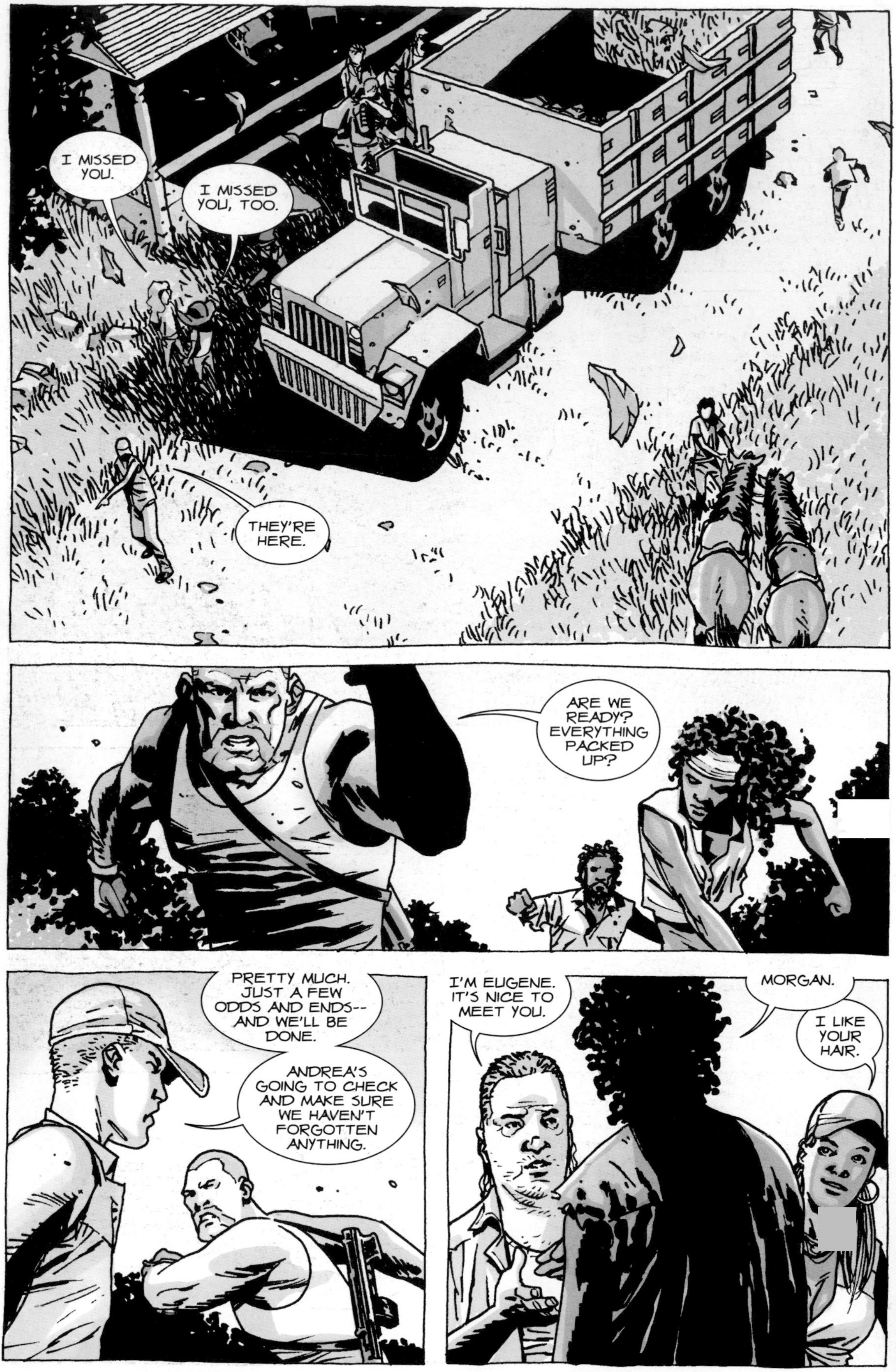
I MISSED YOU.
I MISSED YOU, TOO.
THEY'RE HERE.
ARE WE READY? EVERYTHING PACKED UP?
PRETTY MUCH. JUST A FEW ODDS AND ENDS-- AND WE'LL BE DONE.
ANDREA'S GOING TO CHECK AND MAKE SURE WE HAVEN'T FORGOTTEN ANYTHING.
I'M EUGENE. IT'S NICE TO MEET YOU.
MORGAN.
I LIKE YOUR HAIR.

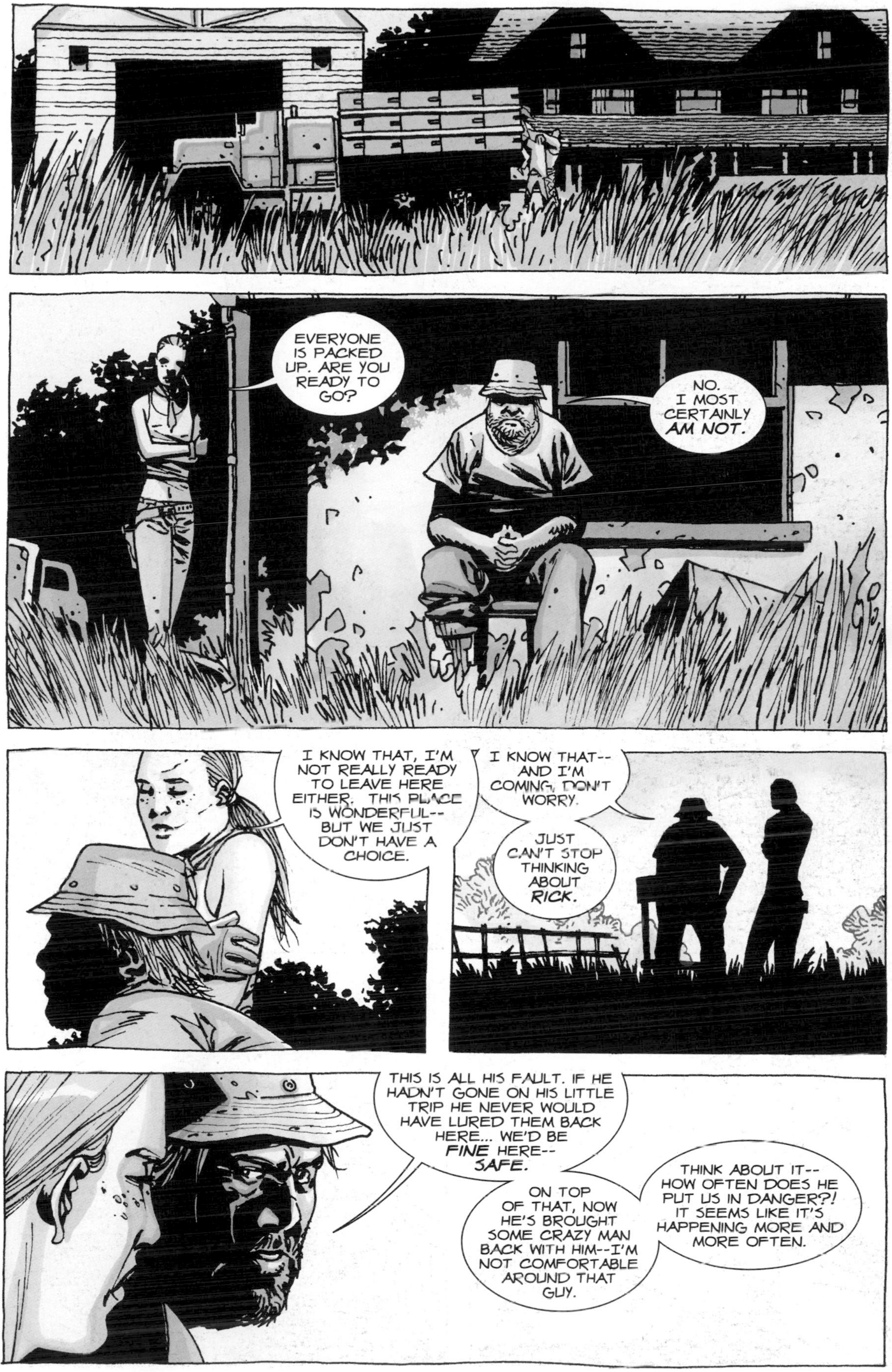
EVERYONE IS PACKED UP. ARE YOU READY TO GO?
NO. I MOST CERTAINLY AM NOT.
I KNOW THAT, I'M NOT REALLY READY TO LEAVE HERE EITHER. THIS PLACE IS WONDERFUL-- BUT WE JUST DON'T HAVE A CHOICE.
I KNOW THAT-- AND I'M COMING, DON'T WORRY.
JUST CAN'T STOP THINKING ABOUT RICK.
THIS IS ALL HIS FAULT. IF HE HADN'T GONE ON HIS LITTLE TRIP HE NEVER WOULD HAVE LURED THEM BACK HERE... WE'D BE FINE HERE-- SAFE.
ON TOP OF THAT, NOW HE'S BROUGHT SOME CRAZY MAN BACK WITH HIM--I'M NOT COMFORTABLE AROUND THAT GUY.
THINK ABOUT IT-- HOW OFTEN DOES HE PUT US IN DANGER?! IT SEEMS LIKE IT'S HAPPENING MORE AND MORE OFTEN.

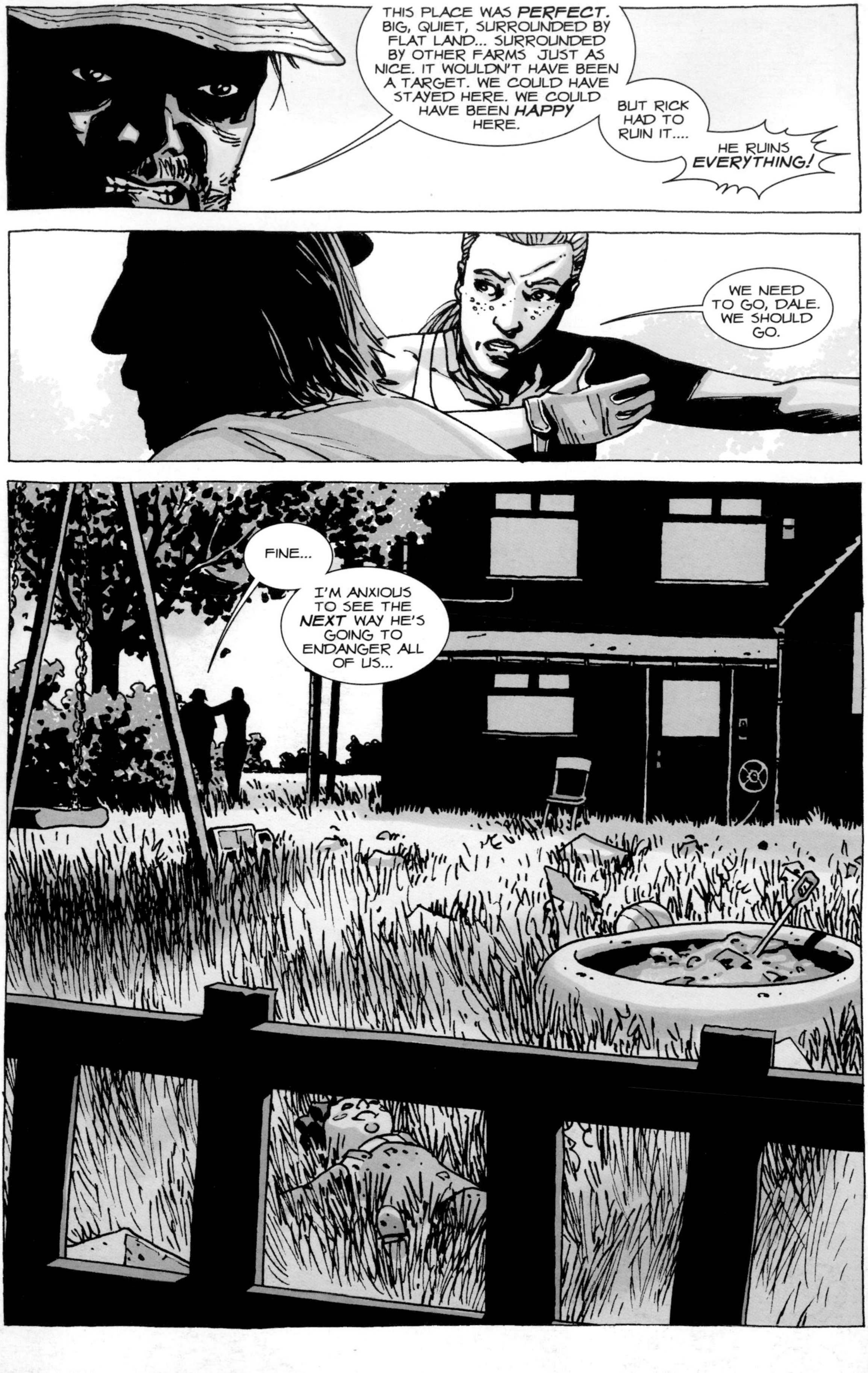
THIS PLACE WAS PERFECT. BIG, QUIET, SURROUNDED BY FLAT LAND... SURROUNDED BY OTHER FARMS JUST AS NICE. IT WOULDN'T HAVE BEEN A TARGET. WE COULD HAVE STAYED HERE. WE COULD HAVE BEEN HAPPY HERE.
BUT RICK HAD TO RUIN IT....
HE RUINS EVERYTHING!
WE NEED TO GO, DALE. WE SHOULD GO.
FINE...
I'M ANXIOUS TO SEE THE NEXT WAY HE'S GOING TO ENDANGER ALL OF US...

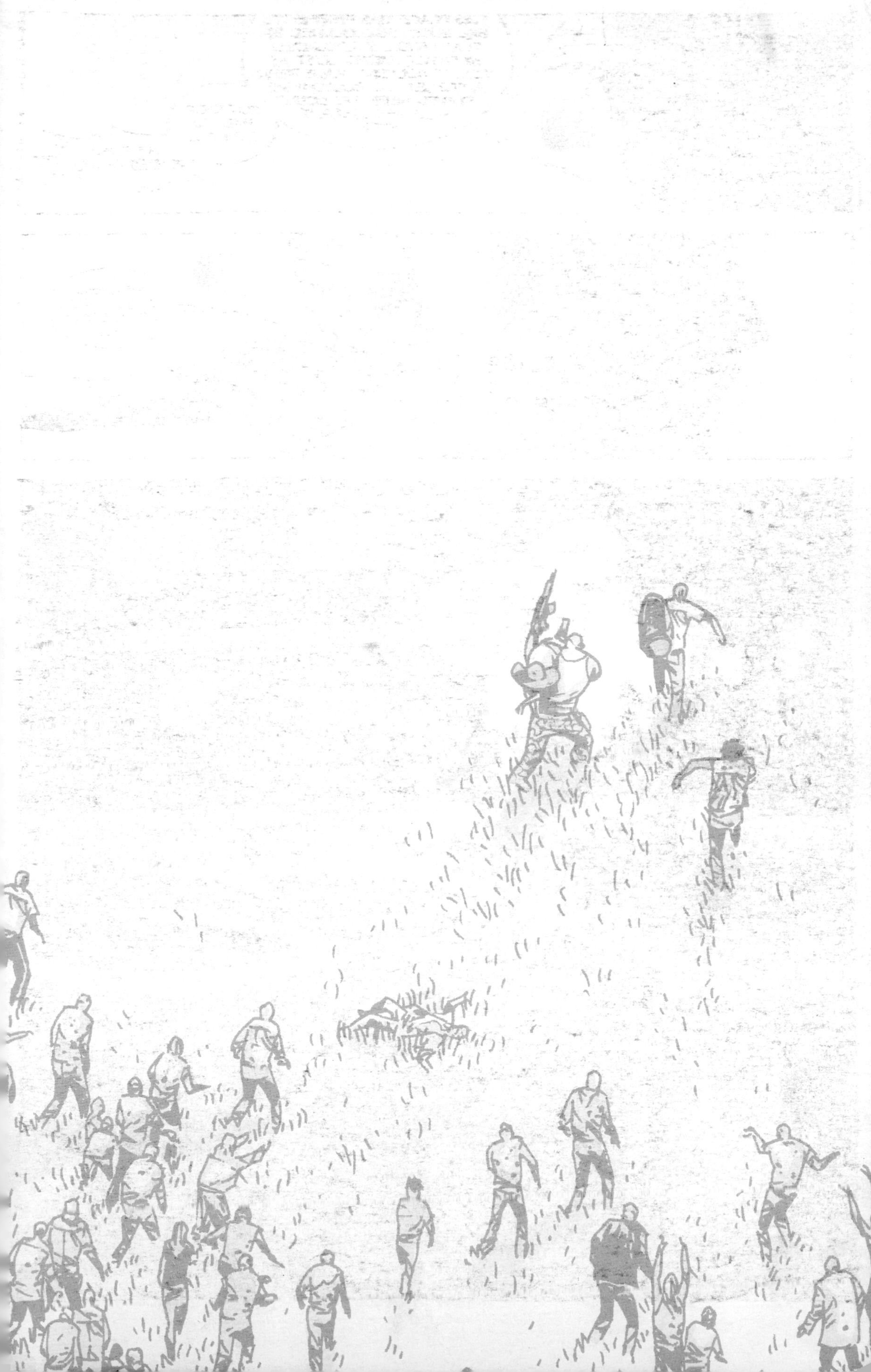

MORE GREAT BOOKS FROM
ROBERT KIRKMAN & IMAGE COMICS!

THE ASTOUNDING WOLF-MAN
VOL. 1 TP
ISBN: 978-1-58240-862-0
$14.99
VOL. 2 TP
ISBN: 978-1-60706-007-9
$14.99

BATTLE POPE
VOL. 1: GENESIS TP
ISBN: 978-1-58240-572-8
$14.99
VOL. 2: MAYHEM TP
ISBN: 978-1-58240-529-2
$12.99
VOL. 3: PILLOW TALK TP
ISBN: 978-1-58240-677-0
$12.99
VOL. 4: WRATH OF GOD TP
ISBN: 978-1-58240-751-7
$9.99

BRIT
VOL. 1: OLD SOLDIER TP
ISBN: 978-1-58240-678-7
$14.99
VOL. 2: AWOL
ISBN: 978-1-58240-864-4
$14.99

CAPES
VOL. 1: PUNCHING THE CLOCK TP
ISBN: 978-1-58240-756-2
$17.99

CLOUDFALL
GRAPHIC NOVEL
$6.95

REAPER
GRAPHIC NOVEL
$6.95

TECH JACKET
VOL. 1: THE BOY FROM EARTH TP
ISBN: 978-1-58240-771-5
$14.99

TALES OF THE REALM
HARDCOVER
ISBN: 978-1-58240-426-0
$34.95
TRADE PAPERBACK
ISBN: 978-1-58240-394-6
$14.95

INVINCIBLE
VOL. 1: FAMILY MATTERS TP
ISBN: 978-1-58240-711-1
$12.99
VOL. 2: EIGHT IS ENOUGH TP
ISBN: 978-1-58240-347-2
$12.99
VOL. 3: PERFECT STRANGERS TP
ISBN: 978-1-58240-793-7
$12.99
VOL. 4: HEAD OF THE CLASS TP
ISBN: 978-1-58240-440-2
$14.95
VOL. 5: THE FACTS OF LIFE TP
ISBN: 978-1-58240-554-4
$14.99
VOL. 6: A DIFFERENT WORLD TP
ISBN: 978-1-58240-579-7
$14.99
VOL. 7: THREE'S COMPANY TP
ISBN: 978-1-58240-656-5
$14.99
VOL. 8: MY FAVORITE MARTIAN TP
ISBN: 978-1-58240-683-1
$14.99

VOL. 9: OUT OF THIS WORLD TP
ISBN: 978-1-58240-827-9
$14.99
VOL. 10: WHO'S THE BOSS TP
ISBN: 978-1-60706-013-0
$16.99
ULTIMATE COLLECTION, VOL. 1 HC
ISBN 978-1-58240-500-1
$34.95
ULTIMATE COLLECTION, VOL. 2 HC
ISBN: 978-1-58240-594-0
$34.99
ULTIMATE COLLECTION, VOL. 3 HC
ISBN: 978-1-58240-763-0
$34.99
ULTIMATE COLLECTION, VOL. 4 HC
ISBN: 978-1-58240-989-4
$34.99
THE OFFICIAL HANDBOOK OF THE INVINCIBLE UNIVERSE TP
ISBN: 978-1-58240-831-6
$12.99
THE COMPLETE INVINCIBLE LIBRARY, VOL. 1 HC
ISBN: 978-1-58240-718-0
$125.00

THE WALKING DEAD
VOL. 1: DAYS GONE BYE TP
ISBN: 978-1-58240-672-5
$9.99
VOL. 2: MILES BEHIND US TP
ISBN: 978-1-58240-413-4
$14.99
VOL. 3: SAFETY BEHIND BARS TP
ISBN: 978-1-58240-487-5
$14.99
VOL. 4: THE HEART'S DESIRE TP
ISBN: 978-1-58240-530-8
$14.99

VOL. 5: THE BEST DEFENSE TP
ISBN: 978-1-58240-612-1
$14.99
VOL. 6: THIS SORROWFUL LIFE TP
ISBN: 978-1-58240-684-8
$14.99
VOL. 7: THE CALM BEFORE TP
ISBN: 978-1-58240-828-6
$14.99
VOL. 8: MADE TO SUFFER TP
ISBN: 978-1-58240-883-5
$14.99
VOL. 9: HERE WE REMAIN TP
ISBN: 978-1-60706-022-2
$14.99
VOL. 10: THE ROAD AHEAD TP
ISBN: 978-1-60706-075-8
$14.99
BOOK ONE HC
ISBN: 978-1-58240-619-0
$29.99
BOOK TWO HC
ISBN: 978-1-58240-698-5
$29.99
BOOK THREE HC
ISBN: 978-1-58240-825-5
$29.99
BOOK FOUR HC
ISBN: 978-1-60706-000-0
$29.99
THE WALKDING DEAD DELUXE HARDCOVER, VOL. 2
SBN: 978-1-60706-029-7
$100.00

TO FIND YOUR NEAREST COMIC BOOK STORE, CALL:
1-888-COMIC-BOOK

THE WALKING DEAD™, BRIT™ & CAPES™ © 2009 Robert Kirkman. INVINCIBLE ™ © 2009 Robert Kirkman and Cory Walker. BATTLE POPE™ © 2009 Robert Kirkman and Tony Moore. THE ASTOUNDING WOLF-MAN™ © 2009 Robert Kirkman and Jason Howard.
TECH JACKET™ & CLOUDFALL™ © 2009 Robert Kirkman and E.J. Su. REAPER™ © 2009 Cliff Rathburn. TALES OF THE REALM™ MVCreations, LLC. © 2009 Matt Tyree & Val Staples.
Image Comics® and its logos are registered trademarks of Image Comics, Inc. All rights reserved.